THE SHADOW REAPER

By
Bob Whitely

COSMOVERSE PUBLISHING
AN IMPRINT OF QT GAMES LLC

Another tale from the

Cover painting
Mike Antrim

Book design, logos and illustrations, except where noted
Bob Whitely

Also by Cosmoverse Publishing
**Arcane Synthesis: A Blended-Genre Anthology
Sea of Worms**

THE SHADOW REAPER

ISBN 978-0-9907903-7-2 [EPUB]
ISBN 978-0-9907903-8-9 [MOBI]
ISBN 978-0-9907903-9-6 [TRADE PAPERBACK]

All characters in this book are fictitious.
Any resemblance to actual persons, living or dead, is purely coincidental.

First Printing: July 2019

10 9 8 7 6 5 4 3 2 1

Join our newsletter to get a free novella and to stay up-to-date on
upcoming Cosmoverse fiction and tabletop games set in Toonaria.

Website: qtgames.com | Email: info@qtgames.com

In loving memory of my father, who encouraged me to never stop writing, and passed away before I could finish this tale.

PROLOGUE

More than four thousand years had passed since the reaper slipped out of the shadows and was ambushed by a being immune to his peculiar talents. A hyper intelligence encased in metal, the entity had defeated the reaper using a simple array of floodlights linked to a solar generator.

Trapped within the searing light, the reaper became inert, able to think, but not act. He wished not to remove the light, only diminish it, for without light, there can be no shadows.

Explorers came along and found the solar generator and disabled it, unaware of the creature they were releasing. In his impatience, the reaper made another miscalculation and found himself stranded, unable to escape the tiny world that had become his cage. Determined not to repeat his mistake, the shadow reaper went into hiding, knowing it was just a matter of time.

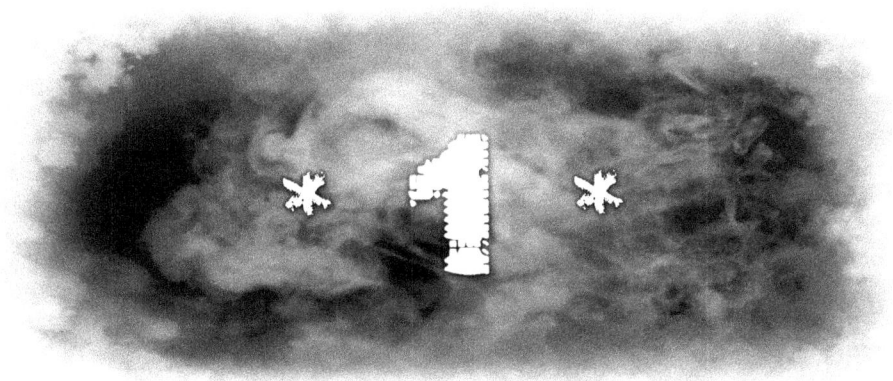

Galactic Date: 08.12.7039 [Pantara calendar]
Galactic Spatial Coordinates: -156,+46,0
Western edge of the Dark Nebulae
CDF-E179 Dauntilus

In the distance, thousands of mammoth asteroids spun and collided, stirred up by dimensional tornadoes. Thus far only a few of the skyscraper-sized boulders had broken off from the pack and tumbled toward them, prodded by the tornadoes. Hemmed in on five sides, the *CDF-E179 Dauntilus* remained steadfast.

We all knew the Dark Nebulae was a dangerous region. No wonder the Interstellar Alliance never committed serious funds to exploring it. I wonder what makes the Colonial Defense Fleet think we're up to the task? Lance Bendrik wondered.

Captain Raeden doesn't seem overly concerned about the tornadoes, Lance thought. *Perhaps I'm overreacting. I dunno. Maybe he's right. I am only the XO. He's a decorated soldier with many more years of experience than I have. Well, I've said my piece and he refused to head for safer skies until his precious probes return from retrieving data on the dimensional phenomenon.*

Ensign Lorego was the nav officer on duty and Lance trusted him. He had worked with him previously on another ship and Lance had recommended him for a promotion, but his captain had disagreed. Now XO aboard the *Dauntilus,* Lance found himself in a similar situation. Once again he was working alongside Lorego, and once again he was at odds with his superior.

Before the tornadoes had escalated in size and intensity, the *Dauntilus* had only been hemmed in on three sides. That alone had been enough to inspire Lance to suggest they pull out. *Our force shields should be able to handle the smaller annoyances, but I still say hanging around here is too risky. I'm sure Lorego would agree, but the Captain isn't taking his advice. He doesn't seem to think much of mine, either. Lorego's talented, despite his age. I'm sure he'll do everything he can to keep us out of harm's way. Even so . . .*

When Raeden addressed the crew, he painted a rosy picture, not only insisting they were already maintaining a safe distance, but suggested it was their duty—no honor—to gather intelligence. He called it a historic occasion.

Looks like we won't be going anywhere for the next thirty-six hours, so I might as well try to relax while I can. Lance thought. He sat in his favorite mess-hall booth alone with his thoughts. He found them more than enough company, at least while his wife was still on duty. Their downtime usually overlapped by only a few hours, but he favored their time together immensely. Even when they were too tired to do anything but sit together in bed and read, he found satisfaction in it. Being newlyweds, even when they were tired, they regularly found the energy for more intimate pursuits.

Lately, something had been chipping away at Lance's peace, but he hadn't been able to zero in on just what it was that had him in a funk. *My home life isn't the problem,* he decided. *There's not nearly enough of it, but it's not as simple as that.* He sighed deeply and tried to relax. Glancing around, he was pleased to see the cafeteria had finally emptied out.

I have dreams just like anyone else. I do! But talent tends to favor those who don't deserve it, while opportunity often comes when you're ill prepared to capitalize on it. Or maybe it comes to awaken a potential you didn't know you had?

Yeah . . . right. One can hope, but I swear sometimes it comes just to remind me I don't have what it takes.

I'm not in this to get rich. Having little is more than the rich enjoy. They just don't get it—the burden of chasing after wealth or fame, as if either brings even a sliver of peace or happiness. My father was the happiest person I've ever known, and he wasn't rich. I have no grand aspirations.

Lance removed his badge and set it down on the table before him. He stared at it, as if for the first time. A moment later, he picked it up and read: "Commander Lance Bendrik." Above the name was the logo of the CDF: a stylized helm over a pair of wings encircled with stars.

Setting the badge back on the table, Lance sighed. *I chose neither my name nor my title. I'm not sure how I even managed to attain the position of Commander. I didn't want it, but no matter how hard I tried to blend into the background, I kept getting promoted.*

Is it lazy to just want a regular paycheck and quiet evenings alone with my wife? Is that really all you want? Isn't that enough? Maybe. It'd be a great start—certainly more than I deserve, but is it a crime to chase my own dreams, rather than those ascribed to me? Fact is, even if I had the talent, I'm not sure I'd want the opportunities that keep popping up.

There's a reason for everything, just no simple explanations. He shook his head, recalling some of the opportunities he'd let slip away over the years—doors he hadn't realized were open till they'd shut again. A friend once told him some opportunities disguise themselves as tribulations. *Is this one of them? If it is, I just don't see it. I know I ought to be grateful for the opportunity to explore the Dark Nebulae. Few have ever laid eyes on this region, and most never will,* he reminded himself.

At this moment I want nothing more than peace and quiet and the comfort of my favorite booth, and favorite drink. Lance took a sip from his Dragon Mocha and enjoyed the view. A great window wrapped around two thirds of the semi-circular, domed eatery, so the view was naturally spectacular.

Although he couldn't see the force shields, he knew they were there protecting them. He also knew they weren't fail-safe or foolproof. *I still say we're too close. We can always return later to pick up the probes and study the phenomenon, but there's no convincing Raeden. Don't know why I bother. Still,*

I'm glad I'm not the one in charge. I have no desire to take on that much respon-sibility. I'm just glad my shift is over and I can relax a little before heading back to my quarters.

Private Telly came out from behind the bar, wiped down the tables, and then retreated to the kitchen. She was a shy, nervous girl, but nice. The officers liked her, but as far as Lance knew, she hadn't dated any of them. She mostly kept to herself.

A few minutes later, the cafeteria doors sighed open and three officers walked in talking loudly amongst themselves.

". . . never heard of Toro?" Corporal Harding said, his tone skeptical. "The guy's stronger than an Althean bull!"

"I seriously doubt that," another said.

Lance recognized the second speaker from Med Center and frowned. *Doctor Nevins,* he recalled. *Ever since Janys told me about his bedside manner, I haven't liked him. Considering I've never actually spoken with him person-ally, I suppose that's not really fair,* he realized, but something about the man rubbed him the wrong way.

Harding motioned with his head at the Commander and told his com-panions to keep their voices down, which Lance found amusing. He knew Harding well. The corporal was usually the loudest among the company he kept, but was pleasant enough, at least.

Waiving at Lance, Harding said, "Evening, Commander."

Lance nodded and then took another sip from his mug. He avoided eye contact with the others, as he wasn't fishing for a conversation.

Harding said, "I'm telling you, the guy can lift a bus!"

"A bus?" a burly officer said, walking a pace behind the others.

"That's right," Harding answered, as he turned to look over at the bar. He glanced back at the burly fellow and said, "Kord, I thought for sure you'd have heard—"

"Nope. Never heard of him," Kord said and shrugged. He glanced momentarily at the Commander.

Nevins chimed in, shaking his head, "Harding, I've never heard of an orc superhero, period."

"We talking a full bus, or empty?" Kord inquired.

That Kord's a big boy. Big enough to be a superhero himself, Lance thought. He could have been a masters-at-arms instead of a biome technician, but I'm glad he's doing what he enjoys. He reminds me a little of those wide-bodied xeelotians from the Alliance.

"You sure he's a superhero?" Nevins asked.

"Oh, I don't know if he's a superhero per se. He did rescue that dwarven diplomat on the sky train, but I think Toro was just a passenger at the time. He is an augment, though. Confirmed," Harding said, his voice carrying over the others.

Lance continued listening, having given up on any notion of peace and quiet. He knew it was within his authority to order them to lower their voices further still, but didn't want to impose. It was their downtime, too. Besides, he preferred to get along with everyone, when possible. The Captain had called that a flaw, but Lance didn't like confrontation.

"Was this Toro fellow ever confirmed medically?" Nevins questioned.

Harding nodded and got to his feet. "You know, I think I saw a vid once where he lifted a bus. It was empty, but he lifted it as easily as you lift a mug of beer, Nevins."

"You sure he was an orc?" Kord asked, adding, "I thought only humans could be born with the augment gene?"

"Apparently, you haven't learned yet how to read," Nevins snapped. "The gene is in all of us. It's been found in numerous species. Augmentism—the manifestation of augment powers—it's just far more common among humans—and humanus. For whatever reason, it manifests far less frequently in non-humans, but there have been cases on many worlds."

"Really?" Kord said. He seemed surprised.

"Perhaps if you spent more time reading than playing games on your wristcomp . . ."

Kord frowned. "For your information, Nevins, I learn all sorts of things from playing games. And in case you've forgotten, I could break you in half like a toothpick if I wanted to."

Harding laughed. "That he could, Doc," he said as the corporal strolled up to the bar.

Lance couldn't help but smile.

Nevins gave the burly fellow a dirty look and then joined Harding at the bar.

Private Telly emerged from the kitchen to take their orders. Harding pointed at a glazed donut in the display case. Telly put it on a plate and slid it toward him. Glancing over his shoulder, he said, "Can I get you something to drink, Kord?"

"Sure. I'll take two of whatever you're having."

Harding nodded and placed their order.

Kord turned and stared out the window for a time and then glanced back and called out, "Hey, Nevins? What does it take to become an augment?"

Nevins gave him a sideways glance and said, "Why do you ask? Kord, aren't you pumped up enough on Metamaxall?"

"I'm all natur—al, baby," Kord said. "Just curious is all."

"Ah, I thought maybe you were hoping to moonlight as a superhero. I'd avoid the black market if I were you. Plenty of wrong ways of activating the gene—most of them will get you killed."

"I meant legally, of course."

"Oh, well there are two common triggers, birth being the first. The other I don't think you'll ever reach."

"What's that?" Kord asked as Telly set their drinks up on the bar.

Nevins took a gulp of beer, glanced at Harding and then back at Kord and said, "Puberty."

Kord's eyes narrowed. "Don't make me come over there and pound you into butter."

"Ever seen a xeelotian up close?" Nevins asked. He continued before Kord could respond. "Standing next to a xeelotian you'd look like a little girl."

Lance thought about it and agreed. Even the orcs weren't as big as the xeelotians.

Kord sneered. "Ever seen the inside of a trash can? Better yet, how 'bout I just toss you out an airlock? Just answer my question, Nevins. Aren't there any other ways to become an augment? I thought I read somewhere about a guy getting powers after being bitten by a bug."

"I'm pretty sure that came from a comic book. And no, comic books aren't scientific journals, in case you were wondering."

"Never know when to stop, do you, Nevins?" Harding said and finished off his glass.

"You try working in Med Center!" he said, glancing between Harding and Kord. "Nobody ever cracks a joke. Talking boring? Kord, you know I don't mean anything by it, right, big guy?"

Nevins took a sip of beer, set his glass down and asked, "Now, what was the question again?" He immediately raised his hand and then pointed at Kord. "Augmentism, right? I believe in some cases, a physically or mentally traumatic event activated the gene. Augmentism only manifests powers in roughly one in a million humans."

"Huh," Kord said, seemingly satisfied. He downed the rest of his glass and then picked up the second.

Nevins returned to the table with his glass and sat down.

Turning to Nevins, Harding said, "You forgot about the Pulse of 6120 and the GodStorm."

Nevins shrugged. "It's true that the Pulse simultaneously manifested powers within thousands of humans on numerous worlds, and affected several other species in smaller numbers. But that was an extraordinary event. Who knows when it will happen again? Now the GodStorm? There's still not enough evidence to confirm it is linked to augmentism. We just don't know enough about that phenomenon yet. I've read some compelling accounts, but again, they haven't be confirmed."

Kord gulped down his second glass and set it down on the table and frowned.

Nevins glanced over at him and said, "Don't worry, Kord, maybe I'm wrong and you'll reach puberty one of these days. Anything could happen."

Kord stood up and cracked his knuckles, staring down at the mouthy doctor. Harding got up and took his donut with him. He wandered back over to the bar and sat down on a stool to watch his companions, shaking his head.

Private Telly vanished into the kitchen.

"Don't make me have to intervene, gentlemen," Lance muttered under his breath, not wanting to get involved. He'd seen Kord in a fight back on Taeros. The brute won the fight, but he hadn't thrown the first punch. Lance had been there long enough to watch him throw the last. It had been a short fight. As far as Lance knew, Kord had never actually started a fight on his own. At least not since joining the CDF Academy.

Most folks were smart enough not to provoke him.

I think I've seen them in here before, so maybe Nevins knows how far he can push him. *Don't be stupid, Doctor*, he thought. *Anyone can be pushed too far, and sometimes you don't know it till it's too late.*

Nevins remained seated. "Relax, Kord, my friend. Let me get you another—"

A teeth-jarring vibration and bright flash of light silenced Nevins as it rocked the ship, slamming the doctor to the floor. Harding's donut went rolling off into the shadows, but the corporal had managed to grapple the bar in time to keep himself from falling off his stool. Lance was thrown onto his table, spilling the last of his Dragon Mocha.

Kord staggered backwards a step, but remained standing.

"Commander?" Harding shouted in alarm.

Lance's ears were still ringing and there were halos before his eyes as he got to his feet. When the ship rocked, his badge slid off the table. As his vision began to clear, the wristcomp on his left arm flashed an emergency signal, followed by Raeden's voice. "Commander? Get your butt up to the bridge. The One Above All has seen fit to drop the GodStorm on our asses."

Lance doubted the GodStorm was the One Above All's doing, but now wasn't the time to argue particulars. *I hate when I forget to put the comm on privacy mode.* He rushed over and retrieved his badge. "On my way," he said and snapped the badge back onto his uniform. "Everyone okay?" he waited for the officers to confirm their status before continuing. "Nevins, check on Private Telly. I want all three of you back at your stations. Let's move!" he shouted, as he ran toward the exit.

Overnight, the orc's eyebrow hairs had grown down past his chin, his nose and ear hairs farther still. Through a curtain of wavy black locks, he stared at himself in the mirror, shaking his head in disgust. "Dreadlocks are one thing, but this? I look like a girl—a human girl with this head of hair!" he said through gritted teeth. "How is this even possible?" He shuddered when he thought back over the past forty-eight hours. "The GodStorm . . . it did this to me," he whispered, as if to speak of it louder might summon the magical anomaly. He recalled the stories he'd been told in his youth of Deamond, Ariam, Lorel, Vomix and other gods who were swept up in the storm, lost forever, their spirits becoming one with the storm. He shuddered again.

"You say something, Mardag?" came a muffled female's voice.

Behind him, a large mound in the center of his bed stirred. Parting his eyebrow hair, Mardag watched the mound through the mirror. *She's still under the covers. Good. She must not see me like this!*

"Go back to sleep, Rodna. You were dreaming," he said as he walked into the restroom. The door slid shut behind him. Mardag listened for his companion and sighed in relief when she began snoring again. Opening a drawer, he pulled out a trimmer. First, he trimmed his eyebrow hairs and then shaved his head, eager to rid himself of the long locks.

I wish I were dreaming, but the GodStorm taints everything it touches.

The magic-spawned GodStorm first appeared in the Audrysi system more than two centuries ago. Since then, it had resurfaced numerous times across the Pantara Galaxy. Hundreds of ships and humanus space mechs had been disabled by the arcane storm. Dozens had gone missing and some of them had still not been found.

The exploration ship, *CDF-E179 Dauntilus,* was just inside the Dark Nebulae, only three parsecs from the orc homeworld of Taeros when the devastating GodStorm appeared. The anomaly immersed the *Dauntilus* in arcane energy and supercharged the dimensional tornadoes now raging all around them. Blindsided, and struggling to navigate a shrinking corridor, the *Dauntilus* was faced with few options.

The *Dauntilus'* crew attempted a short jump, hoping to escape the arcane storm. Instead, their jump was magnified by it, catapulting them over thirty-five parsecs, through the hazardous Shipbane Expanse and into the dimensional rift located there. When the ship's sensors came back online, the *Dauntilus* found itself hurtling toward a largely unexplored ringworld in the Cosmothereal dimension. It was a region about which precious little was known. Regaining control of the ship, they reassessed their situation from orbit.

Mardag had heard of the ringworld and knew it was called Cathor, but as he was only a supply officer, he figured his superiors weren't in any hurry to share details. *Grandfather told me there were orcs on Cathor. If the legends are true, Chronus, the god of knowledge, came to our world and built an arcane stargate and then left. Decades passed before my brethren figured out how to activate the gate. An orc scout went through and came back telling of fertile valleys, forests and lakes. Then many went through, hoping to find a more hospitable world. Few returned. As is our lot, wherever we go, we find war. Or make war. I know not what the case was on Cathor, but I doubt I'll ever set foot on it regardless. If I do, I certainly don't want any orcs to see me like this. It would bring shame upon my clan.* He sighed and continued repairing his appearance, removing his dangling nose and ear hairs.

Once satisfied that he was more or less back to normal, he opened the restroom door. Rodna was still snoring, but one of her meaty arms had slipped out from under the covers. Mardag gasped when he saw that it was covered in a thick rug of black hair. He was about to wake her with the news, but decided to let her sleep.

Being a farmer is far less stressful than life in space—a simple life has simple problems, he realized. Father was right. I should never have joined the CDF.

With a deep sigh, he slid down in front of his terminal and contacted Med Center. He soon learned that Kord, the only other orc on board, had also reported explosive hair growth, while several dwarven and human personnel experienced severe hair loss. Mardag was relieved that he wasn't the only one suffering. He was encouraged to remain calm and was reassured that most GodStorm side effects were only temporary.

Most?

Tangible aberrations were not uncommon during GodStorm manifestations. One ship might report the sudden appearance of flowers or butterflies on board, another, feathers or even snowfall. The *Dauntilus* had been filled with motes of light that danced and changed colors as they drifted about the ship for hours. The motes were all gone now, but more than a few of them had exploded into harmless, but annoying clouds of confetti.

The GodStorm often played havoc with ship controls, fouled up sensors, drained power plants, and caused other bizarre effects. Arcane shapers—or mages as some call them—were assigned to capital ships as advisors. They usually took on other roles as well, since the GodStorm was thankfully still an uncommon hazard. The *Dauntilus* had no such magic advisor.

Mardag made his way down to his station. *Far from home in another dimension . . . could things possibly get any worse? he wondered. I doubt we'll ever find our way back home.* Turning a corner, the orc was sideswiped by Ensign Dromo riding inside his shell, an antigrav hoverball. The little frog-like orynii was moving faster than he could properly steer.

Realizing he had tempted fate with such negativity, Mardag blurted out an orcish adage, "On my way to a perfect day," but it was far too late for that. The orc sighed, wishing he'd taken a different path.

Plagued by agoraphobia like most of his kind, the bulging-eyed Dromo would sometimes make a nasty remark and then hide inside his hoverball until the offended left the area. No one on board liked Dromo, and the feeling was mutual.

The shell whirred to a stop and then backed up, almost hitting Mardag a second time. A tiny portal slid open and the green-skinned orynii poked his head out. "Mardag! You wouldn't believe what I've had to put up with already today!"

The orc kept walking and avoided eye contact.

"Mardag? Mardag. Mar—dag!" The orynii called out in his annoying nasal voice.

"What is it, Ensign?"

"Have you noticed that most everyone on board is going bangy?"

"I just left my quarters."

"Well, everyone's going—"

"Bangy?"

"You've noticed it then. Not you too, I hope?" He didn't wait for Mardag to answer. "My fellow high elven and human officers have been demonstrating severe mood swings and I just bet they're going to blame it on the GodStorm!"

Mardag shrugged. *It probably was the GodStorm,* he thought. He knew better than to comment, as that would only prolong their interaction.

"I haven't experienced any side effects," the orynii said haughtily. Leaning forward, he rested his elbows on his portal frame and cupped his chin in his hands. Dromo stared at the orc with enormous eyes and it was creeping the orc out. What's worse, Dromo's fully extended, worm-like arm nubs were tapping on the orynii's temples as he had a nervous habit of doing when he was thinking hard.

"What now?" Mardag said, growing irritable.

"Nothing. I just didn't remember your ear hairs being so freakishly long. You should braid those or something."

Embarrassed, Mardag turned around and ran back to his quarters without saying another word. Arriving late to his station, he was pleased to find his commanding officer wasn't around.

Only one other officer was present and mostly kept to himself. Glancing up from his terminal, the officer said, "Mardag, you're lucky you weren't here earlier. Our illustrious leader made me clear all the shelves of confetti. Right after that, things went seriously bangy."

"How so?" Mardag asked, glancing down at the floor. Clearly his fellow officer had merely brushed the confetti off the shelves and let it fall where it may.

"We were in her office going over the inventory log and she . . . well, her irises just vanished."

"What do you mean, vanished?"

"I'm telling you they vanished. Her corneas started glowing red like a banshee's—it was so extra-dimensional!"

"You serious? Where is she now?"

"She became dizzy and went back to her quarters."

"Unbelievable," Mardag said and leaned back against a shelf. He felt his nose hairs twitch and rested a hand on the pocket of his uniform jumper, to confirm he had remembered to bring his trimmers with him.

"You think we'll ever make it back to Mortalis? Back to our own dimension?"

"It can't happen soon enough for my tastes," Mardag said, as he reviewed his shift schedule.

The other nodded and held out a broom. "Here, you can finish up."

Glancing down at the broom, Mardag frowned. His ears itched and he was in a foul mood.

"Hey, might as well keep ourselves busy, right?" the other said, eyeing Mardag strangely.

Mardag sighed and took the broom, then understood the strange expression on his comrade's face and rushed off to the restroom.

Once the GodStorm's bizarre side effects appeared to have finally wore off, some of the crew members became excited over the prospects of exploring the ringworld—no one more so than Captain Neal Raeden. Neal was confident he could turn over the situation and come out on top. "Commander, I hope you have some good news for me," Neal said, as he entered the bridge.

"Captain on the bridge," Lance announced, and everyone stood at attention. As he exited the command station, the commander added, "Sir, the status report came in from Engineering."

Neal met the commander halfway up the ramp separating the upper and lower bridge stations, eager to move on to other matters.

The officers on deck saluted and then returned to their stations, avoiding further eye contact.

"Summarize it for me, Commander," Neal said, as he continued up the ramp. Lance followed him. As soon as he stepped onto the upper bridge, Neal snapped his fingers to get Ensign Lorego's attention, and then pointed to a piece of confetti on the floor.

"Sir, yes sir," the ensign said, and rushed over to pick it up.

Neal had never lost his taste for power. Turning back to Lance, he frowned. "You're the XO—take pride in our ship."

"Yes sir," Lance said.

Looks nervous, Neal realized and found himself smiling. He masked his amusement and motioned with his head for the XO to continue. Impatient, Neal said, "The report?"

"Yes, sir," Lance said, nodding. "The *Dauntilus* is in relatively good shape despite the GodStorm, but the JumpGate Drive suffered significant damage. Chief Engineer Rojyr Maeson said repairs and calibration will take approximately three weeks, assuming nothing else goes wrong."

As the captain listened, he noticed his XO casually rest his hand over another stray piece of confetti laying on the top of the rail surrounding the upper bridge. When a moment later the commander withdrew his hand and slipped it into his pocket, the confetti was gone.

"I figured as much," Neal said, staring at his subordinate, smiling knowingly.

"You seem in a good mood, sir," Lance said after a moment, giving the captain an odd glance, but he said nothing further.

Neal had already spoken with the Chief Engineer and knew about the damaged drive, though he refrained from admitting he had actually been pleased when he heard the news. Even so, he realized Lance might have guessed he was in no hurry to leave the Cosmothereal dimension. "While waiting, we owe it to the Republic to take advantage of this unique opportunity, wouldn't you say, Commander?"

"I'm not sure what to think at this point, sir," Lance said, without a hint of enthusiasm.

Ensign Lorego glanced over, eyeing them, until Neal turned his head and Lorego quickly returned his attention to his nav screen.

Neal was barely able to contain his excitement and frowned at the XO's response. He knew Lance believed it was in their best interests to focus on reviewing their data on the hazardous Shipbane Expanse in preparation for their return voyage through the rift.

"Sir, about the probes . . ." Lance started, falling silent when Neal gave him a warning look.

The captain turned to his XO and motioned for him to join him in the Ready Room. "Lieutenant Commander Falorin? You have the bridge."

"Yes, sir," the young lieutenant commander said, glancing up from reviewing a report with an officer on the lower deck.

As the door to the Ready Room closed, Lance said, "Sir, I recommend sending out two probes . . . record some vid, analyze the data. That should be sufficient, don't you think?"

"Have a seat," Neal said and walked over to his desk. When he glanced back, Lanced seemed about to say something, but took a seat instead.

"That would leave us with only five probes. If you recall, we lost three probes in the Dark Nebulae."

"True, but—"

"Something to drink, Lance?" Neal interrupted, hoping his relaxed approach would derail the commander. He stood, waiting.

"Thank you, sir. No, I . . . I'm fine," Lance said, relaxing his posture slightly.

Lance was tall. Neal preferred to stand while talking with his crew, but never felt comfortable sitting for long regardless. He needed to keep moving, and so he walked over and poured himself a drink, then strolled back over. Neal was in no particular hurry to engage the commander, enjoying the tense atmosphere his silence was creating. Neal knew the commander felt uncomfortable in his presence. All of the officers did. He also knew Lance would eventually back down. Leaning on his chair's backrest for support, Neal sipped his wine as he glanced at the star map projection on the wall behind Lance. *Now for some fun . . .* "There's a trash receptacle in the corner. You may dispose of the confetti in your pocket there, if you wish," he said, unable to resist revealing what he had seen earlier.

"Thank you, sir. I'm fine."

"Go on. It will ease your mind."

Lance stared at him for a moment and then sighed. "Yes sir," he said, and quickly disposed of the tiny strip of confetti. He returned to his seat looking deflated. "Thank you, sir."

"Neal, please."

Lance seemed nervous, uncomfortable, and sat up straight in his chair.

"Sir—Neal . . . the Alliance is ahead of us on every front. They have superior technology. They have bases set up along the northern edge of Dwarven Space, much closer to the dimensional rift than the Republic, and—"

"All the more reason we need to get down there."

"But the Alliance has considerably more experience handling extra-dimensional affairs. We have little intel on the hazards of Cosmothereal space. The Alliance found the ringworld first and quarantined Cathor after only a single trip to its surface. My guess is they must have had a good reason for doing so."

"Lance, you worry too much. Caution is a good thing, but frequent caution starts looking like cowardice," Neal said, grimacing.

"Why don't we send out the probes and see what they find, then decide?" Lance urged.

"We're going to send out the damn probes, Lance. I already know what they are going to find."

"You do?" Lance said, and leaned forward on the edge of his seat.

"Yes—something we'll want to take a closer look at."

Lance shrank back into his seat.

"This isn't your decision," Neal said, taking another sip of wine.

"I know, sir—uh—Neal. I appreciate your willingness to hear me out. By the way, I spoke with Ensign Lorego this morning. He took it upon himself to scan the Keth Rudar system in his spare time and it looks like he may have gathered some promising data. I believe he intends to double check his findings before approaching you with them."

"I'm aware of the Ensign's activities," Neal said, lying. "He has initiative. We could use more of that around here." He stared disapprovingly at the commander over the lip of his glass. After a moment, he set the glass down on his desk and said, "Aren't you at least a little curious?"

"More than a little, but—"

"Have you considered that the Alliance might be simply trying to discourage us from going down there because they found precious metals or caches of architechnology, and want to hoard it for themselves? Maybe they set up secret mining operations and not even the Galactic Senate knows about it. The fact is, they have no jurisdiction in the Cosmothereal dimension—nor in the Shipbane Expanse for that matter."

"It sounds like you've already made up your mind, but I have to advise against setting foot on Cathor. Neal, we're just not ready for this. We don't even know how we're going to make it back home yet."

Neal slammed his fist down on the desk. "Why can't you see we've been given a gift?"

"Frankly, I—"

"We may never get another chance to find out what juicy secrets the Alliance doesn't want to share with the Republic." Neal's frustration was mounting. Knowing Lance was generally liked by the crew, Neal had hoped the commander would support him publicly on this. He didn't need it, but he wanted it. More than anything else, he wanted someone to take the blame if things went poorly. "We're going, Lance, and that's the end of it," Raeden said. *No matter what the probes find.* "Tell Ensign Lorego I want that report," he said with an edge to his tone, adding, "and shut that door on your way out, Commander."

"Yes sir," Lance said and exited the Ready Room without another word.

Neal watched him leave and then sighed deeply.

He glanced at the map projection, and then poured himself another glass of wine. *Would you have agreed with my decision if I had revealed there had once been dozens of primitive, magic-centric empires of elves, gnomes, dwarves and other species across the habitable portions of the ringworld? Or that those empires apparently thrived for millennia, and then for reasons unknown, fell into war and ruin, leaving behind scattered pockets of civilization? Would that have made a difference, or would that knowledge have only bolstered your reservations? He'll find out soon enough,* he thought, and slipped down into his high-backed chair and sipped his wine.

Well, at least he had the backbone to speak his mind. I'll give him that much. Didn't think he had it in him. As he finished off his glass of wine, Neal stared at the star map, wondering what they would find on Cathor.

When years before he had befriended an Alliance dignitary with a fondness for wine, Neal was pleasantly surprised when he started talking about Cathor. The dignitary claimed an organization funded by the Alliance government had made several unofficial trips to the ringworld. Neal had found his descriptions of Cathor amazing, but wasn't sure how accurate the tales were, or how he would ever make use of such information. He was pleased to have such knowledge now, but wondered if Cathor was really as dangerous as the dignitary claimed.

He had no intention of revealing that the ringworld supposedly had an active defense network, nor had he planned on sharing evidence suggesting its structure underwent repairs within the past century, despite the alleged absence of the ancient Architects. *They'd just get cold feet if I told them. Lance, that frikkin' coward . . . he can find out what's what along with the rest of the Away team.*

Returning to the bridge, Neal took his place in the command chair. He noticed Ensign Lorego glance over at him nervously from his sensor display then look away. Knowing the ensign was working feverishly at his report, Neal held his tongue and reviewed his notes.

Five minutes passed and then ten, before Ensign Lorego approached and stood at attention.

"What is it, Ensign? You know I don't like it when you hover over me like a bloatfly. I'm busy."

Ensign Lorego flicked on his wristcomp, and displayed a holo of one of the moons of Cathor. "Sir, if I may? During my downtime, I've been mapping the Keth Rudar system."

"You stole access to expensive CDF equipment without my permission?"

Ensign Lorego's eyes widened. He glanced over at the XO.

"Don't look at him. I'm the one in charge here, Ensign."

"Sir, yes, sir. Sorry, sir."

"Commander Bendrik?" Neal called out, spinning his enormous chair around to face Lance. "What is the typical punishment for violating Article 42?" *Is it 42? Who knows? Ah, the pleasure of power. I was born for this.* He winked at the commander. Turning away from the ensign to address Lance, Neal allowed himself a smile.

Lance didn't respond right away.

"Commander?" Neal prodded.

"I'm sorry, Captain, but you said the ensign stole access without your permission. I'm not aware of a regulation requiring authorization prior to stealing access, or for stealing anything for that matter."

Neal exchanged his smile for a frown. "Careful, Commander, or should that be Lieutenant Commander?"

"My mistake, sir. Did you say Article 42? Ah yes, that one," Lance said, looking nearly as nervous as the ensign. After a moment, he added, "Sir, Ensign Lorego did seek my advice regarding the matter, and I believe his research may interest you."

"It better . . ." Neal said as he spun back around to face the ensign. "Lorego, don't compound your mistake by keeping me waiting. If you show me something worthy of my time, I'll consider forgetting your breach of conduct this once."

"Sir, I thought—I'm sorry, sir. I . . . It won't happen again, sir." A trickle of sweat ran down his cheek.

Neal glanced back at Lance and frowned. He shook his head at his XO and stood up, feeling uncomfortable with Lorego looming over him.

Lorego motioned with a hand and the holo responded, zooming in on one of Cathor's moons. "Sir, the sensors located three enormous, geometric structures on the surface of Moon Thirty-Seven," he said, pointing at a highlighted region of the moon on the holo.

"I have eyes, Ensign."

"Sir, yes, sir. I encountered some scanning interference, making progress sluggish, but I pinpointed the source to this structure here. I compensated for the signal degradation by alternating the—"

"Bottom line it, Ensign."

"Sir," the ensign said and wiped his brow. "My scans revealed significant subsurface construction." He displayed the subsurface structure model, pointed at potential areas of interest and smiled.

Neal found himself smiling, too, and decided to end his taunt. "Well done, Ensign. Your sins have been forgiven."

"Thank you, sir."

"We will investigate those structures prior to setting down on Cathor."

"Sir, yes sir. I should be done with subsurface mapping by—"

"Yes, yes," the captain said dismissively, and motioned for Lorego to return to his station. After a final glance at the main viewscreen, Neal said,

"Ensign? As soon as you complete your report, send the XO and myself a data link and alert Bay 1 to prep a shuttle. I'll be waiting in my quarters for your report. Contact me when we're in position and ready to deploy."

"Sir. Yes, sir!"

"Commander, notify the rest of the Away Team." Approaching Lance, he added in a lowered voice, "On second thought, don't mention anything to Master-at-Arms Valenora until shortly before launch."

"Sir, Master-at-Arms Valenora—"

Neal glared at the commander and added, "I'm fairly certain my order was clear enough for you to understand."

"Yes, sir. I—"

"XO, you have the bridge," Neal interrupted. He turned and walked down the ramp to the lower stations.

Lance nodded as Neal passed. "Yes, sir."

Neal exited the bridge and headed for a lift. He couldn't suppress a smile, but as he got to thinking about setting foot on one of the ringworld segments, he also became more than a little concerned. *Lance is right. We should wait and send out probes, analyze the data—the whole nine yards.* Neal had never understood the ways of magic and knew there might be worse things in store for them down there if half of what his dignitary friend had said was true. He hoped he wasn't putting the Away Team in harm's way, but felt compelled to uncover Cathor's secrets.

Upon arriving at his quarters, Neal activated his holodisk, one of his favorite mementos from his only trip to Alliance Space. The tiny, floating holo projector displayed a massive, three-dimensional model of the ringworld. He lay down on his bed and stared up at it. *Are we getting in over our heads?*

Some of the greatest minds and most powerful ships in the Pantara Galaxy belong to the Alliance. They had everything going for them, it seemed, but their greatest scientists, the taagers, had retreated into the shadows after numerous blunders. Their absence sent shockwaves across the galaxy.

The Alliance must be kicking themselves to have let the taagers go—but they'll be back in the mix soon, if there's anything to the rumors, he thought. *If I'm going to make a name for myself, I need to act now. The Alliance won't sit on the fence for long. With or without their precious taagers on board, they'll return to Cathor soon, if they haven't already. I just don't know how much we can accomplish without their help. The CDF—the whole Republic—wouldn't even have JumpGate Drive technology without the Alliance's help, though we paid dearly for it. They showed us that monsters were real and we became their meat shields against the Hordaq Imperium. Frikkin' Alliance. I think we earned this.*

He rubbed his temples to assuage a throbbing headache and tried to sleep, but he couldn't turn off his thoughts. He felt old and his eyes ached, begging to close. Instead, he reviewed the CDF records on Cathor and on magic, in hopes of finding something he'd missed in his earlier readings, something the Alliance dignitary hadn't shared with him. *How could primitive cultures pose any serious threat? Sure, they know magic, but just how powerful is their magic? We may be an exploration vessel, but we have advanced technology and weapons.*

The moment he thought it, he recalled reports he had read of the troublesome grey elven mages of Seluthenara, and realized magic-wielding mages could indeed pose a serious threat regardless of their level of technological sophistication. *What marvel or horror did the Alliance discover there? If the Alliance deems Cathor too dangerous, what can I hope to achieve?* Neal wondered.

Unable to sleep, he got up to take a shower to refresh himself and calm his nerves before briefing the Away Team.

While stepping out of the shower, he slipped and broke his ankle in two places. He never made it to the moon, much less down to Cathor.

Two successful missions to Moon Thirty-Seven passed while Neal was recovering. The crew found evidence of an ancient Architect Base. It was a valuable find, for the Architects were the most advanced AI's in the known Cosmoverse, and it was assumed that Cathor was their handiwork. Neal was pleased to hear there were no active defense systems on Moon Thirty-Seven.

Ultimately, he acquiesced to Lance's wishes and had authorized the use of probes. The vids they had acquired suggested the ancient ringworld was incomplete, its creators nowhere to be found. Two great parallel rings held seven equidistantly spaced rectangles of metal, earth, and water. Each segment was framed with high mountains and held an atmosphere. Their surfaces were dotted with the ruins of ancient civilizations and newer ones, too.

The ringworld circled an artificial sun—such technology was far beyond anything the Humanus Republic had or hoped to have within the foresee-able future. Many moons orbited the vast structure, some of which Ensign Lorego theorized had been moved there, apparently as additional building material, but were never utilized. Lorego found evidence of ruins on three of the moons, but Neal was losing interest and wanted to get to the surface of Cathor.

Though still recovering from the broken ankle, he was losing patience and announced he would be the first member of the Republic to set foot on the ringworld. Stalling while he healed up, and because the team had found a huge Architect machine on Moon Thirty-Seven, he sent them back to retrieve the machine, and several smaller devices they'd found there. Although two members of the team were scientists, they were not taagers, and had no clue as to the architechnology's purpose and function. Even so, the *Dauntilus* had standing orders to bring back architechnology whenever crew members found it. Lance wondered what new ship he'd be given to command to go along with his assured promotion.

Neal glided toward his wine cabinet, pausing the hoverchair close enough that he could lean on the counter for support. Behind him, the holo projection on the wall displayed the structures Lorego found on Moon Thirty-Seven. Though it pained him to stand, he glanced over his shoulder at the Ready Room door, and then gingerly got to his feet and opened the cabinet. Putting more weight on his bad foot than he'd meant to, he winced with pain. *Frikkin' pain meds are wearing off again,* he realized. *Another glass of wine should help take off the edge.*

The captain rarely shared his wine with others and never let anyone—not even the commander—touch his wine cabinet. The crew knew better.

He removed three bottles and reached his hand in and felt around the back of the cabinet. He glanced once more at the door and then pulled out an oddly shaped metal object, long and thin with strange protrusions on one side. He had no doubt if others saw it, they would know it was exotic and he didn't want anyone asking questions.

Master-at-Arms Manning had owed him a favor, and the object was payment, a minor bit of architechnology the master-at-arms brought back from Moon Thirty-Seven and conveniently forgot to put in Lockdown with the rest. There was no official record of it being on board. It was a smaller memento than Neal would have liked, but one that he was confident he could sneak back home without getting caught. He hoped to sort out a way to sneak back even more of the valuable artifacts, and was itching to get down to the ringworld.

What the hell is this thing? It's metal, but it's warm. Why were you made? Frikkin' thing doesn't seem to be broken. Sure is an odd gizmo. He turned it at different angles hoping to guess its purpose, but was at a loss. *Why were you on that moon? I'd toss you out an airlock if you weren't architechnology. Probably worth more than I'll make off this trip, unless I find something truly fantastic.* He set the strange object down on the bar with a sigh, as he poured himself a third glass of wine. I'm definitely tossing this frikkin' hoverchair out an airlock once I'm healed up.

Neal stared at his treasure while he drank, taking his sweet time. Upon finishing the glass, he hid the object back in the cabinet and put the bottles of wine back in front, then closed the glass doors and returned to the bridge.

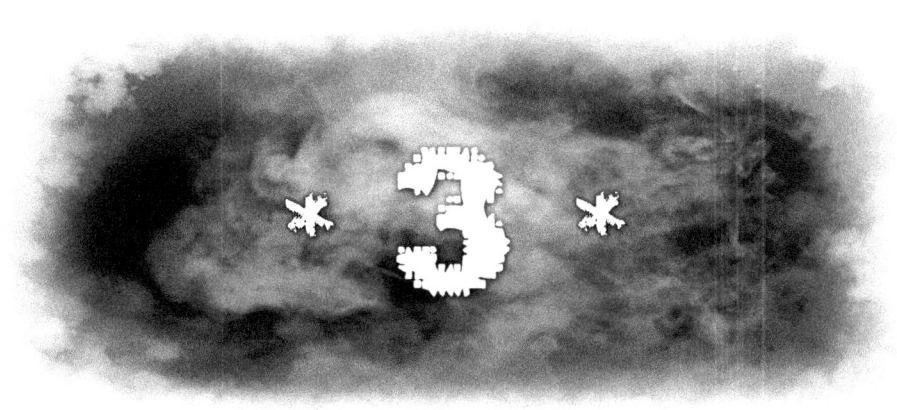

The final trip to Moon Thirty-Seven went by the book. The Away Team reported no significant hiccups in safely bringing on board the much coveted architechnology. All had returned in excellent health, including their team leader, Commander Lance Bendrik.

Shortly after Med Center authorized the Away Team's release from mandatory quarantine, crew members all over the ship began manifesting painful, running sores. The captain was the first to die. A nurse stopped by to check on him and found him in bed, covered head to toe with sores.

Early on, a few members of the crew blamed the GodStorm, even though time had passed since their encounter with the magical storm. Most suggested it was the Away Team's fault, claiming they brought back a xeno virus, but the team had followed all safety protocols, including extensive medical examinations. Med Center found nothing out of the ordinary during their routine safety procedures. Neither team members nor medical personnel became sick while in quarantine.

The science team had isolated the architechnology brought on board, and encased it within force screens, just to be safe. Only the science team had direct access to the exotic technology, and they dismissed rumors of a techno or techno-organic virus. They further made assurances that no one was in any danger from the exotic technology as long as it was kept inside Lockdown, away from the crew.

Not everyone was convinced the architechnology was safe, however. As a result, the science team ran additional tests, all of which came back inconclusive. Eventually, one of the Away Team manifested sores, too, and died soon after.

Reports came in daily of those who had succumbed to the strange, running sores. Dozens of deaths were reported during those early weeks, including all of the nurses and doctors save one: Dr. Janys Bendrik, Lance's wife. Janys became immersed in caring for the sick.

All spare moments were devoted to the living, not the paperwork of the dead. Everyone was devoted to finding answers.

As per CDF protocol, except in times of war, when a crew member died, a funeral was conducted. It wasn't a protracted affair, but elements of the deceased's listed religion, if any, were included and the person was honored. Then the body was released to the sea of stars beyond. A considerable amount of paperwork followed, and personal effects were inventoried and stored for eventual return to their family. When things began to move faster than anyone expected, there was neither the time nor energy for funerals and extensive paperwork. As in times of war, they cut corners. They made do, telling themselves they'd pick up the pieces later.

Lance had reassigned two force screen technicians to assist in Med Center. They seemed leery at first, having no official training, but seemed willing to learn. Aki Yamasura was slow, but careful and thorough. She asked too many questions, but maintained a calm, friendly attitude, for which Janys was grateful. The other, a nervous young human named Ford Mulder, was bright and showed potential, but was so afraid of getting sick that he was almost paralyzed, unable to be of much use.

Morale was diminishing and the crew was on edge. The possibility of getting sick or stuck in a foreign dimension and never finding their way home was ever present on the minds of the crew of the *Dauntilus*.

The dead were removed from the ship using Med Center's own evacuation hatch—sent adrift on the Cosmothean Sea inside chemical decomposition accelerant body bags.

Deep space in the Cosmothereal, unlike space back home, was awash with color, like those gorgeous color visualization images served up to the public in those early days of space travel, as if space up close and personal really looked that good to the naked eye. Such images were representational only, colorized to give the public warm fuzzies and help them dream. And they made everyone feel good about shelling over billions of credits to support the space program. Those doctored images were beautiful, but they were displaying colors visible only to special equipment, and some of the colors were even added, to note celestial details or simply to enhance an image's appeal.

Here, however, the majesty of Cosmothean space was visible for all to see without special "visualizers," though it too had surely been doctored in some way by dimensional energies, the wayward gods and the ever-shifting GodStorm. The view outside the *Dauntilus* was enchanting. Kaleidoscopic gases and shimmering arcane particles swirled about the vast sea. But who had the time to stare at it when there was so much work to be done? And who was in the mood when so many were dying all around?

Lorego had promised to share the images the probes had taken of the Cosmothean Sea during his scans of the region. Despite the chaos, Corporal Torrey also had managed to take some amazing shots when they first arrived in the Keth Rudar system.

Janys had seen glimpses of the Cosmothereal herself during those early days of removing bodies to the vast skysea. Her small viewscreen had given her a taste of the dimension's grandeur, but it was nothing compared to an image Torrey had shown her when they'd passed in the hall one night, before things had begun to slide downhill at an alarming rate.

Although Janys analyzed the data from each new case, none of the data conclusively revealed any known diseases. Aside from the blisters, common symptoms of known life-threatening conditions, especially skin conditions, were absent in most cases. Few of her patients suffered from sores that started in the mucous membranes; few displayed scaly patches, rashes or known skin coloration identifiers. Fewer still complained of pain in their muscles and joints or other telltale signs. The blisters were oddly colored around the edges, but that was their only distinctive quality—that, and the corpses they left behind.

While the sores seemed to respond to antibiotics, some patients actually developed new sores while being treated, and seemed resistant to further antibiotics. Only one patient had recovered completely and returned to active duty. Everyone's hope had been renewed, then just two days later, he was back in with another sore and died within minutes of being received.

Janys had only been away for two hours to grab a bite and take a nap. Upon her return, Ford explained what happened. Without a word, Janys retreated to her new office, shut the door and cried, then came back out like nothing had happened and went back to work.

In all cases, infection was a major concern, despite her best efforts to keep her patients and Med Center sterilized. When an antibiotic seemed ineffective, Janys tried another and even tested the antibiotics for signs of tampering and contamination. She found the whole matter baffling and frustrating.

This thing has ballooned into an epidemic and I don't have a clue how to stop it. I can't tell anyone how I feel—that would just make it worse. We can't afford to have people panicking any more than they already are.

She was grateful Lance hadn't become infected. They had met a few months before the mission had been announced, lost track of each other, and then met again later and became romantically involved. It was because of him that she had, after weeks of straddling the fence, finally volunteered for the mission.

With awkward schedules and being moved around a lot, she found meaningful relationships difficult to start, much less nurture while serving in the CDF. She knew they were moving too quickly, but was lonely and tired of the dating scene. Lance was good to her and they got along well. He was hardly perfect, but she knew such a thing didn't exist.

We're choosing to love each other, and are learning how to along the way, she realized the night he had proposed to her. It was an exciting, whirlwind time in her life and as both were coming from old school families that still believed in the archaic notion of marriage, they were committed to making it work. Their friends thought they were foolish, but then none of their friends were married. The concept was slowly vanishing across the Humanus Republic.

They married a few weeks prior to leaving Humanus Space on a year plus tour of the Dark Nebulae. They were practically strangers, but in the time they courted, they surprised each other with how close they had become. The Colonial Defense Fleet had allowed the event, as the duration of their mission was potentially longer than a year and the crew members' positions were unrelated. Lance was the XO, almost living on the bridge. Their shifts barely overlapped and they rarely saw each other. But they both enjoyed private time and no one had ever said exploration missions were easy.

Stepping inside her office, Janys closed the door and locked it. Her breathing quickened as she removed her scrub top and peeled off a HealTab on her left arm. She snapped a picture of a nasty looking blister on her bicep. Superimposing the image over one she had taken earlier, she was relieved, but also confused to find it still hadn't gotten any worse. While it was still large and painful, if anything, it was showing signs of improvement. *Why am I still alive when everyone around me is dying from the same condition? Death would be easier than dealing with . . . no, don't even go there. It's never the answer.*

Janys had been very careful around the infected patients, but woke up one morning to find she had developed a small running sore. She had self-administered antibiotics and continued to work as though unaffected, telling no one, not even Lance, for fear that he would become distracted. She figured he had enough to worry about with his own, expanded responsibilities. She didn't feel right about keeping it a secret, either, but whom would she tell? There were no other doctors on board. No one she could trust. *It is what it is, girl. Just keep going. Don't even think about it,* she told herself, cradling her head as she rocked back and forth, trying not to cry. *Maybe you'll find a cure. Anything's possible.*

She sat down in her chair, took several deep breaths to calm herself, cleaned the wound and put on a fresh HealTab. Donning her top, she headed back into the fray.

Now the senior officer on board, Lance found himself in a difficult position. In the best of times, he felt ill-suited to be the XO, and now he was Acting Captain and responsible for the fate of the *Dauntilus* and what was left of her crew. Med Center had become inundated with dying patients. Lance felt helpless against a medical emergency.

He feared for his wife's health and knew she was under tremendous pressure. The rest of the medical personnel had joined the list of the dead or dying. Like himself, Lance's wife had been thrust into a position of high authority, and was working around the clock. He had barely seen her over the past two days. Stopping by Med Center to check on her, he waited in her office.

Lance smiled apologetically when Janys walked in, closed the door and sat down across from him. "I really hate to bother you when you're so busy, but—"

"I don't know what's killing the crew," Janys said plainly. She slid down into her chair, leaned back, closed her eyes and took a deep breath.

Lance said nothing. He waited impatiently and tried not to think about his own to-do list.

After a moment, her eyes still closed, Janys said, "There's nothing typical about what my patients are experiencing. There's no precedent—at least none I'm aware of."

"I'm . . . sorry. I wish there was something I could do. Any ideas?"

Opening her eyes, Janys glanced over and said, "About how you could help me, or about the nightmare we're currently living?" Her wristcomp lit up and she swiped her hand over the interface to bring up a holo projection and began reviewing her patient log.

"I've been worried about you. You feeling okay?" Lance asked because it was the sort of thing one is supposed to ask, not because he expected an answer. He knew Janys usually kept her feelings to herself and wasn't the complaining type.

Janys nodded. "I'm fine." Glancing up briefly, she said, "It's good to see you, but I'm really busy."

She smiled, but he could tell it was forced. Lance managed to find a smile, but it didn't last. "Tell me you've found something and I'll be out of your hair." He wished they had time for more than just business, but that luxury ended the moment the GodStorm flung their ship into the Cosmothereal dimension.

"I feel like I've done ten years worth of research in the past three days. I've considered various possibilities—autoimmune disorders, bacterial infections, fungal infections, micro-xenomorphic infestations, dimensional poisoning, nano—"

"I get it. I'm not complaining—really—but I could use some answers. I'd even take a wild guess at this point."

For the first time since she entered the room, Janys looked him straight in the eyes—just a quick glance, and then back to her work. "Lance, we aren't trained to make wild guesses. I'm a doctor. My decisions are supposed to be based on statistically proven data. We ask questions, gather as much data as we can, consider the patient's medical history, search for patterns, check conditions off our list, and conduct examinations. If nothing neatly points to a diagnosis, we look for other conditions that might cause the same symptoms. We dig deeper and attempt to treat the top suspects, and then check more things off the list." She shook her head, clearly upset—maybe even ready to cry, from the look of her, but she held it together.

Lance was miserable for her and wished there was something he could do to lessen her burden.

"The worst part is, before I can even slog through all that, my patients die on me," she said, her voice escalating as she spoke. "Every. One. Of. Them." Her eyes were tired. She was a wreck, and the whole crew was looking to her. Oh sure, he was the top dog, but they were all counting on her. He was, too.

"I'm so sorry, sweetheart. I hate it that you have to deal with all this."

"I swear sometimes my patients seem to get worse when I'm around. Yesterday? I had a patient tell me she was feeling much better. Her numbers were looking good. She'd been responding to antibiotics, so I focused on other patients. Dehydration is always a concern, so I walked over and handed her a cup of water and she got two sores while I was standing there. Nothing all day, and then bam—two sores. She was dead within five minutes."

"That's depressing. It wasn't your fault, of course, but what a bangy situation we're in."

"Yes, we are. We get them on antibiotics the moment they walk in the door, and some of them still die before we can get through our list of questions." Janys stood up, her eyes still riveted to her patient log.

Lance stood as well, not wanting to take any more of her time. "Well, I'll get out of your hair. You're smart. I know you'll figure this out." He knew it was a shallow comment, but they were out of time. Kissing her on the cheek, Lance moved over to open the door for her. She didn't respond, head still in the game.

That's how she is these days—most of the time. There must be something I can do. His heart sank. Although he desperately wanted to hold her in his arms, to comfort her, order her to get some rest, he said nothing. He couldn't imagine how she made it through each day, but she'd always been stronger than he was. As soon as she stepped across the threshold into the main room, a patient flagged her down. The soldier's face was contorted in pain. Lance couldn't get out of Med Center fast enough. Putting on a mask of confidence, he returned to the bridge.

Ever indecisive, Lance's way was to second-guess himself even on simple matters. While leadership was something he'd never aspired to, he kept finding himself promoted over the years. He preferred following orders, but that luxury was no longer his. Most of those under him were young and scared—just like he was, but he tried not to let it show.

Chief Engineer Rojyr Maeson was different. He'd been in the CDF a long time and had a chip on his shoulder bigger than a xeelotian's shoulder horns. He seemed to be ever looking for new ways of making his fellow crew miserable.

Sitting across from him in the Ready Room, Lance was reminded why. Maeson was a whiner, too. And he always assumed he was the smartest one in the room. He usually was, since they didn't have any taagers on board—and precious few in the CDF. But that didn't make the situation any more pleasant. *I don't like him, but I do need him,* the acting captain reminded himself. The engineer had been working hard and deserved more breaks—they all did, but in an emergency like this, you do what you have to do. You do what you're told.

"Repairs to the JumpGate Drive are nearly complete," Maeson said. "No thanks to the rest of Engineeering. If nothing else goes wrong, I figure it will take another two weeks, unless you keep calling me in for these little chat sessions of yours, as if I don't have enough on my plate already."

"That long?" *He looks like he's going to blow a blood vessel. Maybe I shouldn't have said—*

"You know I'm alone in there, right? I have to do everything myself because those whiners have a few sores . . ."

"Crew members have been dying from these . . . sores," Lance said, folding his arms. He'd had to feign some of Raeden's confidence since taking over command of the ship.

Maeson sneered. "You are aware, sir," he snapped, "that I can't run Engineering all by myself? I still have to calibrate the drive and it's not like parking a shuttle in a launch bay. That's why we have specialists."

"Are you not a specialist, Chief?" Lance said, tired of talking. His face hardened. *It's fight or die with this guy. I know this is a messed up situation, but I still need results!* he thought. "Your personnel file says—"

"I know what my file says!"

Just go back to engineering and get it done, Lance thought.

"We'll need a miracle to even make it back to Humanus space on a skeleton crew."

"What are you saying, we just give up?"

"No . . . I'm just saying . . . I don't need you questioning my every move. I could use some room to breath, some sleep, some food—and better than that crap they serve in the cafeteria."

Realizing that trying to pretend he was Raeden wasn't working, Lance softened the edge when he spoke next, hoping to yield a better return. "I understand you've been under a lot of pressure, Maeson, but we all have. We're in this together and—" he paused to speed-think his way through, deciding if he backed down now it might hurt him later. "The fact is, we need it done, so do it."

Lance was as surprised to hear himself say it as Maeson was. "What else are we going to do, just sit here and wait to die?" *Now I've done it. I was too harsh. He's really going to let me have it and my bravado is going to blow up in my face!*

Instead, Maeson smiled. "Didn't think you had any backbone. I'm glad to see I was wrong—sir," Maeson said, adding, "I'll see what I can do." Glancing over at Raeden's bar, he licked his lips. "I could use a little something to drink, though . . ."

Lance walked over to Raeden's wine cabinet, took out a bottle of wine, and handed it to the engineer. "Drink on your own time, not during your shift, and try to remain calm. That's an order."

"Sir," Maeson said with a nod, and got up to leave, then paused and turned around. "What if the GodStorm is still there waiting for us when we get back?"

"One thing at a time, Chief," Lance said, and followed him out of the Ready Room, taking a seat at the command station.

Ensign Lorego glanced over at him and nodded, then went back to his work.

Lance stood up and stared at the viewscreen momentarily then walked over to the edge of the upper deck and glanced down at the stations below. *It sure is a lot emptier on the bridge than when Raeden was running the show,* he realized. They were missing a number of key personnel, including Lieutenant Commander Falorin, who had passed away a few days after Raeden. *If the Alliance is thinking about swinging by to visit Cathor, I sure hope they pick this week to do it. We could use a savior about now.* He couldn't stop thinking about his wife. Returning to his command station, he sat down and pretended to review files on his wristcomp. The weight of his own fears and responsibilities made it difficult to think and what he needed more than anything was to rest. Setting foot on the ringworld was the furthest thing from his mind.

Days passed. Med Center continued to receive new patients and his wife continued to tell him she didn't have any answers. By that point,

Engineering wasn't the only part of the ship running on a skeleton crew. Non-critical stations around the ship had been shut down due to insufficient staffing. As some stations relied on others, they too had to be shut down, except for critical stations, of course.

Maeson desperately needed help in Engineering, but there were precious few on board with the right skill set. Staffing the kitchen was easy. Lance doubted the food could get much worse than it already was. He felt it was important to keep the crew focused and busy. The last thing they needed was idle time to stand around and worry about their future. There had already been a few disciplinary problems. It was hard to blame anyone from flipping out and going bangy with the madness they were facing, but of course he couldn't allow that. He had to maintain order. Despite the many losses, the acting captain continued feigning confidence, hoping it would ease the minds of those he worked with. *One thing at a time,* he reminded himself of what he'd told Maeson earlier, but his stomach was in knots.

"Doctor!" force screen technician Aki Yamasura called out, her voice trembling, as she stared through the isolation room window. "It's Petty Officer Gomitch. He just collapsed!"

Janys rushed over and glanced at the medscanner mounted to the wall. "Yamasura, I just checked on him just five minutes ago." *Or was it ten?* she wondered. She felt overwhelmed and needed sleep badly.

Like Ford, Aki lacked any formal medical training. Even so, she was doing her best, and Janys was grateful for both their help. With all her years of training, Janys knew she wasn't ready for what they were facing. *I can't imagine what's going through their heads . . . they're young—not used to seeing blood, much less having to do something about it . . .*

"Sir, he's not moving," Aki said, peeling her eyes away from the window. "Should I open the door?"

"No," the doctor said firmly, not taking her eyes off the medscanner. "This doesn't make sense." She activated the hovercam inside the room. A panel on the wall slid open and a golf ball-sized camera drifted out and waited for instructions. "HCam, zoom in on patient Gomitch's face. There. Stop." She swiped her hand over the screen and the close up of Gomitch's face was overlaid with a med interface providing additional data. Turning to Aki, she said, "The patient sustained a rapid onset of blisters. A 3.2 centimeter blister on right cheek, five smaller sores ranging from 2.3 to . . . it doesn't matter at this point . . . he's dead."

"How is that possible, sir? He's been in isolation the whole time, hasn't he?"

Janys nodded. "Gomitch became paranoid and belligerent shortly after we entered the Dark Nebulae and began suffering from hallucinations." She dismissed the hovercam and turned to Aki. "His condition only worsened during the GodStorm's appearance and he became violent. Former Chief Medical Officer Hampton had him placed inside for observation. Hampton was conducting psych evaluations, but sadly passed away before . . ." she paused to double check the Isolation Room's records. "No one's been in or out. Even his meals were scanned for contaminants and were provided via transfer panel."

Stepping away from the monitor, Janys leaned against the wall and sighed, closing her eyes momentarily. A nearby patient moaned and her eyes snapped open. "There's nothing we can do for Gomitch now," she said plainly, noticing a patient across the room waving his hand in the air. She motioned for Aki to check on one patient, while she attended to the other.

The two civilian force screen technicians were on ten-hour shift rotations. They had proven helpful, but were slow out of their element. They often woke her up during her short sleep cycles to ask questions or relay the latest emergency. To keep from having to babysit them, she assigned them simple tasks, including interviewing incoming patients, maintaining a vid of each for her to review, changing linens, and inventorying personal items of the deceased.

Janys had instructed each thoroughly on safety protocols and on operating the ultrasonic purifier and sterilizer unit. She even prepared an emergency protocol for them to follow should anything happen to her. Early on, the protocols were reviewed daily. Despite her strict sterilization policy and aggressive antibiotic treatments, the patients were still becoming infected. She knew she was stretched too thin and there was only so much the technicians could do without proper training. Janys began having them review medical tutorials, administer antibiotics, and other med tasks.

More than a third of all interviewees reported similar stories: The victim woke up and noticed blisters had appeared while they slept, or while going about their day. Some reported noticing a shadow move across their path and then vanish. A moment later, painful sores began to manifest. The shadow was sometimes humanoid in shape, bearing a tail, sometimes formless.

A few of those who said they saw a humanoid shadow claimed it spoke to them in Traders Tongue and told them all sorts of things—usually focusing on how inevitable their deaths were, how meaningless resisting was, or asking whether they had a preference on who should be "shadowed" next.

Ford became obsessed with analyzing the accounts, looking for commonalities. There were several cams set up throughout Med Center monitoring activity. Janys didn't buy the notion that there were one or more gaseous creatures on board, as many had suggested. Even so, she approved his request to begin reviewing Med Center security vids. It seemed to calm the technician, and he was quick to stop and lend a hand whenever she found something he could handle.

Over time, Ford became obsessed with stories of "shadow people" and spent most of his on-duty time analyzing Med Center vids when not otherwise busy. A few times he thought he might have seen something in a vid and showed the doctor. Once he did show her something that looked curious, but later, she guessed the odd, moving shadow had almost certainly been a swinging sling lift used for moving patients. Checking the patient log, she saw that around the time of the odd shadow movement, she had indeed been using a sling lift, so the matter was dropped. A patient in the bed beside the one where she had been working died during that time frame, but she said it was only a coincidence. Ford wasn't convinced. He kept looking.

Some crew members had either been too scared to leave their quarters or stayed away until it was too late, perhaps fearing they would get even sicker in Med Center, since so many had died there. Janys knew it wasn't a fair assessment, since Med Center was where most crew members had gone because they were already sick.

She recalled when Lance addressed the crew over the intercom system. He had ordered all crew members to do regular self-examinations and to report to Med Center at once if they discovered a sore. Even so, a few severe cases died almost on arrival, admitting they had been too scared of Med Center.

Lance had also reassured the crew that Med Center was the safest part of the ship and encouraged them to remain alert and calm, and to practice good hygiene and check in on each other. Further, he announced that Med Center was hard at work resolving the epidemic. Privately, Janys had a growing concern about her ability to resolve anything.

After two patients died while she was out of the room, she reviewed the security vid herself, looking for any clues that Ford or Aki might have done something inappropriate by accident, and was pleasantly surprised to find how zealously they had been adhering to her safety protocols. She even reviewed her own actions just to be sure, but found no transgressions.

Despite the increase in the number of stories told about shadow creatures and the number of deaths, neither Security nor the obsessed Ford had any hard evidence of the presence of his so-called shadow people. In time, as the security team thinned out, Ford received special permission to review vid footage of halls and common areas as well. Janys saw no reason to suspect either Ford or the Security team of lying about the state of affairs on board. She had some suspicions, too, but kept them to herself.

Janys puffed up her pillow and slipped under the covers without bothering to remove her long sleeve undershirt. *Oh man, this feels soooo good. A real bed. I was beginning to think I'd spend the rest of my life sleeping in Hampton's chair,* she thought. She listened for her husband. *Still in the restroom. Good.* She sat up and checked her undershirt to make sure the HealTab was still covering the blister properly and wasn't leaving a stain Lance might notice. Satisfied, she covered herself back up.

Oh, Aki . . . Janys' heart sank at the thought of the technician's recent death. *I have no idea how I've survived this long, but so far, so good. I should have made an excuse, came back for a nap later after Lance left. I didn't think he'd manage to get away and . . . well, I think I would have gone bangy if I stayed in Med Center another hour. I know that's the last place you wanted to spend your final moments.*

She heard the restroom door open. Lance called out from the adjoining room, "I appreciate your finally taking a break. You need this."

"It was either stop or put up with your constant complaining," she said, half serious. "I know. It was for my own good."

"You can thank me later."

"Uh-huh . . ." *He's right. I need this as much as he does. I just don't know what his expectations are, and that's what scares me. I don't want him to see the HealTab and I don't have the energy to—*

"I'll be there in a minute, sweetheart." Lance said.

She heard shuffling about. It continued for a time and she wondered what he was up to. *I should just tell him. No, I can't do that—not yet.* She took a deep breath and tried to quiet her mind. *Maybe I should pretend to have finally fallen asleep when he comes in? It would be believable after how little sleep I've been getting. No,* she decided. *That would be such a let down to him after all this time. He deserves—what is he fussing with?* "What are you doing in there?" She immediately thought of the shadow creatures. *You don't believe in them, remember? Of course I don't. Then why is your heart racing? Don't be silly. Stay calm. It's only Lance. He's just—why is it so quiet in there now?* "Lance?" She heard movement again and listened, trying to determine if it was something she should be alarmed about.

A minute later, Lance walked in shirtless, carrying two glasses of wine and wearing a big grin. Janys pulled her covers up higher and frowned. She was about to scold him for not answering when she saw the wine glasses. Handing her a glass of wine, Lance walked around to his own side of the bed and pulled the covers back. "Aren't you going to be hot in that thing? Since when do you wear jammies to bed?"

"I have been for awhile." *Lance . . . I agree it's been way too long since we—well, I hope you're not thinking—*

He got in bed and said, "Can you believe we're in bed—together—at the same time?"

She eyed him suspiciously. "That is the only definition of together I'm aware of."

"You know what I mean," Lance said, his smile only vanishing for a moment. He looked tired, but even after a long day, she knew he sometimes still wanted to mess around.

Lance sat up, turned to her and said, "Isn't this surreal?"

She nodded. "It shouldn't be, but yes, it is. Lance, I—"

"When was the last time we've actually been in bed together?" Lance interrupted as he reached over and stroked her long, dark hair.

I shouldn't be here. What are you doing, Lance? You can't seriously think I'm in the mood? They had only been married a short time before the epidemic broke out. Lance had been in the mood more frequently than she thought possible since their wedding day—she didn't disapprove, but it had surprised her. Their shifts kept them apart more often than either of them had preferred, but he had usually been the initiator. She missed hanging out together, even when they weren't doing anything special, but missed their lovemaking, too. Apart from their whirlwind honeymoon shortly before the GodStorm changed everything, they'd barely found time for each other.

She felt guilty for depriving him the few times they'd found a moment together recently, but couldn't imagine being intimate with all that had been going on. In truth, she struggled to think about anything beyond fighting the epidemic most of her waking moments.

I haven't even managed to save anyone yet. For all I know, I'm coming about it all wrong. Missing some vital piece of evidence. There was a reason I wasn't the ranking medical officer on board. I wasn't at the top of my class at the academy. I'm just . . . average. He's looking at me funny. "Lance, don't get any ideas. I don't have time for anything but sleep. I'm sorry," she said, and meant every word.

"I know," Lance said, defensively. "How can you think I have the time or energy for anything but a nap myself? I'm exhausted!" He kept staring into her eyes, still smiling.

"I just thought . . . you did bring me wine, and you keep smiling."

"I'm just happy to see you finally relaxing. It's been too long since either of us have done that. We're both still healthy. I'm trying not to think about the rest right now. Let's just—"

"Relax?" she said, searching his eyes. *He's telling the truth—I think.*

"Exactly!"

"I feel guilty."

"About what?"

"Us . . . I know it's been awhile since we've—you know. And Ford . . . I hope he's going to be okay without me for a little while. He's been stressing."

"He and that other technician—Aki? They were friends right?"

Janys nodded. "Ford's been more stressed out than usual since her death." She looked into Lance's eyes, searching. *Ford feels it. I bet Lance does too, but he keeps up the mask. We all do. Nobody talks about it, but it's like we all know we're going to die and it's more a guessing game of who's going to be next.* She glanced down at the glass in her hands. "I shouldn't even be drinking this . . . not to mention we were saving it for our one year anniversary."

"It's just one glass and it's from Raeden's private stash. I wouldn't open our anniversary bottle without asking you."

Janys leaned over and kissed him, then licked her lips. "Yum, a blend of mouthwash and wine, my favorite," she said, and then rested her head on her pillow and stared up at the vent over her head. Janys sighed pleasantly, enjoying her husband's touch, his warmth, and most of all, the knowledge that he wanted to spend time with her over anyone else. Even so, she didn't want to encourage his affections, knowing they would have so little time together, and was exhausted. She smiled and took a sip of wine.

"Raeden stocked up good before we left for the Dark Nebulae. You need to relax, and the wine will help."

Janys took another sip and said, "That it will. Thanks for this. Lance, you're right. I did need it. We have a lot to talk about, but not right now. You wanted me to get some sleep," she said, and rolled over on her side facing away from him. "Good night, or good morning, or whatever it is."

"Goodnight, sweetheart," he said.

Janys detected a trace of disappointment in her husband's voice—only a slight trace.

Lance gently ran his hand from the tip of her left shoulder down to her hips, gave her a squeeze, and then rolled onto his side.

Janys held her breath the whole time, that he wouldn't feel the HealTab or accidentally elicit pain from her blister that would make him ask questions. She knew he really did want her to get the sleep she desperately needed, and loved him dearly for it. *I'll make it up to him later,* she thought.

When Ford's call woke her up three hours later, she glanced over to find her Lance had already left. She had been so out of it that she hadn't heard him get up. She wiped the drool off her cheek, quickly dressed and headed down to Med Center.

She saw a patient in need and hurried over to help. Ford was nowhere to be found, so she began to panic. She rushed into the backroom, then checked the restroom, but it was empty. Next she stopped to get another patient a cup of water and then walked over to check her office. *What'd he do sneak off to grab a bite to eat?* Her mood soured quickly.

Janys apologized to one of the patients and walked into the office. Ford was sitting in her inside. "Mulder, why aren't you out there? Your wrist-comp is lit up like a Christmas tree. There are patients out there needing help!"

"I'm . . . sorry," he said, adding, "It's been a rough day . . ."

Janys shook her head and rushed back to the door. She paused and said, "I know it hasn't been easy for you, but I was hoping you'd keep going till I arrived. I wasn't gone that long. We'll talk when I finish up out there." With that, she flung open the door and rushed out.

Ten minutes later, she returned to her office. Ford hadn't moved an inch. The moment she entered the office, she said, "I know you weren't trained for this, Mulder, but the Captain reassigned you to me. You agreed to help, and—" she stopped in mid thought, realizing what had happened.

Ford glanced up to her. His eyes were red and she saw two HealTabs on his right hand and another on his right ear.

"I'm so sorry," Janys said, and walked over and put her arms around him. "I've got one too," she heard herself say, suddenly feeling a kinship with the screen technician.

Ford stared unblinkingly up at her, but said nothing.

Having revealed the truth, Janys continued, "I've had one for weeks. It almost went away a couple times, but then got worse again. It's like a really bad joke. I don't know why I haven't . . . I'm just saying, I—"

"It's okay. I've been expecting it. It was just a matter of time," Ford said calmly. "I'm sorry you got one too. You deserve better than that."

Not really, but . . . whatever. I was really hoping . . . "You've administered an antibiotic, right?"

Ford nodded. "I didn't see a creature. I still believe they're real, but I didn't see one."

"If you didn't see one, then how can you—never mind. I'm sorry . . ."

There was silence between them. Janys desperately wanted to fill the void, but didn't know what to say.

"I've already filed a vid interview."

"Thank you . . ."

"I know we haven't always seen eye to eye. A lot of people think I'm strange . . . bangy, even."

"I don't think you're bangy," she said, feeling miserable for him. "You want to lie down on one of the beds? I'll help you in any way I can."

"No . . . I think I'll just go back to my quarters. Stay there until . . . you know . . ."

"You sure?"

Ford nodded.

She felt terrible about yelling at him, knowing what an emotional toll the sores can take. "Don't worry about anything, and please don't hesitate to contact me, okay? Promise?" she said, and gave him a hug.

"Sure . . ." Ford said and sighed. "Don't worry, I've made my peace. I'm done with this life and am ready for the next. Doctor, just do me a favor and read the messages I sent you when you get a breather. Especially the ones where the subject lines are all caps."

"I will," Janys said, and she meant it. She figured it was the least she could do. It was during moments like these that she'd heard others offer to pray for the afflicted, but she hadn't prayed since she was a little girl. To her, prayer had always been a tool of the unenlightened.

When Ford left her office, he checked on one of their patients and then somberly walked out of Med Center. She never saw him alive again.

Ford had introduced her to a number of concepts that would have caused the scientific community to shake their heads. That fact didn't seem to bother him in the slightest, which told her he had either been a fool, or was on to something others had overlooked. It wouldn't have been the first time. Still, while she had scoffed at many of his theories, she also admired him for taking a stand for what he believed in. As time passed, however, Janys realized many of the things she had once thought absurd, carried more weight than she'd previously given them credit for.

Every time she consulted her wristcomp, Ford came to mind. Because she hadn't been taking him seriously, she had allowed dozens of his messages to pile up, and her message alert was always beeping.

As promised, she slowly began plodding through the messages, articles, pictures and vids he had left for her. In them, she found information on arcane accidents, magical injuries, legends of shadow people, as well as considerable documented evidence on the power of prayer.

Several times, she stopped reading, and considered erasing all of his messages. *Some of them seemed reasonable,* she realized. *His discussion of magical injuries might be dead on, but these others . . . if he's wrong on some, how can I trust the others?* When she thought some more about his ramblings, she knew she couldn't prove he was wrong. She only wanted him to be wrong, and this notion concerned her more than his controversial messages.

Finally, she took a break and visited the other messages between her regular duties.

When she sat down again to fulfill her promise to Ford, Janys tried to do so with an open mind, knowing there were highly intelligent people on both sides of every debate. She had never seriously considered prayer before, and was surprised to find it had been so well documented. Even so, she couldn't imagine herself actually praying. *Intelligent people simply don't pray. They know better,* she had always told herself, but now she wasn't sure what to think. The answers of the enlightened no longer smacked of truth at every turn as they once had, not when she considered the bigger picture. She continued reading, though her stomach was beginning to revolt for lack of food.

The more she read, the more she realized Ford hadn't been as bangy as she'd thought. *All these years, I assumed people who prayed were foolish, but where have the greatest brains in the galaxy gotten us? Both the Alliance and Republic are slowly collapsing from within. The other galactic powerhouses are no better off. We're as screwed up now as we've ever been, despite our technological advances. No, what's foolish is thinking we're always right, just because those we disagree with can't prove every facet of their side of the story. What if we're both wrong, or what if there really is only one way—one truth, but we've been too stubborn or preoccupied to find it?*

More than once, she had caught herself rejecting the gods simply because her colleagues did so. Religion had become a dirty word, and so she had spent her whole life trusting in herself and in those she respected. She had no doubt the gods were real. Even the much-vaunted taagers admitted as much, but few seemed willing to take the next step and actually follow a god wholeheartedly. *I'm only human, operating with limited wisdom, experience and understanding. That hardly qualifies me to make judgment calls about spiritual matters, but can I afford the luxury of unbelief, just because I have doubts?*

If there's anything to all this, I'm going to find it, she decided, and exited the app, unable to ignore the grumblings of her stomach any longer. A moment later, one of her patients' bed monitors went off and she rushed out the door.

Dodging security cams had not proven as difficult as the reaper thought it might be, especially after shadowing a master-at-arms while he was using a security terminal. None of the private quarters were monitored, nor were the restrooms or showers. The reaper also discovered the cams were absent in ventilation shafts and other small openings that he could use to move about the ship unnoticed. Even where cams were present, he sometimes found gaps where he could slip between shadows. The reaper preferred joyriding invisibly in a host's shadow, but as he was shadowing a number of crew members at once, he began using the ductwork more frequently.

Sometimes, out of boredom, and at other times, for the thrill of the challenge, the reaper had exposed his position intentionally to various crew members, most of whom were now dead. When some of the crew members began trying to capture him on vid, the reaper was more careful. That sort of activity inevitably ended poorly for the foolish paparazzi, but the reaper preferred being a rumor to most.

I don't need the entire security team hunting for me at once, he thought. *Right now, they aren't even convinced I'm real. If they become too much of a nuisance, I'll have to make their deaths a higher priority. Till then, I'm having much more fun taking my time, toying with the fools, and making each kill count.*

Glancing down at the small, olive-skinned body on the shower floor, covered in sores, the reaper said, "You were particularly delightful. Of course, you never should have opened your hoverball, poor orynii." The reaper shook his pointy head at the corpse. "I thought you'd never come out of there. I could have come in there for you, but you'd probably have had a heart attack. Besides, half the fun is in the waiting—watching you squirm!"

Reaching down, the reaper willed his body to become corporeal and lifted the orynii's bulbous head to stare into its enormous eyes. The dead crew member's nose was almost completely eaten away by a giant blister that reached all the way up to its left eye. "I have to admit, I almost regret taking your life. You were an easy kill, but oh so deliciously puerile. So many phobias! Fortunately your shell was sound proofed. No one could hear you scream. The look on your face? Priceless!"

When he released the orynii's head, the lifeless bag of flesh hit the shower floor with a sick, smacking sound. "Yes, I think you've been my favorite kill in a very long time. It's a shame you became paralyzed with fear and just gave up in the end. Where's the fun in that?"

A knock came at the front door of the tiny quarters and the reaper glanced up through the open doorway. "I would have let you survive a while longer if you'd have gone to Med Center, but no, you couldn't stop wetting yourself hiding in the shower. I know you thought I was gone by then, but . . . well, hindsight and all that . . ." The reaper paused to listen for the knocker, wondering if whoever it was had left, then turned his attention back on the orynii. "That Dr. Bendrik is pretty sharp. She knows what she's doing, not that you would have been safe there indefinitely. She could have healed you—well, that is, if I didn't stop her. I make sure nobody gets out of there alive. That's my favorite playground!"

Another knock came at the door followed by some dreadful jingle that made the reaper blanch. "Is that noise orynii music?" The reaper asked. The sound ended jarringly. Its absence pleased the reaper immensely.

"Dromo?" someone on the other side of the door called out. "You in there?" The voice was muffled and the reaper couldn't be sure who it was.

Glancing down at the body, the reaper whispered, "Dromo, should I

answer the door since you're incapacitated? Maybe it's your orc friend—
what's his name—Mardag?" The reaper glanced over at the door, then back
at Dromo's body. "I haven't decided who to shadow next, so it might as
well be Mardag, or whoever that knocker is. Hmm, maybe I'd better get
back to Med Center. The last time I stayed away too long a patient fully
recovered. We can't have that, now can we? Ah well." The shadow reaper's
form dissolved into a puddle of shadowstuff, slid up the wall and vanished
into a vent in the ceiling, as orynii music filled the quarters once more.

The chief medical officer's office was spacious, unlike the rest of Med
Center. Lance understood why Janys slipped inside at times, even when
she didn't need to. The privacy was calming. Lance knew well the pressure
of being seen. Someone always has a question, a report or a complaint.
Constantly having to make important decisions and interact with others
is mentally exhausting. Even though the bridge was now mostly empty,
Lance still enjoyed retreating to the Ready Room. He didn't enjoy coming
to Med Center anymore, however. When he'd first come on board, there
was only the occasional patient, but now . . . he tried not to think of all the
crew members that had already succumbed to the sores. It was depressing.

Peeling his wife away from her patients was never easy, but he rarely saw
her outside of Med Center these days. He came as much to find an excuse
to get her to take a break as to see her, though he needed to keep abreast of
her progress. Sitting across from her at her desk, he sensed she was more
tired than usual, and that was saying something. "Let me guess. They saw
shadow creatures?" he said.

Nodding, she confirmed, "All three of my latest patients shared the same
basic story. Lance, I don't know what to think anymore."

"We'll get through this," Lance said, despite his plummeting confidence.
She and the rest of the crew needed a strong leader. They weren't getting
one, but he made a point not to express his own fears, not to give them
more reasons to doubt him, or her, for that matter.

Janys looked like a child in Hampton's tall-backed, sim-leather chair, so
small and slender, but she was competent, sharp. While he wasn't convinced

she could rescue them, he never cared for Hampton and figured if anyone could sort things out, she could. But lately, her confidence seemed to be slipping. He told himself all she needed was more sleep to stay sharp, but suspected the situation was graver than either had imagined.

She sat staring out the window at her patients, and rarely looked over at him.

Lance realized how much he missed her company, her touch, just being together. He wanted nothing more than to sweep her into his arms and hold her tight. He yearned to shower her with affection, to tell her what was on his heart—what she meant to him, but instead he asked for a medical report.

They were working so many hours—*that's not living, just existing*— he knew, but too much was riding on them. They worked on the same ship, shared the same bed—though rarely at the same time, and rarely talked— really talked—about something other than death and how to prevent it. And now it seemed they didn't have the luxury to talk about much else.

Their romance had been short, but thrilling. He knew she was the one for him, but he couldn't give her any assurances he was right—nothing that would hold up in a court of law. Maybe they should have taken more time. But he also believed that he could make it right, even if he wasn't. She had doubts—always the analytical one, and said they should wait until they got to know each other better—until they were sure. Ultimately, he didn't understand why she had agreed to marry him. *Maybe I wore her down. I dunno*, he speculated.

I just want to be there for her—be the sort of man she needs . . . I just don't know if I have it in me. I thought I did, but . . . all this time . . . I think my strength was in her. And now . . . to see this new side of her . . . the confidence slipping away and there's nothing I can do to show her things are going to get better . . . it kills me. I can't help but wonder if she feels the same way about my own insufficiencies—if she suspects I've been depending on her for strength all this time. How can I give her something I've been lacking myself?

When he knew he was faltering, he always reminded himself that she was still there—still moving forward. She had always been his anchor, and now, it seemed, he was hers. She had given him the courage to keep going, but now he was also responsible for the surviving crew members and needed answers. Lance knew every decision was critical and every hesitation could result in lost lives. The thought was suffocating.

These days it seemed even eye contact was uncommon. *She's always got her eyes on a screen, desperately researching, studying or looking after her patients.* He stared at her. Minutes passed as she fixed her eyes on the one-way glass at the rows of beds beyond. It was like she wasn't even inside anymore, but had left the ship and was somewhere floating around the Cosmothean Sea. She was slipping away and he felt helpless to pull her back. *Just talk to me. Tell me some good news. I really need some good news. Don't just fade away. Stay in the game, sweetheart . . .* "You okay, sweetheart?"

Janys nodded, but her eyes were still elsewhere.

When we first discussed the possibility of shadow creatures on board, she laughed. Now she's openly considering it. Get her to talk. Say something . . . "Don't tell me they made a believer out of you?"

Janys simply shrugged.

"Mulder never found anything definitive while reviewing the Med Center cams. Janys, we have surveillance cams all over the ship—"

"I know, but—"

"We have yet to see anything remotely convincing to assume there's a creature on board."

"I didn't say I believed them, Lance, but when so many people tell the same story, I don't think it's helpful to just ignore them," she said, turning to him finally.

"Fair enough," Lance admitted. "I haven't told Security to stop searching, but if they haven't seen anything suspicious by now . . ."

"Maybe it's nothing. Anxiety can manifest in a number of ways. We could be dealing with an undetectable airborne contaminant, something bleeding through the force screens emitted by the architechnology, or something else your team brought back from your trips to Moon Thirty-Seven, but was never discovered."

Lance shifted uncomfortably in his chair. He felt warmth on his leg and ran his hand casually down the side of his pants leg to a cargo pocket where he stored something that wasn't supposed to be there. He patted the pocket and sighed, his eyes never leaving hers. *I don't want any more theories.* He thought. *I want—no, I need answers.*

"Whether it's an airborne contaminant or simply fear, paranoia, anxiety—we're dealing with something very real—a belief in a creature capable of doing all this. Whether the creature is real or imagined, fear can be crippling."

Lance sat up. His mood and patience was crumbling. *I know we're in a world of hurt. Spit! Come on, sweetheart, I need something tangible to go on,* he thought. *She's drained, emotionally and physically,* he reminded himself, *and this situation's a train wreck.* "Janys, if it was an airborne contaminant was to blame, the ship-wide decontamination cycle you ran awhile back should have removed it, right?"

"That's assuming the architechnology isn't still emitting it—if it ever was."

"Good point." Lance still couldn't make up his mind on what to do about it. He didn't feel there was enough proof to blame everything on the architechnology, but wasn't sure if they could afford to keep it on board either. But there were other factors at play that made him want to steer clear of acting on the architechnology.

Janys returned her attention to the window. She leaned forward, apparently watching one of the patients. After a moment, she turned back to him and said, "We need to be crossing causes off our list."

"Exactly," Lance said, and smiled, pleased they were on the same page.

"Regardless of whether that huge machine your team brought back is the culprit, even if it stopped emitting a contaminant, the effects of exposure could potentially last for weeks after the contaminant was removed from the air."

Lance's smile quickly faded. *You've got to be kidding me!* "So, what do you think we should do?"

"I wish I knew. I'm still searching for answers. I meant to tell you yesterday, but I've stopped admitting every patient that comes down with a sore. If their condition isn't advanced and they seem mentally stable, I've started just giving them antibiotics and sending them back to their stations."

"You sure that's a good idea?"

"My tests suggest the condition isn't contagious, and there's only so much I can do. I tell them to contact me or return for a visit once per day, if that will ease their concerns. At least keeping busy helps keep their minds on other things. Believe me, worrying never helps."

"Yeah . . ."

Janys swung her chair back around to face him. It had been weeks since he'd seen her trademark confidence, the strength in her presence, or her smile for that matter. "I'm not making a lot of progress, and the more patients I have in Med Center, the less time I have to solve this. Those that feel the need to remain under my care, I never turn away, but I encourage them to keep clean and keep busy."

"Whatever you think is best."

He became aware of a chemical odor. It beat the smell of death and dying, but it wasn't a pleasant smell. It pervaded not just Med Center, but her office as well. *It's the Thirty-first Century. You'd think by now we'd find a way to make hospitals smell like roses.* Sometimes she brought the smell back with her after a shift. He didn't have the stomach for blood and wounds and death and couldn't understand how it didn't seem to faze his wife.

She glanced at him briefly, then back out the window and said, "I've been working under the assumption that the shadow creatures were merely the result of hallucinations, perhaps related to the epidemic, since they started at about the same time. Cure the disease and the mental condition follows."

"And?"

"Well, they could be linked, but they aren't necessarily—or at least not in the way I was assuming." She leaned back in her chair and took a deep breath, then glanced at him. "Lance, the mind can seriously screw with you, make you think all sorts of things, and see things that really aren't there. Now, I'm not ready to buy into this—it's just a theory, but maybe what we're dealing with is simply a folie à plusieurs. At least I hope it is, because I can't stand the idea that monsters are running around on board."

"Wait, a folie what?"

"Folie à plusieurs. A madness shared by many—or shared psychotic disorder," she said. "Maybe we can treat that. If nothing else, having a non-violent option to tell crew members what might be going on could diminish panic. And if it turns out to be true, all the better. We'll focus on that and find an answer. But we can't ignore the other possibilities, either. I'm going to interview the remaining, healthy crew members, not just those who have shown symptoms or reported seeing apparitions. If there's no pattern, then we can cross that off our list. It couldn't hurt."

Lance shrugged. "The remaining crew members are already working extended shifts. I suppose if you can snag them during their downtime. That's fine by me—if you think it'll help."

"Like I said, it couldn't hurt."

Lance shrugged. "With so many sightings on board, I'd assume the creatures were real if it weren't for the fact that we've not once caught them on cams—and there are cams all over the ship."

She said nothing at first, but seemed to be considering his words. "There aren't any cams in the restrooms or the quarters," she corrected.

"I know, but we should have caught them traveling to those locations, if—"

"Them or it—if they exist. Of course there's a freakishly large number of monstrosities living in the Cosmoverse. I don't recall reading a single report on any that are gaseous. If there are creatures on board, maybe they are invisible or can teleport, not that either of those options is any more encouraging."

"Tell me about it."

"I won't pretend monstrology is my specialty," she said, leaning back in her chair once more and closing her eyes. "I'm beginning to wonder if medicine even is at this point."

"Sweetheart . . . I doubt Chief Medical Officer Hampton would have faired any better. As for monsters, we don't have to look any further than the Hordaq Imperium, but I'm sure we've got some nasties in the Republic, too. There are still a lot of planets we haven't visited, especially on the frontier, and from what I hear, the HDF left hundreds of systems unexplored due to budget cutbacks. Who knows what threats lie west of Humanus Space?"

"And the CDF hasn't?" she countered.

"We're not as bad as they are, but we have big borders to protect against threats we already know are present. The HDF has no excuse. At least we haven't given up on exploration."

Opening her eyes, his wife sat up. "They haven't given up. They just approach the potential of danger by amassing a bigger mech army, just in case something is out there."

"Anyway, we aren't ignoring the potential threat of hidden creatures on board. We just haven't found anything yet," Lance said, frustrated. He felt like they were running in circles and still hadn't arrived at a concrete course of action. *Sure, she can interview crew members, but what am I supposed to do?*

She stood up and stared out the window for a moment, before turning to face him. "If one can believe the reports on board, we're dealing with something gaseous. That's out of my ballpark medically and seems hard to believe."

"But a foly plus sores is more believable?"

"It's folie à plusieurs—I think—and I didn't say it's more believable, but it does seem more reasonable than a gaseous creature."

Lance shook his head and spread his arms wide, motioning around him. "How's that a more reasonable theory? Out there—somewhere—is the GodStorm, a magical force that never goes away—it just moves from place to place, tainting everything, slowly tearing apart the Cosmoverse for all we know. Spellcasting is real. Bizarre monstrosities have been found on planets, supposedly left behind by the Architects—beings far beyond our own intellect. Superheroes walk on the surface of Galandria and many other worlds. Janys, anything's possible."

Janys nodded and said, "Okay, okay. You're right. Or, for all we know, there's a shapeshifter augment on board masquerading as a crew member, a being with the power to cause infectious sores or worse."

Back in the game, but we need answers, not just theories. "Okay, Janys, I'm glad you're thinking outside the box, but we seriously need to start narrowing down the possible causes, not dreaming up new ones. I don't think we're dealing with an augment. The CDF has gotten pretty good at spotting augmentism. If there was an augment on board, it would be in its personnel records."

"That's true . . . unless one of their powers was the ability to conceal their Augmentism. But for what it's worth, I think a shapeshifter is less believable in this instance than a gaseous creature. A shapeshifter would also have to be a damn good actor, and I don't see a motive. And if a shapeshifter were killing off the crew, how does it expect to ever get home again?" she said as she stood up.

"Why bother looking out the window when your wristcomp alerts you that one of the bed monitors went off even if you didn't hear it?"

"I don't want to take any chances."

"You mean you're keeping an eye out for shadow creatures?" Lance asked, half-smiling, toying with her, but also a little curious. He still wasn't sure what he believed about the notion there were creatures on board.

"Are you trying to get me to make up your mind for you?" Janys asked.

You've always been better at reading me than I am, you. You're smarter than I am—why haven't you solved this yet?

With a shake of her head, Janys pressed down her white coat, frowning at a spot on the left arm. Lance thought it odd that she would fuss over getting some blood on her coat at this point. Turning toward him, she said, "We don't have an arcane shaper on board to tell us whether we're dealing with some new GodStorm residual so let's just set that one aside, agreed?"

"Okay."

"I did discover one oddity—well, Ford found it, actually."

"Oh?" Lance sat up in his chair, hoping to hear some good news.

Janys walked over to a small fridge and took out two bottles of water, handing one to Lance. He smiled, realizing how thirsty he was.

"Sorry, but I don't have bottles of wine sitting around to crack open when the mood strikes," she said. Returning to her side of the desk, she opened her bottle and took a swig as Lance waited impatiently.

She's been holding out on me? "You were saying?"

"There's something about these sores that doesn't seem natural. The coloration around the wounds isn't quite normal in appearance. It doesn't match any sores I've ever seen."

"But that's not new. You've told me that before."

"Right, but hear me out. It has been bothering me, but it wasn't leading me to answers. Ever since I told Ford the coloration was odd, he wouldn't stop talking about it. He did some research and kept trying to get me to read some articles of his—they weren't even from a medical journal. One of his conspiracy sources, I figured. I have to admit I wasn't really paying that much attention. Ford always had a theory—usually something completely bangy—"

"Yeah, I sensed the same thing."

"When were you talking with Ford?"

"You do sleep sometimes. I've come in here a few times when you were catching a nap to check on him. But recently I ran into him in the halls between shifts and he started talking about what he called, 'Shadow People'. He seemed really into it. He said he'd done some research, but was afraid you weren't reading his messages. He claims methamphetamine addicts suffering from sleep deprivation sometimes claim they've seen shadow people."

"That's actually true. Or rather, they can hallucinate while using—and claiming such nonsense isn't unheard of. What we're probably dealing with here is a ship full of methamphetamine addicts," she managed with a straight face.

That's the woman I married. Lance tried not to smile, feigning the same seriousness, though he hadn't believed Mulder for a minute. "He also said they have appeared on numerous worlds by various names. I think he may have just stumbled onto something really important. He said something else—it's on the tip of my tongue. Terribly important . . . ah, right. He also told me if a Shadow Person lives under your bed, it wouldn't hurt you."

"How comforting. Anyway I *was* in the middle of a story, remember?"

"Oh, yeah . . ."

"I had just finished a sixteen hour shift. Frankly, I was a bit out of it at the time."

"Not surprising."

"Quit interrupting!"

"Sorry!"

"I was going through Ford's messages and found one he sent me about a bank robbery of all things. The subject line was in all caps and I promised him I'd read them, so I did, even though I thought it was a waste of time."

Lance was about to say something, but held his tongue and listened for a change.

"There was a picture of a boy with strangely colored marks on his body. He and his father had been waiting in line at a bank—I think it was on Endama—no, Neo Earth. Anyway, apparently the bank robber was an arcane shaper. He started casting spells at a security guard and the mage's spell accidentally hit the poor kid's arm, leaving the skin around the wound discolored—not unlike most of my patients."

"What are you saying, you think the wound might be magical?"

"All I can say is that it was interesting. I haven't had much experience with magical injuries, I'm afraid. We don't have any shapers on board. I'd know it if we did. Ford sent me another picture and an article about the GodStorm. It's all in our database, of course, but who has the time to go through that massive beast with a room full of patients to care for? I've been trying, but it's only gotten worse now that I'm back to doing everything on my own. I hadn't realized how helpful Aki and Ford really were . . ."

"I know it hasn't been easy, sweetheart. What about that other picture you mentioned?"

"I was getting to it. The other one was from a security cam in the bank. The mage's fingertips were also discolored in the same way. The article Ford sent me indicated that once the GodStorm started popping up regularly, magic became less reliable. It also said there's really no limit to how much magic even an inexperienced shaper can cast, but if they go beyond a certain amount, it can get very dangerous."

"You mean more dangerous than usual."

"Right," she said with a shrug. "Their spells can misfire and manifest bizarre, unpredictable consequences. Sometimes, the spellcasters burn themselves—not with fire per se, though almost anything can happen with magic, but I'm talking about an arcane burn."

"Like the sores—the coloration, I mean?"

Janys nodded. "Uh-huh. Those marks were found in other areas of the bank. Apparently, the burns have been found in many areas where magic has been used. After reading that, I searched the medical database some more and found other examples of the arcane burns, but they weren't labeled as such. I'm sure that's what they were, though. It's something to keep an eye out for."

You mean besides the bodies? Lance thought. "I'll have Anders do another sweep of the ship and keep an eye out for strange marks, and also see if he can sort out if there are gaps in their security cam coverage. I think I'll also have him start to monitor who is going in and out of which quarters—make sure we don't have a crew member doing a lot of wondering, in case we're dealing with a shapeshifter."

Janys showed him the images Ford had sent her. "I transferred them to your wristcomp."

"Thanks," Lance said, blanching at the gruesome burns on the boy's arm.

Janys returned to the window and glanced out. "What about the archi-technology?" she asked, her voice flat, her back to him. "Are you going to dump it, so we can mark it off our list?"

"Janys, I have standing orders to bring back any architechnology we find."

"Whose orders? The CDF? They'll never know—you don't have to tell them! None of us are even going to make it back to tell on you if we don't turn this situation around."

"I know . . . but I'm not ready to make that kind of decision yet—I'm close, but . . ."

"Lance, we're running out of time. I may be off base on the magic end of things, and regardless, some architechnology has been found to implement magic as a component."

"I don't think that's been confirmed," Lance said. *She's desperate. She doesn't think she can find a cure . . .*

She walked up to him, folded her arms and said, "If the architechnology is at fault, every day we delay means—"

"You think I don't know the risks?" Lance said louder than he'd meant to. "That's all I can think about. Janys, it's not that simple."

"It's not? Lance, you're the captain. It's your call!"

She doesn't understand. But she knows I've never been good under pressure. I have a hard time deciding what to eat for breakfast. How can I command a starship? I can see it on her face. She doubts my abilities. The worst part is, I don't blame her. I just wish . . .

A gulf of silence grew between them and lengthened as she returned to the window. A moment later, she said, "I'll be right back," and exited her office.

Lance watched her walk up to a patient as the door sighed shut.

Don't I have enough troubles of my own? So, the masters-at-arms aren't the only ones who think I'm unfit. Lance wished he could explain his fears, help his wife understand, but he doubted she would listen. *When she gets it into her head there's a way for them to resolve something, she never backs down. It doesn't matter. Even if I told her yes, she has neither the time, nor energy to solve all of our problems. Janys has enough on her plate and needs to find a cure. I can't bother her with my problems—not when everything's riding on her to find a cure. She has to be allowed to focus on her work.*

When Janys walked back into the office, she looked over at him and said, "Lance, I really need you to be strong. This is not the time to . . ." she paused as she crossed the gulf between them, an odd look on her face that made him wonder if she were about to shout at him or cry. She frightened him at times like this. There'd been very few of them since he'd known her, but she was never quick to back down.

He was completely caught off guard when she stepped forward and sank into his arms, wrapping her slender arms around him. "I'm sorry," she said. "Just decide soon, okay?"

Lance held her close and nodded. Her warmth and emotions flooded over him, and as ever before, sealed whatever request she made of him.

He knew it was just a matter of time before he removed the architechnology from the *Dauntilus*. Now it was more a matter of how. He knew there were those on board who would support his decision, but others who might cause trouble. "I will," he said finally, not wanting to seem like a pushover by revealing he'd just decided.

She kissed him on the lips. With her so close, Lance pressed her closer still and slipped in and kissed her on the neck. It had been so long since they'd held each other. She moaned softly as he kissed her, startling him. Immediately, without dwelling on it, his body reacted. A moment later, it seemed she was trying to pull away again as he continued to kiss her and hold her close. *Does she actually think I'd try to have her right here in the office? Why's she—* "What's wrong?" he said, releasing her.

"Nothing," she said, seeming out of breath, her face difficult to read. "It's just this new pair of scrubs. Mine are all dirty . . ."

Yeah, so why are you pushing me away? he thought, confused.

"I had to wear one of Aki's. It doesn't fit right. She was a couple sizes smaller than I am. It keeps pinching me." Reaching inside her open coat, she tugged on the hem of her teal scrubs. "Anyway, I've got to go." She leaned forward and gave him a kiss.

Already, his excitement had faded. Their lips barely touched, and then she was off and running, back to her patients.

That was weird. Hopefully it's nothing a nap couldn't cure. Lance remained in his wife's office for a time, staring at the wall, his own breathing slowly returning to normal as he considered his next move. He faced numerous decisions, some more critical than others. None of them were easy. *I hate this! I never wanted to be in a position of authority. The Masters-at-arms don't respect me. I can tell by the look on their faces. Their tone—most of them, anyway—they know I'm not cut out for this. They won't let me just walk in there and order them to dump the architechnology.*

Miserable, the realization of his situation weighing heavily upon him, Lance sank into Janys' chair, brooding. *Chief Master-at-Arms Anders doesn't trust me, and I know he doesn't like me. He's made that clear more than once. And he knows as well as I do dumping the architechnology is against protocol. The CDF won't come out and say it, but they are perfectly willing to lose soldiers if it means getting their hands on architechnology, especially in light of the rumors floating around indicating the Hordaq Imperium has been stepping up their efforts to kidnap augments and build an army of augment slaves as they rebuild their fleet.*

Disobeying a direct order under any other circumstance would ruin Anders's career. With so many lives at stake, they might side with me, but I can't be sure, he realized. *Not when we're talking architechnology. Way out here in another dimension? If Anders doesn't trust me . . . I'm not sure what he would do. I think Master-at-Arms Valenora would support me. She seems all right. Manning? I dunno—maybe, but the others? They follow Anders like he's the captain.*

Janys doesn't realize the situation I'm in. Maeson thinks I'm an idiot. How much sway do I really have over the crew? Sometimes I wish I could just crawl into a hole and hide—wait things out, but things don't seem to be getting any better.

As he sat there trying to make up his mind, he realized he'd been staring at an AC vent for over a minute and didn't even notice it. That gave him an idea, and he stood up, overcome with excitement. All the way back to the bridge, he role-played in his head how he would present the idea to Anders. *First I think I'll run it by Ensign Lorego and have him bring up some schematics. See how feasible it is. I need to think things through and present them intelligently if I'm going to expect the crew to get behind my decisions.*

The great cube stood silent in Lockdown, surrounded by force screens. Seamless, the huge, ten-ton machine offered no hints as to its purpose, only questions. Completely covered on five sides with levers, knobs, buttons, and other strange protrusions, the cube was just one more architechnological mystery to be solved. The smaller items in Lockdown, though less impressive, were equally mysterious. Many crew members suspected one or more of the ancient artifacts was responsible for the deaths on board.

The science team had attempted deep scans, but something was interfering with their equipment. Even if they had found something, CDF protocol was explicit that minimal information be released, in order to assuage concerns and thereby reduce resistance to having potentially hazardous technology on board.

In matters of architechnology, the chief science officer on board enjoyed special authority even surpassing the captain in certain, limited instances. This fact had been a thorn in the side of every CDF captain since first discovering the exotic technology. Aside from the science team, the Captain, XO and masters-at-arms had limited access. Many of them were now dead.

Ultimately, the science team announced it would be safest to lock up the architechnology and let the CDF specialists take a crack at it upon return to Humanus Space. The architechnology was stowed behind force screens as much to protect it from harm as to protect the crew members. The CDF prized each and every architechnological find.

Turning off the force screens without proper credentials was grounds for severe disciplinary action. Such an act also activated an alarm system and automated turrets. Even if a crew member managed to get into Lockdown and turn off the alarm, force screens and the automated defense system, a proximity alarm would sound as soon as anyone got within three meters of the coveted technology.

On an exploration ship, typically two masters-at-arms would be stationed in Lockdown. With their numbers dwindling and the other on duty masters-at-arms sweeping the ship for potential invaders, on this particular day, Master-at-Arms Jon Deliiri alone guarded Lockdown.

Lately, the chief science officer had been visiting the cube regularly, though he never stated his reasons for doing so. His presence didn't sit well with any of the masters-at-arms, but because they were only guarding the architechnology, he reminded them of his special authority. Even so, he had been acting particularly paranoid and emotional lately and Jon kept an eye on him. When Jon heard the news that the chief science officer had succumbed to the sores, he was not overly upset.

Jon was pleased the CDF had assigned him to the *Dauntilus*. Having no living family, nor other emotional attachments, he accepted the isolation of a long-term mission readily. It was decent pay, after all, and he preferred working in the field, as fewer eyes were on him.

An exemplary soldier, Jon had shown himself to be resourceful, which led his commanding officer, Chief Master-at-Arms Anders, to question why he hadn't taken a different path within the CDF.

Anders was not aware that Jon had been a securities expert and software engineer before joining the CDF. No one knew. Gifted, Jon had become successful at a young age. When the firm he had established on Fargate came under suspicion of illegal and unethical practices, he managed to destroy the evidence and the investigation was eventually dropped. Even so, the negative publicity had hurt his company's reputation. Within a year, he shut the doors, moved to Taeros, changed his name, and started a new life.

Living on the fringe of Humanus Space, he enjoyed anonymity, but soon grew bored. He regretted his failures and reinvented himself, joining the CDF. Those that knew him as Jon Deliiri might claim he was easy to get along with or that he was lucky at card games. They might even say he was a decent artist, for he could sometimes be found sketching and painting during his downtime. Jon never publically showed any interest in computer science or defense systems beyond the role he played in the CDF.

Anders knew Jon had come into contact with architechnology before. Three years earlier, Jon had been assigned to a security detail sent to pick up a Humanus diplomat who for unknown reasons had landed on A032, a minor, unexplored world, and then became stranded there for equally mysterious reasons.

The diplomat had been found in possession of an architechnological device that according to Jon's report, emitted a lethal nanite swarm. Jon alone survived. The others were wiped out by the nanotech nightmare within minutes, along with the diplomat. The swarm had also rendered Jon's recon ship inoperable. Nearly a month passed before a CDF vessel arrived to pick him up.

He languished in a military hospital for three months. During that time, he reported several times what he seemed convinced were prophetic dreams. Jon claimed the Architects were communicating through his dreams to warn the CDF of a coming apocalypse. Such comments were not well received, and resulted in his removal to a psychiatric ward to receive counseling.

Tired of being treated as someone who was damaged, Jon learned to convincingly portray himself as having fully recovered from the traumatic event. Although he continued having nightmares related to the event, he stopped mentioning them and also stopped asking questions about the diplomat and A032, which pleased his superiors. Jon worked hard to gain their approval and excelled at every turn. After nine months, he returned to active duty. When the time came, he reenlisted for another tour of duty.

When Raeden authorized the Away Team to bring the architechnology on board, Jon expressed his concerns, but was careful not to cast himself in a questionable light. He continued to perform his duties respectfully and calmly, without complaint. Inside, however, he felt like he was ready to explode and began having nightmares again.

Jon stood on the other side of the force screen and stared at the giant cube for well over an hour, working up his nerve to do what he felt needed to be done. By the time he made up his mind, he had also gotten it into his head that he could not delay a moment longer, for he firmly believed the cube was responsible for numerous deaths on board.

In his mind, the longer he waited to remove the architechnology, the more people that would die. He deeply regretted forgetting to reprogram the door code, as Chief Master-at-Arms Anders walked in on him right as he was about to disarm the security system. Pretending to be in pain from a sore, he lured Anders closer and then caught him by surprise and killed him. Immediately after, Jon changed the door code. With Anders out of the way and the rest of the team on other assignments, Jon sat down at a security terminal and hacked into the defense and force screen programs and deactivated them.

Turning off the proximity alarms and other fail-safes, he donned protective gear and then climbed inside a power loader to move the smaller, controversial technology into the airlock. Such close proximity to the exotic technology elicited a painful memory of his time on A032. He began to shudder uncontrollably, and almost dropped one of the smaller devices. As he did this, he worried about what would happen if they did make it back to the Republic, knowing he would be in a great deal of trouble. But he also felt compelled to act. *There has to be something I can do to minimize the fallout from my actions, in case they don't understand I was trying to save them. Anders forced my hand. His death was an unfortunate necessity, but they won't see it that way.*

Jon walked around the cube twice, then a third time, staring at the numerous protrusions on each face. *Did someone on the team accidentally bump one of them, causing the cube to release airborne contaminants that are killing off the crew? What if a button merely needs to be pressed to shut it down?* He had already taken pictures of the cube at various angles and spent more than a week studying them when he knew others weren't watching.

It was exhausting work, trying to find a pattern in the number and positioning of levers compared with knobs and other protrusions. He compared sizes, recorded the number of levers in up, down, center, left and right positions, and counted the number of buttons and the positions of the knobs hoping to find a clue. He had spent many hours trying, but finally gave up and decided to dump the architechnology out of an airlock instead.

Jon paused before the cube. It scared him, but excited him, too. *How could one possibly know which button to press, lever to flip, or knob to turn?* From his own research, most architechnology the CDF had found thus far appeared simple externally, but housed complex, advanced machinery within that even the brightest taagers struggled to understand. It was almost as if the Architects had intentionally over-complicated their creations in order to baffle the unenlightened. This cube was only typical in that it was a simple shape and its purpose was a mystery.

Over time, taager scientists managed to unlocked many architechnology mysteries, resulting in great bursts of technological progress. It was dangerous business, but one the taagers apparently relished. Reports popped up regularly showing new caches of architechnology uncovered across the Pantara Galaxy, revealing the Architects had visited far more worlds than anyone had previously thought. Even some of the CDF scientists managed to stumble upon the truth behind some of the technology they had acquired, and they too were eager to learn more, despite the danger.

Few taagers lived in Humanus Space. There were none on board the *Dauntilus*. Long before the Taager High Council pressured their brethren into withdrawing from the Alliance after several very public blunders, a number of their top scientists had uncovered the secrets behind key technologies that made it possible for ships like the *Dauntilus* to travel the stars in weeks instead of centuries. It also enabled the taagers to build colossal structures in space, reverse-engineer powerful weapons, gates, terraformers, and other useful technologies, only a few of which ever made it into the hands of the Republic.

Through the Alliance, the taagers had shared many lesser technologies with both their CDF and HDF allies within the Republic. Someone had to guard the Southern and Western borders of the Republic from the Hordaq Imperium, after all. If the Hordaq were on the move, the Alliance wanted to know about it. They relied on the Republic to share intel and continue to help defend the galaxy in exchange for occasional tech upgrades.

As Jon knew well, some of the more advanced technologies shared were slowly falling into disrepair. With the Republic struggling to maintain the advanced taager technology, he didn't trust them to be fooling around with architechnology.

Of the taagers who had remained behind, rejecting their High Council's wishes, they were now uber rich, for they alone understood how to repair the technologies they had developed by reverse-engineering architechnology. They were hounded by megacorporations, private militaries and other groups that wanted help with existing technologies, and a leg up on new technologies. The taagers further proved useful whenever a cache of architechnology was discovered.

When the Taager High Council finally ended their self-exile, the taagers were welcomed with open arms, but by then, they had decided to severely limit their involvement in the affairs of other species. Again, those taagers who refused to acquiesce to the council's wishes were ostracized, but continued to live like kings—or, in some cases, as well treated prisoners, forced to work for covert organizations. The taagers had changed the technology landscape of the Pantara Galaxy forever, but as Jon knew well, not all exotic technology was beneficial.

He was certain the Architects were clever enough to manufacture a contaminant capable of leaking through a force screen. *Surely they included a way of turning the thing off! They may have been thoughtless and irresponsible, but evil?* He doubted that. *Maybe they created it as a puzzle designed to test those who find it. A contagion might have been included as an incentive to sort out the answer to the puzzle—to get us primitives using our heads. If they did, then it is reasonable to assume they also left behind clues, knowing we're only mortal.*

There was much debate as to whether the Architects were still around. The humanus worshipped them, and their priests claimed to commune with one or more Architects regularly, though they were not able to provide proof. They suggested the reason most, if not all architechnology discovered was ancient was due to the Architects spending most of their time in distant corners of the Pantara Galaxy and beyond.

The humanus built a fleet of colossal Mechs in honor of their metal gods, and much of their art and architecture reflected their passion. Whenever architechnology was found, the humanus claimed it had been left for them to find as a gift from their gods, and strongly encouraged all architechnology to be handed over to them. This rarely happened.

While the humanus were not nearly as advanced technologically as the taagers, HDF AI and robotics development was superior to the CDF's and they had always been more successful at making use of the architechnology that did make it into their hands.

When the genetically identical humans arrived in the Republic, the humanus welcomed them with open arms and shared both their sector of space and their faith in the Architects. The humans gladly colonized numerous worlds, but few humans turned to the Architects. Unlike the humanus, who claim to have been visited numerous times over the centuries by their so-called gods, the humans didn't trust AI.

Rather than turn to the Architects, the humans clung to their old gods, primarily the One Above All, and they rejected the humanus notion of an AI controlled government. The humans had seen too many movies, read too many books and had stumbled too many times with artificial intelligence to ever trust them in positions of power. Instead, they insisted the Architects—if they were even real—were not to be worshipped, but feared.

Tensions grew between the two factions, but fell just short of civil war. They needed each other and the distance between their capitals helped maintain the peace. The Republic, protected by the Humanus Strategic Command, was a union of two great fleets: the larger, predominantly humanus, mech-focused fleet of the HDF and the CDF, the mostly human remnant of far away Earth. In time, the tiny CDF grew into a powerful force, but their stance on the Architects never changed.

Jon, like most humans, believed in the Architects, just not that they were benevolent. He figured they were still around, but likely in hiding. Just as the taagers had admitted to monitoring galactic events from their corner of Alliance Space while in exile, Jon believed the Architects were doing the same thing. *They want us to find their valuable technology or they wouldn't leave it lying around. But why? And who made the Architects? The gnomes would say they did, but who can trust them? The elves know them better than anyone else and they don't trust them. What the elves would agree on is that the gnomes once wielded advanced technology. Of course the elves aren't ones to judge, having no significantly advanced technology of their own. And where is all the allegedly advanced gnomish technology? The gnomes can't even build a decent hovercar!*

Glancing at the time on his wristcomp, Jon began to panic. *I don't have forever to figure this out. Just dump it out the airlock and be done with it! No, I should at least attempt to solve the puzzle and turn the cube off. Are you bangy? Dump it! If I can stop this, we just might make it back home. I would be viewed as a hero. No one can prove I killed Anders. I just need to come up with a good story. He went bangy and tried to dump the architechnology? That might work. When I tried to talk him out of it, he attacked me and accidentally shot himself. Or maybe—spit! How do I turn this thing around?*

A thought came to him. He combined the images of the cube he had taken in secret using the graphics program on his wristcomp. The digital art board was divided into five sections: one per cube face bearing protrusions. The cube itself was a deep, metallic purple, but the protrusions on its surface were varied in color. He isolated the cube itself and deleted it, leaving only the protrusions. Near as he was able to determine, all of the knobs were colored red, black or white. They were otherwise identical. Using the graphics software, he began isolating the protrusions by color, starting with red. Nothing leaped out at him as significant among the red protrusions. He isolated the red knobs from other red elements and looked for patterns.

Nothing.

Repeating the process for both black and white knobs with no success, Jon also separated out the other protrusions by color. The software couldn't identify the difference between protrusion types, but isolating by color was simple. After twenty minutes, he became frustrated.

Still nothing.

He decided the knobs were irrelevant to solving the puzzle and hid all of the knob color layers in the app, so only the other protrusions were visible. He also hid all of the tiny glowing protrusions, which seemed to have no moving parts anyway.

Next, he considered the buttons and began checking for patterns, but soon manifested a terrible headache. *It's probably poisoning my brain. I wonder if sore victims get a headache just prior to becoming infected?* Jon paused his analysis to check on the locations of the other masters-at-arms, knowing he only had so much time to sort things out with the cube. Out of frustration, he dismissed the buttons as irrelevant, and hid them as he had the knobs and lights. He had already extracted the red, black and white protrusions. There had been only half a dozen or so levers among those colors on each cube face. None of the levers were colored the same as any of the buttons, for which he was grateful. He made the isolated red, black and white levers visible again so that the only visible protrusions on the digital art board were levers.

As time passed, his headache grew worse, and he seemed no closer to an answer. Deciding he had wasted precious time, he was about to close the file when he saw it.

There!

Having removed all the other colors, much of the five cube faces were now empty. One of the cube faces bore a cross shape composed of levers. Deliiri knew crosses were used as religious symbols in numerous cultures, but on some worlds they had also come to be associated with hospitals and healing. *The answer is on that cube face. It has to be!*

He quickly separated out the rest of the levers by color, feeling miserable and worried he was running out of time. Even so, he was driven to continue.

Eleven colors. No, twelve. There are twelve! That one's purple! There are multiples of all the other lever colors, but only one purple lever, and the cube itself is also purple! I found it!

Before he could change his mind, Jon rushed around the cube to the face with the purple lever. It was in the Up position. He pulled it downward and stepped back expectantly. His head was on fire and he felt a little dizzy. *I've done what no one else could do. It's over. The contagion—the madness!*

Nothing happened—at least nothing he could detect.

Spit! I must be going bangy. How would I know if something did happen? Well, it didn't explode. That's a good thing, he reminded himself. *I was hoping all the lights would turn off or something. Did the hidden contagion emitters close? How would I tell if they had? This has been a complete waste of time!*

Breathing hard, he sat down on a force screen exhaust manifold and tried to calm himself. Moments later, his wristcomp sounded. He considered not answering it, but knew that would have been suspicious.

"Yeah?"

"Deliiri?" Why aren't you on visual?"

"I'm on the pot," Jon said, thinking fast. "What is it, Manning?"

"You always say, 'Lockdown' whenever I call in."

"Okay, Lockdown—whatever. You know it's me, Manning," Jon said, his tone impatient, nervous. In the background, he could hear someone weeping.

Manning responded, "You sound out of breath. That must be one big—"

"Spit, Manning. Would you give me a break here? I'm just . . . it's nothing. Just a little nauseous from lunch. What do you want? I assume you called for a reason?" *Get off the comm,* Jon thought. *Finish this!*

"It's Lenning," Manning said. "He just—"

"I frikkin' came down with three sores, Deliiri. Three!" Lenning interrupted, shouting.

"I gotta take him to Med Center," Manning said.

"Then go. You don't need my permission," Jon said, his eyes locked onto the cube.

"Spit, that's harsh, Deliiri! You know what a sore means. Anyway, we're supposed to check in, remember? What's with you today?" Manning asked.

". . . nothing. Med Center—got it," Jon said and severed the connection. He made his way to the observation deck, crossed the bridge leading to the upper deck and sat down in the crane's control pod. His hands were still trembling. He had never operated the crane before, but as he suspected, the controls were fairly straightforward. What he hadn't counted on was the locking mechanism preventing unauthorized use. It wasn't overly difficult to bypass—certainly much easier than hacking the security terminal, but it took time.

Once he had the controls unlocked, he moved the crane into position over the cube. As he was lowering the locking clamps, the door to Lockdown shot open and three masters-at-arms rushed in. "Hands in the air, Deliiri. Don't move!" Manning shouted.

Jon knew he was out of time. The moment the door opened, he fired his pistol twice. He was trembling madly and it didn't help his aim, but he got one lucky shot in, catching Manning in the chest. The master-at-arms crumpled like a doll into a heap. The other two masters-at-arms went for cover. Jon fired again and again to keep their heads down as he lowered the clamps into place. "Please, I have to do this," he shouted. "This cube is what's killing everyone!"

"You don't know that," shouted Bronin, a dwarven master-at-arms, who was a little rough around the edges, but had never once given Jon a reason not to like him, much less kill him. The dwarf continued, "Drop the pistol, and let's talk."

The other officer was a fair-skinned high elf. Deliiri had once been interested in her, until he found out his commanding officer had a thing for her, too. Ultimately, she had rejected them both. She called out, "You know we can't let you do this. Not without orders. You don't have the authority to make this kind of decision. Maybe Acting Captain Bendrik will agree with you. He's light years more understanding than Raeden ever was. Don't make things worse, Deliiri."

Jon was largely obscured by the crane's control pod, but the elf kept her side arm trained on him through the plasteel glass.

"Worse? Angelina, it can't get much worse!" Jon was certain the architechnology was to blame and felt he had to at least attempt to save the ship. And if he was wrong and the architechnology wasn't at fault, he figured there was more than a decent chance they wouldn't make it home anyway. Jon had briefly considered stealing a shuttle and heading down to the ringworld, but knew he'd never make it now. His piloting skills were atrocious and he wasn't so sure it was any safer down there anyway. Though he had intended to give himself up after dumping the architechnology, Jon now felt trapped.

Spotting Bronin making his way up toward his position, Jon fired, missing. The dwarf had to cross a short, exposed bridge to reach the crane level, which put him at a disadvantage. From Jon's vantage, he could see down at the half circle staging area dominated by the giant cube, as well as the main and side entrances. He was a better than fair shot most days, but was still shaking badly, and fired several times before hitting Bronin as he was crossing the narrow bridge. The bullet lodged in the master-at-arm's leg. That alone wouldn't have killed him, but he fell to the floor below, smacking his head on something on the way down.

Jon gasped at the sound and knew Bronin was dead or soon would be. He hadn't wanted to hurt anyone—quite the opposite, but he couldn't let them stop him. "I'm sorry, Angelina, but I have to do this!" He shouted. "We should never have allowed Captain Raeden to bring the architechnology on board. It's too dangerous!" His eyes were red and tears ran down his face. "Please, I don't want to—" his words died in his throat as he felt a sting and his neck become wet. Heat spread out across his body and he turned to stare into the eyes of Angelina who had gotten into a good firing position while he was distracted with Bronin.

"Damn it, Deliiri, drop your weapon—now!" She shouted, but he just stood there staring at her, his mouth agape. *Not you, Angelina . . .*

Blood was running steady as a faucet out of his neck and down his uniform. Angelina fired again, catching him in the shoulder and he fell back against the bulkhead and then slid down into the growing puddle of his own blood.

Time passed. He could hear muffled footsteps drawing nearer, but couldn't turn his head to see. *I have to explain to her,* he decided. *Make her understand how dangerous architechnology is.* By the time Angelina reached him, he could barely think. Everything was fuzzy. His wounds were too grievous. Angelina knelt down and rested a hand on his arm. "You left me no choice, Jon. I didn't want to—"

The heat dissipated and a cold chill washed over his whole body, everywhere except where she was touching him. Her touch felt good. He couldn't remember the last time he felt a woman's touch. "I . . . I always liked you Angelina," Jon said, his voice little more than a ragged whisper.

"Try not to talk," Angelina said, as she pulled a HealTab out of her breast pocket and placed it over the wound on his neck. From the look on her face, the HealTab wasn't big enough. The blood was still flowing. She cupped his neck in her other hand, presumably to stem the flow.

"I did it for you—for all of us," he lied. His concern had always been focused on ensuring his own survival. Their continued survival was merely to assist his own. He knew he couldn't make it back on his own. *I am doing it for them. For you,* he told himself. It rang hollow, even in his mind. He repeated it, soundlessly mouthing the words, trying to convince himself. *For you, Angelina.* "You could finish for me . . ." he said, nodding slightly. It was a strain to talk, to breath. Instead, he focused on her touch, her warmth, until he could no longer feel and everything faded away.

Lance was on his way up to the bridge when he came upon a young orc officer sitting up against a bulkhead, whimpering like a child. The broad-shouldered orc was staring down at a huge, oozing blister on his left hand.

He knows what getting a sore means—everyone does now, Lance thought. *It must be a horrible thing to realize you're going to die and know there's nothing you can do to stop it.* Kneeling down beside the orc, Lance tried to think of something comforting to say, but found it hard to focus on anything besides how freakishly huge and pus-filled the sore was on the orc's hand. He felt miserable and hopelessly underqualified. "I'm sorry, son," he said, finally.

A large bubble of pus in the center of the wound had formed a rivulet that ran down onto the officer's jumper. The sore covered most of the orc's left palm and the space between his index and middle fingers. The orc cradled his injured hand in his other and began to weep. "Sir, I was just washing my hands—trying to keep clean in case I came in contact with something tainted." He raised the hand up to show Lance, but the Acting Captain leaned away, not wanting to get too close. He knew his wife said the sores weren't contagious, but with so many getting sick, he didn't want to take chances. Further, he didn't have the stomach to be so close to something so horrible. *I could never be a doctor*, he realized. *I don't know how Janys does it.*

"I've been washing them a lot lately—just to be safe. I even used soap!"

Soap? It took Lance a moment to recall that orcs had different standards of hygiene, though they were still expected to follow CDF health protocols.

"Last time I washed them I saw a huge bulge in the center or my palm. I pushed on it and it burst open." He gasped and lowered his hand down onto his lap. "Then I felt an itch on my stomach and went to scratch it with my good hand, and found this . . ." the orc said as he unzipped his jumper.

"That's okay, I . . . I get the idea," Lance said, but it was too late. The orc had pulled up his undershirt revealing two nasty wounds near his belly button. Lance blanched. Once he regained his composure, he continued. "Did you notice anything odd shortly before the wounds appeared?" "You mean a creature in the shadows? Nuh-uh, but my friend Rodna went yesterday, after talking about hearing things in her room. So I got out of there fast—just in case!"

"Corporal Rodna?"

"Uh-huh," Mardag said, frowning. "She refused to go to Med Center. I tried to convince her to go, but she wouldn't get out of bed. I found her shortly before she . . . it was awful. I stayed with her—held her hand, as she was passing. She told me he—it—whatever that thing was, kept touching her with his tail, each time leaving a mark, a wound. Nobody deserves that!"

"You think she really saw something?"

"She had been drinking, but . . . well, I've never known her to make up something. I sure hope you find whatever it is and kill it. So many people on board are . . ."

"We're still looking. I'm really sorry . . . we're doing everything we can. Try to remain calm."

The orc nodded, but his eyes never left his ruined hand.

"What's your name, soldier?"

"Supply Officer Mardag, sir," the orc said. "I'm going to die, aren't I, sir?"

"I . . . we all are at some point," Lance said, struggling to think of what to say. "Every day's a gift, but let's just get you down to Med Center. You'll be in much better hands there, than out here."

"That's where I was headed. I just . . ."

"Come on," Lance prompted, helping Mardag to his feet. Rather, he tried to help, but Mardag must have weighed well over three hundred pounds. Lance accompanied him to Med Center, scanning every shadow along the way. *Why haven't I seen it yet, if it really exists?*

Upon arriving at Med Center, Lance immediately spotted his wife rushing between patients. She appeared exhausted.

Seeing them enter, Janys pointed to an open bed. Once Mardag was settled in, she came over and began evaluating the orc's condition, talking with him calmly and pleasantly.

Janys, you're amazing. I don't know how you can remain so calm, so gentle, with all the madness going on around you, he thought, watching her work. Lance heard someone moan and turned to look, noticing a master-at-arms lying on a bed. *When did Lenning*—Lance's wristcomp sounded, interrupting his thoughts. He stepped out into the corridor to answer it. "Acting Captain Bendrik."

"Captain, this is Manning."

"Sorry about Master-at-Arms Lenning," Lance said, frowning. He glanced back through the glass wall at the master-at-arms twisting in pain. He turned away and walked further down the hall.

"Sir, I was on the comm with Deliiri a few minutes ago and he was acting strangely."

"Everyone's been on edge lately, Manning. They're scared, and—"

"Pardon sir. But, he's the only one in Lockdown, and he's stopped all communications." There were some odd noises in the background and then Lance heard Manning say, "How much longer, Bronin?"

"What's going on? Manning?"

"Sorry, sir. Deliiri sealed Lockdown, but we'll have the door open in a moment."

"Did you inform Chief Master-at-Arms Anders?"

"I've been trying, but he's not answering his comm. Sir, yesterday I discovered evidence Deliiri had been reviewing—"

Silence.

Lance started heading down to Lockdown.

A moment later, Manning continued, "Sorry, sir. We have a situation. Bronin, Valenora and I are going in."

"Be careful. I'm on my way," Lance said, and rushed off. By the time he got to Lockdown, it was all over.

"Sir, the fusion reactor on Moon Thirty-Seven is active. Since it's a Class Six, I knew you would want to know immediately, but under these circumstances, any active reactor is alarming," Ensign Lorego said as Lance entered the bridge with Master-at-Arms Angelina Valenora at his side.

Lance turned to the master-at-arms and said, "I need to look into this matter before we discuss what just happened in Lockdown, Master-at-Arms."

"Yes, sir," the attractive elf said, and stood at ease.

Lorego was standing at the top of the ramp leading to the upper bridge and glanced at the master-at-arms briefly, then returned his attention to a holo schematic on his wristcomp.

Lance recalled reading in the ensign's report about a fusion reactor, but there was no mention of it being active, much less on the scale of a Class Six. "Are you sure it's a Class Six?"

"Sir, yes, sir," Lorego said, but he seemed nervous.

"One sir will suffice, Ensign."

"Yes, sir."

"Tell me, Ensign, how could you miss a Class Six power plant in your earlier sweeps?" *It doesn't make any sense. The Dauntilus is only running a Class Two. The greatest warships of the Alliance are only running Class Fours!* "You must be mistaken. When's the last time you got some sleep, Ensign?"

"It has been awhile, sir, but it's no mistake. I checked it twice. The reactor is only the size of a Class Four which is what threw me at first, but, well, you know the Architects . . ."

"That still doesn't answer my question," Lance said. He knew Ensign Lorego was very talented. He also knew even a rookie could have detected an active fusion reactor. They hadn't managed to explore but a fraction of the structures Lorego had found on the moon—they were too expansive, but there was nothing in the ruins to suggest a need for a reactor of that magnitude.

"Sir, I'm afraid I don't understand. As you may recall, when I first started scanning the moons I encountered sensor interference. I've been making adjustments to the sensor sweeps ever since to accommodate for it, but as I said in my report—"

"You assured me your scans were accurate, and now you're telling me we have a Class Six right under our noses?"

"Sir, I updated the reactor's class in an addendum to my initial report."

"What addendum?" Lance asked, his frustration mounting. *I knew Raeden wasn't telling me everything, but a Class Six? What else was Raeden hiding from me?*

"Captain Raeden ordered me to share updates only with him, sir. I thought it strange, but that was his order. When you became acting captain, I assumed you had full access to—"

"If you thought I had access to that information, why are you reporting it now? You said you told Raeden about it earlier."

"Sir, I'm sorry. But to clarify, I told him about the Class Six. But it wasn't active before. Now it is. That's why I said—"

"You're telling me a ship landed on Moon Thirty-Seven and activated a Class Six reactor? You should have told me the moment you detected a ship."

"With all due respect, sir. I'm doing the best I can, but sensors didn't detect a ship. Unless it was cloaking its presence or someone down on the ringworld was using long-range teleportation technology . . . or maybe the reactor was remote activated somehow . . . well, I don't know what to tell you, sir. I haven't detected any ships in the area."

Lance realized his lack of sleep and stress over the Lockdown situation was affecting his performance. He'd been harder on Lorego than the ensign deserved. "I see. Well, good work, Ensign," Lance said and took a deep breath, trying to calm his spirit. "Continue sweeping the sector and monitor that reactor. I'll be in the Ready Room. Alert me the moment you detect anything out of the ordinary."

"Yes, sir." Ensign said.

"Carry on." *Madness. When will it end?* Lance wondered. He felt emotionally and physically drained. Turning to Master-at-Arms Valenora, he motioned for her to join him in the Ready Room.

His heart sank as she gave a verbal report of the assault on Lockdown. Like him, she was exhausted and was pushing upwards of eighteen hours on her feet. Considering she had just come out of a battle, she was well composed and coherent, where as Lance felt overwhelmed.

Angelina sat across from him in the Ready Room and waited quietly for his response. Deliiri had shut off the Lockdown cams so there was no vid record of the event.

Lance saw no reason to doubt her. The master-at-arms had always conducted herself in a professional manner and had a clean record. Her version of what happened reasonably fit with what he had seen when he entered Lockdown. From what he knew of her, she was level-headed and an excellent soldier. She had become somewhat emotional during the GodStorm event, but not as pronounced as the other elves on board. And none had passed through the GodStorm unscathed. Afterwards, she was calm and professional as usual, and always pleasant to be around. If he had to complain about something, it was that she made little effort to interact with the crew members during her downtime.

"You all right, Master-at-arms? Why don't you to stop by Med Center?" Lance suggested.

"I'm all that's left, sir," Angelina said, sounding defeated.

Lance knew how she felt, and sighed in despair. "You did your job. I have no complaints. I just wish . . ." Lance fell silent, not ready to express his thoughts and appear weak. "I'm sorry," he said, and smiled sympathetically. "We lost some good people today."

Whenever he saw her out of uniform, Angelina always wore her hair down and loose. Her golden locks were stunning. During her shifts, as now, it was up in a bun so as to prevent it from becoming a liability in combat.

Even with her hair up, she was striking in appearance. Lance made a point not to stare out of respect for his wife, if nothing else. It wasn't easy.

While there was diversity among elves, as with any other species—some attractive and others not—Lance would have had to be blind not to notice Angelina's beauty. She visually fit the fairy tale elven princess stereotype. *No wonder all the officers keep going on about her.* But she can fight too. He'd seen her sparring with the other master-at-arms during Anders' practice sessions, and that's where the fairy tale ended. Angelina could hold her own in combat, with or without a weapon. *Emotionally? No one's immune to what we've been through, but Angelina has held it together, externally, at least.*

Upon entering the Cosmothereal dimension, the master-at-arms had expressed great interest in joining the Away Team. She cited numerous tales of both high and grey elves who crossed vast distances of space to reach the ringworld, and settled there, building great kingdoms. As the elves had first come to Humanus Space and only recently began settling on worlds within the Interstellar Alliance, Raeden questioned how her people could possibly have gotten to Cathor before him. Lance had already guessed correctly, and wondered if Raeden knew as well and was just stalling, to keep her talking. She was easy on the eyes after all, and the way he talked, his probing was more prurient, than fact-finding.

Angelina explained that her brethren traveled to many worlds long before the Republic existed. She told of how a great many elves created stargates and fled the Mortalis dimension when their homeworld, Prax, fell during the Elven/Gnomish wars. If she was right, the elves discovered numerous worlds in their flight to evade a devastating gnomish war machine, settling on Adara, Vandoon, Cathor and others, including those of other dimensions. The way she talked, there were scores of dimensions the humans weren't even aware of that her kind had already colonized. She then claimed it was predominantly because of her people and also those who used the gates that languages like Traders Tongue found their way into the far corners of the dimensions.

"But your kind didn't create all of the gates," Raeden had countered. "Surely you aren't taking credit for the work of the Architects or the gods?" To that she conceded, but insisted neither the Architects nor the gods participated daily for thousands of years with other cultures, sharing art, magic, music, language and lore. Had Raeden been a gnome, instead of a human, he would probably have scoffed at that. If Lance knew gnomes even a little, he would have said the elves rarely shared anything with anyone, and likely impaired, more than contributed to, the welfare of others.

Raeden had always enjoyed taunting the crew, and started badgering Angelina, insisting her people had never set foot on Cathor. He told her he had already assigned Lance to appoint the Away Team and the commander had no room for additional members. Lance couldn't correct him without making his superior out to be a liar. Angelina knew as well as he did that crossing Raeden had never been a good idea. Now that Raeden was no longer around, Lance felt no such compulsions. Fortunately, Angelina seemed not to hold anything against him for keeping his mouth closed.

He couldn't imagine what made her seek a security path, but Raeden had commented more than once about her martial art and melee combat skills. And he recalled Anders bragging about her accuracy with pistols, claiming she was the best on board. Lance had seen her in action too and was glad to have her on the Away Team. And if there really were elves down on Cathor, he would have been thrilled to have her on the team again, if he had any intention of setting foot on the ringworld. But that no longer seemed an option. *I can see why Raeden wanted her at his side.*

Once when she wasn't around, Raeden had confided in Lance that Angelina had actually been the first master-at-arms he had picked for the team—not because of her enthusiasm, but because she was even more capable of protecting them than Anders. Enjoying her frustration over not being allowed to go, he hadn't planned on revealing her position on the team until shortly before they were to get on the shuttle. That was Raeden.

"He told me he was doing it for us, sir. He was trying to save us," she said, staring blankly at the floor.

"Deliiri?"

"Yes, sir," she said, making eye contact. "He pleaded with me to finish the job, but you know as well as I do that CDF protocols are very strict regarding architechnology. He was convinced it was emitting or leaking out some hazardous substance causing everyone to get sick."

"He could be right."

Angelina stared at him wide-eyed, then looked away. "I didn't want to take him out, sir, but it was the only shot I had . . ."

"You did nothing wrong, Master-at-Arms. The thing is . . . I've been looking for a proper way of removing the architechnology myself."

"Are you telling me all that was for nothing?" Angelina said, her emotions rising.

"I would take full responsibility, of course."

"You really think we'll make it back, sir?"

Lance hesitated. He didn't want to lie, but lately he was having serious doubts. There were only a handful of them left, after all.

Once disaster struck the *Dauntilus*, Lance noticed Angelina no longer mentioned journeying to the ringworld. *She must have sensed it had become a low priority.* He felt sorry for her, but they had to concentrate on staying alive.

I wonder how she feels to have potentially come so close to visiting other elven cultures only to have that opportunity vanish? I wonder if she realized we'd have to leave orbit as soon as Maeson calibrates the drive? We won't have time for Cathor. Not now, with all that has happened.

"Chief Engineer Maeson is nearly finished repairing the JumpGate Drive . . ."

"If we go back, we'll be bringing whatever is infecting the crew with us," Angelina said.

Lance frowned. "Trust me when I say I will do my best to prevent whatever's happening on this ship from getting back home, or anywhere else for that matter."

"Sir, Chief Master-at-Arms Anders told me it would take months to make it back to Republic Space, if we can even get back through the Shipbane Expanse."

"We aren't heading home."

"We aren't?" There was an odd look on her face.

For a moment, Lance wondered whether she was still hoping there might actually be a chance they'd make it to Cathor after all. "Not directly," Lance said. "Anders was right. It's too far. We will attempt to cross the rift and stop at Gahruk or G7, hopefully Gahruk. Both are far closer than Taeros."

"Gahruk? Sir, do you think the dwarves would be equipped to handle something like this?"

"No, but the Alliance has a colony on G7 and a military base on Gahruk. I will apprise them of our situation as soon as we make contact."

"May I be frank, sir?"

"Please do."

"We're in a foreign dimension. There are only a few of us left. Even if we find the rift again, we'll be lucky to navigate the Shipbane Expanse. I don't see that happening, not at the rate crew members are dying."

Lance knew the situation was bleak. *We're lucky to be alive and it kills me to think we lost several good people today.* He felt guilty, too, and wished Deliiri had brought his concerns to him.

Chief Master-at-Arms Anders, and Masters-at-Arms Bronin and Deliiri were dead. Master-at-Arms Manning had been taken to Med Center in critical condition. Along the way, he developed several sores and died a short time after arrival. Master-at-Arms Lenning who had been taken to Med Center shortly before the attack, had preceded him by only ten minutes. Other masters-at-arms had perished during the previous weeks.

"If you thought we weren't going to make it back anyway, why did you risk your life to stop Deliiri from dumping the architechnology?"

"I'm just doing my job, sir. You give the word, and I'll dump it right now, but until then, it stays put."

"I appreciate your honesty, and your loyalty. Anders would never have supported dumping the architechnology."

"No, sir. He wouldn't."

"I was trying to avoid a mutiny on board. I wanted to be certain . . . Well, there's nothing we can do about it now. It's a shame, but we need to contain this ASAP. Do you know why Anders never got back with me on the drones? I ordered a drone sweep of the ventilation and access shafts yesterday."

"Anders said it was a bangy idea. He doesn't—I mean he didn't believe there were any creatures on board."

"Fine, but did he do a sweep or not?"

"No, sir. He was just coming off a fourteen-hour shift. I offered to do it, but Anders said he'd take care of it at the start of his next shift. He didn't live that long."

Lance shook his head. "Spit! You have considerably more experience flying the drones than Anders. He should have assigned the task to you."

"I agree sir, but I wasn't in a position to—"

"No, I understand, it's just . . ."

"I'll take care of it right away, sir."

"Thank you, Valenora, but are you up to it? I know you haven't slept since—"

"I'll be fine, sir. If the creatures are in there when I run the drones through, I'll find them and then we can decide what to do next."

Lance nodded. "Excellent. Keep me apprised."

"Yes, sir, but what about the architechnology?"

"I'm going to move it all into Shuttle One myself. I'll remote pilot the shuttle and park it away from the *Dauntilus*.

The elf's eyes lit up. "Smart thinking, sir."

Lance couldn't help but smile. It had been a long time since anyone had paid him a compliment. One of the elf's pointy ears was poking through her long, dark hair, reminding him of a lovely, scantily clad elf Raeden had introduced him to on the night he was to marry Janys. However breath-taking, Lance hadn't found the image productive to be looking at back then, and he wasn't keen on entertaining the memory now. He recalled how Raeden mocked him for getting married, but Lance still felt it was the best decision he'd ever made. Even so, his heart began to race. Angelina was looking even more alluring than usual. Lance frowned at the thought.

"Is something wrong, sir?"

Lance glanced away and sighed. It amazed him how even in the worst of times, the base nature could rise up. Avoiding eye contact, he managed to refocus and said, "If we determine the architechnology isn't to blame, we'll retrieve the shuttle before heading to Dwarven Space, if possible. If we can't be sure it isn't hazardous, I'm leaving it behind."

"Sounds wise, sir. I do wonder though . . ."

"What's on your mind?" he said, turning once more to face the elven master-at-arms.

Angelina stood at ease, concern marring her otherwise pretty face. "If we haul the architechnology into Dwarven Space, won't the Alliance try to take possession of it? I can't see them letting us haul architechnology across their borders. And it's not like we'd be in a position to oppose them."

"It's still on our shuttle, and they can't take our shuttle. Well, I suppose they could insist on transferring the architechnology—"

"For our own safety, of course," Angelina said. "Sorry for interrupting, sir."

Lance shook his head, dismissing her minor infraction. "Yeah . . . they'd probably claim it would be safer for them to transport it across Alliance Space."

"No doubt they'd study it all the way across, taking their sweet time."

Lance nodded. "I'm sure. They would be doing us a favor, after all, helping us get the *Dauntilus* back home safe and sound," Lance said and shifted uncomfortably in his seat. He didn't like their options. "If we leave the shuttle here in high orbit, the Alliance is bound to find it before we can get another ship out here. If we take it with us, there's at least a chance that we can get the architechnology home, and as you know, that's a high priority for the CDF."

"I understand sir. Of course there's also a decent chance we'll lose the shuttle entirely while crossing the rift or the Shipbane Expanse."

"We're going to have to risk it. I'll take full responsibility," Lance heard himself say for a second time. He couldn't imagine the Republic risking another ship. It was too far, but if he told them there was more architechnology on Moon Thirty-Seven, they just might try it, despite the danger.

"We'll make contact with the Republic as soon as we get to Alliance Space and see what they want to do. No doubt the Alliance would be able to crack our transmission, and I don't see that there's anything the Republic can do to stop the Alliance from getting first peek, but maybe they'll share their findings with the Republic in exchange for additional time with the architechnology."

"If they give it back."

"Right. If they give it back, but I think they will. We're the ones who found it and they're still our allies. I don't know. Hopefully that's the right move. It will be too late to change our minds when we reach Dwarven Space. I don't think we should even mention Moon Thirty-Seven until we're back home, just to be safe."

"For what it's worth, sir, you kept your cool and handled all this better than Raeden would have."

"I don't know about that, but I appreciate your vote of confidence." *It kills me that I spent weeks scratching my head accomplishing nothing. It's really only been in the past twenty-four hours or so that I've thought of anything intelligent to act upon.* "Once the architechnology is safely offship, I'll have Chief Medical Officer Bendrik run another shipwide decontamination cycle—see if we can end this."

Angelina's lips curled up in a smile, then quickly flatlined.

It had been a brief, but pleasant thought, knowing she was pleased with him. He looked away before his mind lingered where it shouldn't. His wife came to mind, enabling him to refocus faster.

"Sounds good, sir. The sooner the better."

"Right. We'll know before long what we're really dealing with here. That will be all."

"Yes, sir," Angelina said. She stood and saluted.

Lance stood as well and returned the gesture.

Pausing at the Ready Room door, the elf turned and said, "Sir? I know you feel like you let us down, but you didn't. You did what you could, and that's all anyone can ask for."

"Yeah? Well . . . thanks," he said and smiled. "Be safe and try to get some sleep soon."

"Yes, sir," Angelina said and added, "I hope you find some time to sleep too, sir."

Lance couldn't recall the last time he had slept. He knew he needed sleep badly, but he didn't dare acquiesce. Not yet. There was too much to do, and like Angelina said, they needed to act, *"the sooner, the better."* Lance went into his private restroom, splashed water on his face, dried off and made his way down to Lockdown to prepare to move the architechnology into one of the shuttles.

Bay One was directly below Lockdown. Lance opened the cargo hatch and used the crane to lower the huge cube into the shuttle. He then removed the smaller devices from the airlock where Deliiri had taken them and lowered them inside the shuttle as well. He sealed the shuttle doors, closed the hatch to Bay One and sighed in relief. *Now to get the shuttle off the ship without damaging anything in my compromised state . . .*

Lance took the personal lift down to Bay One's control station and stood in front of the terminal. He leaned against the terminal and closed his eyes. His mind was foggy, his cognitive skills diminished. He rested for several minutes and then set up the remote link and opened the airlock. His adrenaline was pumping, and with it, his heart began racing, knowing what was at stake. This gave him the edge he needed to remote pilot the shuttle out of the bay. Closing the airlock, he parked the shuttle. *Finally. With any luck, we're one giant step closer to ending this.* "Janys?" he said, activating his vid comm.

A moment later, her face materialized on his holo screen. "All done?" she asked, looking as tired as she sounded.

Lance nodded. "The architechnology's offship."

"Finally, she said with a sigh, then smiled. "You did good."

Lance smiled as well.

"I'm initiating the shipwide decontamination cycle now. Just remember, even after the cycle is complete, it could still be weeks before it's truly over. If the remaining crew members are carrying the contaminant in their systems and just haven't developed sores yet."

"I understand."

"Have you heard anything from Master-at-Arms Valenora yet?"

"No, but there are miles of ventilation and access shafts to check. Hopefully we'll hear good news soon," he said, realizing that even if Angelina didn't find anything, that didn't mean there were no creatures on board. *They could be inside quarters and other private areas.* Still, he was pleased they were finally making progress.

"Lance, are you going to move everyone into Med Center?"

"I think it's best—until this is truly over. There aren't many of us left. It will be easier to keep an eye on everyone that way. Get some rest when you can."

"You too, Lance. I'm your doctor, so that's an order."

"Will do," he said and stepped away from the terminal. She would be concerned if she knew just how long I've gone without any sleep. Back home, I would have won a record by now. He sank down into a chair to rest and closed his eyes.

Lance's wristcomp sounded, rousing him from a deep sleep. He yawned and stretched, looking up and realizing he was still in Bay One. *How long have I been sleeping?* His wristcomp chimed again. He didn't bother using the vid comm. "This is the Captain."

"I'm sorry, sir . . ."

"Valenora? What is it, Master-at-Arms?" Lance said, wiping sleep from his eyes. He stretched and sighed deeply.

"I . . ."

"You sound out of breath. Are you okay?"

"No . . . no, I'm not," she admitted. Her voice was weak. "I was running the drones through the ventilation shafts. I got about forty percent through the sweep and started . . ." she sniffled. To Lance, it sounded like she were in tears. "Sir, I haven't seen any sign of intruders yet. I'm going to try and finish, but . . ."

"Valenora?"

Silence.

"Valenora?" Lance shouted and ran out of Bay One, heading for Security. By the time he got there, she was too far gone. She was hunched over the drone terminal, covered in running sores. He held her hand until she passed.

Janys closed her eyes and leaned back in her big chair, but couldn't switch off her mind. *I can't go back out there. I'm no closer to finding an answer than I was a month ago. What can I tell them? What hope can I offer? Mardag is my second patient to beat the sores. He fully recovered, but how long is that going to last? The first patient to do it got sick again right away, and died faster than any of the others.* Her breathing quickened, and tears ran down her cheeks. She no longer felt up to holding them back.

I can comfort them, but they're still going to die. I can't beat this. I envy those who believe in God, those who have hope. What do I have? I can't even protect myself! If Lance hasn't gotten a sore already and is just hiding it like I am . . . then he's bound to get one soon.

"I wish I could just sleep," she muttered, out of breath. *I don't even care if I wake up again. I've been fighting to stay alive to protect Lance and my patients, but I'm not making any difference.*

Why have I been spared while so many others have died? She took a deep breath, let it out slowly and then took another, and another, trying to clear her mind and psych herself up to do what was expected of her. *Lance ordered me to get some sleep, but I can't. I've tried and it won't come. There's too much at stake—I might stumble upon a cure yet. No, it's more likely we'll die by the sores of the shadow people or the architechnology's curse than be saved by my hand. While I'm still here, I can at least comfort the survivors.*

Her condition was almost laughable. The sore on her left arm had responded well to antibiotics, but just as the skin healed over, she got a second blister beside it, and it became infected immediately. This happened repeatedly. She'd even found a dried mark of grime around the wound, and that had really scared her. It baffled her too. *I've done everything I can to provide a sterile environment and proper medical attention. I wash my hands all day long. It doesn't make sense.*

There should be a logical explanation for what's been going on, but I can't find one. A lingering spell effect would be a reasonable theory, at least if one of the crew members was a spellcaster. If the GodStorm left behind some magical contagion, I'm at a loss as to what to do about it, other than to abandon ship in the remaining shuttle. But we don't know anything about Cathor. Would it be any safer down there on the ringworld than up here? It has to be, but I can't just leave Med Center. It's our only hope of overcoming this—if there is any hope.

Applying a fresh HealTab, Janys donned her scrubs and coat, and walked out of her office.

Lance and Lorego had just returned from removing the two latest victims of the epidemic, sending them adrift in the Cosmothean Sea. Intentionally avoiding her husband, Janys went straight to the restroom to freshen up.

In an effort to keep a closer eye on the remaining survivors, all crew members were moved to Med Center. Additional beds were crammed inside, wherever they'd fit, along with foodstuffs from the Biome, additional staples from the cafeteria and storage, including chairs and tables. Of the eight remaining crew members, only one was sick, Private Telly, from the cafeteria. She was immediately quarantined, with the focus on minimizing opportunities for infection, and quelling the objectors.

Chief Engineer Rojyr Maeson was the loudest dissenter. "You're trying to kill us off, aren't you, Doctor? Move the cook out into the hall. What? Don't look at me that way. Doctor, if I die, who's going to run Engineering, the cook? Fact is Private Telly's going to die anyway."

"Chief?" Lance said, his tone laced with a warning. He stood up from the security terminal.

Stay out of this, Lance. Janys shot her husband a look and he fell silent. *He's wiser than I'd been giving him credit,* she thought. Turning to the engineer, she said, "This is Med Center, Chief Engineer Maeson! Telly is in quarantine. She has a single sore. I'm not even convinced it's the same type we've been dealing with. It's more than likely just a coincidence. Regardless, this isn't a democracy. It's my Med Center. Don't tempt me to put you in quarantine instead," Janys said, in no mood for Maeson's attitude. She immediately regretted her comment.

Maeson shook his head disapprovingly. "Great bedside manner, Doctor. They teach you that at the academy?"

"Maeson, for your information, sores were common prior to bringing the architechnology on board, so there's no reason to assume Telly is—"

"I could tell by the look on her face. I'm telling you, she'll be dead soon."

That's probably true of all of us, Janys thought. Instead, she said, "You're out of line, Chief. Telly offered to go into quarantine or I would have kept her out here with the rest of you, regardless of your comfort levels." She knew that wasn't quite true. There had been some concern over morale, and she'd run into Maeson before and knew he was a grumbler. She folded her arms, then released them quickly upon feeling pain from the compressed sore on her left arm.

Ensign Lorego seemed to notice her reaction and gave her an odd look, but said nothing. The others were oblivious, even Lance.

Okay, I'm doing a miserable job of instilling calm. Maeson's right. I shouldn't have mentioned quarantine, not to him of all people. He had always rubbed her the wrong way, but she usually managed to hold her tongue. *Cool it down* . . . "As I've said before, Maeson, there's no reason to suspect the sores are contagious."

The engineer sneered. "Oh, so you know what we're dealing with then, do you, doctor? Do you have even the slightest idea what's going on?"

"Shut it, Chief," Lance warned again.

"I know I have antibiotics," Janys said, and tried to make eye contact with each of the survivors before continuing. "And I know they help. They really do. I also have pain meds and I know the most important thing we can do right now is to keep clean and to remain calm. Pray if you're a believer, but remain calm."

Janys routinely evaluated her patients' emotional states, looking for clues to assist her in responding to their needs, though she was no psychologist. Maeson was the one she was the most concerned about. Thus far, his emotional state seemed largely unchanged. He was annoying, as usual. She knew he was afraid—they all were. He seemed more nervous than usual, but that too was normal under the circumstances. Still, she made a point to keep an eye on him.

Finally, the engineer quieted down. A few minutes later, she walked over to him. "I'm sorry about what I said, Chief." She would never have put him in quarantine, but knew her comments had been unprofessional.

"You of all people should know better."

"I didn't mean it. I'm doing my best, and you've been questioning me at every turn. We're all tired and—"

"That's no excuse," he said, and found something to distract him on his wristcomp.

"You're right," she said, resisting the urge to throttle him. Maeson made no move to continue the conversation or apologize for his earlier behavior. She hadn't expected him to. *Okay, let's try this again . . .* "You feeling okay, Chief? No sores, I hope."

"No sores—yet," he muttered, eyes glued to an obscure holo display on his wristcomp.

She walked away without another word.

A short time later, she saw Lance walk over to Maeson. When her husband spoke, he was calm, something she found very difficult around the engineer. "Chief . . . let's talk."

Maeson glanced up and said, "What a cozy arrangement you've created for us. I feel so much safer now."

"You know as well as I do what's at stake. Something's going on and until we sort out what it is, we're safer together than apart. If there's something out there, I have a gauss rifle and a pistol."

"All the masters-at-arms are dead. You know we're sitting ducks out here in the middle of nowhere. Everyone's dying and I'm supposed to be comforted that you have weapons?"

"We've also got cams all over the place."

"Cams looking at empty halls."

"Get some rest, Chief. That's an order."

Maeson shook his head and frowned, muttering under his breath, "You have to sleep sometime." His tone was difficult to read, but Lance seemed to take it as a challenge.

"What was that, Chief?" Lance said, getting up in the engineer's face.

Everyone was tired and uptight. It was natural, but it was also far from ideal.

Janys continued to monitor them. She stared at Maeson, who hesitated to answer his superior officer.

Finally, Maeson's features softened and he half-smiled. "So there is some spunk in you. Good, we'll need that if there really are shadow creatures on board, which I find hard to believe, but I suppose it's possible." He glanced over at her and the others, then back at Lance before continuing. "I only meant that you're tired like the rest of us. Why don't you give me the pistol? That way we can both guard, just in case the shadow creatures are real. Gyria! We should just go down to the weapons locker and arm everyone while we're at it."

Janys watched them, hoping neither would overreact. Maeson might be sincere, but she still didn't trust him, and hoped Lance would decline. *Maeson's right though. Lance does have to sleep sometime, but if there were shadow creatures on board, why all the sneaking around? Can they even be hurt? Why not just sweep in here, infect us all and then wait for us to die, or maybe they've already done that?*

"When was the last time you fired a pistol, Chief? Besides, I didn't say rest was optional. I said it was an order," Lance said, staring down the engineer.

Maeson wasn't a fighter, but he was bigger than Lance and not easily intimidated. He sniggered, but said nothing. Finally, he took a seat in a corner away from the others.

Janys was pleased to have one less distraction, but wondered how long it would last. She was sure Lance's concern wasn't over Maeson's abilities with a weapon. Stifling a yawn, she sat down before her med terminal and saw a notification on her screen to check in on Telly. She stood up and walked over to the Quarantine door. Glancing in the window, she found the young woman lying on the floor in the fetal position. Her jumper was smeared with blood. Around her neck, a puddle of blood had formed. After checking the biohazard sensor, Janys slipped inside, but it was too late. The young woman had found something sharp and slit her own throat.

Checking the body, Janys found no new sores. The one Telly did have hadn't gotten any worse. In the privacy of quarantine, she sat down beside the girl and wept. When she was able to compose herself, she returned to the others and told them the news.

Everyone was scared. Crewman Kelsa Tanners in particular, seemed distraught. The young crewman shuddered visibly and after a few moments, began to cry.

Maeson glanced over and said, "Don't act like you care, Crewman. You didn't say a word when she went into quarantine."

"That doesn't mean—"

"Save it. Not once did you go over and talk to her through the door comm."

"It wasn't like that. I did care, but like Dr. Bendrik said, she went in there willingly. I didn't know her real well, but she was nice. I liked her. There are only a few of us left. Grow a heart, Chief!"

Maeson stood up and glared at the young woman and then turned to Lance. "Acting Captain Bendrik, I presume you were witness to Crewman Kelsa Tanley's disrespectful remark?"

Lance looked up, but didn't answer right away.

"Acting Captain?"

"I'm afraid I'm unfamiliar with any crewman by that name, Chief. Did you mean Crewman Kelsa Tanners?"

"You know exactly what I—yes, Tanners, sir," Maeson said, softening his tone near the end.

Lance shrugged. "You can file a report once we get back to Humanus Space, if you wish. Perhaps I'll file my own report at the same time. We can do it together. I may need you to confirm the spelling of your last name for me."

Maeson's face went red. "Me? Without me, you'd never make it out of this dimension. How typical," Maeson said under his breath. Turning back to Kelsa, he said, "Watch your mouth, Crewman."

"Sir, yes, sir," Kelsa said, but it sounded hollow.

Maeson shook his head and returned to his seat. A few minutes later, Janys heard him badgering Ensign Lorego.

She continued to keep an eye on him, worried emotions would start running even higher the longer they were cooped up in Med Center. There was still so much they didn't know about what had happened, and she didn't feel at all comfortable yet about what they should do next, aside from getting proper rest, nutrition, and remaining calm and clean. As for the bigger problem, she felt no closer to finding a solution than when she first began tackling it. That wasn't true, of course. She had made some progress, but worried that the important questions might not be answered until it was too late to do anything about them.

Four days had passed since they shut themselves up in Med Center, and no new sores had appeared. Everyone but Maeson's spirits had visibly improved. The engineer felt claustrophobic and spent most of his time to himself, when he wasn't complaining. Everyone was glad to give him the extra space.

Janys began filling out reports on those who had passed away. It was unpleasant business, but she didn't mind terribly as she was hopeful that it was finally over. After all, they had lost most of their crew, so they were past due for a turn of luck.

Taking a break from documenting her cases and reviewing her notes, she stood up, back aching, and stretched. Then she walked over to check on Lance.

As she approached, Lance glanced up and smiled. "Everything okay?"

Janys shrugged and looked away.

"Besides the usual, I mean." Lance clarified, before continuing. "Things are looking up, right? No new sores in several days. Smile. That's a good thing. It means this whole mess may be over."

Janys nodded. "I was just filling out reports of the deceased and mulling over what-if's in my head."

"Oh?"

Janys glanced past him at the others, and then motioned with her eyes for him to follow her into her office.

Lance closed the door behind them.

"What's up," he asked, as he set his pistol down on the desk. He leaned the gauss rifle against the wall and then sank down into a chair on the other side of her desk and sighed.

"Nothing alarming," she said and plopped down into her big chair. "I mean, it would be alarming if it was true. I was just being morbid—thinking about what sort of creature could have evaded our security cams for this long."

"I've been thinking about that too, but I'm reeeaaallly hoping we're wrapping up an architechnology problem. Otherwise . . ."

"We could be looking at more deaths—if something or several somethings are out there and we just don't have the technology to spot them." Janys shuddered.

"Yeah . . ." Lance frowned. "That is morbid."

"Most of the eyewitness accounts were similar." Janys snapped her fingers over her wristcomp and a holopage manifested in the air above it. She began reading. "When I woke up this morning, I saw a purplish-red skinned humanoid with a long tail and glowing eyes. It was staring at me from a corner of the bedroom." She glanced up and raised her eyebrows. "Even those that didn't describe it as humanoid often mentioned seeing a tail."

"I know. I've read most of those reports myself, but—"

"Most?"

"I've been busy. I probably read all of them. I'm sure I've read all of them."

"Uh-huh."

"I read everything you send me. I just don't have the greatest memory. There might be something I missed."

"Which is why it never hurts to review," she said, and glanced back at the summaries she'd made. "Smoky—shadowy—slithering out from under my bed—under my desk—in the closet—slipping out of my own shadow . . . that last one was mentioned three times," she said, glancing up from her wristcomp momentarily. "Most of the accounts describe the creature at some point as a shadow . . ."

Lance sat quietly for a moment, elbows on his knees, fingers interlaced. For a moment she thought his eyes were closed and wondered if he were praying. She'd been thinking a lot more about prayer lately, but hadn't known him to do so. Then he cracked his knuckles and said, "If they can slip into our shadows, maybe they can move with us, mimicking our movement, the way our shadows look as we're walking around the ship."

Janys shook her head. "There's no way it could guess every nuance of a person's movement. If such a creature could even exist, it would need magic to pull that off."

"Magic?" Lance said, clearly skeptical. "How about many years of practice? Who knows how long they live?"

"For the sake of argument, let's assume the creatures do exist. I don't think practice alone would be enough. Not every corner of the ship is as well lit as Med Center . . . though lately it's been crowded with people, furniture and supplies that there are plenty of places it could hide."

"Yeah . . ." Lance said as he glanced around the room, his eyes slowly returning to hers before continuing, "but there are also plenty of eyes that could catch it as well."

"Exactly," Janys said. "Perhaps it's using a combination of tactics, but hiding in the shadows of its victims might well be one of them. Of course let's hope this is all just a waste of time and there are no creatures on board."

When she was young, Janys didn't believe in magic. Her father was all about science and always said there was a reasonable explanation for everything. But as she grew up, she began to find more and more things that couldn't be explained. "If there is a creature or creatures on board, I'm convinced they're using magic. At least to inflict the sores. The coloration around the wounds does match similar wounds found on an arcane burn victim."

"So you really believe we're dealing with a creature then?"

"Oh I have no idea—like I said, I hope not! But if it exists . . . well, Ford's the one who got me thinking of the magic factor. I hope we aren't dealing with magic. I don't understand it. At least with gaseous, the creatures would still be matter, which means they can be hurt."

"I sure hope they can be hurt."

"Gas doesn't normally take a shape, but there's nothing normal about what's been happening."

"You got that right," Lance said, frowning. He looked up at the nearest vent on the wall and stared at it.

Janys realized she'd never turned off her holo and glanced at it again. After a moment, she said, "Twenty-three unique incidents—some crew members reported seeing the creature more than once. All of them are dead now." She glanced back at Lance only momentarily and then continued reading. "Like a living shadow—like smoke—shadow—shadow—purplish—hideous mouth—three mentioned enormous claws, four mentioned big teeth—"

"During crime scenes . . . ten different witnesses give ten different accounts of what happened." Lance shrugged. "None of the reports said anything about bite marks, claw marks, nothing. Just sores. There's no physical evidence. No pictures, no vids—not even Torrey's managed to snag a picture of it."

"I know, but—well, we're just brainstorming here, and I'm not sure there's much we can rule out yet, as much as I'd like to," she said as she spun her chair around to glance out the window. "You said it yourself we could be dealing with hallucinations," Lance reminded. "Just like with Petty Officer Gomitch."

"I seriously doubt those events were related. Gomitch was going off the deep end before we even got to this dimension," Janys said, forcing her eyes off the window. She glanced down at the monitoring app on her wristcomp, then back up at Lance. Taking a deep breath, she let it out slowly. *I wish we had answers, Lance, but I just don't know . . .*

"Janys, everyone's scared. Like you've said before, their judgment's been compromised. It's hard to believe in, much less eradicate something you can't see—something you can't even be sure exists. We went through a GodStorm after all. Who knows what that could have done to people's heads?"

"We keep going back and forth on this. It could be anything. But one thing's for sure. We need to figure out what we're going to do if the stories are true."

"Trust me, I've been thinking about it," Lance said.

He seemed worried, unsure of himself. Janys wished she could lend him her strength, but hers was fading fast. She didn't feel she had much left to give. *He has to be ready. If the deaths continue or a creature shows its face inside Med Center, he has to take it down, somehow.*

"What do you want me to do?" Lance said, clearly frustrated.

"I don't know, but we can't just wait for the creature to attack again," she said. Her husband seemed about to say something, but she was certain she already knew, and blurted out, "Yes, I know—if it exists. We need to assume it does until we're certain the danger is over." There was a touch of exasperation in her voice. She loved him deeply, but he was moving more slowly than she felt comfortable with. She knew the last thing he wanted was to be in charge of the *Dauntilus*, but something had to be done. He'd always struggled with indecision. "We need to be proactive."

"I know, but . . . if I can't see it, I can't shoot it. I've already sealed off all non-critical sections of the ship. I even turned off life support for those areas."

"You did? Really?"

"Yes. I also had additional security cams put in place awhile back, and even had some auto turrets set up in key areas. They won't fire on a crew member, so there are no worries there. There's an app on my wristcomp that will inform me if a turret activates. I'm not saying any of that will help, but I did do it."

"Why didn't you say something?"

"I didn't know I was supposed to. I'm doing my best," Lance said. The frustration in his voice was clear, and Janys felt bad about giving him a hard time. She realized he didn't just need to prodding, but affirmation as well. "I'm sorry, I thought—doesn't matter. That's great, Lance. If we really are dealing with creatures as intangible as smoke, we're screwed. They could be anywhere, but I'm glad to see you taking action."

Lance leaned back in his chair and stretched, letting out a tremendous sigh. "I had Valenora searching the vents. There are miles of little shafts and little spaces all over the ship. How are we supposed to defend ourselves against something like that? And if they're gaseous, how can they hurt us? You think their composition is acidic or poisonous or something?"

"We don't have anything in our records about a creature like that. Of course our records aren't as exhaustive as the Alliance's library, but none of the known gases produce the symptoms I was seeing. Of course we've never heard of a sentient gas. That doesn't mean the creature isn't gaseous. Its composition might by toxic like you said." A thought came to her and she ran with it. "Maybe it's capable of switching states, just as water can be a liquid, solid or gas. In that case, maybe it evades detection in gaseous form—using our own air vents and then solidifies inside crew quarters."

Lance rose from his chair and paced about the room, stopping occasionally to stare at the knickknacks of the previous chief medical officer.

Janys glanced over to see what her husband was doing, and noticed the Hotaki ball sitting on a shelf and was reminded that the office was still almost entirely Hampton's stuff. The former chief medical officer was a huge sports buff. Janys couldn't care less about sports, but redecorating was the furthest thing from her mind.

Finally, Lance turned to her and said, "You know there are other places a gaseous creature could slip through, like our water system. They could popup out of a commode," Lance said, frowning.

"The commode? Please don't ever say anything like that again. I'd never be able to—just don't!"

"So I shouldn't mention sinks, showers . . . hey, you started it."

They sat in silence for several moments. Lance glanced at the wall and stared at a vent while she turned to check on the others. Maeson was arguing with Mardag about something, as usual. The orc looked embarrassed. *The others were just watching, no one wants to be in his line of fire*, she surmised. She stifled a yawn of her own. She needed sleep and was tired of hypothesizing. She just wanted it all to be over. Briefly glancing over at Lance, sadness came over her. She turned and glanced back out the window.

Maeson finally wondered off toward the supply bins. *He's always eating. No, he's always complaining. He even complains while he eats.* "That guy's always hungry," she muttered. "I wish I could eat like that and not gain weight. I'd have to use meds or nanotech implants." Yawning again, she looked away, tired and feeling in a rut. All she could think of was closing her eyes and going to sleep. *I could sleep for a week. Maybe two,* she thought.

Lance walked over and leaned against her desk, deep in thought. Staring at a vent, he said, "If there is a creature on board, how do you think it's—or they— are hurting people?"

"Maybe its touch inflicts an arcane blister of sorts," she said, spinning back around to see the back of Lance's head. He was still staring at the vent. She thought for a moment and said, "You've seen the vids of the Hordaq. Those are some seriously freaky-looking aliens. The Cosmoverse is filled with oddities, but you don't have to look any further than the sea to find some bangy—spit, Lance—take the sea cucumber, for example!"

"Does that seriously exist?"

"Afraid so. They're like fat worms with tentacles. They can change their shape, squeeze into really tiny places. They can even expel a toxin to kill predators."

"So, we're being slowly killed off by shadowy cucumbers?"

"Be serious for a moment. There are a number of creatures that store poison in their bodies as a defense mechanism, and Ford told me that some arcane shapers have access to poison spells. There was one arrested last year. Took out thirty people in a restaurant, before someone noticed he was using magic. The creatures could be using all kinds of bangy tricks to take us out," she said. Just talking about it was starting to scare her. *The Hordaq are real. The shadow people could be real, too.*

"Okay . . . but we're not predators. We aren't attacking them. If they even exist, they're preying on us, not the other way around. We've done nothing to provoke anyone."

"You don't know that, but I didn't say I have any answers. I said I was mulling over what-ifs. Lance, We could have done something without realizing it, or maybe it's protecting something."

"You mean the architechnology?"

"Maybe."

"You think we picked something up on Moon Thirty-Seven?"

"The epidemic did stop when we removed the architechnology from the ship. If creatures snuck on board to stop us, maybe they stopped when we removed it," she said.

"We're still in possession of it," Lance said, adding, "it's just not quite as accessible, but if you're right, maybe the Architects created a gaseous or nanotech creature or something, and they no longer deem us a threat. If they were on board, then they were most likely spying on us and must have realized we're in no position to do anything with the technology. Maybe they left with it and are waiting on the shuttle, in case we come back for it."

"Let's not do that. Can we agree we aren't touching that shuttle again?"

"I don't have the authority to . . ."

"Lance?" *You'd better not be thinking about retrieving it.*

Lance shook his head, sat back down in his and closed his eyes. "I don't know what I'm doing," Lance said and sighed, turning his eyes to the floor. After a moment, he glanced over and said, "You should have been acting captain. You'd have done a better job."

"I was busy," she replied with a shrug, knowing full well the chain of command didn't work that way. She wouldn't have wanted the position anymore than Lance did. As it was, they were all looking to her to find a cure and she doubted her own abilities. *I'm no skin specialist and I've a feeling this is well beyond anything I could handle if I was one,* she thought.

"Trust me when I say I have no intention of getting anywhere near that shuttle. But I am trying to decide whether we should leave it or tow it back with us," Lance said, and she knew he meant it. "If we don't tow it back, that will probably be the end of my career with the CDF."

She considered that. *I'd rather we remain alive than remain with the CDF.* "If you do bring it back, many more may die."

"We'd tell the CDF, the Alliance, anyone who got remotely near it that it isn't safe, but they'll want it. They are far better equipped to sort this all out than we are."

"At least they'll think they are. If something like that gets loose on a space station or planet, Lance, who knows how much damage it could cause?"

"Let's just put that on hold for now," Lance said. We've got time to figure out that one. What do you want to do? You want me to retrieve the drone control board and set it up in Med Center and give the drones a spin for myself? I'm not as good with those things as Valenora was. Tell me what to do. I'm all ears."

Don't go soft now, Lance. You've been making some decisions on your own. I need you to continue. I don't have the greatest track record of success myself lately. Mardag's my only lasting success story and he might still . . . don't go there. Don't— "You can handle the drones, Lance. You're an excellent pilot."

"You think so?"

"I know so. I'm just not sure it would be helpful. After all, if it's gaseous or incorporeal, it could easily slip away at the first sign of drones." she said, pausing to stifle a yawn. She glanced over at Lance and was pleased to see he was sneaking a peek at the vent again and didn't seem to notice. "Hey, I wonder . . ."

Lance glanced back over. "What's that?"

Janys brought up the database she'd made on all the bizarre reports that came in. "Not sure," she said as she scanned the list and made an inquiry. "Just checking to . . . that's interesting . . ."

"What is?"

"None of the alleged events involving the shadow people or whatever they are, took place at the same time, so maybe we're dealing with a single entity."

"It could also mean the victims weren't careful with reporting the time," Lance said, as he scanned the wall. Finally, he turned his attention back to her.

"You're a ship half-empty kind of guy, aren't you?" she said, then wondered if her comment was in bad taste. "I'm sure they were all pretty distracted," she said, as she opened her desk drawer and glanced around inside. Finding what she was looking for, she pulled out a candy bar and ripped it open. "Been saving this," she said and smiled at Lance. He seemed very interested. "Can you believe xeelotians can't eat chocolate? Well . . . they can, but most of that species has a severe intolerance for it, which is a shame considering how wonderful it tastes."

"Hard to believe anything can harm those stone heads," Lance said. "They look indestructible." He never took his eyes off the candy bar.

"This is my lunch, Lance. Breakfast, too, actually."

"Doesn't look very healthy."

"I'm the doctor and I'm prescribing myself chocolate."

"There's plenty of food in the other room and more in storage down below."

"I need something now. Something yummy," she said. With a sigh, she broke the bar of chocolate in two, handing the smaller half to Lance. "On second thought, you're right. There's food in the other room. Here," she said, and waited with hand outstretched for him to return the candy bar. She knew he wouldn't.

"Nah, I'm good," Lance said, smiling, and took a bite.

"That's what I thought," she muttered and took another bite.

"So . . . you think there's just . . . one creature on board, then?" Lance said in between bites, his eyes once more on the nearest vent.

She finished her bite and said, "I'm not sure of anything. I'd like to think whether there's only one or a dozen, they're on the shuttle rather than here."

Lance shrugged. "Definitely, but as far as the attacks go, there's nothing saying they have to attack all at once."

"You're right. We're probably dealing with polite aliens who took turns so as not to steal each other's thunder," Janys said. They both laughed.

After sitting in silence while they finished eating, Janys walked over to the disinfectant dispenser mounted on the wall. She stole a glance out the window and then turned on her heels and said, "I think we're dealing with a real creature—maybe only one, but from now on, we need to assume there are several. We also need to assume they are still on board, just to be safe."

Lance turned back from the vent and looked her in the eyes.

Good, you were making me nervous constantly staring at that vent, she thought.

Lance nodded. "Yeah . . . I just wish I knew why they haven't attacked over the past four days. You think they're afraid of getting caught, with so many of us in close proximity? We're a lot harder to sneak up on now."

Janys rubbed the disinfectant into her hands, as she stared absently at the vent. "Well, that's definitely true, but it could be the lights," she said after a moment. "Med Center is more lit up than any other part of the ship, except maybe the biome."

Lance shifted in his chair. "Actually, with all the extra beds and supplies, we probably have more shadows than ever. They could just be toying with us—taking their time."

The thought made Janys' stomach turn.

"Of course that assumes intelligence," Lance said.

Janys shrugged. "Given the state of affairs, I think that's a fair assumption."

"Yeah," Lance said. "If nothing else bad happens, we'll keep an eye out for invaders, but assume it was the architechnology all along, and head back home."

With or without the shuttle? Janys wondered. She closed her eyes and rubbed her temples. "We've had more than our fair share of death," she said as she turned her chair to face the window again.

"Yeah we have."

"Almost lost the whole ship," Janys muttered. She thought back on all the crew members that had come through Med Center and left out the evacuation hatch. Her stomach was cramping up and she felt miserable. "Mardag's the only one who's gotten sick and is still alive." She turned to face him. Lance was in deep thought, leaning forward, elbows on his knees, fingers interlaced. "I'm sorry, Lance. I know you don't like being in the limelight, especially under such extreme circumstances. How long do we wait?"

"Let's give it a full week and see how things go, unless you think we should wait longer."

"Two weeks would be safer, but Maeson won't make it two weeks trapped inside Med Center. He's driving me crazy besides. His claustrophobia will only get worse."

"One week it is. We can always change our minds later. I've crunched some numbers and options with Ensign Lorego and the Chief. It wouldn't be easy—hell, it would be far from easy, but I think we can make it back, at least to Alliance Space. That's assuming things start to go in our favor from here out."

Staring out the office window, Janys followed the engineer with her eyes as he walked toward the restrooms. When he was out of sight, she turned back to Lance. "I hate sitting around waiting for something to happen."

"Let's hope nothing happens. Nothing would be really great about now."

Janys nodded. "I did have some other what-ifs . . . invisibility for one. I've heard about a superhero living on Galandria that can turn invisible. I think his name is Inviso."

"I've heard of him," Lance said. "You think Inviso is on board killing off the crew? And here I thought he was one of the good guys," he said, and smiled. "Seriously though, if there's a creature on board capable of going invisible, I think I'll jump out an airlock. It's hard to believe augments even exist, but they're real, so who knows?"

"Unfortunately, an invisible creature isn't quite as far-fetched as I wish it were. That *would* explain their absence on cams, but not why people reported seeing something, unless the creature has to become visible to attack."

"If the creatures use invisibility, then they're probably solid and can't even fit into the ventilation system," Lance said, adding after a moment, "if they can do both, we're definitely screwed. I think we can safely cancel out invisibility, since no one has reported hearing things they can't see," Lance said.

That's not quite true, Janys realized. "Actually, there have been reports of strange noises on board."

"Well . . . yeah, but in every case, the crew members later reported seeing something, so we can't count those," Lance corrected.

"That's no guarantee invisibility isn't a factor. You're probably right though. And someone would have mentioned a strange smell. They have to have a scent if they are only invisible," she said.

"Did you say, 'Only'?"

Janys chuckled. "This is so bangy, like a dream—no, a nightmare. I sure hope it was only the architechnology and not—don't say it! I said only.

Again. Whatever."

Lance didn't say anything. He only smiled.

Janys yawned again and turned toward the window, lost in thought. *Please don't be real. If I knew there were really creatures sneaking around in the shadows—that one might have actually touched me—gave me a sore somehow while I slept? I don't know if I could ever get to sleep again—not that I've slept much over the past few weeks. I don't know how Lance does it. I never see him sleep. He swears he's been sneaking naps, but I haven't seen him. I can see that he's tired, but I haven't actually seen him sleep in a long time. I don't know how he does it. It has to affect your cognitive functions after awhile. No, I know it does. Just the other day I almost—*

"Maybe they just enjoy stressing out their victims," Lance said.

"What?"

"They could just kill us in our sleep. Instead, they're either clumsy or loud and keep getting caught, or maybe they just enjoy scaring their prey before killing them."

"Oh, that's a comforting thought," Janys said. "Okay, I think we have more than enough what-ifs for one day."

"Me, I'm betting on the sea cucumber," Lance said. Maybe a magical sea cucumber, or—"

"Enough," Janys said and shook her head.

"Thankfully, we haven't seen anything yet. Maybe the shadow creatures don't even exist."

"Unfortunately, we can't afford the luxury of choosing not to believe in something just because we haven't seen it."

Lance stood up. "Okay. We'll start guarding the vents."

Janys nodded. "Better safe, than sorry."

"Yeah. I'll round up the troops."

When they returned to the main room, they didn't see Maeson anywhere. Janys walked over and started counting the vents. *I never realized there were so many.* She was also surprised at how many dark corners there were, despite all the lights. *No,* she corrected herself—*because of all the lights. Lance was right. Even here, we don't have enough lights, at least not if there's something trying to hide in the shadows.* As she looked around the room, a knot in her stomach formed. She walked over and whispered in Lance's ear, "Maybe we should try sealing off a few of the vents. We don't need all of them."

Lance nodded and walked over to Lorego. Together, they blocked off two vents. Lance was just finishing a third when Maeson returned from the restroom and joined the others. Once everyone was together, Lance walked over to the center of the main room next to the surgery table and said, "Listen up, people."

Lorego stood at attention. Mardag stood as well, though at ease. The others glanced over, but didn't move.

"I know things have been really bangy since arriving in this dimension. We've been through a lot—more than I'd want to ask from any of you. I appreciate your maintaining a positive attitude during these difficult times."

Except for Maeson, Janys added in her mind, as if Lance had said it.

"You've all been doing your self examinations. No new sores, I assume?"

Janys' own sore was healing well and she had no intention of mentioning it.

"I want to get back home as much as the rest of you, but we still don't know if it's safe yet. We need to nail down a few things before we can attempt a return journey. We'll be holding up in here for a full week—longer if we have to, but I'm hoping the threat is over. We'll know soon enough."

Maeson and Kelsa began grumbling. Mardag sighed. He looked tired and frustrated. Even Lorego appeared tepid about the idea. Torrey was hard to read, but she said nothing.

Lance continued. "While we're waiting, we need to be as productive as we can, but also step up our guard, just in case the architechnology wasn't at fault. I need volunteers to guard the vents. Two vents each."

Silence.

Lance glanced between the survivors, leaving Janys out of it, for which she was grateful. She saw Lorego's face. The ensign made a slight nod at her husband, but Lance either didn't see it, or didn't call on him for whatever reason.

"Now, before anyone gets antsy, while there've been more than a few rumors of shadow creatures on board, we've never once caught them on security vid. We don't even know if they exist. The whole thing could simply be a case of folie à plusieurs—hallucinations."

Janys looked away to hide her smile. *That's not quite how you say it, my love.*

"Anyway, I doubt we'll see one, but I'm not asking you to confront it if you do. If you see anything suspicious, just back away and call out. Probably just the boogey man, but if they're real, I want more eyes than mine on the vents. Three vents have been blocked off. Obviously, we can't block them all."

Maeson turned and looked at Lorego, Mardag, Kelsa and Torrey. "Well? Aren't you going to answer him? Surely guarding vents shouldn't be too difficult for you. How about you, Mardag? Torrey?"

Torrey looked like she was about to fall over from exhaustion. She stood off to one side and muttered, "I'm too hungry to focus and too tired to think."

"Who isn't," Maeson asked, sneering.

"I'll do it, sir," Lorego said, stepping forward.

"Thank you, Ensign," Lance said and smiled. "You and Maeson will do just fine."

"Me?" Maeson said, clearly taken off guard, his voice annoyed.

"That's correct. You have eyes. Surely guarding vents shouldn't be too difficult for you."

Watching the look on Maeson's face, Janys suppressed a smile.

"Sir," Maeson said, rooted to the floor.

What is it, Chief?

"With all due respect . . . Acting Captain, shouldn't a higher ranking officer like myself be assigned a task more fitting to my training? At the very least, I'll be needing proper rest if you expect me to get Engineering up and running all by myself so we can attempt a trip home. You do want to get home don't you?"

Lance turned to Lorego and said, "Thank you for volunteering, Ensign, your services have been commendable. Did you get the remote sensing link working on your wristcomp?"

"Yes, sir."

"Excellent. Let me know if you detect any changes in energy readings on Moon Thirty-Seven. For that matter, keep me informed of anything else you think I should know about."

"Yes, sir. I took the liberty of setting up a notification system and can operate most of the sensor equipment remotely."

Lance nodded. "Very good, Ensign. That will be all."

"Sir," Lorego said with a nod and walked off.

Maeson remained where he was. "Sir—"

"Chief, we won't be leaving orbit until this is over, so I'm reassigning everyone new duties in the interim. The rest of the vents are up for grabs. Pick any two you like."

"You can't be serious."

"That will be all, Chief."

"Wonderful . . ." Maeson said, devoid of enthusiasm. He returned to where he had been sitting, grabbed his chair, carried it over to the wall of supply crates and sat down. He folded his arms and swung his head from vent to vent, rolling his eyes as he did so, in an exaggerated fashion like a bobblehead, as if the whole thing was the silliest thing he'd ever heard of.

That will stop soon or he'll get neck cramp—and a well deserved one at that, Janys thought. *He could easily have positioned his chair better, but at least he'd thought to bring a chair. Laziness will do that to you, but the chair was a good idea.*

Lance crossed the room and sat down on a chair facing the vents near the decontamination unit, across from the restrooms.

After five minutes of standing vigilant, Ensign Lorego leaned against one of the beds for support. A few minutes later, he turned to Lance and called out, "Sir, can I grab a—"

"Yes, Ensign, You can leave your post to get a chair," Lance said.

"Thank you, sir."

Maeson sniggered.

Janys began peeking at a vent near her as well, alternating between staring at it and reviewing Ford's theories on shadow people and magic. After reading half a dozen messages, and reading an article, she glanced over at the others and saw Mardag had moved his chair to face a vent, Torrey had climbed up on one of the beds and was snoring, and Kelsa was dozing in her chair. Maeson was rummaging through a supply crate for munchies, glancing every so often at the two vents nearest him. Lorego and Lance looked bored, but vigilant. Janys walked over to her husband and kissed him on the cheek, then whispered, "Keeping them busy is good for their mental health. I must admit I love how you rolled Maeson into it."

Lance glanced up at her, smiled, and wrapped an arm around her waist, pulling her onto his lap. She jerked her head over toward the others, pleased no one was looking in their direction.

"Yes, I enjoyed that," Lance said. "I'm enjoying this even more." He kissed her on the neck.

"I can tell, on both counts," Janys said, as she squirmed to get back to her feet, worried that one of the others might catch them.

Lance held her firmly, but not uncomfortably so. It felt good to be in his arms, but the reality of the situation quickly diminished her excitement.

"Lance, please. You know Maeson's looking for an excuse to—"

"He's busy raiding our supplies," Lance said. He softened his grip, but tried to kiss her on the lips. She turned her head to the side, dodging and said, "Don't forget to let the others get some sleep. That's healthy, too."

"Right," he said, and continued his quest for a kiss.

"I'm betting Maeson is much more pleasant when sound asleep."

Lance nodded. "Kissing is healthy, too. A smart doctor once told me it provides numerous health benefits."

"Then why don't you kiss Maeson?"

"I'd rather kiss—" Lance paused and released his hand from around her waist when she turned to face him and smiled.

Janys darted in and gave her husband a quick peck on the lips, before he was able to respond in kind, and then stood up before he could wrap his arm around her waist again. "There, satisfied?" She asked, and was answered by his hand locking around her wrist—not painfully, but he wasn't letting go. "I'm on the clock you know," she said and glanced back. Lorego had seen them, but quickly averted his eyes.

Lance frowned at her. "That one didn't count, and besides, you're always on the clock these days," he said, finally releasing her with a pat on her bottom.

She gave him a look of mock anger and then sighed. *He knows I don't like public displays of affection!* She glanced back at Maeson. He was leaning forward with an elbow on his leg, supporting his head with the palm of his hand and looked about to fall asleep. When she turned back, Lance was in her face and stole a kiss. She didn't mind, but frowned at him anyway. Backing up, just out of reach, she said no louder than a whisper, "I take it you didn't call on Lorego because he was ready and willing?"

"Exactly. I knew Maeson wouldn't volunteer, so he was the first on my list."

"Good move," Janys said and smiled again.

"Why don't you take a nap while you can?"

"I will—soon," she replied, and smiled. "I just want to do a bit more reading first."

Lance shook his head and smiled. "If you don't take one soon, I'm going to have to put you in the brig." He glanced over her shoulder—at Maeson if her guess was correct— and then leaned forward and kissed her on the lips. He made no attempt to capture her this time and she didn't resist. She winced when Lance bumped her left arm. Thankfully, he didn't seem to notice. His eyes were already back on the nearest vent. Without looking up, he said, "Is it stupid for us to watch the vents?" He looked up at her once more. "I feel stupid staring at a vent."

"Better safe, than sorry," she said, pretending she wasn't in pain. She hated keeping secrets from him, but saw no good that could come from revealing her wound, either. Not now. She didn't want him worrying about her. "It's only stupid if nothing ever crawls out of one of them. No offense, Lance, but I'm hoping you're stupid, so we only have to worry about out-waiting the last of the architechnology contamination. Hopefully it's already ended. I'm looking forward to getting back to worrying about something more pleasant, like finding our way home."

"You and me both."

As she walked away, Janys casually moved her hand along her left sleeve and began feeling for the HealTab when she noticed Lorego was staring at her oddly. He said nothing as she returned to the med terminal and sat down. She desperately wanted to go straight to the restroom or her office to check on the blister, but waited fifteen minutes, in case Lorego was suspicious and was watching her. When she did check her arm, she found the HealTab had shifted and was hanging off, providing zero protection. She was relieved to see the wound was healing nicely and replaced the HealTab. To her knowledge, Lorego never said a word to anyone.

Five days and no new sores. If Raeden hadn't ordered a team down to Moon Thirty-Seven, what would we be doing right now? Janys wondered. *I suppose we would have gone down to the surface of the ringworld. Probably more than once. I wonder what it's like down there?* She found it hard to believe they'd been in orbit for over a month. Their mechanized biome continued to grow, process and store food, and additional staples had been brought in from the cafeteria.

One of the hardest things about being cooped up away from the viewports and other common areas of the ship was psychological. Being stuck in a room—even a big room, and not knowing whether it's safe to go outside can be unnerving. They weren't even convinced it was safe to be inside, and being in a room made it easy to loose track of time. The day-night cycle is soothing. It's constant. Familiar. On board a ship, especially confined to a single area, one can feel a little trapped.

Stress was understandable, but also unpredictable. Maeson flared up every time she turned around, but even Lorego slipped on occasion and became irritable. Kelsa complained about not being allowed to retrieve certain personal items from her quarters. She also complained about being bored and about how Mardag smelled, among other things.

Janys' thoughts shifted to Maeson. Though she hated giving him an inch when he seemed to live to annoy, she knew he was having a harder time dealing with confinement than the rest of them. Further, long periods of mindless staring at vents weren't helping. It was neither engaging, nor good exercise. But she knew they needed to keep busy while they waited, and even when they did get chances to sleep, falling asleep wasn't easy—not when you are worried there might be invaders on board.

Janys was pleased to see Ensign Lorego and Supply Officer Mardag getting along so well, despite all that had happened. Unlike Maeson and Kelsa, Lorego was almost always friendly and eager to please. He seemed like he could get along with anyone, but even he wasn't as enthusiastic as he used to be. Mardag was cordial—nothing like the stories she'd heard of orcs. She recalled a pleasant conversation she had with him over lunch and realized how much of what she had been told as a child about orcs was wrong.

There weren't many orcs in the Republic, not compared with humans and humanus. There were even fewer in the CDF until more recently. Racism still thrived after all these years.

The Orc Empire had remained aloof for centuries, the orcs keeping to themselves in the quieter, northern frontier of the Republic, far from the clutches of the Hordaq Imperium. They fought amongst themselves and were considered barbarians by most at the time. Only in the past thirty years had their kind finally been accepted among the CDF and the remnant of Earth.

Very few orcs lived in the HDF half of the Republic and were forbidden to join the military. While genetically identical to humans, the humanus had followed a very different path than the humans and were slow to accept the brutish orc race. There were many things the two great fleets of the Republic didn't agree on. Orcs were one of them.

Like many species, the orcs had discovered and used ancient stargates to colonize other worlds, including Reeko, Vanis, Adara, Vandoon and others. Mardag believed there were even orcs down on Cathor, too. The CDF first encountered orcs on Fargate. War almost broke out several times, but after three years of negotiations, they became allies. Even so, the humanus had been wary of their inclusion and to this day only tolerate orcs.

The CDF shared with the orcs their lesser technologies in exchange for certain architechnology the orcs had found on the worlds they had settled. Aggressive in combat and peculiar in their customs, orcs fought better in teams of their own kind than spread out among the humans. In time, some orcs rose to levels of prestige—not many, but a few. One of the greatest dog fighters in the history of the CDF was an orc, as Mardag in a proud mood sometimes reminded his fellow comrades. The supply officer had never risen to a position of honor or power, but he was much liked aboard the *Dauntilus*.

Janys was pleased to see him so happy. She still found his scent disarming, but his smile was contagious. She was also pleased to note he had acquired no new sores. Things were looking up.

She knew little about Kelsa and even less about Corporal Torrey, until recently. Torrey was a year younger than Kelsa, not nearly as bold and opinionated, but easygoing. She usually kept her opinions to herself. Janys had made it clear to Torrey when they first met that she didn't want her taking pictures of patients in Med Center and Torrey had complied without argument. Torrey was on board solely to record their adventure. When she wasn't taking pictures or vid, she was often recording her thoughts on the events around her.

Torrey had completed a tour of duty as a combat videographer and had been elated to become a member of the crew, away from the hazards of combat. Thus far, most of her pictures and vids had been candid shots of the crew, and of space, from the vibrant, arcana-infused asteroids of the Dark Nebulae to dynamic footage of the GodStorm raging just outside their ship, to the Cosmothean Sea, and the ringworld. She was always ready with her wristcam and maintained a good attitude. Janys liked her.

Finally completing reports on each of the crew members who had died from the sores, Janys stood and stretched her legs. Glancing around to see how the others were doing, she found Kelsa asleep on one of the beds, Lorego and Maeson eating in silence, and Mardag and Lance watching vents. She glanced around and realized Torrey was in the restroom.

Five minutes passed and then ten. She walked up to Lance and asked, "How long has Torrey been in the restroom?"

"I dunno. Five or six minutes, maybe?"

"It's been at least ten," she corrected."

"Okay, ten," Lance said and glanced toward Torrey's assigned bed. He turned back to her and added, "Isn't that her wristcam sitting over there? I've never seen her without it, so she's got to be taking a shower."

"Nevermind. Sorry to bother you."

"No, it's fine. Staring at vents for hours isn't my idea of a good time. You're always a pleasant distraction."

"Is that all I am to you," she asked in a convincingly offended tone.

With emotions running high, she realized she might have been more convincing than she'd meant and so she finished it with a wink. Lance smiled. "No, you're so much more than that. I love you, sweetheart."

"Love you, too. It's hard to believe this is almost behind us." She wasn't lying. The sore on her arm was doing worlds better and she had high hopes for the days ahead. "Have you decided whether you are going to leave the other shuttle behind?"

"I think we should try to tow it back with us if we can."

"There's no way the Alliance will let us cross their borders without at least searching our ships. If they take even temporary control over the shuttle with the architechnology, they could be exposed to whatever attacked our ship."

"I've thought of that, but I put a biohazard warning beacon on it. Even if we lost it while crossing the rift, on the off-chance someone found it, before they could access it, they would receive a Class X biohazard warning."

"Good thinking," she said. "Torrey had the right idea with a shower. I think I'll take one as well, and then you should get some sleep. I don't mind taking a turn at the vents, but I assume you'll be stopping that before long."

"Like I told the others—"

"We're really going to wait a full week?"

"Don't you think we should? You said the contaminant can stay in our systems for up to two weeks or so."

"You're right," Janys said. "We still don't know if we're out of hot water, but so far, so good, huh?"

Lance smiled. "Let me know if you need a hand in there."

She knew he wasn't serious. Not when he was on guard duty and the others would know something was up if they both vanished. She immediately thought of her sore. It was healing nicely, but she didn't want him seeing her without clothes on while she still had it. "I think I'll manage, but I'd be lying if I said it wasn't tempting. I'm looking forward to getting back to some semblance of normality."

"I'm definitely looking forward to that," Lance said, as she walked off.

She grabbed a fresh jumper and a towel and then entered the restroom. The sinks were off to her right, ending in a wall. The stalls were to her left. At the other end of the room was an opening to the showers. The water wasn't running, but the restroom was steamed up, which told her Torrey was in one of the stalls changing or on the commode.

"Hey Corporal," Janys called out as she removed her shoes and slid her fresh jumper into a cubby on the wall. Stripping down, she tossed her soiled jumper into the shoot below the cubbies and draped the towel over her left shoulder, hiding her HealTab in case Torrey walked out and asked questions.

"Man, do I need a shower. Hope you didn't use all the hot water," she said, making small talk, knowing full well there was no way that could happen. Panic shot through her like a knife. *No-no-no-no-no! Please don't be—*

The stall to her left swung open, and Janys jumped, dropping her towel. In her mind, she watched Torrey fall into her arms covered in running sores, all life drained out of her, and hovering over the commode, a great, shadowy humanoid grinning from ear to ear, its long clawed hands covered in blood. Its rumored tail motioning her to enter. She was breathing hard when Torrey stepped out in perfect health and said, "Sorry, I didn't answer."

Wearing only panties, she was vigorously toweling off her hair. After a moment, she glanced up and said, "I don't like to talk when I'm—"

"Torrey!" Janys called out, relieved and feeling foolish for panicking. Her heart was racing and she almost started bawling. She fought to regain her composure.

"What's wrong?" Torrey asked, looking confused. Then her eyes went wide and she frowned. "Please tell me none of the others got sick, Doctor!"

"No, no. I'm just . . . I'm sorry. Everything's fine," she said. "I thought—never mind. Everything's fine."

"I'm glad it's you, doctor. No offense, but Maeson gives me the creeps. I saw him staring at me the other day like—never mind. I'm sure it was nothing." She moved over in front of the mirror, grabbed a brush from her cubby and started running it through her hair.

Mindful of her exposed HealTab, Janys blurted out, "I think Ensign Lorego likes you," and bent down to pick up her towel. She rushed past Torrey and darted around the corner into the showers, still breathing hard. *I shouldn't have said that. I wasn't lying! You still shouldn't have said it. You were just saying it to distract her.*

"You think so?" Torrey said from down the hall. Her voice was muffled.

"Yeah. He's a nice guy," Janys responded, but she was barely holding it together. She slung her towel over the hook and stepped in front of the showerhead. She tried to catch her breath as the water ran down over her.

Torrey said something, but Janys couldn't hear it over the shower.

"Sorry, I can't hear you. I'll be right out," she said and then closed her eyes and cried as the water ran over her. She didn't know why she was crying, relief maybe, but the tears came just the same. When she got out of the shower, she toweled off and then wrapped the towel around her bosom, in case one of the men walked in.

Janys found the corporal's towel on the floor halfway up the row of stalls toward the sinks. When she reached down to pick it up, she noticed a smear of blood on the stall door beside it and drops of blood leading into the stall. The door wasn't latched. "Lance!" Janys shouted at the top of her lungs.

She flung open the stall. The floor was smeared with blood. Torrey sat against the back wall beside the commode, her legs pulled up tight about her chest. She was hugging herself as she rocked back and forth.

"I'm here, Torrey . . . I'm here . . ." Janys said as she draped Torrey's towel around her shoulders. She held her in her arms and they cried together. As she held Torrey, she noticed the woman had splotches of grime all over her. Janys' first thought was to rush back into the shower, but instead, she remained at the videographer's side.

Moments later, Lance burst into the restroom. "Janys!"

"In here," Janys called out, her voice shallow, drained. Knowing Lance would be scared, she said, "It's Corporal Torrey . . ."

A moment later, Torrey stopped crying and Janys realized she'd passed.

Finally running out of tears, Janys continued to hold the woman in her arms until Lance managed to pull her away. "Don't touch me!" she shouted.

Startled, Lance backed away.

Janys was covered in blood and grime and was afraid her husband might get some on him.

"I'm so sorry, sweetheart. I . . . I was really hoping it was over . . ." he said.

"Me too," she said in a small voice, her whole body trembling. She was breathing hard and struggled to think.

"Janys?"

I've got to get this grime off of me. If any got in through a cut or the sore on my arm . . .

"You okay, sweetheart?"

"I'm . . . I'm sorry for shouting at you," she said, as she got to her feet. "I was afraid." Tainted blood dripped down her bare legs.

"You and me both. You sure you're okay?"

Miserable, her emotions were flying in all directions. She was about to admit to having a sore, but managed to pull herself together enough to nod.

Lance rushed through the restroom checking every stall, in every corner, his gauss rifle held in white-knuckled hands as she stood in the center of the room.

"That grime I was telling you about? Lance, she's covered in it, and now I am, too," she said, thankful he hadn't noticed her HealTab yet. Her left arm was covered in blood. "I'm okay, but I need to get cleaned up right away."

All of the blood in Lance's face had drained away and he was breathing hard, too. "I don't want to lose you, sweetheart. You're all I've got."

She glanced down once more at Torrey and almost lost it again. Turning to Lance, she nodded once more, then started heading back toward the showers. "Thanks for rushing in here and being my knight in shining armor, but now I need some time to myself, okay? Just . . . make sure the others are safe," she called out.

"I'm not leaving you in here alone again."

I should tell him. Not now. Now. No, I need to think. I have to— "Torrey was probably carrying the contaminant all this time and didn't know it," Janys said, refusing to admit the nightmare wasn't over. She started walking back toward him, sensing he wasn't going to leave and worried he'd see the HealTab. *All that grime . . . you know Torrey wasn't a carrier. I don't know spit,* she told herself. She paused before Torrey's stall and said, "I don't have time for this. I have my pistol." She intentionally avoided looking to her right, or down. She just stared at Lance, her breathing quickened, knowing she had no time to lose.

"Janys, this is a matter of safety, not me trying to sneak peeks at your body."

"I said, 'No!'"

"Damn it, Janys. In your cubby's not good enough. At least take the pistol with you. Just put it on the towel rack," he said and walked over to her cubby.

I can't let him into my cubby! "I can get it myself!" she said, rushing up to his side and reaching her hand into the cubby, removing the pistol.

Lance took a step back, grimacing.

"You're right. I'm wrong. Now check on the others."

"You sure you're my wife and not some alien doppelgänger?" Lance said, and remained at a distance. "My wife would never be so quick to surrender."

"I said, 'Go!'" she shouted.

"Yep, you're my wife," he said, and rushed toward the door.

"When I'm done taking a shower, I need to get some disinfectant in here and clean the body and stall, then you and Lorego can . . ."

"Gotcha," Lance said, and then pushed through the door.

"I'm just going to leave it open a crack. Shout if you need me."

"Got it," she said, and rushed back to the showers. She quickly set the pistol down on the towel rack and then got under the nearest showerhead, washing off her left arm first. She inspected every inch of her body, relieved to find she had no open cuts or sores. As soon as she was sure she had removed any trace of the grime, she dried off and ran back to her cubby where she had hidden her antibiotic and HealTab, grateful Lance hadn't seen them. She took the antibiotic and put on a fresh HealTab. She then discarded the evidence and dressed in a fresh pair of scrubs and coat.

It's not over. Not even close. Don't say that. There's still a chance it ended with Torrey, she told herself, but she knew the truth. Her heart was still racing when she rejoined the others.

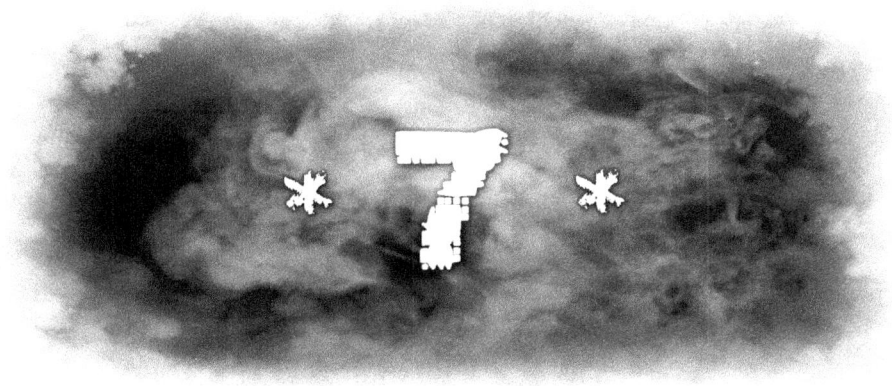

Everyone was panicking after Corporal Torrey's death. To calm them, and because Janys wasn't positive there really was a shadow creature on board, she told them it was possible the corporal had been a carrier, and the contagion finally manifested. In her heart, she had no doubt the creature was real, as she had been unable to explain where the grime was coming from.

Because of the timing of the attacks, she believed there was only one creature on board. Her husband and the others seemed convinced there were multiple creatures running about the ship. *Maybe they're right, but I hope not. One is too many as it is,* she thought. They were already guarding the vents and keeping an eye on each other, but clearly more needed to be done.

During a private moment, she confirmed Lance's suspicions that the grime was not a natural substance that some of the crew members had accidentally stumbled upon, exacerbating whatever sores they might have. She hadn't revealed the truth to the crew as she first wanted to gauge their emotional states. In particular, she was concerned about both Maeson and Kelsa, who were already on edge. Lance agreed with her reservations, but said the crew deserved to know. She studied several samples of the grime she had collected, and then announced her findings.

Kelsa sat down on her bed and cried for five minutes straight. Maeson was surprisingly quiet and busied himself on his wristcomp, as if nothing had happened. Janys worried he might be suffering from depression. The others were quiet as well, though their faces were easy enough to read. Things weren't going to get better until they destroyed the creature—if such a thing were even possible.

"Until the creature is destroyed, I'm afraid safety is by necessity going to have to trump privacy," Lance announced. "Privacy will only be allowed while using the commode. Whenever someone is taking a shower, eating, sleeping—whatever—at least one other crew member will stand guard."

Vent rotations continued. Because of the danger, the survivors tended to keep an eye on vents during their downtime as well. Hours passed and then a day, without any sign of the creature.

Maeson barely spoke a word to anyone and mostly kept to himself, eyes glued to his wristcomp whenever he was off vent duty. No one was in a rush to take either a shower or a nap, despite needing both, saying they felt too vulnerable. The depression was tangible. Sometimes the survivors had to be reminded to eat.

After thirty hours without sleep, both Lorego and Mardag lay down on their beds. Janys suggested they cover themselves completely just to be safe, as previous victims usually only received sores on exposed areas. She wished Lance would sleep too, as she was concerned for his health. He refused to sleep and continued guarding the vents. He didn't even stop to eat, so she brought him his meals. Finally, he took a break long enough for her to give him a medical examination to prove to her he was well enough to guard. *I don't know how he's doing it*, she thought, and walked up beside him and draped her arm around his neck. *"Hey."*

Lance smiled, but kept his eyes on the vents. *"You okay?"*

"Yeah . . . I was just thinking, do you realize we've spent more time in this dimension as husband and wife than in our own?"

"That's depressing," Lance said, frowning.

She nodded. "Sorry. Guess we have enough of that going around as it is.

I was just making small talk, anything to get our minds off—"

"Whose idea was it for us to get married right before going on a dangerous mission?"

"I think it was yours. You wanted to sleep with me and couldn't wait a lousy year," she said. In truth, she hadn't wanted to wait, either. None of their friends had married, but to her and Lance, it was an important step in their relationship.

"Can you blame me? Have you seen you? Never mind, I'd do it again. But seriously, I wish we'd have had time for a real honeymoon, at least."

"You promised me one, and I'm holding you to it!"

A sudden quiet came over them. She knew what he was thinking. They were bringing up old times because the present was too depressing to think about. She didn't want to broach the topic and spoil the moment.

"How about a trip to one of the moons of Cathor?" Lance said, finally. "I hear they are to die for, this time of year," he said and chuckled.

"That isn't funny," she said, as a flash bomb of images cascaded through her mind. *So many have died.* "Lance, that's crass."

"Sorry. I was going for morbid."

"That, too."

"Still, it was—never mind. Sorry, I wasn't thinking."

"See what I mean? Sleep deprivation," she said, but she knew his joke had required too many brain cells to confirm anything. Besides, she didn't need to. He had already passed a medical examination and broke any confirmed record she'd ever heard of for going without sleep, at least among humans.

Trying to think of something pleasant, she recalled their weekend honeymoon and found a smile. It had been a whirlwind, cheap affair. They hadn't had time for anything elaborate, nor did they have the credits to spend. But they did have each other, and it was a wonderful memory. She had hoped they'd make many more together over the years once they finished their tour aboard the *Dauntilus*.

They knew everything was going to change when they agreed to join the *Dauntilus* team, but she had no idea just how profound the change would be. *No one could have imagined this! It seems like it was a lifetime ago since we just sat together and talked about our future—our dreams.* She missed the late night walks holding hands, the dinners out, and the warmth of his body next to hers after a long day. She wondered if he missed such things too. *He must,* she was convinced, *but who could be in the mood at a time like this anyway?* "Why don't you let me watch these vents?" she offered.

"We could watch them together, like going to the movies. Make it a date," Lance said with a wink, more enthusiastically than he felt.

Janys frowned.

"Oh—kay . . . I'll switch over to the vents by the medical cabinets."

That's not what I meant! With a sigh, Janys said, "I was hoping you'd take a break and get some sleep."

"I'm fine," he said, his eyes glued to one of the vents. After a moment, he glanced over at the other nearby vent and stared at it for a time.

"Lance, this is bangy. I haven't seen you sleep in—well, a very long time. Even that nap you told me you took in Bay One wasn't remotely long enough to—you're scaring me. I don't understand. Maybe you've contracted some exotic insomnia condition. I keep thinking you're going to just keel over. The body needs regular sleep, not just cat naps, though even those would be preferable to nothing at all."

"I don't understand it, either. I know I should be tired, but I'm not, at least not tired enough to go to sleep, and the creature's out there, so I might as well stand guard."

"When's the last time you ate something?"

"I ate earlier. Janys, I said I'm fine."

"In cases of extreme sleep deprivation, reports show that some experience hallucinations. As your doctor, I could order you to go to bed," she said, ignoring the hole in her plan.

"That goes out the window during times of emergency," he reminded her.

She sighed. *He's right. Still, going without sleep has got to affect his judgment at some point.* "I can give you something to help you sleep, but natural sleep is better."

He turned to face her briefly and said, "Thanks for caring, but I'll know when I need a nap."

Janys shook her head. *Fine. Let's try a different approach.* "Are you aware that stress and sleep deprivation can cause loss of libido."

Lance turned back to her and smiled. "That's a relief, for a second there I thought you were going to say it diminishes one's sex drive!" He winked and returned his attention to the two nearest vents, sometimes glancing over at a third.

She couldn't help but smile. It was a nice diversion from thoughts of doom and gloom. "I'm sorry we haven't been able to . . . you know. And I wasn't joking about getting proper sleep. It can negatively affect the libido. Cognitive functions, too."

There were dark circles under his eyes, but he still seemed to have a decent amount of energy. "So can having monsters run amok, but it doesn't take a lot of thinking to—anyway, let me get this straight," Lance said, still smiling, "you mean if I take a nap, you're up for going into your office and—"

"Lance!" She said in a scolding tone. She knew he wasn't serious, but was concerned someone might have overheard them. She glanced over at the others and was pleased that Lorego and Mardag were still sound asleep, and Kelsa didn't seem to notice. Maeson was sitting in a chair staring at the sleepers, but at the angle he was sitting, he was staring at them, too. *Who knows what goes on inside that creepy mind of his?* She was thankful, at least, that he was on the other side of Med Center and couldn't possibly have heard what her husband said. She sighed and shook her head. "Maeson's staring at us."

"Let him stare."

She considered what she'd studied on sleep deprivation. *His present state could be due to a rare side effect of sleep deprivation.*

"Sweetheart, you haven't seen me nodding off at my post, have you?"

He's right. He hasn't been struggling with it. But it's got to hit him at some point.

"There's too much at stake, sweetheart. I'll sleep when I'm dead."

"Don't say that. I'm telling you the mind starts doing some strange things when you're sleep deprived. Just because it hasn't happened yet, doesn't mean it won't."

"I'm sorry. I . . . I dunno. Maybe I'm still running on adrenaline, but over the past month or so, I just haven't felt the need for as much sleep. And I'm not stressing out, either. Well, not at the moment. Too bored of watching vents to be stressed out. Anyway, I'm still on vent rotation. I'll nap later," he said, as he handed her his pistol. He unslung his gauss rifle and headed over toward the medical cabinets. Janys immediately turned her attention to the vents before her. *So much for that,* she thought, wondering why she'd bother to ask.

She glanced back at Maeson. The engineer was glaring at Lance like he'd killed his dog or something. The engineer scared her. *Some of the things he's said to the others about Lance's alleged mistakes . . . I just don't trust him.*

She noticed that when Maeson did sleep, he never covered up. *He probably feels claustrophobic when he covers up. He wouldn't have been selected for the mission if his condition were severe. Med Center isn't that small, but it's smaller than Engineering.* Even so, she knew it had been hard on him. *He hasn't been taking being cooped up very well, but at least he's been less talkative lately.* That's less maddening for the rest of us, but I'm not so sure how healthy that is for him. She had to keep reminding herself that it wasn't that he was a jerk—he was definitely that—but that he was also being psychologically affected by his condition. Further, he was scared and felt powerless. They all did, but she knew that fear manifested in different ways.

She glanced over her shoulder at the other vents within her line of sight and sighed. *There's too many.* She stood up and left her post and made her way over to Lance, glancing back as she walked to check her vents. She almost tripped over the surgery cart on her way. "Lance, you do realize even with the vents you blocked off that we're still only watching half of them at a time?" she said.

"I told everyone to rotate between vent locations—"

"I know all about that, but it's not enough." *Now I sound like Maeson,* Janys realized and fell quiet.

"What do you want me to do, sweetheart? Close off more vents? I already sealed off two more last night. You know it's going to become problematic if we keep doing that. At least we aren't making it easy on whatever's out there. Besides, it beats sitting around waiting to die."

"Right," she said, adding, "but don't forget, the creature's intelligent. It could be watching us right now, listening. If it is, then it knows our pattern and then can simply go to a vent we aren't guarding." He leaned forward and whispered, "That's why I sent them a message telling them to switch vent locations every twenty minutes."

Janys nodded and without another word, returned to her station. A few minutes later, she saw Maeson move to another set of vents and moved on as well. As she did this, she noticed Crewman Kelsa walk over and sit on her bed, then stand up and walk around, then return to her bed, only to stand up again and pace. The doctor wished she could think of something to put the crewman's mind at ease. Finally, an idea came to her and she walked over to a cabinet, took out a medical bottle, glanced back at her vents, and then approached the woman and said, "You should try to get some sleep."

Trembling, Kelsa said, "I can't sleep. I can't get my things from my quarters. I can't get out of this frikkin' Med Center. No offense, but it's driving me bangy."

Janys frowned. *Kelsa's file didn't say anything about—*

Kelsa was trembling. "I feel like I'm trapped in a cage and something's going to poke or prod me at any moment. What if one of those creatures shows up and—"

"Kelsa, Acting Captain Bendrik is well armed. I have a pistol, too. I know you've heard a lot of rumors over the past few weeks, but we can't even prove the shadow creature actually exists. We're assuming it does because it's safer to do so. I think they do, but you should be safe here. No one has ever seen it inside Med Center. Worrying is perfectly normal, but it isn't going to fix our situation. Let me give you something so you can at least get some sleep, okay?"

Kelsa shook her head, her breathing elevated. She kept biting her lower lip. Finally she nodded. "I'm not sure if I could even sleep without meds these days . . ."

Janys gave her a pill and pointed her to a sink where there was a cup dispenser. Soon after, Kelsa was lying on a bed sleeping. Janys checked on Lorego and Mardag. Satisfied that they were not in any immediate danger, nor bore any new sores, she returned to guarding vents.

The next time she rotated to a new set of vents, she headed off to get a drink, passing Maeson as he was finishing up his vent rotation. Neither made an effort to make eye contact, much less say anything to each other.

Maeson walked up to where Ensign Lorego was sleeping and started poking him in the ribs. "Hey? Get up. Lorego, you waste of—"

"What?" Lorego said, waking with a start. "Quit poking me!"

"Then get up," Maeson said. He gave the ensign a hard rap on his forearm and pointed to the vents on the wall. "Let's go. Your turn. Start over there," he said, pointing at a vent. Without saying another word, Maeson walked over to his own bed and lay down.

Lorego got out of bed and shuffled over to the vent and sat down. He rubbed his eyes and glanced back and forth between the assigned vent and another.

Janys set her pistol down on a supply cart beside her and repositioned her chair to watch three vents near her. She knew splitting her attention between three wasn't as thorough, but she doubted the creature would manage to slip past her if she kept switching her attention. She sat in silence, hoping it would stay that way through the rest of her watch.

Thirsty, Janys walked over to get herself a drink of water and thought she heard a faint moan. She jerked her head in the direction of the beds. Mardag and Kelsa were still sleeping. Maeson was farther away. *If he isn't asleep yet, he will be soon,* she figured. Maeson always amazed her at how fast he could get to sleep once he hit the pillow. She wished Lance could do that. Maeson had rolled his bed into a corner shortly after being "imprisoned" inside Med Center, and was facing away from them. She didn't like him being so far away from the others. It made it harder to keep tabs on him.

Glancing back at the others, she spotted Ensign Lorego enter the restroom alone with a pistol in his hands. Several minutes passed and he still hadn't returned, so she approached her husband. "Lorego's been in the restroom for awhile. You should go check on him."

"I haven't heard any shots. He's probably fine," Lance said with a shrug.

"Just do me a favor, and check on him."

"Okay . . ." Lance said and got up from his post and headed toward the restroom.

"Be careful," she said, and then forced herself to return her attention to the vents before her. *The last thing we need is an injury by friendly fire.*

In such tight quarters, everyone knew everyone else's business. When Maeson asked for a pistol so that he, too, could go to the restroom safely, she had seen the look on his face when Lance said he would go with him. Maeson was red-faced when they came out, and has been complaining even louder than usual ever since.

The engineer had a military issue pistol in his quarters, but they had been ordered not to return to their quarters. As the days passed, Maeson had become angrier and angrier. Janys had tried to talk with him about his claustrophobia and his short fuse, but it only made him madder, despite her making special efforts to keep the conversation professional and friendly. He was scared. They all were.

Janys watched the sleepers while Lance was checking on Lorego. Kelsa was still, but Mardag turned in his sleep, first on one side, then the other. Lance returned with Lorego and they took up their positions at the vents. A few minutes later, Janys heard a sound she was sure was a moan. "Mardag," she muttered and stood up. *He's probably just having another nightmare,* she told herself, but continued to watch closely. From her vantage, there were no visible sores on exposed areas, or stains on his jumper.

A minute later, Mardag moaned again, louder than before. Janys rushed over to the orc's side. Upon walking around to the far side of the bed, she saw his right foot poking out from under the sheets and immediately found a fresh sore on his right ankle. There were two more on the right side of his neck. She just stood there and stared at the sores on his neck in horror. *Not again. Pleasepleaseplease not again,* she thought, and closed her eyes in despair, fighting to keep from losing it.

She heard something and her eyes snapped open. Glancing over her shoulder, she saw Lance and Lorego talking quietly. "Lance?" she called out, and he rushed over.

"What's wrong?"

"I need you to check Kelsa for sores."

Lance gave her a long look, fear spreading out across his face. He quickly moved toward the foot of Kelsa's bed. The crewman was wearing bed socks, was covered up to her neck, and remained very still, her eyes closed. "I don't see anything," Lance whispered, as he rushed around to the other side of the bed. "I can't tell. She's mostly covered up. Should I wake her, or?"

Sores only on one side of his body. Exposed areas. Far side of the bed from where he was being monitored. The bed partially blocks our view. All three of Mardag's sores are blistering and covered in grime just like with Torrey and—

"Janys?"

She glanced up briefly. "Lance, I need to give him a full examination. Check the security vid for the past fifteen minutes."

"What about Kelsa?"

Janys glanced over at Kelsa. *No sign of discomfort. Sleeping peacefully. She's safe for now,* she decided. "I'll check in on her next. We need to know what's on those cams." She glanced down at Mardag. He continued sleeping, but it was clear he was agitated.

"You see anything, Ensign?" Lance called out, as he made his way to the security terminal, not stopping for an answer.

"No, sir," Lorego said, wide-eyed. "You need me to . . ."

"Mardag?" Janys whispered, resting a hand on the orc's shoulder and squeezing gently.

Silence.

For several moments, Lorego watched them from a distance, and then finally peeled his eyes away to examine a nearby vent.

"Mardag?" Janys said a little louder. The orc opened his eyes and she knew he knew what had happened. His eyes were filled with terror. It would have been easier to treat him while he slept, but she didn't want to startle him. *He deserved to know, and I don't need a four hundred pound orc kicking or punching me thinking he's under attack in his compromised state.*

"It's okay, Mardag. I'm here. Try to relax."

"The sores . . . you said—"

"I need you to take a deep breath, Mardag. Let me help you."

The orc was biting his lower lip and rocked slightly, trembling in pain.

Janys didn't have to explain the situation to him. He already knew better than any of them, so she went about disinfecting his wounds. She had no doubt a portion of the infectious grime had already been absorbed through his wounds. The antibiotics would help, but she was afraid of the greater ramifications. After applying a HealTab, she gave him her best antibiotic. Her heart told her it wouldn't be enough, but she did it anyway. "I'm sorry my friend, but—"

Mardag shook his head, "Just tell me you still have some of those heavy pain meds you gave me before?

Janys nodded. "I'll help you in any way I can."

Lorego kept glancing over. He looked miserable and darted around, looking under beds, behind equipment, glancing at anything that could project a shadow. Everyone's hope had diminished after Torrey's death.

As Janys treated the orc, it became obvious to her that he was depressed and fully expected to die soon. He seemed more interested in controlling the pain, than anything else.

Leaving his side only long enough to get him the meds he needed, Janys then retrieved a field olfactometer from her coat pocket. She detected no exotic scents, so she slipped the device back into her pocket.

Her heart sank. *It's still happening.* "Do you feel pain anywhere else?"

Mardag shook his head side to side, biting his lip enough that it began bleeding.

She whispered. "Now's not the time for modesty. I need to know if you have any other sores. Would you prefer to have Ensign Lorego help you with an examination?"

"I don't need anyone—"

"Whatever you want to do, my friend, but it's important for me to treat any other sores. I've already seen you head to toe."

The orc winced in pain, as he did so, his enormous tusks protruded even farther than usual as his lips stretched back.

Janys dabbed away a dribble of blood that ran down his chin. "Biting your lips isn't helping, Mardag. Try to relax and let me do my job."

"I'd know if I had other sores, Doctor. Just the three, but they hurt something awful."

"You'll be feeling much better very soon. I gave you the good stuff. Hang in there."

Mardag nodded and took a deep breath. He laid his head back down on the pillow and closed his eyes. His hair and pillow were soaked with sweat. When Janys changed his pillowcase, she noticed a smear of grime on it. A tear ran down the side of the orc's cheek and onto the HealTabs covering his neck when she replaced his pillow.

"I'll be right back," Janys said and rushed over to Kelsa's side. "Ensign?" she called out, motioning for him to make his way over.

"Sir?" Lorego said, and came at once. He seemed eager to help.

"I need you to wheel Mardag's bed into the surgery station, across from my med terminal."

"Sir, yes, sir." he said and began moving the bed.

Turning to Lance, Janys said, "Talk to me." She knew it would take time to review the vid, but she was anxious to find out if the cam caught anything. It seemed too much of a coincidence. *Mardag was only injured on the side of his body facing away from everyone else. There's still a cam facing that side. I don't know if it's good or bad for Lance to find something on the cam. At least if there was a sign of a creature, that would give us a clue to what's going on. I can't believe this is happening again!*

She checked Kelsa's neck and hands and was pleased to see there were no exposed sores. Her breathing remained normal and as she expected, she was fine. Just to be safe, she went ahead and woke her up. Kelsa wasn't totally coherent, but she was awake enough to know if she was in pain. Janys questioned her and then let her go back to sleep. She breathed a sigh of relief and refrained from telling the crewman about Mardag's condition. Remembering Lance was reviewing the security footage, she headed his way. *Oh my gosh. Maeson!* She spun on her heels and bolted toward the engineer instead. *He's probably just sleeping. No way we'd have two cases in one day.*

As she approached, a groggy Maeson turned his head and glared at her. "What? I'm not dead yet, if that's what you were hoping! What in Gyria's name is up with all the noise? I was trying to get some—" the engineer fell quiet and he quickly sat up, his eyes fixed on Mardag's bed. The orc was moaning in his sleep. "What's wrong with him? Another of his stupid nightmares?" Maeson said, and rolled back onto his side, facing away from them.

Janys didn't answer him. She just stared at the orc, watching him sleep.

"Who would have guessed orcs were such wimps?" Maeson said under his breath and pulled a sheet up over himself.

Drifting back over to check on Mardag, Janys rested a comforting hand on his shoulder, but her mind was elsewhere. She had no doubt that had Maeson been aware of what Mardag was going through, he would have been scared—not for Mardag, but for his own welfare. *Who could blame him? Every sore means another death. Maeson has to be thinking the same thing I've been: We're not going to escape this.*

"Talk to me, Lance. Anything?"

Lance looked up from the terminal and frowned.

"What is it?" Janys asked.

"Nothing suspicious, at least nothing captured on vid. It's what *wasn't* captured that's got me worried."

"Meaning?"

"We've got one dead cam and another that's out of alignment."

"You've got to be kidding me?"

"Wish I was, but that whole area," he said, motioning toward the supply corner and Maeson's bed, "I can't see that at all, and the dead cam would be covering the far side of both Kelsa and Mardag's beds. Both cams overlap a little."

"Are you telling me a shadow creature snuck in here, disabled one cam and redirected another?"

"I don't know what to think, but somebody moved that cam, and the other . . . well, cameras die. They malfunction too, but it is an odd coincidence."

It was no coincidence, Janys decided. "You sure you or Lorego didn't bump it by accident while checking it?"

"I suppose that's possible . . ."

"But unlikely, right? Especially given the other one so conveniently died right when we needed it."

"That's what I was thinking too, but I just wanted to hear you say it." He gave her a defeated look and she didn't know what to say. Just the day before they were thinking everything was looking up. Now . . . she was scared and wasn't sure what to do. Glancing around an idea came to her. "We've got way too many beds in here now. Too many places for a gaseous creature to hide."

He nodded. "I'll get the extras moved out into the hall." From the look on his face, Lance only saw empty beds.

But when Janys looked out, she saw previous patients and blood. They were staring up at her, each covered in wounds and leaking their life's blood down the sides of the bed and onto the floor. She gasped, and put a hand to her mouth and bit her lower lip. The vision faded, but her heart was still racing.

Each bed had held a patient, some of the beds had held many over the past month. Most of the crew was gone. Only five remained. Lance began moving one of the extra beds toward the exit.

Janys shook her head. *Lance, when you said you'd move the beds, I thought— or hoped, at least, that you meant you would have Lorego do it, or even Maeson. Well, maybe not Maeson. He'd do it, but it wouldn't be worth the trouble. That's probably why Lance decided to do it himself,* she realized. She headed over to Lorego. "Ensign?"

"Sir?" Lorego said, glancing up from where he was guarding vents. He stood as she approached.

"Would you please help the Captain move the extra beds out of Med Center?"

Lorego glanced toward the main entrance and then back at her. He looked nervous, but nodded. "Yes, sir," he said, and walked up to the nearest unassigned bed and rolled it over to where Lance was waiting.

"Thank you, Ensign," Janys said and then checked on Mardag. He was sound asleep. The pain meds were doing their thing, but she wondered how well the antibiotics were working. She glanced back up at the cams, shook her head and frowned. Glancing back at Lance, she watched as he took out his pistol and covered Lorego as the ensign moved the beds out into the hall and then locked Med Center down again. They repeated the process for each of the extra beds. Janys pointed out carts and mobile machinery that wasn't likely to be needed and they moved those out into the hall as well. When they returned, Med Center was considerably more open.

Lance then sent Lorego back to guarding vents while he checked on each of the cams himself.

Kelsa awoke and needed to go to the restroom, so Janys accompanied her and then the crewman went back to bed. Janys rechecked both Mardag and Maeson and was pleased that both were sleeping soundly. She glanced around the room and was grateful they'd removed the extra beds. *It's an improvement, but there's still plenty of places a being made of shadow could hide,* she realized.

A short time later, Lance approached her and said, "I reoriented two of the cams to help cover for the dead one."

"Couldn't fix it?"

Lance stared at her for a moment and then shook his head. "They aren't that old, either," he said, glancing over to see if anyone was listening. "I know they were both working fine a couple hours ago." He approached closer and whispered, "While I was opening up the dead cam to check on it. I discovered it had a severed cable."

Janys shut her eyes for a moment, trying not to panic. She felt helpless and miserable. She glanced over at Maeson, then back to Lance. "You don't think he'd cut the cable do you? That dead cam looks like it would have covered our beds as well."

"It did cover ours, though not as well as that one over there," he pointed, adding, "but that's not the problem."

"Think about it," she said, her mind rapidly piecing together reasons why Maeson was guilty. "If Maeson only sabotaged the cam facing our beds, then he might look suspicious, so he changed the angle on his as well. That way, he could claim he, too, was a victim. If nothing else, redirecting his cam might have made it easier to disarm ours."

"He couldn't have cut the cam cable."

"You sure?" Janys said. She wasn't entirely convinced Maeson was out to get them, but she knew he wanted a pistol of his own. *He clearly didn't think*

Lance was competent and didn't like him—or me for that matter, she realized. *He may be a jerk, but I don't think he was trying to set us up for the creature to attack. Redirecting his own cam would also put him at risk.* She didn't think he would try to kill them in their sleep, but she didn't trust him.

"Janys, the cable isn't exposed on this side of the wall."

Janys shot a glance at the nearest cam and saw no cables leading up to the cam. "Then how did—"

"I was about to—forget it. The cable goes directly from the wall through the cam's mount and into the cam. There are no exposed wires or cables. There's probably an access shaft on the other side of that wall," he said.

"So the only way Maeson could have done it was if he—"

"We would have caught him."

"While we were sleeping?"

"I'm sure those cameras were working properly earlier today. There's never a time when he's the only one awake. I made sure of that. Besides, the cut wasn't clean."

"I don't understand."

"It wasn't cut by a tool. Janys, the cable was shredded."

Maeson had been furious when he awoke to find that Mardag was sick and no one had woken him. Kelsa, on the other hand, had been glad she'd slept through it. She admitted she would have been freaking out otherwise. But the orc was sleeping peacefully by the time they awoke, and that had calmed her a little. Maeson, on the other hand, stepped up his litany of complaints.

Well into the next shift of vent duty, a jarring noise reached Janys' ears and her eyes flashed open. Startled, she dropped her pistol and nearly fell out of her chair. Embarrassed that she had apparently fallen asleep during vent watch, she quickly retrieved the pistol. As she did so, she turned to see what had made the noise and saw Maeson walking past her carrying a chair. He paused and turned to glare at her. He continued walking a few steps and then dropped the chair and said, "Oops."

Janys realized it was the same sound that she'd heard moments before and knew what he was up to.

The engineer turned and glanced down at the gun. He slowly lifted his eyes up her body, taking his sweet time reaching hers and said, "Sorry if I distracted you from watching the vents, Doctor. I'd hate to think I was responsible for letting a shadow creature slip through." He moved the chair further along the wall and took up position in front of another vent.

The first thing that entered Janys' mind was the times she'd caught him dozing while supposedly guarding the vents. She had never said anything, knowing it wouldn't make a difference, but wished she had now. *Maybe then he wouldn't have said anything,* she thought, furious at herself. *Even if I told him, he'd still say my infraction was worse. I did drop the pistol after all, and his mistakes don't excuse my own regardless.*

A few minutes later when Mardag woke up and sat on the edge of his bed, Lance called everyone over to Mardag for a meeting. Janys brought over a plate of food and set it beside him, but his usual appetite had diminished along with his enthusiasm. She avoided eye contact with Maeson. She had no doubt he'd be grinning over his latest diatribe.

Lance held up the cam with the shredded cable dangling from it and explained what he learned about the cams, confirming there was an intelligent intruder on board.

Everyone muttered at the news.

After a few moments, he continued. "I need everyone alert as we sort out our next move," Lance said. "According to the Chief Medical Officer—"

"Acting," Maeson corrected, adding, "She's definitely acting, I mean, she's the Acting Chief Medical officer, Acting Captain."

Janys was dying inside, but held her tongue. She avoided eye contact and focused on Lance. From the look on her husband's face, she knew he wanted to punch the engineer in the face.

"Shut it, Chief," Lance ordered. "Apparently the antibiotics are working just fine. It's an aggressive condition."

"That's right," Janys said, stepping forward, her eyes going from Lance to Lorego and back to Lance again, occasionally finding the floor an important focal point. "The creature either carries or excretes a poisonous substance that exacerbates the condition. If you see anything grimy, don't touch it. Report it to me. It's crucial that you continue doing self examinations, and keep yourselves and your surroundings clean. Most importantly, stay calm."

Maeson sniggered. "More people have died in Med Center than any other part of the ship. I'd be safer in Engineering . . ."

Lance had given the engineer a warning glance, but he had been immune to Lance's threats for some time now. And now she had added ammunition to his claims by falling asleep on the job. *Why couldn't Lorego or Lance have found me? Why did it have to be Maeson?* She frowned deeply and returned her attention to the vents. *That's not going to happen again,* she told herself.

There were only five of them left and Mardag was fading fast. The orc was slumped forward on his bed looking weak and a little out of it. Janys walked up beside him and rested a hand on his shoulder to help steady him, but knew she couldn't keep him from falling if he started leaning too far forward. She was about to ask him to lie back down in bed when he turned his head to look the engineer in the eyes.

"Chief—," Mardag said, pausing to catch his breath, " I know your mom died a few months back, and—"

"Who gave you permission to speak?" Maeson retorted. You don't know anything about me, orc!"

Mardag sighed, nodding. "I don't know you, but I know about your mom."

"Shut up," Maeson said. There was spittle on his lips. Janys glanced over at him, only for a second and then over to Lance.

"I heard Captain Raeden talking to another officer about what happened. I was in the elevator and . . . anyway, I just wanted to say that I'm sorry about that. I am."

Maeson looked furious, but he didn't say a word. He just stared hatefully at the supply officer. Janys noticed the engineer's fists were clenched tightly. She didn't dare make eye contact. She didn't need to. She knew.

Lance started to say something, but fell silent, as Mardag continued. "Thing is . . . bitin' off people's heads isn't helping anyone. I know you're hurting inside, but . . . well, I said more than I should've, I suppose."

"Like I said. You don't know spit about me," Maeson said, and walked off.

"Chief…" Lance started, but Janys shook her head and he said no more.

No one said a word for nearly a minute and they all seemed to find something to look at other than each other.

Mardag was the one who broke the silence. Turning to Janys, he said, "Sorry, Doc. Captain. Guess I'd better lay back down before I fall down. I'm not feeling so good all of a sudden."

"It's okay my friend," Janys whispered. "You did good."

Lance nodded and shared a sympathetic smile. Turning to Lorego and Kelsa, he said loud enough for Maeson to hear, "No more solo trips to the restroom. Always take someone with you. If you see an intruder, don't engage. Fall back and call out, understand? I'll confront it myself."

Janys, Lorego and Kelsa nodded.

"Yes, sir," Lorego added.

Lance turned to address the orc and said, "Mardag, I don't expect you to stand guard."

The orc looked up at him and nodded. "I'm sorry, I haven't been much help."

"You have. More than you know," Lance said and then something must have caught his attention, because he glanced past the orc and stared. Janys didn't look, but she knew where her husband was looking and her stomach tightened. She tried not to think about Maeson.

"Mardag, I need you to stay in bed and get as much rest as you can. Your body needs to fight, and for that, you need plenty of sleep. And with the meds you're on, you'll be drowsy to boot."

"Yes, sir," Mardag said with a deep sigh.

"Don't worry, Mardag," Maeson said. "I'm sure we're completely safe as long as the good doctor doesn't drop her pistol again and shoots one of us by accident. By the way, Acting Captain Bendrik, wise move giving the doctor a pistol. Why are we even bothering with guarding the vents? Let them come, whatever they are. The way you talk, you can handle them all by yourself."

Lance stabbed a finger in the engineer's direction and said, "I'm getting tired of your lip, Chief."

Lance, please don't go there, Janys thought, knowing it wouldn't do any good.

"Aren't you even a little concerned about what happens when we get back to the CDF and I post my report?" Lance said, taking a step toward the engineer.

"Not really," Maeson said, folding his arms.

"You should be."

"Why? We're not going to make it back. We're all going to die out here!" Maeson shouted.

"Your complaining isn't helping the situation," Lance said.

"And you are? What have you done, Acting. Captain. Bendrik?"

"I can tell you one thing I haven't done," Lance said, his eyes locked on Maeson's, "I haven't given up."

Fists clenched, Maeson growled in obvious frustration.

The room was jarringly silent as Lance and Maeson stared each other down. Maeson was bigger and looked stronger than Lance, but Janys knew that wouldn't stop her husband from throwing a punch if it came down to it. She knew that was the last thing he wanted, but from the look on Maeson's face, the engineer was hoping he'd try it. Lance didn't back down, neither did he taunt the engineer.

To the room's surprise, Maeson turned and walked away a second time. Everyone followed the engineer with their eyes and then started their next shift of eating, sleeping or guarding. No one said a word for over an hour. Janys wondered if they were all thinking the same thing. *We can't keep going on like this. Something has to change.*

Stopping by Mardag's bed to check on him, Janys was pleased to see he had developed no new sores on the exposed areas of his body. His meaty left hand was sticking out from under the sheet and she tucked it back in and covered him up to his neck.

I'm no expert on orc physiology, but Mardag seems pretty resilient. Its not him I'm worried about, she realized. *It's the bacteria. It's extremely resistant. There's no way I could develop some new, super antibiotic in time—I don't know if I'd be able to given another two decades and I'm starting to wonder if we'll last another two days.* She walked around the circumference of his bed and checked his vitals. *So far, so good, but that's just the outside.*

She knew inside his body, a war was raging. Her antibiotics would likely win the battles, but the war itself? *Whatever that nasty garbage is the creature dumps on his victim's wounds infects the whole body and weakens their immune system. I've analyzed it. Damn thing replicates like bunnies. Never seen anything like it.*

Some of the antibiotics work. Or maybe the bacterium just goes into an inert form so the body stops detecting it as foreign and harmful, and stops fighting it. After a period of time, the foreign contaminant reawakens, maybe even morphing itself into a new strain that's highly resistant to the antibiotics, and attacks again, stronger than ever. Who knows? I'm so out of my league here. She realized she was staring at a vent, but not really watching it. She'd zoned out and wondered if a creature had come through, if she'd have even noticed. *At least I haven't dropped the pistol again.* She kicked herself all over again over that blunder.

Before long, she was once again lost in her thoughts. *Maybe the creature has to keep visiting its victims and applying its grime—or magic—or both, to up the ante. Maybe that's why the antibiotics aren't enough.* She found no pattern among the various species on board—no age, gender or other factor that she could pinpoint as a negative or positive impact. There was nothing special about her own blood or health history she could point to.

It kills me that I haven't found a cure yet. If we don't kill that thing or things soon—oh, Lord, I pray there's only one, and that Lance will be able to figure out how to kill it! She jumped when she heard Med Center's twin doors slide open. She turned and watched her husband walk in wielding his gauss rifle, escorting Lorego from a quick run to the weapons locker. Lorego rolled a cart into Med Center and headed over to the lockers. Lance quickly locked the doors behind them. Maeson was waiting by the door for them, but as she suspected, Lance wouldn't give him a weapon. Maeson's face turned red.

"Crewman Kelsa isn't getting a weapon either, Chief."

Janys listened as her husband delicately explained that the engineer was rusty and had been emotionally compromised by their situation. She was proud of the way her husband calmly handled the confrontation, but she knew it had only infuriated the engineer. He reminded Lance of her blunder dropping the pistol. He struggled to answer that one, but noted that at least she'd kept the safety on and had been pulling extra vent rotations on top of taking care of Mardag, unlike the engineer. Lance reassured Maeson that he would make sure she got plenty of rest from here out. He also told him that he didn't want him confronting the creature as he was too important to put in harm's way. Maeson stormed off.

Lance rejoined Lorego by the patient and staff lockers and together they stowed the extra guns and rifles. By the time he reached the lockers after squaring off with Maeson, Lance found Lorego had nearly finished putting away all the weapons. Lance set two pistols on the counter. Once they were finished, he handed one to Lorego and then walked over to Janys. He gave her a kiss and a pistol, and said loud enough for Maeson to hear, "Acting Chief Medical Officer, I don't want to see this firearm in your hands unless you've had proper sleep."

"Yes, sir," she said, and handed him his pistol back and then slid the new one in its place in the holster he'd given her earlier.

Her husband's back was to Maeson. "Understand?" Lance winked at her. "I mean it," he said in a serious tone, and she knew he was. She also knew he was trying to soften the blow with Maeson. *That's probably wise,* she thought. *He's becoming a liability.* After a moment, she realized, *I will be too, if I don't get more sleep. I thought I could keep going—like Lance, but I don't know how he does it.*

Janys nodded. "I understand, sir. I'll take a nap shortly and be more careful."

"Be sure you do," Lance said, and strode off.

As she turned to sit back down in her chair, she noticed Maeson look away, shaking his head.

A few minutes later, Janys heard Maeson and Kelsa arguing for the umpteenth time. Lance told them to stop, but they ignored him. You can threaten a soldier with charges of insubordination, but like children, if they don't think their parents are going to follow through, orders can only go so far. Only yesterday Lance had asked her if locking Maeson up in quarantine was going too far given the engineer's claustrophobia, and she suggested against it.

Lance told Janys that short of tossing him out an airlock, quarantine was the only option. She knew he'd never toss anyone out an airlock, but was worried he'd do something they'd all regret. Lance agreed, but wasn't sure what to do about it. "We'll put him in quarantine by gunpoint if we have to, but I think it's only going to make him worse, and away from the rest of us, he would be a sitting duck for the creature."

Morale was lower than ever.

Finishing her vent rotation, Janys walked over and talked with Kelsa while she ate, then told Lance they needed to use the restroom. "Chief, you and Lorego guard Mardag while the rest of us take a restroom break, unless you need to go too?"

"No. You three have fun. I'll remain here and guard the orc with my bare hands."

Lance escorted the ladies to the restroom and had them wait outside while he quickly scanned the showers and stalls. He returned a minute later and accompanied them inside and waited by the sinks.

Knowing her husband was so close by and was waiting for her, Janys found she was unable to relax enough to pee. She quietly took out a new HealTab from her coat pocket, rolled up her sleeve and the peeled off the old one, ditching it in the commode. She was grateful to see the blister was all but gone. She flushed the commode as was expected of her, and to cover the sound of ripping open the HealTab package.

Removing the HealTab, she pressed it in place and shoved the empty package into her coat. She'd managed to dodge undressing in front of her husband for over a month now, to keep her secret. *The creature marked me. I doubt he's forgotten about me. Unless something drastic changes—like killing whatever the hell that is out there, I'm going to die with the rest of them. I should have died already.* This wasn't a new thought. It was on her mind every day.

Rolling her sleeve back down, Janys rejoined the others, determined to get some sleep, come what may.

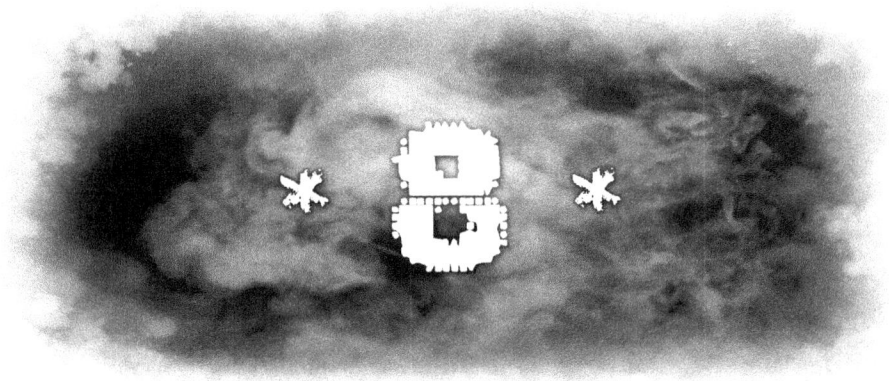

Maeson became unusually quiet, his stabbing remarks less frequent, which worried Janys. *What changed? Has he given up completely?* She kept stealing glances at him when she was sure he wasn't looking, but couldn't read him. He often sat with his back to them and even when he ate, he usually climbed up onto his bed facing the wall and ate alone, quietly.

Hours later, as Maeson sat down on the edge of his bed after vent rotation, Janys made a point of walking past him carrying her meal, taking the long way to her next set of vents. She was determined to communicate with him, however painful it might be, deeming his silence unhealthy. As she drew near, however, she found him weeping.

"Chief?" Janys asked, hoping she wasn't opening a can of worms. *If he doesn't want to talk, I certainly won't pursue it, but the look on his face . . .* "You okay, Chief?" she asked again, setting aside her plate. She waited for the snide comment, but it didn't come.

Maeson said nothing. A few seconds passed and then he gingerly pulled up the leg of his jumper to reveal two sores around his ankle. They were covered in grime and were already oozing puss.

"Please . . . do something," he said in a shallow voice, whimpering, but a moment later when she tried to inspect his sores, he jerked away from her.

"Here, let me take a look, Chief," she said and stood beside him, but he wouldn't even look at her, and cursed under his breath. She'd been around grouchy patients before. It came with the territory, and waited for him to send over a volley of verbal abuse, but knowing and experiencing aren't the same. She knew he needed help and so, she pressed the issue. "We need to get that cleaned right away, Chief," she said.

Maeson began trembling. His face contorted with anger. He shoved her aside, grabbed a nearby scalpel, and slashed at the air around him, to keep anyone from coming near. He stared at the Acting Chief Medical Officer with wild, bloodshot eyes. "This is your fault, you stupid witch! Everyone who comes to Med Center gets sick, and now you've killed us all! Did you cook up this frikkin' virus? You get some sick pleasure out of doing this?"

"Maeson, please. Calm down," Janys said, taking a step back, but remaining calm, at least externally. "We're all tired. You aren't thinking clearly."

Lance aimed his gauss rifle at the engineer and stepped in front of Janys to protect her. "Put it down, Chief. She's not the enemy. None of us are."

"You're in this together. I must have been bangy not to realize . . ."

"Maeson . . . she can't help you if you don't calm down. Put it down. That's an order!"

"An order? You think your rank means spit right now? Most of the crew are dead and you sit around watching vids and staring at empty vents. You want me to relax? Easy for you to say! Funny how neither you nor your wife have so much as a single sore after all this time. And you were on the Away Team! What happened down there? You make a deal with some shadow devil not to hurt your family?"

Janys began rolling up the sleeve of her left arm to reveal that she too was a victim.

"You sold us out, didn't you?" he shouted.

"Maeson, please . . ." Janys said, changing her mind. From behind Lance, she rolled her sleeve back down. "Whatever is causing this condition is aggressive. I need to dress those sores before they become infected." She took special care to keep her voice calm and even, despite how she really felt.

Lance motioned for her to stay back and she hesitated. "Maeson, I can help you but only if you let me," she said.

"You can't help me. Who have you managed to save so far? Can you name even one?" Maeson asked, his eyes were like flaming arrows launched toward the couple. Breathing hard, he held the scalpel in his hands like a weapon, ready to lash out at any moment. Lance, Janys and Lorego had weapons, but they weren't out. The engineer had them by surprise, and in truth, Janys knew none of them wanted to hurt the engineer, no matter how much they disliked him. Besides, in such close quarters with everyone surrounding Maeson, getting hurt by friendly fire was very much a possibility. *There must be a way to diffuse this,* Janys thought. *Before it gets worse.* Lance may be the most experienced at firearms in the room, but he'd been only in combat simulations up till this point.

Kelsa was flipping out screaming at everyone. Lorego seemed frozen in fear, standing off to the side, staring wide-eyed. The closest to Maeson was Mardag, but he was a mess. He lay on his bed miserable. He was due for another round of pain meds, but Janys couldn't reach him. The blisters on his face and neck began rapidly spreading the moment Maeson flared up. The next time Janys peeled her eyes off of Maeson, she saw that the orc's wounds were oozing, infected. *I think the creature's in here with us—somewhere . . . I'd swear it can accelerate a victim's condition . . .*

"Maeson," Janys called out, "Mardag just took a turn for the worse. I think the creature's in here with—"

"Shut up! I'm so sick of your lies. You're just trying to distract me."

Lance glanced over to Janys only briefly. He seemed confused, and quickly turned back to face the visible threat, his hand hovering over his side arm, not yet apparently willing to draw it.

If Lorego and I bring out our pistols, it might just exacerbate the situation. Maeson might go over the edge, Janys realized. Her eyes darted around, but she saw no sign of the creature, yet as she watched in horror, Mardag's condition rapidly deteriorated. She felt helpless.

Despite his injuries, the wide-shouldered orc supply officer sat up and slowly slid his legs over the side of his bed. It looked as if he were about to attempt to lunge at the engineer standing nearby. But it was also clear the orc was in a great deal of pain.

"Stop it, Maeson! All of you!" Kelsa shouted, her face red and wet with tears.

Janys watched as Kelsa fell silent, her eyes now riveted to Mardag. The crewman stood with mouth agape, her breathing erratic, the front of her jumper soaked in sweat, her whole body trembling.

Janys was right behind her husband, her back up against the surgery table. "Mardag," she mouthed, unable to find her voice, fearing the orc would get stabbed trying to intervene, but she was unable to respond. She desperately tried to make eye contact with the orc, to warn him to stay back, but his eyes were boring a hole in Maeson's back.

Mardag's sores continued to spread. Blood and pus were running down the side of his bed. He tried to stand, but seemed to be having trouble. He just sat there swaying, his eyes blinking in confusion. Blood and spittle were running down his chin and his face had lost its color.

Jany was afraid to move or say anything for she knew Maeson didn't like her and might respond badly. She stole a peek at Kelsa, who was glancing all around them now, jumping at every shadow and screaming at the top of her lungs, flailing madly with her arms as if fighting some invisible creature.

After several tense minutes, Mardag made one final move to stand, but then his muscles visibly relaxed and he lay back down and closed his eyes for the last time.

Maeson never looked back. He kept jabbing at the air before him. "Stay back. Don't you frikkin' touch me."

Kelsa finally calmed down somewhat. She sunk down onto the floor and cried instead. Janys wanted to go to her, to comfort her, but she was afraid to leave Lance's side.

Maeson slowly backed away until he bumped into Mardag's bed. He must have sensed something was wrong because he reached back with one hand and felt behind him, then quickly withdrew his hand and stared at it in obvious horror. Blood ran down his fingers.

"Dr. Bendrik wasn't lying, Chief. Mardag's—"

"Shut up. Just . . . shut up!" Maeson screamed, trembling.

"Just take it easy, Chief," Lance said.

After several tense moments, Maeson's breathing finally slowed and he seemed about to drop the scalpel, when Kelsa cut the silence with a scream.

Lance and Janys looked over and saw the crewman was holding her arm and staring in horror at a trickle of pus running down it. She had three sores, one was a large bubble of stretched flesh, the other two were oozing. Janys peeled her eyes off Maeson for a moment and rushed to Kelsa's side.

Maeson must have used the distraction to charge Lance, and caught him off-guard. Janys looked back in time to see Maeson's scalpel bite deep into her husband's side. In the commotion, Lance's gauss rifle slipped out his hand and skittered across the floor.

Lance gasped in pain and gripped the emergency table for support. His free hand fumbled to draw his pistol.

Amidst the chaos, a shot rang out. Lorego had drawn his pistol and fired at the engineer and missed.

Maeson stumbled forward, carried along by his own momentum and struck his head on the metal lip of the surgical supply cart, scattering instruments and gauze everywhere. His scalpel spun off into the shadows. Lance turned to face Maeson, not realizing the extent of what had happened, and wrenched in pain, his breathing ragged.

Janys reached into her pocket and pulled out gauze and a packet of wipes and pressed them into Kelsa's hands, then rushed to her husband's side, tears in her eyes, her bottom lip quivering. She glanced over at Lorego and shouted, "Ensign?"

Lorego didn't seem to hear her. He just stood there staring wide-eyed at Maeson lying on the floor, his pistol aimed at the engineer's head.

Janys handed her husband a swath of gauze and said, "I need you to put your hand right here and apply pressure."

Lance nodded, his face contorted in pain.

She turned to Lorego and shouted, "Ensign Lorego, I need you to stay in the game. The creature's still in here. Check the area. Every shadow, understand? Lorego?" Janys said. "Lorego!"

The ensign finally lowered his weapon and he nodded. "I'm on it," he said, finally.

Having watched the engineer fall, Janys assumed the worse. She wanted desperately to patch up her husband, but instead she knelt down beside Maeson and checked his pulse. "He's dead," she announced, and then rushed back to her husband to check the severity of his wound."

"Flush him! What about me?" Kelsa shouted.

"I'll be right there, I promise."

"Husband first. I get how things are . . ." Kelsa said, with tears still running down her face.

Without looking up, Janys said, "He's losing a lot of blood. You can do the first part easily enough. Just go over to the sink and rinse off."

Kelsa walked over a few feet and then collapsed into a chair and stared at the pus dribbling down her arm onto the floor.

Janys heard Lorego running around Med Center checking every nook and cranny, every vent and shadow. "I don't see anything," he shouted, pistol still in hand. "It's gone!"

All the color ran out of Janys' face. She'd been doing her best to remain calm in an insane situation. Taking several deep breaths, she let them out slowly as she tended to his Lance's wound. Her husband stood there looking miserable, his eyes fixed on Maeson's body.

"Hang in there, Lance. You've lost some blood, but you'll be okay. I need to help—"

"Go. I understand," he muttered.

Janys realized she wasn't hearing water running at the sink and glanced over her shoulder. "Kelsa, I need you to go over to the sink and wash off that arm! Don't touch the wound, just put it under the water. It's going to sting a little. The sooner you get cleaned up, the better."

"It's too late! Spit, I can't believe—"

"Damn it, crewman. Every second counts. I said to—"

Lance squeezed his wife's arm and she fell silent. He whispered, "I'll be all okay."

She turned to him, tears welling in her eyes and nodded. "I'll be right back. Keep applying pressure." Realizing it would take too long to coax Kelsa to get up, much less get her to the sink in her state, Janys rushed over and grabbed a tray of medical supplies and set it down on a bed beside the crewman. "We have to get your wounds cleaned immediately," she said, and brought out a disinfectant and began prepping her for HealTabs. She then gave her an antibiotic and covered her wounds. Kelsa continued to weep. As soon as she was finished, Janys rushed back to her husband and began dressing his wound.

A moment later, Lorego returned to her side and said, "If it was here, it's gone now."

Janys shook her head. "I want you to stand guard beside Kelsa while I finish patching up the Captain."

"Yes, sir."

Janys glanced back at Kelsa, who was holding her wounded arm, her eyes darting around, looking at every shadow, tears still flowing, though more softly now.

Lorego walked up to the crewman and rested a hand on her shoulder. "I'm sorry, Kelsa," he said.

He still had his pistol out when Janys glanced over. "Careful with that thing, Ensign. I don't want anyone to get hurt."

"Yes, sir," Lorego said, his breathing starting to return to normal. He slid the weapon back into its holster after a final glance around them.

Janys realized there was no one to spare to remove the bodies, and there was still grime on the floor. She finished patching up Lance and suggested he lie down to get some sleep while she stood guard.

"I'm okay."

"You need to rest. That scalpel had a lot of momentum behind it. You have a deep wound."

He frowned. "I figured as much. You are going to give me pain meds soon, right?"

"I already gave you one. It'll kick in shortly. Now get some rest. I'll watch over you."

"Janys, I don't need sleep. I want to check the security cam."

She knew she wouldn't be able to talk him out of it, and ordering him to sleep seemed fruitless. He was coherent, if in a good deal of pain. She nodded and went back over to check on Kelsa. "No new sores, I hope?"

Kelsa said nothing. She just shook her head and stared at the HealTabs on her arm.

A few minutes later, Lance called his wife back over and she stood beside him as he played back the vid of recent events. "Ever since we started doing vent rotations I haven't been checking this as often," Lance said. "Looks like it killed two of the cams. The whole far side of the room is offline, but if we switch to the cam behind us . . ." Lance paused as he split the screen to show all the active cams and then tapped on one. Shifting in his chair, he gasped softly.

"Lance?"

"I'm all right."

Janys stared at the screen as the horrible events that just happened began to unfold again before them. Lance gestured at the terminal and the scene fast-forwarded until he made another gesture with his hand. "Here," he said and pointed at Mardag. "Watch around his neck area."

"What is it?"

"You'll see . . ." Lance said with a sigh. "This is the cam behind us seeing pretty much what we were, but as our eyes were on Maeson, we didn't notice—shoot, I need to—" He motioned again briefly, then quickly made another gesture and the vid switched to normal speed again. "There. See it?"

As she watched, she saw a purplish-red tentacle come into view—*no, a tail,* she realized, remembering the reports. The tip of it was bulbous and rose up from behind the bed to linger over the orc's neck. It began dripping something that she realized was the toxic grime she kept finding on the victims.

"Zoom in thirty, quadrant three," she said, and the vid displayed a close up of Mardag's neck. The tip of the tail was covered in suckers. It slid over Mardag's cheek, then slipped down across his neck and chest and into his open jumper. After a moment, it slipped back out and vanished behind the far side of the bed into a trail of smoke—*no, living shadow,* she thought.

"Well, that's that," Lance said. "We've finally seen it. Now how do we kill it?"

"For one, we don't ever let it catch us by surprise again," she muttered, knowing it was no small order. "Is there any more?"

"No, it's gone. Zoom out full," Lance said.

Janys turned to Lorego, who was now holding Kelsa's hand, trying to comfort her as his eyes sought out every nearby shadow. "Everything okay over there?"

He glanced up, "No sign of a creature."

"It was here. Captain Bendrik just found it on the security cam. Keep a sharp eye out."

"Yes, sir."

Turning back to Lance, Janys said, "I want to see it again. The whole thing."

"Okay, but the creature doesn't show up until around seven minutes and—"

"Humor me."

Lance restarted the security vid from the beginning of the incident with Maeson. After a few minutes, Janys said, "What's that?"

"What's what?"

"By the foot of the bed."

I don't see—"

"Right there," she said, pointing. Impatient, she blurted, "Zoom in 30, quadrant 1." A smoky cloud appeared, just barely poking up above the sheet near his right foot. A moment later, it dissipated. "Back up five seconds. Play." The smoky cloud appeared again, only for a moment, and then vanished.

"You think it's generating its own smokescreen of sorts?"

She considered this for a moment and said, "That might have been the creature in gaseous form—or part of it, and then it solidified in order to use its tail."

Lance nodded. "Back up five seconds and play," he said. After watching it again, he said, "I have a theory."

"I'm online. Talk to me."

"Maybe it can only enter well-lit areas by generating a shadowy covering—you said it yourself, it might be magical."

"I was guessing, Lance. I don't know. Maybe. Whether it's a part of its body or a magical covering, it might not be capable of turning it off any-more than we can tell our bodies to stop sweating in the heat. We don't know much, but we know more than we did before, and that's a good thing."

"Yeah . . ." Lance said. "Now to figure out how to kill it."

Janys glanced back at Lorego and Kelsa. They were talking about some-thing, but every few seconds, Lorego glanced around, making sure the creature wasn't anywhere to be found. Lance called them over and showed them the creature.

Afterward, Lorego said, "We were right there, Kelsa and I. You didn't see anything, did you, Kelsa?"

The crewman was quite for a moment. "I may have noticed the corner of Mardag's bed smoking a little, but I thought it might have been a mechanical short, nothing important, not under the circumstances—so the foot of his bed stops tilting or something. So what? I was going bangy. I kept thinking Maeson was going to rush over and grab me, try to use me as a hostage so he could return to his precious Engineering like he used to go on about. You were all scaring the hell out of me . . . and then *this* happened," she said, glancing at the HealTabs on her arm.

"Kelsa, I'm so sorry," Janys said. The others offered her sympathetic glances and nods.

"Me, too," the crewman said. She glanced around at each of them and then returned her gaze to the doctor. "You were right, Doctor, that pain med does its job well . . . but I'm still going to die. And to think, I joined the CDF so I could visit worlds I could never afford to take vacations to. I never thought . . ." She fell silent and stared off.

"We were all focused on Maeson. It was the perfect time to strike. It could have been there for five minutes and we'd never have known," Janys said. "If we can keep the creature away from you, those antibiotics should do their job. Just stay clean and let's all stay close together."

She looked to each of the survivors for agreement. She saw the determination on Lance's face and knew he aimed to make sure no one else died. *Everyone has to die sometime,* she thought. *I'm not giving up, but I know when it's my time. And that time is coming. It will come for Kelsa too, before long.*

Janys glanced down at the bodies. "Lance?" she said, and motioned with her head at the bodies.

A few minutes later Lance and Lorego had placed the bodies into burial bags and moved them onto the evacuation hatch platform. Janys and Kelsa accompanied them. Lance shut the airlock and said a few words. He activated the launcher and they all stood before the small window in the airlock watching the bodies of Maeson and Mardag drift out into the

Cosmothean Sea. The sight was depressing, and breathtaking at the same time. Janys noticed her husband step back and scan the small room. He was holding a gauss rifle and slowly swung it back and forth everywhere he looked. She kept glancing back to check on him. Lorego and Kelsa continued to stare out the small window. After being cooped up in Med Center for so long, she understood why they continued to look. She glanced back. Lance was still searching the shadows for signs of movement. There were plenty of places to hide.

We need to get back into the light, she thought. On their right was an incinerator, and rows of shelves lined with linens, extra pillows and other supplies. On their left was a backup decontamination chamber, backup generator, ultrasonic purifier and sterilizer unit. Each cast heavy shadows.

"There are too many places for the creature to hide in here," Lance said.

Janys agreed. "Let's go, you two," she said.

Everyone looked at each other and then pulled out their pistols. Kelsa winced, no doubt bothered by the sores on her arm.

Several hours passed and they saw no sign of the creature. Instead of watching the vents, they sat or stood in the center of the room, all together. Finally, Kelsa said she was hungry.

"Why don't you bring it back over here to eat," Lance suggested. "That way . . ."

Kelsa nodded. Lance seemed about to say something, then fell quiet as Lorego stood and accompanied the crewman to the supply bins.

Janys turned to Lance and said, "That creature could have killed every one of us." She knew she wasn't far from losing it herself.

Lance sighed deeply. "I can't protect us," he whispered. "I don't know what to do. It's playing us."

"I know." Janys didn't have any answers either. Her stomach was raging so badly, she thought she might hurl. She took several slow breaths and tried to calm herself. Finally, she said, "I'd like to think it hasn't just been waiting us out. We've been making it harder and harder for it to find a crack in our defenses, but whenever we let our guard down, it takes one of us. I stood there and watched Mardag die."

"You didn't know the creature was there and you couldn't have saved

Mardag even if Maeson hadn't—"

"We should have shot him when we had the chance," Janys heard herself say, and was shocked by her own words.

Lorego and Kelsa were just returning with food enough to share. They stopped and just stared at her.

Janys felt ashamed for even thinking such a thing, much less saying it. "I didn't mean that," she said, looking up at them. "I'm just . . . I wanted so badly to go to Mardag—to hold his hand while he passed, if nothing else. I think the creature has to touch you to give you new wounds, but if it can get close, just its proximity can make them worse. I don't know. Maybe if I'd have been with Mardag, the creature wouldn't have come. I . . . I should have been there for him . . ."

"It's not your fault," Lance said.

Janys looked away. She could taste the bile in her throat and walked over to get a drink. When she returned, everyone was quiet. She approached Lance and whispered in his ear, "I'm having a hard time thinking straight. I'm too tired. I don't know if I can sleep after what just happened, but I have to try."

"Whatever you need to do, sweetheart."

"Lance, if you get a chance, kill that thing, but don't die on my account. If it takes me in my sleep, that's not such a bad way to go. I've been luckier than I deserve."

"Don't talk like that!" Lance said louder than he'd meant to, she realized by the expression on his face.

He was clearly upset, and she considered telling him right then and there. After all, the sore on her arm was nearly gone again. She didn't want him to worry. She put a finger to her lips to remind him they weren't alone. Devoid of energy, she could barely keep her eyes open, having slept horribly on her previous attempt. "Whatever happens, it's okay," she said, staving off the tears. "It really is."

She climbed up onto the surgical table, rested her head against the pillow and closed her eyes. She felt Lance's hand envelop hers. She squeezed his hand, releasing him. Rolling onto her side, she pulled the covers up to her neck and feigned sleep until it finally came.

"You set up motion detectors across the whole Med Center?" Lance asked, hopeful their luck was finally changing.

"Just the main room, sir," Lorego said, smiling.

"Still, that's great news!" Lance said. He glanced down at the four tiny motion detectors in the ensign's open palm. Each was smaller than an earbud. "What are those, extras, in case one of the creatures finds a way to disable some of them?"

"Oh, no, these are for the ceiling vents. I was just about to put them into place. I think I can make a few more before I run out of parts."

"Wait, how are we going to move around? We'd be setting them off all day long!" Lance said, beginning to sour on the idea.

"That was my concern initially as well. But the range is short and the cone is very narrowly focused. I have them aimed at the vents. We would need to stay at least point five meters away from them. That ought to be enough to avoid triggering the detectors." Lorego got an odd look on his face and smiled. "That assumes no one takes up cheerleading to pass the time. That would trigger a ceiling alarm. But simply raising your hands shouldn't cause a problem."

Lance chuckled. "Excellent work. Be sure to let the others know. I meant to ask you what you've been working on these past few days."

"They're very fragile, sir. But hopefully they'll help."

Over the following forty-eight hours, one or more of the detectors went off three times. The first was when the air conditioning came on. Nearly all of the detectors went off and it took Lorego several minutes to kill the ear-jarring beeps. He recalibrated them and promised it wouldn't happen again. The second time, only one of the detectors had sounded. They didn't know why, but Lorego analyzed it, and said it was working perfectly. Everyone agreed it must have been the creature, which they started calling Shadow Men, inspired by Ford's obsession.

The compromised vent was in one of three locations that Lance had discovered were out of view of all of the cams. They sealed up the vent, but Janys said they'd need to keep the others open. Pleased that they seemed to be keeping the creature at bay, they continued their daily routine. Lorego was able to make four more motion detectors from unused bed monitors, but said he would have to tear apart more bed monitors to assemble additional ones, and there were only so many bed monitors left. He assured them the creature would have to come into the room to damage a detector.

The third time the motion detectors went off was odd and disturbing. Kelsa and Lorego were sleeping while Lance and Janys stood guard. Lance was walking wide circles around their beds feeling like he was going to go bangy from boredom when Kelsa lifted her head and said, "I'm supposed to be able to sleep with you marching circles around me?"

Lorego continued to sleep undisturbed.

"I was being as quiet as I could," Lance said, feeling irritable. "And you forgot to say, 'sir,' crewman."

Kelsa shook her head. "Sorry . . . sir, but I hate this! Sometimes I just frikkin' wish that creature would have finished me off when it had the chance. Flush, waiting to die is worse than—" Kelsa gasped and went statue still for a moment. Eyes wide, her face contorted in fear, she reached over her shoulder and brushed her fingers across the back of her neck and then screamed just as a motion detector started beeping wildly. Lorego bolted upright in bed and looked around in confusion.

Lance held his pistol in two hands and glanced all around, then realized the motion detector that was sounding was directly over Kelsa's bed. The next thing he saw was the crewman throwing herself off her bed onto the floor.

Kelsa gasped again as she landed hard on her bad arm and continued screaming as she flailed her arms wildly across her back. "Get it off of me!"

Lance rushed around the side of the bed, almost slamming into his wife, who was converging on Kelsa's location at the same time.

Everyone looked up and locked eyes on the vent directly over Kelsa's bed. Smashed into the grillwork was a dead rat covered in blisters and blood. Lance trained the pistol on the vent and fired. He heard a noise in the ventilation shaft above, then silence.

Ensign Lorego scrambled out of his bed and took his pistol out of the drawer below it.

Lance stood in horror watching as blood dripped down onto Kelsa's bed below. *I don't think I hit a Shadow Man. That blood's from the rat.* Dirty drops of tainted blood stained the sheet. *Was that supposed to be a warning, or was it really trying to infect Kelsa?* Lance wondered.

Janys was checking Kelsa's neck, cleaning up the mess and trying to calm her down.

The crewman was trembling. Every other word out of her mouth was foul. Lance had heard worse in his time in the CDF, but not much.

There were tears in the crewman's eyes. "Who the hell moved my bed back under that vent?" She looked up at the dead rat smashed against the vent. "Just kill me and get it over with you frikkin' coward! Do it already! Flush you!"

"It's okay, Kelsa," Janys said, trying to calm her. "The grime can't hurt you unless there's an open sore. You're patched up good and I think the Shadow Man's gone."

"My arm burns," Kelsa said, blanching. From what Lance could tell, she'd fallen on it pretty hard.

She moved her bad arm this way and that, looking for new sores, still cussing up at the vent.

Janys started checking the crewman's arm for a sprain or break when several yards away, another motion detector went off. The light over a low vent started beeping, its tiny red light blinking on and off. Lorego spun around and ran toward the vent.

"Careful, Lorego," Lance shouted as he ran to meet him. They waited outside the vent, but nothing came through.

"Are there more of them up there? Flush this!" Kelsa shouted.

Janys put a calming hand on her shoulder, but the crewman shrugged her off and then lurched forward, and threw her arms in the air. Her whole body splayed out in an exasperated proclamation, "Just frikkin' kill us already!"

Why aren't they coming through? Lance wondered. *If there are several of them, why don't they rush us? We couldn't possibly stop them all. I'm not even sure if our weapons could hurt them.* He glanced behind him at the others. They seemed in no immediate danger. *What are the Shadow Men waiting for? Maybe Janys was right. Maybe there really is only one of them.* On a whim, he started counting. Several seconds later, another motion detector went off near the Med Center's front entrance. Lorego ran toward the vent. Lance started following after him, then stopped. He turned and glanced back at his wife and Kelsa. Janys drew her pistol and shouted, "You want me to get out a gauss rifle?"

Lance shook his head. "Just stay with Kelsa," he said and continued counting. Another vent detector sounded, and soon another.

Kelsa was hyperventilating. Sweating profusely, the crewman was trembling and Lance stole glances as his wife calmly talked her through it. He couldn't hear what the doctor was saying, but knew she was the best one to be with the crewman during all of this.

Lance watched them for a moment to be sure they were safe, knowing Kelsa's breathing wouldn't improve by much no matter what his wife said or did, until the alarms stopped going off. He glanced around at the vents. *Nothing.*

A motion detector near the entrance to the storage room and airlock went off.

"They're all around us!" Lorego shouted, turning to Lance for direction.

Lance said nothing. He began counting again. He waited and then another alarm sounded. *I think Janys is right. We're only dealing with a single Shadow Man. It's racing from vent to vent, deliberately setting off the alarms. I'd have to see a schematic of the vent shafts to be sure, but I bet that's what's going on. There!* He pointed to one of the vents and said, "I saw its tail for a second sticking out of that vent. It pulled it back in before I could take a shot!"

"Where?" Ensign Lorego asked, frantically converging on Lance's location.

Lance pointed again to the vent and shouted to be heard over the alarms, "Lorego, can you control those detectors by remote? Reset them?"

The ensign thought for a moment and shouted back, "Not yet, but I can set that up with a bit of work."

"I think it's just trying to scare us."

"It's working," Lorego admitted.

"Stay sharp, everyone. Lorego, stay close," Lance said, returning to his wife's side. She looked like she could use a hand with Kelsa, who was still flipping out. She was trying to retrieve a pistol from the drawer below her bed, but Janys had positioned herself in front of the drawer and was talking her down.

Good girl, Lance thought, grateful his wife had intervened, knowing it wasn't safe for Kelsa in her condition to wield a weapon. Lance couldn't hear what his wife was saying over all the noise, but trusted she'd do a better job than he would. Even so, he wanted to be there, just in case Kelsa got out of hand. By the time he got there, the crewman had stormed off, still cussing and shouting at the vents.

"You got this?" he asked his wife upon reaching her. She glanced over at the crewman as she pulled the pistol out of the drawer and handed it to Lance. "No problem. Put this somewhere safe."

Lance nodded and said, "I'm almost positive we're dealing with a single Shadow Man. I counted the time it took to get to each vent."

"That's what I thought," she said, shaking her head. "Just promise me you won't stop till you kill that thing."

Lance nodded again and then ran over to where Lorego was disarming a detector. The ensign showed him how to do it, and together they rushed around resetting them all. A few minutes later, it was nearly over.

"Just the ones on the ceiling left," Lorego said, still shouting to be heard above the beeps. Already it was far less ear-piercing than when they were all sounding at once. Kelsa seemed to calm down once most of the alarms had been reset and sat down in a chair staring down at her arm and rocking back and forth. Everyone else kept glancing over at the nearest vents as they rushed around, in case the Shadow Man returned.

Lorego moved a bed into position below one of the motion detectors and then climbed on top to reset it. Lance walked over and held the bed steady while the ensign worked. Watching him as he worked, Lance said, "All this time we've been assuming—hoping at least—that we've been dealing with lower tech predators . . ."

Lorego nodded. "Now we know better."

Miserable, Lance wondered how much longer they could hold off against a very stealthy, intelligent predator. "I'm pretty sure there's just one, Lorego. I can't swear to it, but I was counting the time between motion detectors going off and the gap was longer the farther away a vent was from the last." *I'm surprised the Shadow Man hasn't already killed us all off.*

"If that's the case, that's the first bit of good news I've heard in awhile, sir, but I'm afraid if the creature knows even close to what we know about this ship, it could sabotage a number of critical systems. If that rat we found was from the Biome, the Shadow Man may have already compromised our food supply."

"Let's hope not," Lance said.

Lorego climbed down and headed over to another ceiling vent. "Just two left," he said to Janys when she glanced over as the ensign was climbing up to reach the motion detector.

Lance followed Lorego over and said, "You know we have a ladder for this sort of thing." As before, he reached out and held the bed from rolling around.

"Sorry, sir. I didn't realize."

"No, I should have said something. It's in the backroom and I didn't feel like getting it out earlier when you were installing them."

"Well, that room is full of shadows, sir. We're almost done, at least until I can set up the remote control," he said. A moment later he climbed back down. "I'll get the ladder if you want me to, sir, but there's just one vent left."

Lance shook his head. "Nah, let's finish this."

Lorego nodded and they moved over to Kelsa's bed.

"Careful not to get any of that stuff on you," Lance said, staring down at the blood stains on the sheets. "And careful with that vent," he added as he pulled out his pistol once more, in case the Shadow Man reappeared, though he suspected it was off hiding somewhere, no doubt pleased with itself.

Lorego pulled the bed just far enough away from the vent so he could be sure to reach the motion detector without fear of any blood dripping on him. He quickly reset the detector, ending the infernal beeping. It took him much longer to get the dead rat out of the vent.

When Kelsa's breathing returned to normal, she started chewing out Lorego. "You're the one who moved my frikkin' bed back under the vent!"

Lorego's face blanched. "I'm . . . sorry! I used it to reach the vent to install the motion detectors!"

"You didn't put it back where you got it! I had specifically moved it so it wouldn't be directly under any vents! You could have gotten me killed, you frikkin' idiot! I can't believe you—"

"Crewman!" Lance shouted. "It was an accident!"

Kelsa glared at the ensign and muttered something unpleasant under her breath.

"I . . . meant to move it back, Kelsa. But I noticed it wasn't lined up in a row like the other beds and thought . . . I'm really sorry!" Lorego said, red with embarrassment. The ensign turned to Lance looking as miserable as Lance felt. "Sir, I'll get right to work on reprogramming the motion detectors so I can reset them from my wristcomp."

I wish you would have thought of that to begin with, Lance thought, but he knew he couldn't give the ensign too hard of a time. The idea of using narrowly focused motion detectors had never even entered his mind.

Kelsa remained upset. Lance felt bad for Lorego and when the crewman finally stormed off after a second round of beating him up over moving her bed, Lance pulled him off to the side and said, "She'll get over it. When she gets a chance to think, she'll realize you're the reason these past few days have gone by relatively peacefully. You've remained cool-headed and disciplined throughout this crisis."

"Thank you sir. I know I wasn't always pleasant to be around."

"We've been under horrific conditions and you've done admirably. Frankly, you've been a lifesaver, Lorego. If you hadn't made those detectors, who knows how many of us would have become infected?"

"I wish I could take all the credit, sir," Lorego said.

"What are you talking about?" Lance asked, confused.

"Sir, when you were in the restroom a few days ago, I caught Maeson taking apart one of the bed monitors and asked him what he was doing. He told me we were being stupid to watch the vents and he was making a motion detector. He'd taken out the parts he needed from one of the unused bed monitors, and planned to make a bunch of them."

"Why didn't you tell me when you found out?" Lance asked.

"Sir, I'm sorry. I thought . . . well, it seemed harmless enough, and he said he didn't want to announce anything until he was sure they would actually work. He really seemed to be enjoying it, and he wasn't making a bomb or anything. There was no danger, and he kept mostly to himself. I figured it was a win-win."

"I see . . ." Lance realized he didn't like the idea of having to think there was something he should be grateful to Maeson for. He liked far better the idea that Lorego was solely responsible.

"Maeson said he was going to test one in the restroom. After he died, I found his prototype. I checked his wristcomp and found some notes he'd made. It took me a couple days, but I figured it out and tested one to see if it worked. So many things have happened since then, and like Maeson, I didn't want to get anyone's hopes up if it didn't work. As soon as I tested it, I started making enough for all of the uncovered vents."

"You should have told me sooner, Ensign. Maybe I could have helped you assemble them."

"It's rather delicate work, sir. Electronics has been a hobby of mine. It was my major at the academy before I switched to navigation. I mean . . . you're right, sir. I'm sorry, sir."

"That will be all, Ensign," Lance said and walked over to check in on his wife. Kelsa frowned at him as she passed by heading straight up to Lorego.

"How can you be so smart and so dumb at the same time?" Kelsa said, folding her arms as she stood before the ensign.

The ensign said nothing. He just frowned and stared down at his feet.

Lance turned around, hoping to derail the crewman. "Kelsa, nobody's perfect. If Lorego hadn't put those motion detectors in place the other day, we could all have become infected by now."

This didn't pacify Kelsa. She wouldn't speak to Lorego for the rest of the day.

With fewer survivors, the edibles they'd stocked Med Center with were lasting much longer. Even so, they knew they would need to restock soon. They hardly felt safe in Med Center, but knew beyond its walls, an ambush would be even easier.

At least once per day, Lance reviewed the cams throughout the ship. To his dismay, he discovered the Shadow Man had managed to get into the Biome and found a way to keep it from closing. That meant various little critters were beginning to make their way around the ship. More importantly, some of the machinery had been damaged, but not all was lost. There was still the cold storage and the cafeteria, which hadn't appeared to be touched yet. There were no cameras inside cold storage. On his last check, he'd found the smoldering remains of a dead chicken in one of the areas defended by an auto turret. He decided not to tell the others about the Biome, as he didn't want to alarm them. *I'll tell them when they need to know,* he decided.

Janys and Kelsa slept as Lorego and Lance sat in silence eating. As they were finishing their meal, Lorego's wristcomp lit up. A warning sounded. Lance recognized it. The sound was a snippet from a horror RPG he knew Lorego had enjoyed back when there was time for such things. In the game, it always sounded whenever a character died. A moment later, the ensign announced, "One of the life pods just launched."

"How is that possible?" Kelsa asked, sitting up in bed. "I don't understand. Did the creature just take one of our life pods back to the moon . . . or down to the ringworld?"

"I doubt it could get inside," Lance assured them.

Then Janys woke up and slid her arms into the sleeves of her white coat, then slipped out of bed.

"What's going on?" she asked.

"One of the life pods just launched," Lance said. "The doors only open by entering your ID into the launch terminal."

"Sir, if the creature disabled the pod's airlock, there's a chance the pod could have launched empty," Lorego said.

"Why would the creature want to do that?" the crewman asked.

Lance thought about it, finding the whole matter disturbing. "I'm not sure. Maybe it got confused or it was simply an accident."

Kelsa shook her head, and muttered vulgarities under her breath.

"Don't worry, Kelsa," Lorego said, "We still have five life pods and the smaller shuttle. Even if it attacked all of the life pod airlocks, there's no way they'd all launch."

"Like the Captain said, 'maybe it was just an accident'," Janys offered.

"Speaking of which," Lance said as he drew his pistol, "We shouldn't assume the creature isn't already back in here hiding, waiting to catch us off guard."

"Sir, there's no way the creature could have gotten all the way back from Launch Bay," Lorego said.

"It's possible," Lance corrected. "Teleportation would be the most exotic answer, but there's a simpler one. We know the creature's intelligent. It might not fully understand our technology, but it's possible it rigged a pod to launch after a period of time, and then came right back to make us think it was elsewhere. It could be watching us as we speak. I've also done some thinking about its prank on the motion detectors earlier. I started counting when it was going from vent to vent. I'm not positive, but I checked the distances on a schematic afterward, and it can move through the vents very quickly, much faster than we could—of course some of the vents are too small for us to even enter, but that didn't stop it. The thing's fast. I'm not saying it's here, just that it's possible. Something else got me thinking. Earlier, the creature stuck its tail through a vent, presumably to taunt us, but since the vent is small, that tells me that it can simultaneously cause a portion of its body to become solid while the remaining portion is still gaseous."

Kelsa shivered visibly. "What does it want with us?" she asked, her frustration evident. From the looks on their faces, Lance knew they were all scared. That emotion had been as common as eating since entering the Cosmothereal dimension.

Everyone muttered.

"Maybe this is just yet another attempt to scare us," Janys said. "We don't know much about it, but it seems obvious it hasn't been in any hurry to kill us off."

What chance do we have if the Shadow Man knows our technology? Lance wondered. *Little to none, would be my guess.*

Lorego's wristcomp just lit up again. "Sir, we just lost another one."

"Kill me now. Just frikkin' kill me now. I swear!" Kelsa said.

"Sir, do you think it's trying to remove all of our modes of escape?" Lorego said.

"I'm not sure. Maybe it's trying to lure us out of Med Center and into a trap. But it can get inside Med Center whenever it wants, especially now, with so few of us to stand guard."

"Is that why you never sleep?" Kelsa asked.

Lance shrugged. "Ever since we left the Dark Nebulae, my sleeping pattern has been thrown off."

"More like way off, I'd guess," Kelsa said.

"All but non-existent," Janys said.

"With all due respect, sir, that's not human," the crewman said, folding her arms.

"Anyway," Lance said, trying to derail the conversation, "She may be right. This could be just one more scare tactic." *Am I sick? Seriously, what is wrong with me? Could this be another subtle attack of the Shadow Man? What purpose would it serve?*

"You should check the cams in Launch Bay," Janys said.

"Great idea, he said. "We should be able to see what we're up against."

"If it's still there," she said.

"Even if it isn't, the cams are set to auto record, and my guess is, the creature hasn't been as worried about keeping itself a secret anymore. We know it's out there," Lance said.

"True," Janys said and turned away from them to slip out of her underwear and put on a fresh pair, her coat acting as a dressing room door. These days, there wasn't a lot of room for privacy, and such luxuries also raised the risk of being attacked.

Lance knew what she was doing, but the others were focused on him. His mind jacked open a file in his head about a conversation they had had prior to getting married, and it sat there demanding his attention. He recalled how he had tried to convince her to volunteer for the mission, and now felt miserable for it. By her signing up, they were able to get married a year sooner, something he wanted even more than she did. *At least she's managed to stay healthy,* he thought.

"Just because the creature is no longer a secret doesn't mean it wants us to know its every move," Janys pointed out, as she straightened the sheet on her bed and puffed up her pillow.

"True," Lance said, watching her make her bed, all the while thinking how meaningless it was. Lately, he felt that the majority of their time was spent doing meaningless things. Even worrying about the creature's actions seemed pointless. *It's just going to keep coming for us until we're all dead.* Calling Kelsa over to the lockers, he got up in her face and said, "I know this situation is flushed. I get it, but if we don't hold it together . . ."

"I know. I'm sorry, I know . . ." Kelsa said, adding, "But—"

"You will keep your head on straight, soldier," Lance said more firmly. "You will keep your head in game. If we ignore our training, allow this spit to overwhelm us—if we give up, we're dead meat."

"Right," Kelsa blurted, her breath catching in her throat. Nodding, she added, "I get it, sir." A tear ran down her cheek and then another.

With less less intensity, Lance said, "I know you can do this. We have to do this." He glanced back at Janys, and saw that she was watching them. After a moment, she nodded and he opened the locker. "We have to stay focused."

"I know . . ."

Lance pulled out a pistol and holster and handed them to Kelsa, but he didn't let go right away. "I know you've been trained in firearms and it's been awhile. Keep the safety on and only use it if you absolutely have to. Understand?"

Kelsa stared at the pistol for a moment and then nodded.

"What did you say?"

"I mean yes, sir."

Lance let go and sighed, closing the locker. He turned and walked over to the security terminal. The others followed. Lance brought up the vid feed for Launch Bay. Moments later, he said, "The only cams responding are pointing at insignificant areas. None of the cams facing the Launch Bay doors are active."

"Great . . ." Kelsa muttered, holstering her pistol.

"Everyone, stay alert," Lance ordered.

"Yes, sir," Lorego said.

"Yes, sir," Janys and Kelsa said in unison.

"Lorego, lock down Launch Bay so the shuttle and pod moorings can't be triggered without

"Yes, sir. Doing so remotely will take longer, but not long."

"Good. I'll start reviewing the footage leading up to this point, in case there's something to see," Lance announced and slid into the chair in front of the terminal.

Everyone stayed together and watched the vents, ceiling, anywhere they thought something could sneak up. They also watched each other, in case the creature got through.

Hours passed uneventfully. Lance found nothing worth sharing with the others upon reviewing the security vids. Sometimes the creature made noises in the ventilation system, and once, Lorego even shot at it when it poked its tail through a vent to scare them again. The ensign had missed, but the creature left for a time. Later still, while Lance was doing a sweep of the ship, one of the corridor cams revealed a damaged access panel to Engineering. The panel and surrounding wall had been defaced. Long, deep scratches marred the surfaces and the panel appeared to be disabled. The light on the cover was blinking sporadically.

Lance split the display to view the inside of Engineering and everything seemed intact thus far, but he was concerned about the fusion core. He continued to monitor Engineering, and found no significant traces of vandalism. *I wonder if the creature resisted damaging Engineering significantly, fearing it might blow up the ship by accident?*

One of the supply shelves in Engineering had been emptied, its contents strewn across the floor, but that was about it. He'd found that sort of thing in other areas over the past few days. *The Shadow Man could have found a way to damage the fusion core if it really wanted to. Guess it doesn't have a death wish,* he realized.

Lorego walked up to Kelsa as she was sitting on the edge of her bed. "You doing okay? How's your arm?"

Kelsa peeled off the HealTabs as he watched.

"They look . . . a little better," Lorego said.

Janys walked up with fresh HealTabs and said, "They are better. You're making good progress, crewman. If we can keep the creature away from you, you'll be fine."

Lance was watching them and knew his wife meant it, but Kelsa said nothing. She was self-monitoring, but just barely. Lorego looked miserable as well.

My wife's treatments work. The real problem is, the Shadow Man's still alive. It keeps coming back to reinfect and scare us. The only time I've had it in my sights, I haven't managed to even injure it, much less kill it. Why does it keep coming after us like this? He thought about the creature further and decided that its absence wasn't merely to taunt them. It had also been tactical. It had to be careful to remain in shadow form whenever it was seen, which meant he had to catch it both in solid form and by surprise. *Or I'm totally off base. I wish we had more intel. I searched the CDF database, but couldn't find any mention of a species like it. We're dealing with something completely new. The Cosmoverse is big. Who knows how many creatures are out there like this one, or worse?*

Lately, it seemed to Lance that his wife had given up any hope of finding a cure and was more interested in finding a way to kill the creature. So when she spent the better part of her last shift researching again, he was pleased to see she hadn't given up hope. It was late when she finally gave up her research for the night. *Or was it day? Who can remember?* Lance watched her for a moment, concerned for her health, mentally and physically. Most of the crew had died under her care and he knew it was a heavy burden to carry. He too felt the weight of those lost under his watch.

She wasn't acting herself these days. Lance couldn't identify anything specific. The color of her skin was paler than usual. Even when she managed to sleep, she awakened tired, her exhaustion cyclical. He felt like she was slowly fading away—*we all are. The creature takes a toll on us even when it doesn't attack.* Lance watched as his wife got up from the med terminal, walked over and slipped into bed without a word. What few conversations they had shared lately were all business. They were merely surviving, not thriving. *It can't keep going on like this. Something has to change . . .*

As soon as Janys and Kelsa woke up, Lance sent Lorego off to bed and he stayed up with the others to guard. *There's something wrong with me. This goes beyond insomnia. If that's all it was, I wouldn't have so much energy. I don't have as much as I did yesterday or the day before, but I'm still going. Kelsa was right. It's not human. Am I just going to keel over one day from lack of sleep? Janys herself said I should be suffering the effects of sleep deprivation, but I'm not. Beyond being tired, I'm fine. How can I go nearly a month without significant sleep and not be sick? She's right to be worried about me, but at least I've been able to stay awake to help with guarding. Right now, sleep is the least of my concerns.* He glanced over and watched the sleepers, his eyes routinely darting into every shadow, searching for movement, a wisp of smoky shadow, anything out of the ordinary. Nothing.

Once Lorego finished his sleep cycle, Kelsa said she wanted to take a shower. Janys reminded her husband it had been four days since anyone had showered and she opted to take one at the same time. That meant Lance and Lorego had to accompany them. They stood guard outside the shower room.

Lorego kept his eyes trained on the restroom stalls, as Lance stood with his back to the wall of the shower room, his gauss rifle held limply in his hands, waiting for time to pass. He was bored, but not so much that he was hoping for anything bad to happen. He thought about what would happen during an attack if he and Lorego had to rush in as the women were showering.

Lorego would see my wife naked! He didn't like the idea, especially when it had been over a month since he'd seen his own wife disrobe. He was proud of the ensign for not once peeking into the shower room. It helped curb his own interest, not wanting to be a bad example, and so he tried to think about something else. Soon, his mind began to wander and he started thinking about his wife and Kelsa in the showers again. *You're such an orc sometimes,* he thought, and then felt guilty for the comparison.

When he was growing up, many of his fellow classmates called each other orcs whenever they were teasing each other about a stupid mistake or trying to indicate low intelligence. That reminded him of the orc supply officer, Mardag, and he felt worse for all the pain the orc had suffered both recently, and likely while growing up. *It must have been hard to be an orc citizen of the Republic, even after how far we've come. When I was growing up, I'd make fun of them just like everyone else. Never thought twice about it.* He frowned. He heard Kelsa talking in the shower and for a moment he wondered what she looked like without any clothes on.

"I saw Kelsa's once," Lorego said as if in response. He had spoken low, under his breath, leaning in close, his lips curled into just a hint of a smile.

Lance felt guilty for even thinking of Kelsa. "What?" he said, his introspection interrupted.

"Her—you know . . . her breasts. She was leaning over to pick up—never mind. Sorry I said anything, sir."

Lance frowned, but Lorego's talk made his mind wander further still. He knew he'd regret it, just like he always did. *I should check on them. Make sure they're safe,* he mused, but knew secretly, he was just looking for a legitimate excuse to see their bodies. *Shut up and focus! A wandering mind isn't healthy for a male,* he reminded himself. Poor Lorego's still single and shy and will probably never . . . "Stay alert, Ensign," he said, feeling guilty over his own distractions.

"Yes, sir." After a moment, Lorego said, "It's getting steamy in here. Women take forever to shower."

Lance nodded. "Wait till they go over to the sinks. At least they aren't putting on makeup anymore. But—"

A scream tore through their conversation and Lorego and Lance looked at each other. "That was Kelsa," Lorego said, raising his pistol.

"Lance!" Janys screamed a moment later.

As Lance and Lorego rushed into the shower room, something touched the back of Lance's neck and he felt a small sting. His first thought was an insect had found its way from the compromised biome into the vents and down onto his neck. Something hot dribbled down his back and he realized the creature was behind him. Rounding the corner, he evaded the creature by entering the shower room. Vision was limited, but he spun around and saw a blur of purplish-red. The creature slipped behind the wall moving toward the sinks as Lance fired the gauss rifle in a wide pattern, punching holes in the stalls. This time, both women screamed. Before engaging the creature, for just a moment, he thought he had seen Kelsa on the floor with his wife hovering over her. He feared the worst, but he didn't have time to think about it.

Lance moved back out into the hall, his gauss rifle heralding his approach. Kneeling down, he glanced under the row of stalls, ready to fire the moment he saw—*nothing*. Behind him, he could hear sobbing.

"Sir?" He heard Lorego call out somewhere behind him. "Stay with them," he shouted back. Lance edged forward, swinging open each stall door on his way to the sinks, scanning both high and low. "It's gone!" he shouted, frustrated beyond words.

The showers kicked back on, as he slowly made his way back to the others, once more scanning floor, ceiling, stalls and walls, in case the creature doubled back.

The ensign was standing just inside the shower room, but his head and pistol were peeking around the corner toward the sinks. He lowered his gun as he saw Lance approach. "You sure?" he asked and then stepped out into the hall, relaxing a little.

"What's happening in there?" Lance asked as he approached.

"They're ah . . . in the shower again," Lorego said, shaking his head, frowning. "Kelsa's hurt bad. I have to get the medkit."

Lance nodded and then glanced inside the shower room as Lorego rushed down the hall. For a moment, Lance's eyes desperately sought out exposed flesh—despite everything that had just happened. The room was still steamy, but the interruption had diminished the obscuring mist somewhat. Out of the corner of Lance's eye he saw two bodies out of focus, one standing, the other sitting, but immediately averted his gaze. It had taken more than he thought necessary to force himself not to stare. *The vents are up high on the walls—probably on the ceiling,* he thought, but almost immediately, his mind wandered where he'd forced his eyes to flee.

I think that might have been Janys standing, but I looked away too fast. His heart quickened and his mind began filling in the missing details of his stolen snapshot. *I can't believe I'm—this is ridiculous!* He was shamefully reminded just how dark the mind could get when left unguarded and was surprised that he couldn't get his mind off of them.

He had hoped to accidentally catch a glimpse of Kelsa, if not his wife. *I already know what Janys looks like without any clothes on, but Kelsa . . . what am I doing?* Lance glanced high up on the walls of the shower room and saw two vents on the ceiling. His eyes darted between them. Between the vent in the floor was a drain.

Lance allowed his eyes to drift over to the women and his heart sank upon seeing Kelsa. All thoughts of seeing her undressed slipped away. She sat partially under a showerhead, sobbing. *The poor thing's a mess.* Blood and grime were running down her legs and arms and pooled around her, slowly draining out of the room. *This is so bangy . . .*

Janys was directly under a showerhead. She kept cupping water with her hands and then poured it over Kelsa's wounds. There was blood and grime everywhere. Lance thought it odd that his wife would be under the showerhead, instead of beside it, but surmised Kelsa had been in too much pain and refused to move closer. The crewman hugged herself as she wept, her body heaving with each breath.

Maybe Janys got some of the stuff on her, too—like last time, and that's why she's under the showerhead, he thought. *Lorego only mentioned Kelsa getting hurt. Praise the One Above All my wife is okay. This time . . . but Kelsa . . .*

Briefly—only briefly, did he allow his eyes to wander, first to his wife. He confirmed that her eyes were on Kelsa—*which means she doesn't know where I'm looking. It's not my fault the attack was in the shower. It's only natural to want to see them . . . make sure they're all right,* he told himself, but knew there was more to it than that. *We only rise above depravity by fighting our baser instincts. I'm better than this.* It was only a minor slip, he knew, but wondered if he had been more vigilant earlier whether it would have made any difference. *Probably not, but still. Their lives are at stake. I have to stay focused twenty-four seven. That garbage I told Kelsa earlier. That pep talk was as much for me as it was for her.*

He looked upon Kelsa again, this time determined to merely apprise the situation, and was surprised by how many exposed sores he found on the crewman's legs and arms. *How could she have gotten so many sores so quickly?* he wondered. Both were sobbing.

Janys glanced up at her husband and stared at him strangely.

She knew I was checking out Kelsa's body! No . . . it's something else. She looks so . . . there. He spotted sores on both her arms and shoulders, and realized the real reason she had been under the showerhead. *Lance's* world erupted into flames. That's when he remembered it.

Without another thought, Lance slid his gauss rifle onto a towel rack, unholstered his pistol and put it alongside it, and then rushed under a showerhead and began stripping off his jumper. The shower immediately kicked on and he frantically washed off his neck and back. He moved his hand toward where his neck stung and gasped when he touched a fresh blister there.

"Lance, what are you—I'm so sorry," Janys said, concern in her voice. She did not come to him, however, and he didn't want her to. He couldn't stop thinking about the wounds he saw on his wife's body and on Kelsa's and felt miserable. The other shower was still on and he knew his wife was still pouring water over Kelsa's wounds and her own. He heard the crewman moan in pain, but didn't glance over, knowing she was in good hands and there was nothing he could do.

Lance kept glancing up at the nearest ceiling vent and was ready to grab the gauss rifle or at least the pistol, if needed, but his hands were wet and his vision compromised. He glanced down at the drain too, but reminded himself the Shadow Man always spaces out his attacks for maximum impact. *He's already taken it further than usual, attacking both of them at once,* he thought. He was confident it wouldn't return for awhile. *I never should have let them—no more showers. It's too dangerous . . .*

Lance's own breathing became ragged as the pain in his neck and side grew worse. *I must have torn open my wound,* he realized, noticing the blood in the water at his feet. He was grateful his stab wound was dressed and hoped none of the grime his wife had been talking about got into it, but knew he was infected now. It surely went straight into the blister. He only had one sore and it stung badly. He couldn't imagine what his wife or Kelsa were feeling right now.

The pain meds had helped, but now he was feeling the stab wound again, made worse by recent events. *Maeson really put his whole weight into that blow. I can't believe that little scalpel did so much damage. It's hard to believe a sore could be worse, but it is.* His main concern presently was the sore on the back of his neck and the poison that he assumed was shooting through his bloodstream. *I only have one sore. It can wait. Janys said infections are worse than the toxin, but that's serious, too, apparently. They're the ones I should be worried about,* he thought, and glanced over to check on Kelsa and his wife gain.

"You all right, sweetheart?" Lance asked, raising his voice to be heard over the showerfall.

His wife said nothing as she stepped out from under a showerhead. Kelsa had quieted down, but her breathing was still frantic and she moaned softly.

Lance stepped out of the shower, leaving his soiled jumper where it lay on the shower floor. He grabbed two towels off the rack and handed them to Janys, who had a pained expression on her face.

"Where's Lorego with that medkit?" she said as she gently rested a towel on Kelsa's shoulders.

Lorego! I should have gone with him! No, then— "I'll check," he said, and rushed over and tied a towel around his waist. Realizing his wife didn't have her pistol with her, he returned to the rack, grabbed his gauss rifle and handed her his pistol. He returned to the rack, grabbed his gauss rifle and headed past the shot up stalls toward the exit. Before he reached the sink, the restroom door flew open and Lorego rushed inside with the medkit.

"Sorry it took so long," he said, giving his commanding officer a strange look.

Lance realized he'd been wearing his medical jumper when they were last together.

"What happened to your jumper?" Lorego asked as he bolted past his underdressed superior.

"Never mind that," Lance said, holding his towel up with one hand.

Lorego only paused for a moment to ask, "How are they?" and then continued down the hall.

We both know what getting a sore means, ensign. Lance sighed deeply and followed Lorego back into the showers.

Kelsa was moved to a bed and was treated first. Her wounds were graver and more numerous, and she drifted in and out of consciousness. She was on heavy pain meds and antibiotics and seemed confused. When she did awaken, she wasn't very responsive, and seemed to have lost the will to live.

Lorego had stood guard while everyone was being treated, and continued to guard while Kelsa slept. Janys was with her too, despite her own wounds, and monitored her condition closely.

Finally, Lance convinced his wife to get some rest as well and she agreed. He and Lorego kept watch over the others. He was more tired than usual, but knew he could neither sleep, nor did he want to. They took turns walking a circle around the beds and sitting and also kept an eye on each other, in case the Shadow Man targeted one of them. Lance's pain med was wearing off and he realized he wasn't sure where his wife kept the bottle.

Late morning, Lance glanced over and found Lorego dozing. Knowing the ensign hadn't gotten much sleep the night before, he decided to let the ensign nap and continued to circle the beds. He paused beside each bed to make sure everyone was okay. A half hour passed and then an hour. Lance glanced around the room, as he walked around and around. Pausing beside Kelsa, he noticed she was statue still. *She isn't breathing. Maybe it's just shallow? No, she's definitely not breathing!* "Janys?" Lance called out, his eyes locked on the crewman.

Both Lorego and Janys woke up and quickly rushed to Kelsa's side. Janys checked the crewman's vitals, then checked them again. They all looked at each other, but no words were needed. Lorego and Lance moved Kelsa to the Cosmothean Sea. Janys accompanied them. Everyone had their pistols out. Afterward, Lorego walked over to his bed and sat down with his back to them. He seemed to be busying himself with his wristcomp.

Janys turned to her husband and tilted her head, motioning at Lorego and whispered, "He really liked her. I could tell," she said, adding, "If you make it through this, you ought to go down to the ringworld. You can't stay here, and no rescue ship is coming."

"You mean we, right?" he said.

His wife glanced away.

She doesn't believe she's going to make it, Lance thought. *I don't know how we've even made it this far.* Wanting desperately to change topics, he said, "The antibiotics work. You said it yourself. But right now, I could use some more pain meds. Mine's wearing off. Where do you keep—"

Janys pointed to a bottle by the sink. "It's not where it's supposed to be, but I'm not running on full. There's more over there," she said, pointing to a cabinet.

"I'll be right back, sweetheart," Lance said and kept glancing back as he made his way over to the sink. He returned with the bottle and a cup of water. He offered her a sip first, but she waived it away. He took a pill and then drank it down, as she crawled into bed with a brief moan.

"Do you need some pain meds?" Lance asked, his heart splintering over his wife's condition.

"I took some. I just need to be careful not to . . . move anymore than I have to. Lance, I'm sorry I never told you."

"Told me what?"

"About the sores."

"What do you mean? You just got them."

"I've had a sore on my left arm for—I can't remember how long. Weeks? Time is so . . ." her eyes closed and her words became garbled. A minute later, she opened her eyes again and said, "I didn't want to . . . distract you. So many responsibilities on your plate."

"Janys, I don't understand." He picked up her hand and held it in his, gently running his other hand over the back of hers as she spoke.

"I didn't realize at first . . . we didn't need a cure. Some of the antibiotics were working. It was hard. The infection's so aggressive, but . . . I was getting better. They all were, Lance . . ."

"I know. You did good. It's just . . ."

"The Shadow Man kept returning. Infecting us. As long as you have sores, I don't think it has to even touch you again. I think it just has to be nearby to exacerbate the condition. Don't let it come close, Lance. Kill it if you can, but don't let it close and you'll be okay," she said, and closed her eyes again. "I left some instructions on the . . . on the med terminal . . ."

"Get some sleep, sweetheart. I love you."

"I love you too," she mouthed, as she drifted off to sleep. Her husband continued to hold her hand fearing they might not have much time left together. He kept a vigilant guard over her, feeling helpless and frustrated. He didn't even notice that Lorego had begun walking a circle around them, keeping the guard.

A half hour later, Lorego whispered, "It's safer outside. We should put on suits and go outside the ship."

"Lorego . . ." Lance started, but his emotions were a jumbled mess and he wasn't up to talking.

"Seriously. The creature is in here so we should be safe out there, at least till we run out of oxygen. Even that wouldn't be so bad. You just pass out and then your brain dies and your heart stops. It's not very painful, I imagine."

"Ensign—"

"What's worse than that is waiting to die," Lorego continued, "that's terrifying. The anxiety . . . panic sets in as you become desperate for air, but Dr. Bendrik should have something that can dull the mind, make it easier."

"Lorego. It's not over yet," Lance said, but he had a glimpse of how deep the pit of depression was. He felt it, too. "It's not over until we give up. Till then, there's always hope."

Lorego made another circle around them and then paused and said, "Maybe you should just use the gauss rifle on us. It's pretty fast and only hurts for a moment. Or you could just set the ship to self-destruct."

"That's enough of that," Lance ordered.

"Sorry, sir, I talk a lot when I'm nervous."

"It's okay. You're right, though. We need to get off this ship," Lance said. "We'll take the last shuttle down to Cathor. There's a breathable atmosphere down there. The Architects or whoever built that thing made sure of that. You said it yourself there were settlements down there . . ."

Lorego perked up, nodding. "That's right . . . they're primitive, but that doesn't mean they're unfriendly. Anything beats being trapped on this ship. And it beats dying in space or a hole in the head—if we can survive long enough to get there. I don't have any sores yet, but—"

"I just want to give her a few more minutes to rest," Lance said and glanced around the room, wondering how much of the Med Center they could squeeze onto the shuttle.

Lorego nodded.

Lance quickly realized only his wife would know what would be essential to bring along besides the pain meds she'd pointed out. *I should have asked her where the antibiotics were.* "I almost forgot, she wrote a note . . ." he muttered under his breath. "Guard her, Lorego."

The ensign walked up beside her and kept glancing around the bed nervously while Lance checked her med terminal. He found a document labeled with a nickname she called him only in private. He opened the file and began reading. It was part love letter, part instruction manual on what to do after her death. He downloaded it to his wristcomp, glanced over at his wife until he was sure she was still breathing, then continued reading.

She had twenty-three sores on her body and had been preparing for her death ever since the first one appeared. *She can make it,* he thought, then imagined her covered in sores and shuddered.

Glancing at his wife again, Lance noticed how frail she was, but was pleased that she seemed to be sleeping peacefully, despite the sores ravaging her body. *If we get her down to the ringworld, away from the Shadow Man, she'll be okay,* he thought. Paranoid, he rushed over to the security terminal, set his gauss rifle down on the counter and checked for activity on the screens. *Nothing. Good.*

"Sir, with all due respect, we need to get off this ship now."

Without a word, Lance moved to the med terminal and skimmed the remaining instructions before returning to his wife's side. He nodded at Lorego. "Load up what you can."

Lorego shoved wads of bandages and a sterilizer into a bag.

Lance leaned over to kiss his wife on her forehead. *Please don't die on me. Please—*

"Sir?"

Lance glanced up and nodded. "Bring me a hoverbed, Ensign."

"Yes, sir," Lorego said and rushed off. Lance's attention flashed back and forth between his wife and Lorego, then around *Med Center. I need to gather supplies on her list,* he reminded himself, but as he did so, he kept glancing back at her and Lorego to make sure they were okay. Anything that wasn't within a few meters of her bed, he left for when Lorego returned.

The ensign removed a hoverbed from its storage slip on the wall and activated it.

Lance paused beside his wife's bed and took her hand in his once more. He squeezed it gently and said, "Just rest, sweetheart. We're going to get you down to the planet. Ensign Lorego located settlements down there. Hundreds of them. They're primitive, but it's worth a shot. You'll start to feel better once we're away from here . . ."

Lorego returned with the hoverbed floating along behind him.

"Watch her," Lance said and then he hurried back over to the med terminal. He reviewed the color-coded reference his wife had provided, and then started pulling out racks of antibiotics, pain meds and other supplies she knew would be useful, and placed the perishables inside a portable cold storage unit.

Lorego stood watch, his pistol ready should the creature show itself again.

Lance placed the cold storage unit beside the hoverbed. Retrieving his gauss rifle from the counter beside the security terminal, He draped it over his shoulder. Out of the corner of his eye, he thought he saw movement on the security terminal. He turned and stared at his wife's bed. *I'm seeing things,* he thought, reminding himself what his wife had said about sleep deprivation. *It's finally getting to me. I'm hallucinating.* He glanced at the screen again. The bed his wife was lying on cast its own shadow below it. He stared at the shadow. *I'm wasting precious time. The shadow is perfectly appropriate for the lighting overhead. There's nothing out of the ordinary. You're just being paranoid.* A moment later, the bed's shadow shifted almost imperceptibly, yet the bed remained still. Neither Lorego, nor Janys had moved.

I must be finally starting to slip, Lance thought, but something made him back up the vid to replay it. He gasped in horror as a shadowy head slipped out from under his wife's bed and stared up at him with glowing red eyes. He snapped up the gauss rifle and spun around, aiming it at the foot of his wife's bed.

Lorego was startled by his superior's sudden movement and stumbled backwards, bumping into a scissor lamp, activating it. Light flooded the area. The shadowy face was still there. It grimaced and withdrew from the light, vanishing down a drainage port below the bed. Lance trained the rifle on the port and fired three times, but the Shadow Man was gone.

Janys bolted upright, panting hard and frightened.

"I'm sorry—I'm sorry. It's okay. Lie down, sweetheart," Lance said, taking neither his eyes, nor the gauss rifle off the drainage port for several seconds. "Lorego, help me move her to the hoverbed."

Lorego seemed rooted to his spot, confused and scared.

Janys laid back down and closed her eyes.

"Now, Ensign!"

"Sir, yes, sir," Lorego said. He double tapped a panel on the side of the bed and moved the hoverbed into position.

All this time . . . I didn't even know there was a drainage port below the bed. Lance struggled to shake the panic from his mind. *Those eyes . . .* He stared down once more at the drainage port. *Nothing.* "We have to get out of here before it returns."

"It was here?"

Lance didn't answer. He slung the gauss rifle over his shoulder and moved around to the head of the bed.

The hoverbed hung in the air a meter above the floor. The bed sunk in the air slightly when they transferred his wife to it, then ascended to its original height. Lorego lowered the foldable storage racks while Lance retrieved the cold storage unit and slid it onto the larger, bottom shelf, and locked it place.

Lance rushed around and grabbed a few other things from the list—not everything, as he was worried they were taking too long. *There's only so much we can fit under the bed, and we need our hands free for our weapons.* "Don't take your eyes off of her," he said, and then ran across the room, returning moments later with a food crate and canister of water.

After stowing the food supplies, he whispered reassuringly in his wife's ear, then unslung his gauss rifle. "Okay. Let's go. Take the lead, but stay close. Keep your eyes open," Lance ordered. "I'll cover."

Lorego nodded and configured the bed to follow him, then drew his pistol and moved toward the exit. The hoverbed maintained a distance of point five meters behind him. When he slowed, it slowed too, and when he stopped to wait for Lance to unlock the main doors, it stopped.

Lance went out first, glancing at every shadow along the way. Satisfied, he went back into the room. He checked around the bed briefly, and then motioned for Lorego and followed him out of Med Center. The hoverbed floated along silently between them.

It took them six minutes to reach the shuttle. They could have gotten there faster, but they kept scanning every shadow, wanting to make sure they weren't being followed. Janys' eyes remained closed the whole way, but she continued breathing and for that, Lance was grateful.

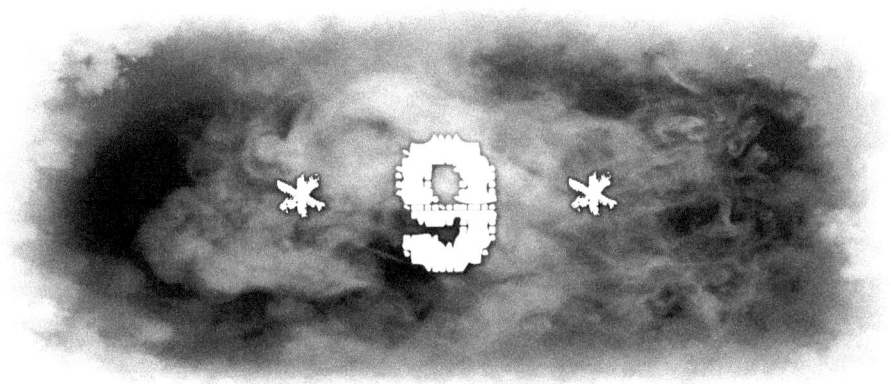

Reaching the shuttle, Lance and Lorego checked under and around the hoverbed and then moved it inside, closing the airlock behind them. Paranoid, Lance turned on every light source in the shuttle and he and Lorego combed the ship for signs of the creature. Once satisfied they were alone, Lance checked on his wife, while Lorego plotted a course for the nearest settlement.

So far, so good, Lance thought, and breathed easier. "I'm right here, sweetheart. You're safe now," he said, as he walked over to where her hoverbed was anchored. His wife's eyes were closed, but she was still breathing. He reached out and held her hand.

Her eyes flickered open briefly and she smiled at him, muttering, "You ordered me to get some sleep. Just following . . . orders." She closed her eyes again. He sighed in relief and smiled, feeling better about their chances.

Lance was a decent pilot. Flying shuttles wasn't normally a challenge, but piloting while stressed out, scared and in need of far more than a short nap, made it challenging. Switching places with Lorego, Lance cleared the bay doors and then slowly edged the shuttle a safe distance from the *Dauntilus*. He glanced through the viewscreen, spotted the other shuttle parked silently nearby, and shook his head. Moon Thirty-Seven came into view as he banked the shuttle away from the ship and headed toward the nearest ringworld segment, following Lorego's course. "How's she doing, Lorego?" he called back, keeping his eyes on the viewscreen and controls, despite his desire to be at his wife's side.

"I'm keeping a close eye on her, sir—both, actually," the ensign said. Lance stole a glance over his shoulder and saw that Lorego had strapped himself in beside the hoverbed. *So far, so good.*

As they descended through the clouds, colossal force projector arrays activated, creating vast, opaque energy walls between the artificial sun and the ringworld segments below. Great rectangular shadows blanketed the land far below them, supplying a night cycle to offset the day. Under different circumstances, Lance would have been eager to get a closer look. The CDF would have wanted him to send out a probe to gather data so the CDF tech gurus could study the technology, but not today. At this point, all he could think about was finding a safe, quiet place for his wife to rest. *If I can find whatever constitutes a doctor or holy adept on this world, all the better. We don't have much on board, but if nothing else, with the antibiotics, she might just pull through this.*

A minute later, the ship's sensors registered a lock on. Lance panicked. "Someone's targeting our ship!" he shouted and immediately began evasive maneuvers.

"Sir, do you want me on tactical?" Lorego asked, scared and fumbling to remove his safety harness. "Maybe I can scramble their lock!"

"There's no time!" Lance called out. A couple seconds later the shuttle was hit by a long-range particle beam weapon. "Just stay with my wife and hang on!" he shouted, and attempted a rapid descent, hoping to drop below the weapon's firing arc.

"Sir, yes, sir," Lorego said out of habit, just moments before a second volley of particle beams flared overhead, shredding the shuttle's roof.

Lance glanced back in time to see Lorego being slammed against a bulkhead. *One of the mooring clamps on the hoverbed had broken free. Lorego must have gotten up to reattach the clamp!* "Lorego?"

Immediately, the shuttle's internal sensors activated its Second Skin defense, sealing the roof and correcting cabin pressure, though the emergency system wasn't designed to withstand attack.

Lorego was crawling back to his seat when Lance forced himself to get back to the business of ensuring they weren't hit again. A moment later, he stole a glance toward the rear of the shuttle and saw Lorego was once again strapped in. The ensign had a pained expression on his face.

"There's nothing on the radar," Lance announced. "Those shots came from a great distance. The ringworld must have an automated defense network. I think we'll be all right now, at least from long-range weapons, but this isn't going to be a fun landing. You two okay back there?"

"Yeah . . ." Lorego said, sounding out of breath. "I think I may have bruised a few ribs and I'm going to have a headache for about a week, but yeah . . . we're okay. So much for the locals being friendly."

Lance struggled to maintain control of the vessel. He was pretty sure he could get them down to the ground, but it wasn't going to be easy. The shuttle had suffered significant damage. Two minutes passed as he focused intently on not crashing the ship. *It's too quiet back there*, he thought. "How's my wife doing, Lorego?"

Silence.

"I know you're trying to let me focus, Lorego, but the silence is killing me. Talk to me. Just tell me she's going to be okay. I could really use some good news."

Silence.

Lance stole another glance over his shoulder, but didn't need to look to know, and began to weep. His breath caught in his throat and he gasped. Lorego was slumped forward, his head bobbing to the turbulence. There were four parallel rips down the front of his jumper, and blood and entrails were pooling in his lap.

The hoverbed was moored beside him. Janys wasn't moving, save for the sway caused by the turbulence. One of her arms had slipped through the bed rail and was dangling. Blood and pus were dripping down from ruined fingers. The side of the bed and racks beneath were wet with blood and dripping. Together they formed a rivulet that ran along the contour of the floor all the way to the back of the shuttle.

Somewhere in the shadows, was the creature, just out of view. This would have terrified Lance any other day, but there were other things on his mind. For a time, he just sat there and stared at the body of his wife, as the shuttle plunged downward. He considered aiming the shuttle at the ground and punching it to make sure the creature didn't make it out alive, but he realized even if he did nothing, the effect might be the same. He could only hope Janys had passed out from exhaustion before the creature attacked. *Maybe she slept through it.* Lance was tired of running and no longer saw a reason to.

Finally, he turned back around in his seat and was about to aim the shuttle at the ground, hoping the creature wouldn't realize what he was doing and become gaseous to minimize or avoid injury altogether. It was too late. While he was distracted, the ship had detected the unsafe descent as he knew it would. It had been flashing a warning, but he ignored it. The ship's autopilot then kicked in and managed to level out the ship, compromised as it was. The moment he made contact with the nav controls, it released control, but he couldn't react fast enough to avoid a large clump of trees directly ahead. He wasn't sure they'd do the job. Given his current state, his reactions were sluggish. Had he done nothing, the ship might have been able to correct in time on its own, but that's not what he wanted.

The craft ripped through the trees, turned sideways, rolled and spun to a stop in a cornfield, flattening everything in its path.

Something hard hit him in the head and everything went black.

When he finally awoke, Lance found himself lying face down. His left leg was pinned down. His face was wet and he had to keep wiping his forehead to see anything. *Blood.* He could taste it on his tongue, feel it running down his neck.

It was dark where he was—not pitch dark, as the moons and distant, Cosmothean stars cast the night in a purplish glow. The blood didn't help. It kept running down over his eyes. He felt for his pistol, but the holster was empty.

A minute passed as he tried to free his left leg from whatever had it trapped, mostly because he wasn't sure how to free it without inviting even more pain than he was experiencing already. Finally he yanked on his leg, and as he did so, a tremendous bolt of pain shot through his body, and he realized he had impaled his leg on something during the crash. Gasping in pain, he lay there for several minutes, able to move his tortured leg, but not wanting to. He waited for death, but it didn't come.

During this time, he made no move to defend himself should the creature still be alive. He didn't care anymore. Reaching into his pocket, Lance took out a bottle of pain meds and dry swallowed some, then shoved the bottle back into his pocket. Almost passing out from the pain, his breathing was ragged and as he lay there, he realized he'd lost everything.

Lacking the energy to move, he listened for the creature, but heard nothing. Finally, the silence was cut by a crow, or something like a crow off in the distance. He heard the flap of wings and a chill breeze rolled over him. The shuttle's roof had been peeled open like a banana.

While he doubted his wife was still alive, he crawled toward what was left of the back of the shuttle and found her. All of the warmth had drained out of her. It amazed him how cold her skin felt. He rested there for some time just holding her, until he heard a voice that was little more than a whisper.

"Lance, you really ought to be more careful."

Traders Tongue. The creature can speak. Lance knew the language well. It had been brought to the Republic by the remnant of Earth. He had never been to Earth, of course, as it had been quarantined over four hundred years before he was born, but he had been to Neo Earth, and was taught Traders Tongue as a young boy. *Who gives a spit what language it knows, kill the damn thing!* But whether by panic or pain or depression, his body remained where it was. He didn't answer at first, nor did he make any move to defend himself.

The creature could have killed me already if it wanted to, he realized, so he just held his wife and let his pain and anger and sadness pour out of him in tears. Managing to pull himself together, he listened again for the creature, but found it difficult to even think. The wound on his head was minor, but that didn't stop the blood from rushing out. The stab wound hurt, too, but not compared to the wound on his leg. Feeling light-headed, he decided to stall and zero in on the creature's location.

Holding his breath, he listened, but couldn't hear anything but the sounds of insects in the cornfield. "You're very good at hiding," Lance said in Traders Tongue.

"And you aren't. Given up, have you?" the creature said from somewhere out of reach. "Where's the fun in that?"

Ignoring the creature, Lance kissed his wife on the cheek and sat down in one of the seats beside Lorego's corpse to catch his breath and take some of the burden off his bad leg. He tore off a long strip from the ensign's uniform and tied it around his own head to stem the bleeding. He squinted in the dark, hopelessly searching for the creature. *Why hasn't it killed me yet? Does it think we're playing a game?* He began analyzing what he knew about the creature. It didn't take long. "You needed someone to fly the shuttle. That's why you kept me alive," Lance said, finally.

"I was beginning to think I'd never get down from that moon, and then your ship . . . It was all great fun, of course, but yes, I needed you, so I had to be careful. I didn't want you committing suicide or doing something else foolish. If I had suspected Maeson was planning to attack you, I would have taken him out sooner."

"Why didn't you take one of the life pods? You don't understand how to use them, do you?"

"You mean the death pods? They kept launching when I tried to get inside, but as I thought about it, the shuttle was maneuverable and you actually knew how to fly it. No, it was the ringworld's defense system I was concerned about. I figured my odds were better with you."

It was quiet between them for several moments. Lance tried to sort out his options. He wondered if the creature was doing the same thing.

"You know, Med Center was my base of operations. Oh, I spent more than a little time exploring your ship, but as the crew shrank in size, I began spending most of my time in Med Center. Lance, I must admit you were very entertaining—and useful as I said, so I kept you alive. I kept your wife alive, too. I could have killed your precious Janys a long time ago."

Lance took a deep breath and stood up. He gasped in pain and stood there for a moment before shuffling slowly around the cabin. Glancing around in the dark, he hoped to spot movement as the creature left one shadow to enter another. More importantly, he hoped to find his weapons. "Am I supposed to thank you?" he asked.

"You can if you want to."

"Why didn't you kill her when you had the chance?"

"I started to, but I was . . . bored. No, that's not it. She was interesting. So convinced there was a scientific explanation for everything—so sure I couldn't exist . . . and she tried so hard to save all those miserable wretches on board—as admirable as it was pointless. I knew she meant a great deal to you, so I let her live for a while. I wanted to make sure you had something to live for, and didn't do something stupid like give up and activate your ship's self-destruct while I was still on board. I never hurt that girl in quarantine, though."

"Telly?" Lance asked, squinting into the dark. *It's a Shadow Man. You actually think you're going to see a Shadow Man out there? I'm trying to keep it talking. Otherwise, I wouldn't have a clue where to look . . .*

"Was that her name? She just had a cold sore, the poor dear. I had nothing to do with her death."

"I wondered about that. Does it ease your conscience that you let some-one live?"

Silence.

Now what are you—

"You're the one who brought me on board. I shadowed you throughout the ruins—you sure took your time getting back to your ship—never seen ruins before?"

"Not just any ruins. Architechnology," Lance said, trying to sound calm, while inside he felt as if he were going mad.

"Is that what you call it?"

"The technology of the AI gods, at least the humanus of Tandem would call them gods."

"Ah . . . yes, plenty of . . . architechnology if you know where to look. Better not to touch that stuff, it can unleash all manner of chaos. Don't feel bad. You aren't the first I've shadowed successfully. I'm rather good at it."

Sounds very close now . . . Lance jerked his head to the side, but didn't see anything.

"Don't bother trying to find me. I can blend in with mundane shadows perfectly. It's only while I'm entering or leaving a shadow that there is any danger of being spotted if I don't want to be. I was very tempted to kill you first, but I resisted."

"You decided to make my life miserable instead. How noble."

"I misjudged you. I admit it. I had to kill more of your crew than I thought I would before you finally gave up the ship."

Lance bumped into a cold, familiar shape and tried not to smile at finding his gauss rifle. He didn't look down at it, but kept his eyes in the general direction of where he suspected the creature was. "So you can become gaseous at will?"

"Incorporeal, actually. It comes in handy, though I had to magically tether myself to your ship to prevent slipping through the hull. *That* would have been problematic."

"Incorporeal?" Lance nodded. "That was my other theory."

"And yet you kept trying to shoot me whenever you got the chance . . . you must realize by now I can't be hurt?"

"Of course . . . except when you become corporeal . . ."

"Well, yes, but your chance has passed. It's over for you. Now that lamp Lorego bumped into in Med Center—that almost did me in!"

"Is that why you raked him with your claws? Got an anger problem, do you?" Having taken the time to reorient himself and get adjusted to the low light, Lance now realized the shuttle was on its side, and he was only eight feet from an safety kit that he knew included a beamer. *If the creature can be hurt by light . . . that might be more effective than my gauss rifle at this point,* he thought. He edged closer to the kit, without looking in its direction. Pain surged through his body with every step. *I sure hope those pain meds kick in soon.* "You got what you wanted. You're on the surface, why stick around? I'm no threat."

"You never were," the creature said.

So confident . . . overconfident, maybe?

"I'm a shadow reaper and a hunter. I wouldn't make a very good hunter if I never practiced my craft, now would I?"

Shadow reaper, Lance mouthed silently. The creature's confidence unsettled him, but he forced himself to remain calm.

"But you're right," the reaper continued. "I have no good reason for sticking around. Of course, I haven't killed you yet."

"True, but humor me. I'm trying to understand something," Lance said, reaching casually for the safety kit as if to steady himself. "You said that when the other guy—Lorego—accidentally turned on a bright light that it hurt you—"

"I didn't say it hurt me, but go on."

"You said it almost did you in."

"Ah, sorry, Traders Tongue isn't my primary language. Mundane weapons can't hurt me unless you catch me off guard in my corporeal state, but that's not going to happen. Light is another matter altogether. What is that you're doing anyway?"

"Getting some gauze. I assume you don't mind if I bandage my head and leg, since you're planning on killing me anyway."

"Seems a waste of time, but sure, go ahead." With that, the creature revealed his position near the back of the shuttle and Lance saw its purplish-red skin and hellish, glowing red eyes for a second time, then the shadow reaper was gone again.

The beamer was within reach, but Lance pulled out a HealTab and the gauze and began wrapping his head, knowing the blood would keep getting in his eyes and compromising his accuracy if he didn't take care of it. "Sorry . . . you were saying something about light?"

"You're trying to get me to expose my weaknesses."

"You were the one who mentioned it. Are you afraid to tell me?"

"I'm not a young child to be tricked by mind games. I've been hunting for a very long time, Lance. I've told you too much as it is, not that you can do anything about it."

"If I'm no threat as you say, then where's the harm in telling me? If you're going to kill me, at least do me the favor of providing a brief distraction from my troubles."

"Fair enough, I suppose, but keep things interesting or I'll grow bored, and you wouldn't like that, trust me."

So it is overconfident. Good. "All right. How do you get around during the daytime—or do you sleep during the day like a vampire?"

"Vampires don't sleep during the day unless they work at night, at least none of the ones I've known. As for light, it doesn't hurt me—well, it isn't pleasant, but it can't kill me."

Wait, was that a joke or are you saying vampires are real? Lance peeled off the backing on the HealTab, pressed it against the wound on his leg, and began wrapping the leg with gauze. He dropped the gauze when he felt hot breath on his neck and something wet slide down his arm and across his ripped open pant leg. *It's right on top of me!*

A wetness dripped down his exposed leg and pooled around his sock.

"Starting to get bored here," the shadow reaper whispered.

Moments after, Lance heard a piece of metal debris clang against the bulkhead beside him and whipped around with his gauss rifle and fired several times, missing as near as he could tell. *Spit! I bet it went incorporeal on me!* The sudden movement had caused his leg to fire its own salvos of pain up through his body and he felt for a moment like he would pass out.

Panting, he rested. *It is treating this like a game.*

From somewhere near the back of the shuttle, the creature spoke again. "You know, for a moment there earlier, I thought you were actually trying to crash this ship."

Catching his breath, Lance gingerly leaned down to retrieve the gauze and finished bandaging his leg as he spoke. "See, I can keep things interesting."

"Even so," the creature responded, "I did promise to kill you when you were done bandaging your wounds, and you are nearly done."

"I don't remember any promise. Was it a promise?"

"Enough! Is that an itch you're feeling on your arm and legs? Did you just break out in sores, by any chance?" the reaper said, his tone turning suddenly playful.

"Which arm?" Lance asked, feigning ignorance. "Which leg?" He briefly ran a hand over the opposite leg from the one the creature had slimed, down to the cargo pocket where he had hidden the architechnology he'd found. He frowned. *It's still in there. I never should have taken it from Raeden's office. I don't know how he got his hands on it, but I can't believe*

I didn't dump it in the shuttle along with the rest, not that it matters now. The architechnology wasn't to blame after all. "I don't feel any sores."

"Sure you do."

"Not really, but then the pain from the puncture wound in my leg and side and the gash on my head would make it hard to notice something as small as sores."

"I know you feel the one on the back of your neck. And now you have more . . ."

"To be honest, with all I've been through today I completely forgot about that little sore on my neck." *Damn, that sore is getting more painful now. Well, it looks like the shadow . . . reaper creature really can make sores worse just by slipping in close. He didn't touch my neck this time . . .*

"Higher up on your thigh where the pants are ripped? You have to feel that. At least you will soon. There's also a few forming on your right elbow and forearm, and another that is starting on your lower back, trust me."

Lance concentrated and indeed felt something on his back. A wetness. *I must have a tear in my jumper. I wonder if it touched me there when I blacked out. It had plenty of time to kill me. Ego. It definitely likes to play with its food before a meal.*

"You'll feel them all soon enough—and more, and then after a short while, you won't ever feel anything again."

Lance felt them, but he wasn't lying. The pain from the sores did not yet compare to the wound on his leg and side, but the pain meds were finally starting to kick in.

If I'm not mistaken, I struck a chord. The creature sounded annoyed. It's going to try to kill me no matter what I do. "That's okay. You'd be doing me a favor," Lance said as he finished bandaging his leg. "Since I'll be dead soon, I have a confession to make."

"Oh?"

"I'm done patching up my leg." He held up the gauze and after a moment, said, "I'm afraid I won't be needing this anymore, but I do appreciate your humoring me."

Silence. *Come closer. I dare you . . .*

Casually returning the gauze to the safety kit, he grabbed the disk-shaped

beamer, just as the creature's hideous tail, first a shadow, and then solidified, wrapped around the arm.

Lance activated the beamer as he shook off the grime-dripping tail.
A bright beam of light lanced out, and despite the pain he knew would
come, he flashed the beamer all around him as fast as he could, first in his
immediate vicinity, then in wider arcs toward the back end of the shuttle
and out into the cornfield. The sudden illumination was almost blinding.
He both felt and saw the grime dripping down his good arm. Two sores
appeared. Gasping in pain, he held his breath and listened.

From a bit further away than he was prior to the attack, the reaper said,
"I can't fault you for trying, but I'm much too fast for you. You're only
human. You'll find there are countless shadows out here, and as I said, you
can't kill me with light. I need light. Without it, there are no shadows."

*It is fast. It may need light, but I'm betting light is a two-edged sword, the
way it tries to avoid it.* With a sigh, Lance slung the gauss rifle over his
shoulder. "So what happens when it gets pitch black?" Lance said, inching
toward the back of the shuttle, the beams of light heralding his approach.
"You cease existing. You die, what?" *Come on, let me see you!*

"I said it can't kill me. I become inert and . . ." the reaper said, his voice
growing more feint. "You're not as clever as the Captain thought he was,
but you're not as inept as you seem to think, either. Glad to see you haven't
given up hope. Where's the fun in that?"

*You're moving away. What happens when you become inert? You really don't
like bright lights, do you?* "So does the same thing happen if the sun is
shining right on you—"

"I become inert, yes. But it's very hard to kill me when I'm inert. It's just
. . . never mind."

Walking up to Lorego's body, Lance retrieved his pistol, kissed his wife
one final time, then made his way to the back of the shuttle. He had to
swing his wounded leg out over the ragged lip and lost his balance when
he did so. Stumbling out into the brisk night air, Lance was breathing
hard and wincing. Daggers of pain shot up his leg with each step. He was
miserable and really wouldn't mind dying at this point, but first, he wanted
to at least hurt the creature.

Flooding the area before him with beams of light, he slowly made his way over the flattened corn stalks and headed for the settlement Lorego had found during his sensor sweeps.

"You really should see a doctor. Gyria's left breast! I forgot. The doctor's dead! Sorry about that, Lance," the creature said in a mocking tone.

I'm going to kill that shadow reaper if it's the last thing I do. Walking around the backside of the shuttle, Lance continued until he reached the end of the cornfield where he found a wooden fence. Beyond it was another field, stretching off into the grim dark.

Lance almost fell over when he felt the creature's tail touch his left cheek. He heard the creature right beside him and quickly flashed the beamer around, keeping it low, assuming the creature couldn't fly. *It better not be able to fly! Damn thing moves too fast as it is,* he thought. *It's somewhere in there among the corn stalks.* His left cheek started to burn from the sore, and within minutes had already become infected and started to ooze pus.

Fatigue set in. He'd been fighting it—ignoring it, but wondered if he would be able to much longer. *No reason to stay awake now. Maybe I'll get lucky and fall asleep before the pain gets worse. I bet that would really annoy it if I took a nap. That is, if I could sleep. Haven't had any luck there . . .*

I'll die even sooner if I don't get this grime off of me. I wish I'd have thought to bring some water from the shuttle. Wiping the grime off his cheek with his sleeve, Lance gasped in pain.

I should have taken some antibiotics. I'm past due for my next round. It's too late. You'll be dead soon anyway. Just keep moving.

"You're a real mess," the creature said, from some distance away.

"Another sore? Are you kidding me? It doesn't matter."

"It matters if you want to live," the reaper said, apparently following from a distance.

"True," Lance conceded. "If I want to live, but you already took away everything that mattered to me."

"Did I?"

Lance continued to slice arcs of light through the air to his left and right, but his arm was beginning to tire. He switched the beamer to his other hand, despite the pain from the oozing sores on his bad arm. *I've lost a lot of blood. I'm covered in sores. I'll be dead soon whether the creature bothers me again or not.* After only a couple minutes, Lance switched the beamer back to his other hand and continued flashing it back and forth. Once, he thought he heard a gasp in the distance. *Did I hit it?* He flashed like mad for a time and then stopped to listen.

Briefly, he spotted the creature's red eyes staring at him from between rows of corn, but he was careful not to reveal that he'd seen him. Minutes passed as he shuffled along beside the wooden fence. Finally, he turned off the beamer and sat down to rest. Once every minute or so, he activated the beamer again and slashed the air in his proximity for a time, then turned it back off when his arm grew tired. He wasn't concerned about running the cell down. He knew the beamer ran on taager batteries and would last far longer than he would.

Taager batteries, like everything else those short, brainy aliens invented, were meant to last forever, or darn near. Lance figured he only needed them to last long enough to scare away the reaper. He popped a few more pain meds and glanced around.

A half hour passed and then an hour and the creature hadn't returned. *It's probably watching me from the cornfield, waiting, toying with me again . . .*

Lance got back to his feet and shuffled further along a fence line, passing one field and then another, moving at a snail's pace so as to minimize the pain in his leg. He hadn't swung his light "sword" vigorously in quite a while as he was in too much pain. There was only so much the pain meds could do. Then he felt the reaper's tail again here and there and slashed with light, much slower than he had been, his strength fading.

It's gone again. Didn't even talk to me this time. If it really is growing bored— no, it's still taking its time. It could have used its claws, but chose not to. It probably enjoys that I'm in pain and is trying to get back at me for letting me live so long before it started attacking me personally. We aren't talking. It doesn't need me anymore. Won't be much longer now. Good. I'm tired of waiting . . .

The reaper had neither visited him, nor said a word in some time. Thinking became a chore. "I'll be dead soon. Seems kind of anti-climactic, considering I'm as likely to fall down from lack of sleep as anything else, and I don't really care at this point what happens to me. It would be a comfort to just sit down, let myself drift off, and never wake up again."

"You're right," the reaper said, breaking a long period of silence. He slapped Lance's good cheek with its tail so hard it nearly knocked him to the ground. Staggering for a moment, Lance leaned up against the wooden fence and held on with one arm wrapped around the middle beam while slashing wildly with the beamer. Sores broke out across his cheek, forehead and scalp. After only twenty seconds or so, Lance stopped swinging the beamer and leaned his full weight against the fence, breathing hard and ready to collapse.

"You'll be dead soon, but you'll be in too much pain to rest."

The voice came from the other side of the fence, dangerously close. Lance swung the beamer out into the field, but stopped after only a few moments. When the creature spoke again, he sounded farther away, and farther still with each word, "I think it's time I find bigger game. You've been an enjoyable distraction, Lance. Thanks for the ride, meat."

Something wet was running down Lance's side. *It's either my scalpel wound or running sores—or both. Not that it really matters. My leg wound never did stop bleeding.* Still, for the first time in a long while, he felt safe. Miserable, but safe. *I don't think it's coming back. Not this time. It knows it's over.* Exhausted, he slid gingerly down to the ground and leaned back against a fence post to rest.

Opening his right cargo pocket, he pulled out a bizarre, oddly shaped piece of metal he found hidden in Raeden's wine cabinet. It was amazingly lightweight.

Lance glanced up at Moon Thirty-Seven and then back down at the strange object. He stared at it, trying to sort out what it was. It beat thinking about his dire situation.

One end of the device was long and flat, the other was a half circle, inside of which were several long protrusions. *What the heck is this thing, a funky alien comb?*

Lance turned it over and over in his hands. *Maybe a giant's hairpin? A bangy fork? A blender attachment for mixing drinks? A worthless trinket? Nah, think bigger. A . . . a bomb?*

A bug crawled onto the back of his neck and he smacked it aside, then whimpered in pain from the blister there. Miserable, he sat for what seemed like forever, exhausted, but unable to sleep.

If I could just get to sleep, then I wouldn't have to put up with this ever again. I just wish I could have taken that reaper with me. It kills me that I'm dying and it's still alive. I've endangered the local populace. I should have stopped it. I responded too slowly . . .

He pinched his eyes closed and rocked back and forth, in more pain emotionally than physically, if such a thing were possible. He was unable to ignore his situation any longer and tossed the odd bit of archi-technology aside and sat there waiting to die.

A cold chill settled upon him, but it took his mind off the sores and dulled the pain.

Convinced the creature wasn't coming back, he turned the beamer back on. Taking a deep breath and letting it out slowly to calm himself, he removed the bandage on his leg. He dipped a finger in the blood and began writing on the wooden fence, wetting his finger again and again as needed. Turning off the beamer, he closed his eyes and listened to the sounds of nature until finally, he drifted off to sleep.

Galactic Date: 20.1.7040 [Pantara calendar]
Galactic Spatial Coordinates: -101,+147,0 [Cosmothereal dimension]
Cathor [Quarantined ringworld], Kingdom of Vraedia, Aedenshire District, Barony of Narchen, Town of Muldon (Outskirts)

The cold deepened. Fog settled over the countryside as the night dragged on. A short, blue-skinned traveler stepped out from amidst a cornfield and made his way along an old, wooden fence. His kind, the skree, were fashioned of shadow and given life to be spies and servants of the Shadow Lord. This one refused to serve the master of shadows. Instead, he walked the worlds of men, not of shadow, and followed after another. He wore a longcoat and carried a bow and a promise he meant to fulfill. But on this night, he sought after something he could use to turn a profit for his money pouch was growing lighter by the day.

Earlier, he had seen streaks of light cross the sky and touch a shadow passing overhead, blotting out the stars. At first, he'd thought the flying thing was one of the great, mythrul dragons, but it had no wings. It was too big to be a battle platform and he knew it wasn't one of the sleek, sky ships of the north, for it had neither sails, nor any clear sign of arcane propulsion. Moments later, it made a thundering sound and he realized it was an offworlder ship. The traveler immediately began searching the area.

Why is it the only time I find these strange ships, I am without a cart to salvage the rare treasures, or they are in blackened, shredded heaps? Well, I suppose it's just as well. I have neither the patience to salvage, nor the tongue of a trader to excel at it, but I still bet I could earn more doing salvage than bounty hunting. He glanced around, but everywhere he looked were rows of corn or empty field.

Pausing to examine a bloody handprint on a fence post, he sniffed at the air and recognized a strong scent nearby. For several moments he stood and listened, but heard no movement, so he continued on his way, his breath visible in the chill.

Hopefully my luck will change when I journey to Delathen. If all goes well, King Laygur will hire me to capture the Masked Man, and other miscreants hiding in the Vraedon Forest. If nothing else, maybe I'll run across more archi-technology, for I hear the so-called wild magic is more plentiful in that forest than any other region in all of the Kingdom of Vraedia.

Above, the sky was bright with stars and moons and swirling arcane clouds. The bounty hunter considered two parallel threads of light laid out across the sky—the Golden Bands of Chronus. The thin bands were said to have been put in place by Chronus to remind the nature goddess, Raea, of his love for her. Gentle Chronus sought to protect the new world and the growing population of mortals there, but Raea desired the world for herself.

When Chronus crafted the Golden Bands, he had enchanted them to repel any who would invade the world. The One Above All had given him much power and authority. Against the Supreme Being's advice, Chronus continued to pursue Raea. His love for her was strong. As a result, the bands helped hold the world together, protecting Cathor from outside forces, including the shenanigans of several wayward gods.

At that time, many of the gods had set their eyes on other worlds where their followers were greater in number. The High Celestial, Mithra, had many loyal followers on Cathor and saw an opportunity to spread seeds of peace and the light of Mithraism across the world. She had found a great glass orb in the sky and filled it with light from her own realm, Palidanea, the plane of infinite light. Claiming the world as her own, Mithra blessed her loyal followers and rose up great paragons there, including the noble Legion of Good.

Chronus had always been kind to her, and she offered to share the world with him. Raea grew angry with him for not opposing Mithra. Chronus explained that Mithra only wanted to protect the world as he did, but Raea wasn't satisfied. He brought the nature goddess to a vast region of Cathor that Mithra had never visited, a wild and beautiful realm he claimed the goddess of light didn't even know about. He offered it to Raea and professed his love for her once more.

Raea rejected Chronus's love and turned her affections to the fallen illuminarii, Xo, the god of magic. According to legend, Raea's fickle ways caused the power of the Golden Bands to fade. Chronus slipped into depression and withdrew to Mortallis where he built countless stargates to connect the worlds of the Pantara Galaxy.

About this time, Mithra's brother, Seth Baal, the serpent god of darkness, began spying on his sister. She was beautiful, and he often hid and watched as she bathed and as she slept. He desired to spoil her purity, as his father Zuledragar had their mother, but he was afraid. Mithra knew her brother's heart and when he refused to turn to the light, she avoided him thereafter.

Seth Baal had always been jealous of Mithra's power and influence over mortals, and despised the great light she had made in the sky over Cathor. With the help of the Shadow Lord, Ranos, Seth constructed a towering wall of shields in the sky to block her great orb, denying the land her warmth.

For a time, the Golden Bands had kept the vile armies of Lucifer's daughter, Gyria, at bay. The demon queen had amassed a great army and invaded numerous worlds. When mortals found Cathor and settled there, building sprawling empires, she swore to sunder the world with her legions, for she had no followers there.

Shortly after construction of the sky shields was complete and darkness fell upon the land, Gyria seduced Seth Baal, and together, they produced numerous offspring—abominations all. She left Seth Baal wounded physically, mentally and spiritually, and from that time forward, Seth swore to never touch a woman again.

The darkness was soon lifted. Together, Chronus and Mithra spun the sky shields around the great light Mithra had created, manifesting a cycle of day and night on Cathor. Chronus warned Gyria many times to withdraw her forces from Cathor, but she ignored him. So, Chronus sought Mithra's help in vanquishing the demon queen, but she refused to take a stand, choosing the path of peace at all costs.

And so Chronus raised up his own army from among the peoples of Cathor. In truth, they needed little prompting and war soon raged across the realms. To make matters worse, Seth Baal opposed Mithra at every turn, including forming the Brotherhood of Seth to hunt down her paragons and destroy her temples. His Brotherhood became powerful, but wherever the Legion of Good opposed him, he suffered losses and withdrew.

Gyria had a much larger army and Seth Baal reluctantly joined forces with her, though they fell into constant bickering. Ultimately, they parted ways. Gyria was furious and turned on the Brotherhood. Heavy losses were inflicted on both sides. The One Above All warned both armies to stand down, yet the war raged on.

Seth's Brotherhood included hundreds of mages and monstrosities, but so did Gyria's army. Hers was a much larger army, though it consisted mostly of poorly trained slaves, skeletons and other undead. She also commanded powerful blood adepts, mounted on elinarka, deadly flying beasts that even gave the great wyrms pause. Few could stand up to them. Only Seth Baal's greatest Death Knights dared face them.

Ranos loathed Gyria and secretly released hundreds of shadow reapers upon the land, instructing them to harass her forces at every turn. The reapers thinned out her numbers on many fronts, remaining hidden so as not to reveal the Shadow Lord's hand. Even so, Seth Baal continued to sustain heavy losses and moved the Brotherhood to Adara, a distant world in the Mortalis dimension Gyria's father knew well, but she had yet to discover.

The One Above All is said to have finally intervened and confronted Gyria's army with a host of angels beyond number. The demon queen fled. Her army scattered, some offworld. Others hid among the mortals and incited them to continue the conflicts she had started. The reapers retreated into the shadows only resurfacing on occasion, with the Shadow Lord's blessing. Those times were known as the Black Death.

Though dozens of kingdoms have come and gone and the skree could not recall a time when one kingdom or another wasn't at war, Seth Baal's sky shields continued to spin, Mithra's light continued to shine, and from time to time, the Golden Bands occasionally struck down an outlander, protecting the realms from external influences.

The bounty hunter had heard such tales as a child and wasn't sure how much of what he'd been told about the gods was true. But he knew the shadow reapers were real. He'd fought one before and had seen its handiwork. It had been a long time ago, but he knew he would never forget it.

Reminded of the bitter cold, the skree pulled his longcoat tight about him and refocused on the task at hand. He sniffed at the air again. Though his eyes were nearly as keen as an elf's, the moons provided more than enough light and the scent was strong.

This close to civilization, the wreckage will be found quickly, and I have no money to buy a cart. Further, I suspect the vessel might have landed in Horgwin's farm. It's the largest in the area and from what I've heard, the fellow is about as ornery as an ogre with a toothache. I'd best not dally on his lands for long. Just as well, the life of a salvager can be as dangerous as bounty hunting at times, and I am far better at hunting monsters.

The corpse drew his attention before the strange pistol lying in the tall grass nearby. Even so, the skree examined the weapon first. He was pleased to find its trigger was not too dissimilar from a pistol he once owned. *The metal is so lightweight and smooth. So . . . perfect! You clearly weren't manufactured on this world.* An offworlder's pistol would be valuable, though he had no intention of selling it anytime soon. There were arcane shapers who could cast spells to replenish exotic ammo, but only if some ammo remained inside the weapon. He hoped that was the case.

Stowing the weapon in his belt, he stared at a strange rifle laying on the ground beside the body. He slung it over his shoulder to investigate later and then squatted down beside the ruined body.

There was something familiar about the state of the corpse. An old memory bubbled to the surface and he frowned. Where the corpse's skin was exposed, it was covered in sores. The rest of the body was concealed beneath a bloodstained uniform of unfamiliar make. There was a zipper running down the front.

Been more than a few years since I've seen sores like these. And the smell! He inspected the wounds and recognized the discoloration. *So, they've come out of hiding again. I wonder how many are left?* This latest victim only served to renew his fervency to rid the world of the reapers.

He heard movement in the adjacent field and eased a dagger out of its scabbard, but saw nothing but a cow. He stared at it for a moment and then returned the dagger to its sheath and continued examining the body.

The stench was considerable, yet he knew the victim had not been dead long. The fingers on one sore-covered hand were wrapped around a strange metal disk. He pried the fingers back and retrieved the object. Noting a depression in its surface, he pressed it. Nothing happened. He slipped it into the pocket of his longcoat, a jacket that had once been his father's, and remained the only warm memory his father had ever provided him.

A weight pressed on his shoulders as he recalled the day he had acquired the longcoat. It had been his thirteenth birthday. The coat was the only present his father had ever given him, and was apparently in expectation that he would become a shadow adept like his father. That path was one he'd never wanted, but the longcoat was a prize he'd coveted since he was seven. Turning down his father had proved more painful than anything he had experienced before or since.

"You're an embarrassment to our kind, Gaerdrik—a blight on our family's name," his father had said, as he roughly pulled the coat over the boy's head and took it. He had said other things too that night, each a venomous arrow targeting his perceived failings and mocking his dreams. At the time, Gaerdrik had been small and the longcoat swallowed him up—its sleeves ran well past his wrists and the garment dragged on the floor, but he adored it. His father said he would grow into it, just as he would warm up to the idea of serving the Shadow Lord, but Gaerdrik refused. His father swore he would never speak to him again. It was the only promise he ever made Gaerdrik that he kept. That was all long behind him now, but such memories were indelible.

Well after his father had gone to bed, Gaerdrik crept into his parents' room and took the coat back. His mother's eyes were closed when he walked around to her side of the bed to kiss her goodbye, but he was certain she was only pretending to be asleep. He knew he'd never see her again, but didn't cry until he was out on the road.

Later that night, when he grew hungry and opened his satchel to take out the apple he hadn't finished at school, he found the warm brownies his mother had made for him. There was also a loaf of sweet bread and cheese. He didn't know when she'd put them in his satchel, but she must have known he would leave that night. He'd fled in such a hurry after taking the coat that he hadn't noticed the extra weight in his satchel.

There was no going back. These days, he felt as much a stranger among skree as among the other communities he visited. Gaerdrik shook away the memories and glanced back at the rows of corn, listening again, for he was certain he'd heard movement. After a minute, he relaxed and breathed again. *Just the night creepers . . .*

Returning his attention to the body, Gaerdrik noticed one of the fingertips on the victim's other hand was covered in blood, yet bore no sores. Then he saw it—above the body, letters written in blood on the top plank of the wooden fence. *How could I have missed that?* He recognized the shapes and knew it was Traders Tongue, but didn't understand it. He could speak the language, but neither read nor write it. Regretting having left his studies early in life, he copied the shapes into his journal. Gathering anything he deemed might be useful off the corpse, he stood again.

Then he saw it, glinting in the moonlight. His own skree eyes were equipped to have seen it on their own, but he hadn't focused in that direction, being so distracted by the corpse before him. There in the grass he saw a shape he recognized, an object he was intimately familiar with. *How clumsy of me. How did I manage to drop it?* He wondered, and stooped to

retrieve his lost device. It had no official name, at least none he was aware
of. Upon closer inspection, he realized it wasn't the same one, though it
was quite similar. He reached into his longcoat, his fingers dipping into
one of many pockets sewn inside, and withdrew a similar instrument. He
walked over to a fence post and laid both objects side by side. The new one
he found was nearly identical, save for certain markings, thinner protrusions that were not hollow like the one he'd been carrying around for years.
But they indeed were meant to be together, that much was clear to him.

Gaerdrik lined up the two objects and slid them together. Like magnets,
once near, the two seemed eager to touch. The thin protrusions of one half
fit smoothly inside the thicker, hollow protrusions of the other. There was
a tiny clicking sound. The two had become one and the device began to
hum and glow with inner light.

Nothing happens by accident, and nothing is beyond the One Above All's reach. I don't know why, but I'm certain I was meant to find this, he thought. Or it was meant to find me . . .

The device only vaguely resembled a key, but he knew from his research that was precisely what it was. *An Architect key!* He had seen a sketch of one long ago in an old book entitled: Fallen Tech: Lore of the Ancients. Circumstances had prevented him from reading about the key, and the ancient tome had seemed out of reach.

Picking up the assembled key, Gaerdrik stared at it, feeling its warmth in his hands. He felt something else too, a prickly sensation at first, which quickly began numbing his fingers. He repositioned his grasp to hold the now circular base. The key cast a purplish glow. The skree squinted and watched as tiny threads of energy arced along the flat part of the key, dancing between the two shafts.

I can't believe I found the second half of an Architect key! After all these years of searching! Now if only I knew what it was meant to unlock . . .

He glanced down at the corpse again. The new half of the key had been found close enough to the strangely adorned body that he assumed the outlander must have dropped it. Gaerdrik tugged on the two half circles and the one became two again. The light faded. With a sigh, he put them into separate, hidden pockets.

Such a find is worth enough to buy a castle, he thought, and smiled, though he had no interest in castles. *Certainly enough to retire on, but what good are my talents if I don't use them, and what good is a rare treasure if one merely sells it for common silver? If collectors knew I had an Architect key, there would be no end to their badgering to acquire it. Sleeping would become risky if they knew. Still, I'd rather have found it than not,* he thought.

"I am sorry for your current state," he said, staring down at the ruined body. "I pray whatever realm your spirit was summoned to, you will find the peace you seek, outlander. I do appreciate the items you left behind, and I will endeavor to make good use of them in due time."

Continuing along the fence line, he eventually came upon a road and followed it.

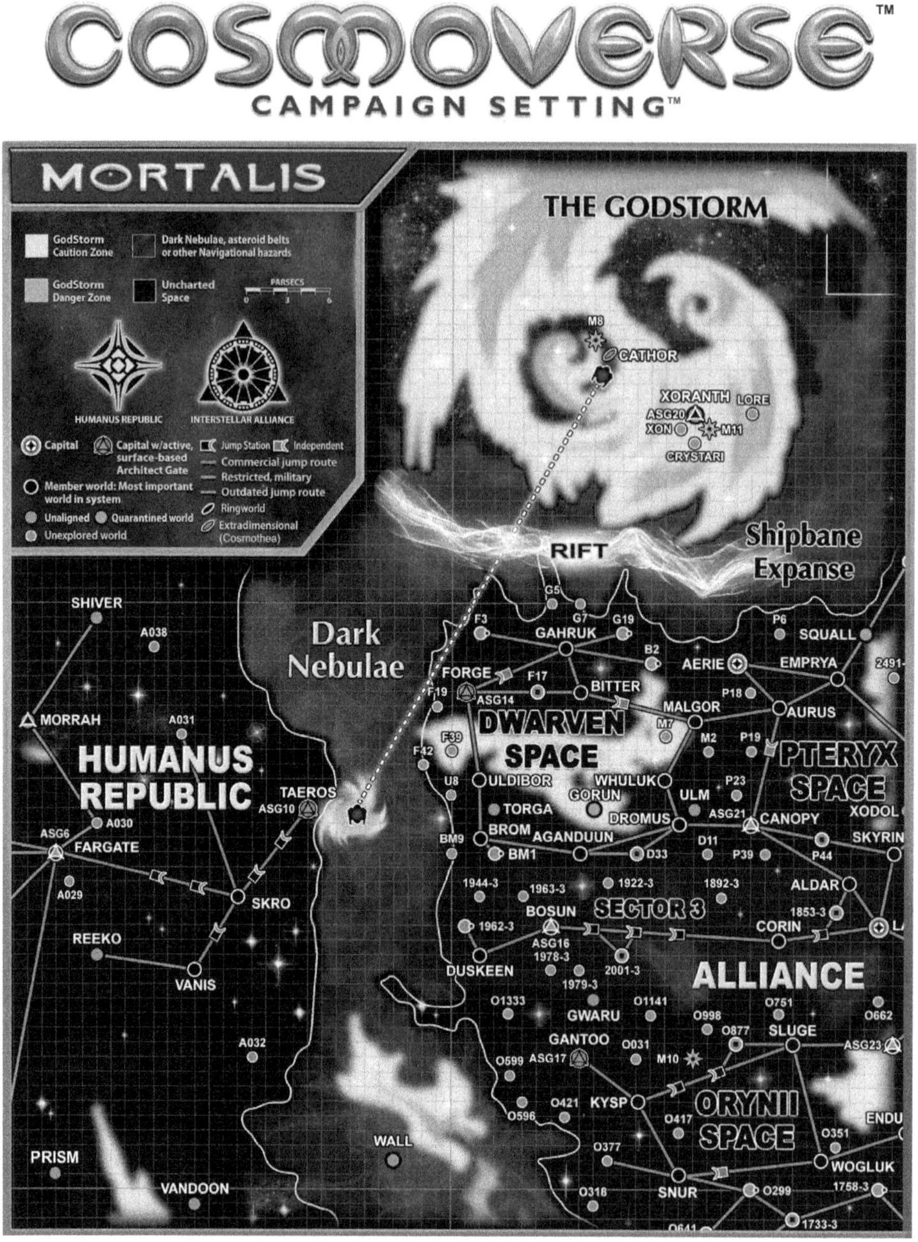

The sun was low in the sky when the cows appeared and spread out across the field. The shadow reaper stepped out from behind a tree and considered a plump cow standing nearby under the shade of another, larger tree on the other side of the fence.

"Dessert," the reaper muttered, as the edges of its purplish-red shadow flesh became indistinct and pooled on the ground where he had stood.

Now a flat shadow, he slithered under the fencing and merged with the plump cow's shadow as it grazed along the fence line, oblivious to the reaper's presence. Once merged, the reaper's form became indistinguishable from the cow's own shadow. In time, the victim rejoined several others of its kind milling about the barnyard.

A young, high elven girl entered the barnyard carrying a bucket in one hand and a book in the other. She scanned the ground ahead of her and made a meandering path around the barn, careful to avoid the cow pies.

Observing the girl with mild interest, the shadow reaper waited until the girl had finished feeding the pigs beside the barn before going to work on his host, employing his art tirelessly, though in no particular hurry. The cow moaned and kept getting up, moving from place to place, confused and weary, unable to rest. While the shadow reaper was capable of killing his hosts more quickly, he enjoyed inflicting pain far too much to rush his work.

Like a doctor, the reaper carefully monitored his host's condition and pain threshold. Occasionally he paused to prolong his victim's life, until finally, the reaper grew bored and slept. By mid-morning, the cow was dead. Restless, the reaper spent the following day slipping from shadow to shadow, sometimes backtracking so as not to be caught out in the open without the protection of another shadow, as he explored his new surroundings.

Besides the girl, the reaper had only seen two others, a seemingly harmless human farmhand, and an aging high elf, presumably the girl's father. Having found the girl to be the most curious of the three, he had decided to shadow her next, leaving the others for later, but as he didn't see her again until late in the day, the reaper regretted his decision and began to miss Lance. *Now he was fun.* Reminded of the hole in his arm, courtesy of Lance's gauss rifle, and the burn from his beamer, the reaper wondered if it had been worth it, but he knew the answer. *Cows are boring.*

It was late in the day when the girl stepped outside to join her father on the porch. The older elf took one look at his daughter's long, plain nightshirt and frowned.

Before he could say anything, she reassured him, "I'm feeling much better, Papa, honest. The pigs will need checking on. I'll just go down and make sure they're—"

"You'll do nothing of the sort, young lady. That was a nasty fall you took this morning. And what, pray tell, were you doing on the roof of the barn anyway?"

The girl cocked her head and smiled. "Writing poetry, of course."

"At five-thirty in the morning?" He shook his head and sighed. "You can slaughter poetry just as efficiently from the porch as anywhere else. Seems every time I turn around, you've gone and gotten yourself into trouble. What am I going to do with you, girl?"

"Papa, you're exaggerating, and why all the fuss? I'm not a little girl anymore. I'll be more careful. I promise!"

"Have you forgotten there's a fire dragon about? It scooped up one of Bartley's cows the other day while he was shucking corn on his porch."

"Who was shucking corn, the cow or Bartley?"

"I'm serious, girl. If the dragon's hungry, I'd rather it eat one of my cows than my only daughter. Course you're so scrawny, you'd only be a snack, but then who'd feed the chickens? The pigs? Not Mather. He's lucky if he shows up at all these days!"

"Mather's not as bad as all that, Father."

"I need you in one piece, Kalisen. I mean it, girl!"

"Papa, you really do care!" Kalisen said in mock surprise, and gave him a hug.

Don't you go trying to change topics young lady, he thought, and squirmed free of her embrace, his frown firmly planted on his face. "Just be careful, you hear? Bartley's is less than a mile up the road, and the dragon's made off with more than a few cows over the past two months. Praise Chronus we've been lucky so far and haven't lost any. But let's not push our luck. Now, back to bed with you. I expect you'll be up bright and early to catch up on your chores — and girl, you're hardly dressed for outdoors besides."

Kalisen grinned. "If I'm *just a girl*, Papa, then why are you worried Mather will see me like this?"

The old high elf wrinkled his nose at her words. Hearing Mather approaching from the barn, he hardened his resolve. "You're dressed for catching colds is all. Now go!"

"Oh, Papa!" Kalisen said, shaking her head, then made a slow retreat back into the house.

Just keeping her out of trouble is a job in itself. And to think she asked me to teach her the ways of magic! She needs discipline, he thought, and sighed. If only her mother were still here to . . .

Reclining quietly—invisibly against one of the two trees casting shadows across the side yard, the reaper listened intently. He didn't fail to notice the girl peeking out of the window, watching as the farmhand spoke to her father. *Such spirit. I will enjoy shadowing her!*

"I tell you Volen . . . it was . . . well, it was a gruesome sight. That's what it was!" the scruffy looking farmhand said to his boss, gesticulating vigorously, perhaps to cover for his meager vocabulary.

Volensidar was staring off into the field as Mather spoke.

That old elf must have infinite patience, or perhaps he's counting his cows? There'll be fewer standing by the end of the week, elf, unless I'm in a generous mood, the reaper thought.

Mather rambled on for nearly two minutes before the high elf cut him off.

The reaper was only half listening. He'd heard Mather talking with the pigs earlier and was convinced the mind-numbed farmhand was incapable of saying anything interesting, and yet . . .

"Dead you say?" Volensidar asked, trying to make sense of Mather's babbling.

Nearly out of breath, the lanky human pushed up his slipping overalls, wiped his nose on his sleeve and continued, again with the hands. "Oh, I dunno for sure. Hard to tell. He was dressed quite strangely—definitely not from around here, a human, I think, but so . . . so—"

"Mather, did the dragon take a bite out of him or not?"

"Dragon?" The shadow reaper muttered.

Volensidar shifted in his seat and turned to glance in the reaper's direction. High Elves have keen hearing, but the old elf's eyes weren't apparently keen enough to parse natural shadow from living, and he simply shrugged at the sound and turned back to Mather and folded his arms.

Mather gazed upward, his tongue dangling nervously to one side as he pondered his employer's question. Finally, looking a bit helpless and staring dumbly at Volensidar, he repeated, "It was gruesome. Never seen nothin' like it!" After a moment, he managed a bit more. "Had sores all o'er him. Even a dragon wouldn't touch him—an' I won't either! What we gonna do with the body, Volen?"

"Sores?" Volensidar asked. "The way you were talking . . ." he sighed, visibly frustrated. "It's late. We'll take a look in the morning. Now get on home."

Nodding apprehensively, Mather took off down the hillside toward the road, startling the cows in the field as he went by.

The old elf watched Mather run off. He shook his head and then went back inside the house.

The reaper slithered onto the porch, up onto a rocking chair and peeked through a window.

Standing beside the table in the kitchen, Volensidar muttered, "If it's not one thing, it's another. All that fuss over sores! As if the Back Death had re—" the thought died in his throat. Refusing to speculate on matters beyond his understanding, he set about preparing supper. There was a faint shuffling of feet on the staircase above, but he didn't look up.

As he sat in silence, his thoughts settled on Kalisen, whose carefree attitude reminded him of her mother. He had been pleased to hear Kalisen had taken up poetry again, something she'd given up when her mother passed away. Unfortunately, she'd also taken to reading her work aloud, which was becoming unbearable lately. It wasn't her voice that tormented his ears, for she had a lovely voice, but the lines themselves that troubled him.

He'd never come to appreciate poetry, not those of the greatest elven bards of Aeden to the north, much less the Lords of Sound, the sonic adept troop from Bashkavar to the west. None of Kalisen's poems rhymed, and while the girl insisted rhyming was not only optional, but unsophisticated, he couldn't help but remember fondly the nursery rhymes her mother used to tell her. Still, he regretted having teased her about her poetry, and worried that he wasn't directing her growth properly. He could hear Kalisen upstairs reading poetry and found himself smiling. It had been seven years since his wife passed away. Volensidar praised Chronus every day that he still had Kalisen, but knew one day she'd be grown, married, and gone. *Knowing her, she'll probably want to travel the world. She hasn't a clue how dangerous it is. Perhaps I should teach her magic, just to keep her safe, but I'd rather she stay close to home where I can keep an eye on her . . .*

He managed to chase away such thoughts before the tears came. The house had been so quiet that he'd gladly taken Mather on board as a farmhand despite his mental limitations and poor coordination. Nothing was worse than sitting around an empty house listening to the walls creak and his favorite rocking chair out on the porch shifting back and forth in the wind. He shook his head, refocused again and set the table.

Withdrawing from the window, the reaper dropped down into a shadow pool on Volensidar's rocking chair. Its tail, now a shadowy whip with a bulbous tip, slashed harmlessly at fireflies as he entertained dangerous thoughts. *Lance and his crew were enormous fun, but it's time for bigger game. There are still plenty of healthy cows left on this farm to attract a dragon.*

Its spirits lifted with the prospect of hunting a dragon. Harming the remaining cows or the girl now seemed a fruitless endeavor. *What if the dragon shows up while I'm off shadowing the girl? No, that wouldn't be wise.*

With his mind made up, the reaper hastily slithered down the porch steps, across the field, and into a healthy cow's shadow, wishing he could somehow magnify his host's appeal above the others. Although he had chosen the healthiest of Volensidar's cows to shadow, that still wasn't any guarantee it would be chosen, if in fact the dragon showed up at all.

As the hours passed, the reaper grew bored and drowsy, but reminded himself that he had waited thousands of years to hunt and had just fed. He could wait awhile longer. For a moment he toyed with the notion of killing off the other cows to guarantee his host would be chosen, then realized the dragon might simply smell trouble and look elsewhere for its next meal.

The following morning, the girl was out gathering eggs, feeding the pigs and enjoying the outdoors. She didn't seem in any particular hurry to finish her chores. Kneeling down in the barnyard, she snatched up a stick and waved it about as if she thought she was some great warrior fending off an evil creature. She laughed and played, but paused whenever Mather or her father came around, or when she was about to drop an egg or step in a cow pie. The reaper found her a pleasant distraction from the mindless cows he'd been associating with lately.

That night, as the reaper watched the sky for signs of the dragon, he heard the farmhouse door creak open, and saw Kalisen out on the porch. She made her way quietly toward the barn, but instead of going inside, she went around toward the back. A noise had come from that direction moments before. Curious, the shadow reaper followed her.

The farmhand was there, and the girl immediately began teasing him. "Mather, you're noisier than a gang of winky dinks."

"What are—"

"Shh . . ." she scolded. Whispering, she continued, "Didn't your mama ever read you fairy tales? Never mind. Just keep your voice down. If Papa hears you, we're both dead!"

"You wanna see the dragon . . . don't you, kid?" The large man wrestled with a lantern in his clumsy hands.

"What are you doing, Mather? It's not that dark out here. I'm an elf, remember?"

"Well, I'm not," Mather reminded, growing irritable. "Stupid piece a junk," he said, trying to wedge open the old, rusted hood.

"That's what happens when you leave it out in the rain. Please tell me you're not still planning to hide up in a tree?" Kalisen asked worriedly.

Behind them, the reaper hid in plain sight in the shadows against the back wall of the barn. While he was closer than he needed to be, he enjoyed the anonymity.

"You scared, Kali?" the farmhand asked with a slight grin, perhaps to conceal his own fears.

"No offense, Mather, but you're not Trendle. I feel safe with Trendle. He's a knight, and you're, well . . ." Kalisen's words trailed off as she walked past Mather and the reaper toward the corner of the barn to take a peek at the cows.

"Trendle's a farm knight, Kali, and that's no kind of knight at all. If he was any good, he'd be protecting a . . . a city . . . or . . . or out on a quest or somethin'. Ah, come on, you," he added, losing his patience with the lantern.

"You're not listening to me," Kalisen said, growing impatient.

"Almost got it. She's lit, but the hood's still stuck," Mather said, lowering his voice as he turned to her. Cradling the lamp against his chest with one hand, he dug at the hood with a knife in his other.

"Mather, the light will give us aw—"

"Oop!" The lantern's rusted hood snapped open, flooding the back of the barn with light. Only Mather had closed his eyes in time. "Sorry, Kali, didn't mean to — shh . . . d'ya hear somethin'?"

As close as that lantern was to the girl's face, she must be as blind as I am right now, the reaper surmised. Already, he felt his body becoming numb, like a statue and was thankful, at least, that he wasn't visible in the bright light.

"Cover that thing, Mather!" Kalisen hissed.

Shifting globes of light floated before the reaper's eyes.

"The dragon," Kalisen whispered, but the reaper did not have her elven ears and had not yet heard the approaching beast.

Completely enveloped by light, the shadow reaper was invisible, but helpless, and cursed himself for abandoning his host. *It's a wonder I ever made it off that moon . . .*

The pigs began squealing, which upset the chickens, while the cows were voicing their concern as the great wyrm descended upon the farm.

Mather killed the light and set the lantern on the ground, then snatched up the pitchfork and held it firmly in trembling hands.

Kalisen glanced over at him and said, "What're you planning to do with that, Mather, offer it to the dragon to use as a fork? I think it eats with its paws."

The reaper's form began to lose its rigidity, though its senses returned more slowly, and the pain subsided more slowly still. Finally, he heard it, too—the sound of great wings flapping overhead was unmistakable. Quietly, the reaper slid around the side of the barn and raced back toward the herd, relying on its familiarity with the farm and sense of hearing, since he was still suffering from temporary blindness. Finally, its eyesight returned, but by then it was too late.

Kalisen's heart lifted as her eyesight sharpened. Although she still wanted to deck Mather for his foolishness, she realized her papa's, if not the dragon's wrath, might still be waiting for her.

"Don't worry, Kali, I have no intention of sticking my neck out for a cow," Mather said, edging slowly along the side of the barn toward the farmhouse, pitchfork in hand. Kalisen followed at a distance, more concerned about getting impaled by Mather than by the dragon, whom she assumed wasn't looking for trouble, just a quick meal. She'd never seen a dragon before, though she'd heard the stories.

Mather stopped several feet short of the end of the barn and just stood there trembling. Kalisen darted past him and peered around the corner, gasping at the sight of a huge fire dragon hovering above the barnyard.

Moving faster than Kalisen thought possible for a creature its size, the dragon swooped down, almost gracefully, and snatched up one of the cows in its enormous claws. With each flap of its wings, the dragon kicked up leaves and dust and scattered the remaining cows and chickens. After the first beat of its wings, the dragon actually sank in the air, almost brushing the ground with its burden, then flapped again and again, building momentum and altitude with each beat.

Out of the corner of her eye, Kalisen thought she spotted movement in the field, but the dragon commanded her attention; all other thoughts vanished.

"Kali?" Volensidar shouted as he burst out of the house so fast the front door threatened to abandon its relationship with the hinges. The elf was carrying a Klandari heavy rifle in his left hand and had a handful of arcane cartridges in his right. Kalisen knew the rifle hadn't been fired in a very long time and the old elf fumbled with the cartridges, dropping two as he loaded one and locked the bolt.

"Kali!" Volensidar repeated, his voice exemplifying fear and concern. He caught sight of the dragon and feverishly cocked the rifle and pushed the locking pin into place. Taking aim, he shouted, "Get down, girl," and fired. The weapon roared.

The dragon was almost fifty yards away when Volensidar fired his first shot, grazing the beast. His hands trembled nervously as he cleared the chamber, loaded and prepared to shoot again.

The first shot barely roused the dragon's attention. The second missed entirely, but Kalisen was proud and surprised by her papas' speed and determination, if not accuracy. She glanced back at Mather, whose wild eyes were scanning the sky as he crouched low beside the barn, still clutching his pitchfork.

"It's gone, Papa," Kalisen said, her chest heaving with each breath, and the sight of her papa now stirring up fear over what would follow.

Volensidar was panting hard too, as he lowered the rifle and rushed over to hold his daughter in his arms.

His voice cracked as he spoke. "You had me so worried, girl. You weren't in your room, and I heard—"

"I'm sorry, Papa," Kalisen blurted out. Embracing her father, she suddenly felt very foolish, and keenly aware of her own mortality. "I'm so sorry." Almost as quickly, she calmed herself and pulled away, suppressing her fears. *I could have been killed,* she realized, but she didn't want to alarm her papa. Although she felt guilty for sneaking out of the house, the whole affair had excited her too, a fact that both surprised and scared her. Life had been too calm for her tastes, but now she felt more alive than ever. Even so, she proceeded to downplay her involvement in the matter, in the hopes of derailing the consequences of her behavior.

Mather's presence at the farm long after he had supposedly gone home for the day, earned him the brunt of Volensidar's attention.

"He was only trying to help," Kalisen had offered, hoping her father would go easy on the farmhand. The fact that Mather was wielding a pitchfork and sneaking around in the dark didn't help his defense, however. Volensidar questioned Mather's proficiency with a pitchfork for its intended use, much less any skill employing it in combat against a dragon.

"Papa, I just thought . . . if the dragon did come, someone should get a good look at it so that they can describe it to Trendle. Size, color, behavior, anything — to aid him in slaying the beast. The more he knows the better prepared—" she caught herself and paused to regroup, realizing her father wasn't buying it. *Why did I come out here? Was it really to help Trendle, or was it just—doesn't matter. Think!* With the cunning of a child caught in a trap, she continued rapid fire over reason, "It's for the good of the town, Papa. Harmless, really. You saw how the beast flew off! Only interested in filling its belly with cow meat. Just a quick look, nothing more, Papa. So, you see there's really no need to get—"

Volensidar's disarming stare halted her words. He was obviously angry, but also clearly glad she was safe. She sympathized with Mather, having no doubt her father wasn't yet finished giving the farmhand an earful for not insisting Kali stay indoors.

"Go to your room Kalisen, we'll talk later," Volensidar said in a firm, but calm voice.

Kalisen lingered, desperate to think of something to say that would quell her father's concerns.

"Now!" Volensidar added, before turning his full attention on Mather, who was still holding the pitchfork, though noncommittally.

The clouds overhead edged slowly across the sky, seemingly in no more of a hurry to pass by than Mather was to reach the body in the distance. Once he came upon the gruesome sight, impatience gripped him. The farmhand swung his head low and stepped through the gap in the wooden fence, eager to show the old elf the body. "It's right here," he said, wrinkling his nose at the smell. Volensidar stepped down from the cart. He tugged the scarf tight around his neck against the cold, buttoned up his coat, and then joined him on the other side.

"I was out walkin' the fence line looking for breaks and found 'm."

Volensidar glanced down at the body propped up against the fence post and grimaced.

"See what I mean, Volen? Covered in sores just like I said." Mather pointed at several blisters on the strangely dressed outlander's body where the skin was exposed.

"I have eyes," Volensidar said, taking a step back.

"And looky there. That's blood," Mather said, realizing his employer was still sore over the previous night's activities.

Volensidar stared at the words written in blood on the top plank and frowned. Several moments passed before the elf spoke again.

Mather was eager to get his opinion and finally blurted, "He don't look like he's from around here. Probably not even from the kingdom. Further West, you figure, Volen? I hear out West, they got—"

"Quiet, fool . . ." Volensidar said and stared at the gruesome scene before them.

Mather wondered what the elf was thinking. He knew Volensidar had traveled extensively in his youth and was a powerful mage, though many years retired. He assumed that's why he hadn't used magic to defeat the dragon earlier. Mather had only actually seen him use magic twice in all the years he'd worked for the elf, but he was convinced Volensidar was one of the greatest of the arcane shapers, and was proud to work for him. *If anyone knows what to make of the outlander, surely Volensidar knows,* he thought. *Not much he doesn't know. I wonder what he's—*

"No, he's not from around here. He's not from the West either. Much farther away, I'd say. Doesn't matter. We can't speak with the dead to find out why he came or what happened. At least it wouldn't be honorable to do so. The dead need their rest," the elf said, his frown deepening.

Mather looked wide-eyed at the elf. He was glad Volensidar didn't use his magic just then. He didn't want to hear what the dead sounded like, and even less what they'd have to say. The whole thought of it made him shiver and he took a step back as well, thinking it safer. He glanced behind them at the rows of corn. The gaps between each row cast shadows and he imagined feral goblins pouring through to devour them. For years, he had suffered from gruesome visions, but most of the time, he could tell the difference between what he imagined and what was so. He took a step closer to Volensidar, just the same, and closed his eyes. He imagined himself invisible, so the goblins couldn't find him. *I wonder what I'd look like invisib—*

"Looks like Horgwin's corn needs looking after. And with him laid low on account of his bad back, it might've been weeks before he found the body," the old elf said, glancing at the rows of corn stretching off in the distance.

"That's what I thought. Doesn't seem right just leavin' it there. Should I go tell Horgwin? He ought ta bury it, that's what he ought ta do."

"No, Horgwin needs his rest," Volensidar said and frowned. "You can bury it."

"But it's not even on our side of the fence!"

"We can't just leave it there. Horgwin can't do it, and it's starting to smell, or haven't you noticed?"

"I don't even want to touch it, Volen. What if it's—"

"There's an old rug in the back of the cart, bring it over here and we'll wrap the body up in it."

"But Volen—"

"You're lucky I don't dock you a week's wages for putting Kalisen in harm's way last night. Now don't just stand there, Mather, the clouds are rolling in. By late afternoon, those clouds will start to leak. I'll help you load up the body and then you can take it to the back field and bury it alongside Kalisen's strays."

"But I still have to clean out the stalls. Volen, you know that bog makes the biggest piles."

"Well then you'd best get a move on."

"But I was hoping to go into town, tonight," Mather said. *It's bad enough I have to clean the stalls, but now I have to bury someone, too?* He thought of Wendili, wondering if she would be at the dance. *She'd looked so pretty the last time in that dress she made!*

He was still upset at himself for not asking her to dance the last time. Of course he had no intention of actually dancing with her. *That would be bangy. I can't dance! I'd just make a fool of myself. No, this time will be different.*

He had it all planned out. *I'll ask her to dance, then ask if she's thirsty. If she says, "No," I'll tell her I'm thirsty! I'll ask if we can get a drink before we dance. She'll say yes to one or the other and we'll walk on over ta the punch bowl together.*

I'll remember to give her a drink first—not like last time, and not spilling it for sure—like last time. Then we'll start to walk over to the dance floor with the others, and I'll pretend to twist my ankle. She'll help me get to a chair and then spend the rest of the night with me, nursing me back to health, refilling my cup and bringing me those little sandwiches Sura makes just the way I like! Maybe Wendili will even give me a kiss, he thought. He felt all warm inside, despite the cold.

" . . . or not?" Volensidar muttered.

"What's that, Volen?" He couldn't wait for the dance and was feeling anxious. "Oh can't I do it tomorrow? I'll get all dirty! I wasn't plannin' ta actually wash before heading in town."

"Mather, you don't smell so good now," Volensidar said. "You think you're going to smell nicer by tonight?"

Mather smelled under his arm and shrugged. *Smells like me.* "Volen, what you're smellin' is the corpse, not me!"

"Then I was smelling the corpse from all the way back at the barn."

"You sure have a good nose," Mather said.

"Yes, well, all the more reason to bury the body now. We don't want any wild dogs showing up, much less ghouls, harpies or worse."

"Worse?" Mather said, his mind imagining all sorts of horrors.

Volensidar nodded, folding his arms.

"I'm on it," Mather said, and without another word, he rushed over to the cart, moved aside some of the old junk meant for the town dump, and pulled out the old rug. "Found it," he said and then hurried back over and laid it out flat beside the body. Then he paused to think and smiled. "I got an idea."

"Oh?"

"I was thinking you could use your magic to move the body onto the rug so we can roll it up without touching it. That way—"

"Magic is not to be used wastefully," Volensidar pointed out. "It is dangerous business. More so since the GodStorm swept through here many years ago."

"I think cleaning up after a bog is dangerous business," Mather muttered, and bent down to examine the body. With a sigh, he walked around to its feet, grabbed the corpse by its boots and pulled it into position beside the rug. It took a bit of work, but they got it rolled onto the rug, then rolled the body up and kept rolling the rug until it was on Volensidar's side of the fence. Then they picked it up and carried it over to the cart.

Once on the cart, Mather checked himself, concerned about the sores. He wiped his hands up and down his pant legs then checked them again to be sure he had no sores.

Volensidar shook his head and cast a maki, a minor spell requiring only a modicum of arcane magic and dowsed Mather over the head with a bucketload of water.

Mather held himself and began shivering. "Than . . . k—k . . . you . . ."

"Don't mention it," Volensidar said and grinned. The elf turned around and strode back across the field toward the distant farmhouse.

Soaking wet and teeth chattering, Mather climbed up onto the cart and headed toward the back field. *Why do I have to . . . do everything . . . just because I'm the employee?* He wondered, and tried to get the bog to go faster, but the great lizard seemed in no particular hurry.

Mather dug and dug until he grew tired and decided to take a break. He was still wet from the dowsing and covered in mud, but glad, at least, that he hadn't become contaminated by the corpse, thanks to the elf's quick thinking. *I'll go home before the dance and change,* he decided. *Put on my best work shirt. Wendili will be pleased to see me all fancied up. Maybe she'll kiss me twice!* He smiled at the thought, and climbed up onto the cart to rest.

Sometime later, Mather felt dozens of tiny things touching his skin. He couldn't see a thing and imagined biters were swarming over his body. His eyes snapped open and he realized it was sprinkling.

The sky was dark and as he climbed down from the cart, a light rain started coming down. *How long was I napping?* He wondered as he grabbed the shovel and ran back to the hole to finish digging. His heart sank, knowing he still had to clean out the stalls. *I'll just clean out the bog's stall. It's the worst, and I know he'll check it. Maybe he won't notice if I skip the others. I hate doing that.* He thought of Wendili, and worried he might not see her for weeks if he didn't go. *She always seems busy when I come knocking,* he thought. *I'm sure she'd be disappointed if I didn't show up for the dance!*

The hole was slowly filling with water, despite his shoveling. Mather's anxiety was mounting as he worked feverishly. *It's getting late and the hole's not near deep enough! No, it's plenty deep,* he decided, knowing he was running out of time. *Ah, Volensidar never comes back here anyway,* he told himself and tossed the shovel aside. Hurrying back to the cart, he climbed up onto the seat. "Come on. Hurry up you dumb bog," he shouted, trying to get the lizard to back up toward the hole.

Finally, the lizard complied. Once in position, Mather jumped off the cart, landing in the mud and hurting his left ankle. He remained down for a moment to catch his breath and then limped to the back of the cart and tugged hard on the rug-enshrouded body until it fell into the mud with a splat.

He thought he heard a moaning sound and stopped to listen. After a moment, he shook his head and muttered, "Like Volen is always sayin', 'Your mind's playing tricks on you, Mather!' Dead is dead!" He reminded himself and glanced down at the hole he had made.

The rug's too big. It'll never fit and there's no time to dig it larger. Oh Wendilli, what 'm I gonna do now? He thought for a moment and then partially unrolled the body, careful not to touch it, then rolled it up tighter. Folding one end over, he shoved the end into the hole. Then he walked around to the other end and dropped it into the hole. "It's not near deep enough, but with how foul it smells, I doubt anything would dig it up to eat it. Not even a ghoul," he said, scaring himself at mentioning the name of the creature out loud. "Oh, I hope there ain't any ghouls in Vraedia. That would be something awful."

After many shovelfuls and hard panting, his ankle giving him fits the whole time, he muttered, "Close enough," and then tossed the shovel aside.

Exhausted and covered in mud, Mather retreated to a nearby tree and stood under its branches to catch his breath. After several minutes of rest, he limped back to the cart, knowing he didn't have time to spare. The rain started coming down in buckets, as he climbed aboard and headed back toward the barn. "Yer gonna make me late, you stupid ole lizard. I hope you're grateful I'm cleaning up after you, and bear that in mind the next time you have to go!"

Lance awoke to the sensation of something touching the edges of his face. This in itself wasn't alarming, though it dragged him out of an interesting, if bizarre dream. As awareness grew and with it, clarity, he soon realized he was being pressed in on all sides and began to panic.

The air was stale and tasted of mud, sweat and old dog. He could neither see, nor move, only feel. And what he felt made him scream. When he did so, dirt and tiny pebbles fell into his mouth. He spat and then shouted for help. Hearing nothing, he shouted again and then was caught up in a fit of coughing, having swallowed up dust.

After that, he listened for a time, gathering his strength and trying to stay calm, but he felt weak and dehydrated. It was cold and damp and was getting colder still. His stomach burned and his extremities were becoming numb. Every inch of his flesh was raw.

Lance's surroundings became moist and then he felt either blood or some other liquid dripping down onto his body in places. His neck was cramping and he tried to lower it toward his chest, but merely brushed up against something rough, odorous and wet. Though he was thirsty, he resisted pressing his tongue up against his enclosure to moisten it.

His arms were trapped at his sides. A heavy weight pressed on his back and seemed to be getting a little heavier. Unable to straighten his legs, his knees ached, but compared to the sores ravaging him, they were merely another thing to focus on, and he had many.

Coherent thought became difficult. He fought to stay conscious and listened. *Nothing, beyond my own breathing. No, I do hear something . . . it's faint . . .*

A continuous thudding grew in volume and frequency and just before trickles of water began to flow down over his head, he realized what he'd been hearing was rain. Desperately thirsty, he licked at the corners of his mouth as the water reached his forehead and dripped down.

It tasted of sweat and filth and dirt. Even so, it was wet, and so he hung out his tongue to catch the drops as they fell. It was then that he realized water was pooling around his chest.

I'm lying on my stomach. My head's higher than my feet, but not by much.

Miserable, he lay there, face pressed against the dank roughness, and tried to think. The surface was soft in places, and furry, like nuzzling a short-haired dog. *It can't be a tarp or even a fur-lined cloak. It's something bigger. A curtain? A blanket? No, a rug,* he thought. *It's an old rug.*

The water continued to rise. He bent his head and lapped at the water until it rose high enough for him to drink. He took several big gulps, coughed and then drank more, but it continued to flow. He felt something like a worm inching along his neck.

If the water keeps rising, I'll drown, he realized. *I should be dead, but I'm not. Someone mistook me for a corpse and buried me alive.*

Thrashing about, he managed to get one hand up near his waist but no higher, and already he was becoming fatigued. As he shifted, water ran down his sides, lowering the level, for which he was grateful, but he knew it was just a matter of time before it would fill back up and over his head.

His lungs were partially compressed. As a result, full breath was beyond his reach. *I'm not getting enough air.* In agony and frustration, he continued thrashing and shouting for help until his throat became raw. Then he realized something was different. His claustrophobic prison was no longer pitch black as it had been. Before he could consider this further, exhaustion claimed him, and soon after, sleep.

Hunting dragons had proven more difficult than Trendle had antici-pated. He'd never actually fought one before, although he'd survived thirteen combat simulations at the academy. His victims had all been impressive, stuffed mannequins mounted to large dollies that could be yanked about quite menacingly by a number of knights-in-training holding ropes attached to the sides. It was all very sophisticated, and nearly useful, except that the vigor with which the other students would pull on the ropes was tempered by the knowledge that they might be up next. To the "dragons'" credit, their claws were dull butter knives tied to short poles sticking out of their sides, and they even nicked a poor sod on occasion.

Even though Trendle hadn't finished at the top of his class, his supe-riors, veteran knights all, assigned him to Muldon, a remote town in the Narchen barony, affording him the confidence that he didn't need the same close supervision as the other graduates. Still, his current path had been arranged by his father when he was very young, and he had never quite gotten comfortable holding a shield, much less a sword. As for wearing armor, it seemed grossly cumbersome compared to a priest's robes, and the "great outdoors" tended to trigger his allergies.

"Ah, well," he thought, stifling a yawn, "Surely I have been called to be a knight, for here I am."

Having spent over an hour removing cow pie from the links of his chain mail after slipping in the stuff while on night patrol, he had nothing to show for his trouble except a stiff back and a concern for the way he smelled. *I still haven't managed to so much as catch a glimpse of the dragon. All I have to go on is rumors and reports. Guess the day wasn't a total loss. At least I managed to repair the farm's threshing machine while I was there waiting for the dragon to show up.*

Trendle was tired and irritable. *Knights don't get irritable*, he thought. *They are . . . knightly.* Finding a shady spot under a tree, he set his armor down, adjusted the straps, and then sat down beside it to rest. His stomach was grumbling terribly however, and so, with a sigh, he stood up again, donned his armor, and then headed down the road to Muldon proper.

With any luck, my clothes will dry before I get there, so no one will accuse me of bathing in my armor again. It did rain. I have that as an excuse, if nothing else, he reminded himself. *Just wish it would have rained after I slipped in the cow pie, instead of before.*

Entering an inn, he sat down for breakfast. Avoiding eye contact to discourage anyone from starting up a conversation he knew would end badly, he reviewed what little he'd learned about the dragon over the past month.

One of the inn's regulars, a stocky old dwarf with too much time on his hands since the mill laid him off last fall, shouted from across the tables, which were mostly empty this late in the morning, "Always lookin' in the wrong place, Trendle," the dwarf snorted, "that's your problem, or maybe that's your plan!"

The knight didn't bother to look up, and continued picking out the hard bits of questionable meat from among his biscuits and gravy. As he suspected, however, the dwarf wasn't finished with him yet.

"You won't find the dragon in there, but if Bartley's son, Willum, hired you to find his missin' bird dog, well—"

"Now, Morse, stop hastlin' my customers. He may not have amounted to much, but that's no cause for scoffing," the wrinkly old woman said as she wiped down a nearby table. "Actually, he was quite useful the other day.

Came over and fixed my sewing machine. Thanks again for that, Trendle, dear," she said as she finished wiping down a table.

"Think nothing of it, Sura," Trendle said, wishing she hadn't mentioned it.

"Any luck?" The old woman asked.

"Yes, do tell, Sir Sewing Knight," Morse chimed in.

Trendle frowned. Turning to Sura, he said, "Some. I have a pretty good idea of the dragon's size, eating habits, and have narrowed down the possible locations of its lair."

"And you been makin' sure you're at one farm when it's at another," Morse chuckled.

"By no means," Trendle corrected. "I've devoted my life to vanquishing evil in every form."

"Like that pig last winter? Ah, now that . . ." remarked Morse, who paused to dig a bit of bacon out of his teeth, "that was somethin'!" The dwarf turned and winked at a young banker who'd been listening from behind the mug he'd been nursing. The two broke out in laughter, and even old Sura herself held her hand over her mouth to stifle a giggle.

"Now how did that one go again?" Flaxton, the banker joined in, knowing the story all too well, but egging on the dwarf, who in truth hardly needed prompting.

Trendle's eyes narrowed. He fought back his anger, feeling embarrassed and wishing they'd let him forget the past. "It was dark—very dark," he said, adding, "and I was told there was a worg running about. Besides, you remember it wrong, Morse. It was a wild boar, not a pig. Three of them actually."

"There was just the one, and it *was* a pig— one of Bartley's. They were always gettin' out," the dwarf said, continuing in an even more demeaning tone, "You fought a pig, Trendle, and if I'm not mistaken, you spent two weeks laid up in bed afterwards. Two weeks!"

"A pig would have had no chance against a knight, Morse." Trendle was trying to retain his knightly composure, but he was starting to lose the battle. Since being assigned to the area over seven years ago, he tried hard to forget that his most difficult and injurious battles had been with the very people he'd sworn to protect.

"Now, you're right about that, Trendle. A real knight wouldn't have been laid up for two weeks after fightin' a pig. Course a real knight wouldn't have—"

"You are trying my patience, old dwarf. Sure I spent time in bed, but it was only because of a bad head cold I'd gotten from staying out in that storm all night. And I did find the worg — killed it, too. Why doesn't anyone ever remember that part?" Trendle said as he got to his feet, too frustrated and angry to remain seated. *At least I think it was a worg. It was dark—very dark!*

"Maybe cause it never happened," Morse countered.

Trendle wondered if the dwarf was hoping to push him into saying something he'd regret later.

"There you are!" said a familiar and infinitely more pleasant voice. It was Volensidar's girl. Trendle could think of no retort that would come back unchallenged, and was grateful for the interruption.

"I've been looking everywhere for you," Kalisen said, from the threshold of the side entrance.

"Hey, Kali," Trendle said, finding a smile for her, and rushing to meet her at the door, his face still red and his heart pumping.

"Papa sent me for you," Kalisen said, glancing over the knight's shoulder to see who else was there.

"Don't tell me the dragon visited your steer last night?" Trendle asked, lowering his voice.

"I'm afraid so. Can you come?"

"Certainly, but it probably won't be back tonight. I've been tracking its movement and eating habits. I'll take a look around, though. Come on," he said, eager to get out of Morse's path.

"So soon? I was hoping . . ."

"I'm heading over there now, Kali. I'll guard your farm tonight if it'd make you feel better. See you after a while," Trendle said as he rushed past, leaving her standing in the doorway, desperate to get out of there. *I think I'd have better luck against the dragon than such as these,* he thought.

Morse turned to Kalisen and grinned. "Hey, kid?"

"What is it, Morse?" Kalisen asked, expecting the worse, but figuring the dwarf would say his piece no matter what she responded.

"A little advice . . . be sure to get your pigs locked up good tonight."

"Why, are you stopping by for a snack later?" Kalisen asked, realizing what he'd been up to. Without waiting for a response, she spun on her heels and ran after the knight. "Trendle, wait up!"

"I don't know, Kali," Trendle began as she came up beside him, "I can't improve my image no matter what I do. I've sworn to protect these people, but they don't seem to want my help."

"They don't deserve it, either, but I believe in you, Trendle, and so does Papa. We know you're a trained warrior. A fine knight."

"Thanks, Kali, but you don't have to say that—really. My father was a knight, and he made me one, too. I didn't have any say in the matter. I would've been happy just being . . ." he paused, taking a deep breath and letting it out slowly, taking his time to answer, as if his next comment was pivotal to their friendship.

Trendle's greaves were clacking together loudly. *He's not nervous, just cold—and rightly so in that armor!* Kalisen thought. There was an awkward stretch of silence. Kalisen wished she could think of some way to comfort him. She knew the reluctant knight didn't want to discuss his upbringing further. *And here I took the long way home so we could talk in private. Your father should never have pushed you into something so dangerous . . .* "You look exhausted, my friend," Kalisen said.

"Just a tad cold is all," Trendle said with a shrug. "I'm afraid my armor's padding is wearing thin in places. I've been tracking the dragon for nearly two months, interviewing folks, following up on leads. I've spent years studying their habits, diet, personalities . . . I've found tracks, Kalisen, and Doniver's oldest boy insists he saw the beast flying over the old mill road a few days ago. I think I know where this dragon's lair is — not the exact location, mind you, but I'm getting close."

In truth, Kalisen hoped he'd never find the dragon. *If only the wyrm would tire of cow meat and move on to Delathen or one of the other baronies before Trendle catches up to it.*

"Don't enter its lair, Trendle." Her words resounded like a command, but were meant as a request.

"You don't think I can defeat a dragon either, do you, Kali?" He didn't give her time to respond. "It's okay. No one else does, either. I'm beginning to wonder, myself, but someone has to try."

"You don't have to prove yourself to anyone. You know that, don't you, Trendle? The dragon hasn't harmed anyone in Muldon yet, and there's no reason to get yourself killed saving livestock. I'd understand if you didn't want to fight the dragon. I've seen it, and—"

"You've seen it?" Trendle asked, excited once more.

"I have," Kali said, carried on by his enthusiasm, "and I can tell you all about it!" For a moment, as they passed Bartley's farm, she forgot her fears.

As they entered her father's farm and rounded the barn, Kalisen saw that her father was waiting for her on the porch. *That's never a good sign.* She smiled reassuringly, waived, and said, "Hi, Papa. Took me awhile to find him. He's been very busy hunting the dragon, but is anxious to have a look around!"

Trendle nodded, smiling, and Volensidar returned the gesture, though with less enthusiasm than the knight.

The second time Lance awoke, confusion gripped him and he began trembling with fear. It wasn't the darkness that terrified him. He'd been able to sleep with the lights off since he was seven. It wasn't the suffocating coffin, nor even the pain. Kidney stones and a hovercycle accident had been among his past sufferings, though this seemed worse by a fair margin.

While all of these factors contributed to his present state, individually, none of them paralyzed him with fear. It was the realization that he had lost everything, and because he brought the creature down to Cathor, countless others would suffer as well.

He'd always feared pain worse than death. But he also secretly feared what might happen following death. Most of his life, he had carefully dodged the topic, but now he was worried that might have been a mistake. *I put off what could be the most important decision of my life. What if there is an afterlife and I pass away before making a key decision? What if . . .* a thought came to him and he shivered.

Maybe I only think I survived. What if I'm already dead? Trapped between life and death? Is this Gheryon—Hell itself? I know I wasn't a saint, but surely I deserved better than this!

A long forgotten vault buried deep in his mind opened and a voice whispered, "All have sinned and fallen short of the glory of God. Only by grace can you be saved."

I recognize that voice, he realized. *It was so long ago . . .*

With the heavy curtains drawn, he had to strain to see in the darkness. Finally, the bedroom door opened, and the old, fuzzy snugglebunny slippers his grandmother always wore appeared in the doorway.

Every day about this time, Mamaw sneaks into her bedroom and locks the door. I've asked her a dozen times why, and she never answers me. He felt a little guilty spying on her, knowing she'd always treated him well, but he couldn't resist. *She'll go straight to the closet. It was the first thing I checked. I should have guessed it would be locked.*

The bedroom door closed and he heard her lock it.

There's no turning back now, he thought. *No way I can sneak out from under the bed and past her without getting caught. She probably keeps the key to the closet in her pocket.* Lance regretted lying to her about going off to play in the backyard, but he was determined to discover what treasure or secret she kept that drove her to return day after day, sneak inside her bedroom in the middle of the day and lock her bedroom door. And because her closet was also locked, he was certain that's where the mystery was hidden.

What's taking her so long? She's just standing there. Open the closet already, Mamaw! He thought. She had only paused a moment, but in his young mind, Lance thought she was taking forever. *Maybe she thought she heard me and stopped to listen?* He pondered the notion, and as he did so, panic gripped him. He could no more avoid it than one of his grandmother's hugs. It was all he could think about. *Don't breath! She would have said something if she was certain.*

Finally, those fuzzy slippers began to move again, but instead of heading for the closet, she shuffled over to the bed, removed her slippers and lay down.

Being of generous girth, his grandmother sank low in the bed. Being old and worn like his grandmother, the bed sank lower still, until Lance was pressed against the carpet and thought he was going to die. Even so, he remained perfectly still and quite. Listening intently, he waited. And then waited some more, wishing he could breath easier, but he didn't dare move.

It was my grandmother's voice, he recalled. No sooner had he realized it, than he remembered a promise she had made. *Or was it a warning?*

"Lance, there is no place you can go where the Lord cannot find you." She had said that after finding him crying when they'd gotten separated at a shopping mall, but he realized it also meant the One Above All knew he was under the bed. Fear of being caught grappled him, but he remained as still as he was able.

Mamaw's the sweetest person I know, and always thinks of something to say that makes me feel better—no matter what. At that moment under the bed, young Lance tried to remember her words. "The One Above All is quick to forgive. As long as you don't give up, there's still hope." Lance had always found such truths comforting. *I have hope. I hope I don't get caught!*

As the weight continued to press on his back, he fought to remember. *For every valley, there's a mountaintop. I know the plans I have for you. Plans to prosper you and to give you hope and a future,* he reminded himself and did indeed feel better, though the pressure was still there. He suspected that he wasn't supposed to just jumble up the verses into whatever order suited his needs.

In those days, he'd feared his grandmother's wrath more than the One Above All's. She had only spanked him once, but Lance remembered the pain well enough. In truth, it had been her disappointment that had stung the most. He didn't want to ever disappoint her again. *Better for me to remain hiding and spare us both,* he thought, and wondered what her secret was. *If you remain quiet, she'll never know you were even here.*

For a long time, his grandmother remained still, and young Lance wondered whether she'd died or merely fallen asleep. *Was that her big secret? She takes a nap every day at the same time?* Having imagined numerous exciting possibilities of where she had gone when she closed her bedroom door—more than one of which included stepping through a gate into another world—he was naturally disappointed.

Ever since his father told him that stargates had been discovered on hundreds of worlds over the centuries, even the farthest corners of the Cosmoverse seemed so much more accessible. The thought that any door—even a closet door—might secretly lead to another world, excited him. It was a notion that occupied his imagination whenever he grew bored. His father had told him that the mysterious Architects and even the lesser gods had built stargates and left them behind on every world they visited. Mages had also built gates and now anyone can go anywhere.

He'd long since decided that someone as wonderful as his grandmother would have been welcomed with open arms wherever she went. In his mind, on a world of the tiny nehi, she was their queen. In Toonaria, candy likely grew on trees and rivers were made of chocolate, and his grand-mother was the steward of an endless garden. The treats she often discov-ered in her "magical pockets" were likely found aplenty in such a realm. *And she had merely to step inside her closet!*

Perhaps she's resting in preparation for a grand adventure! Time probably doesn't pass as quickly beyond her gate. That's how she manages to take a nap and still venture into other worlds. I wonder where she keeps the key? He had found neither magical nor mundane keys while glancing around her room before seeing the time and crawling under her bed to hide. *I bet she visits the nehi on Field Days and the dwarves on Guild Days. In the realm of the dwarves, she's The Great Baker,* he decided, recalling her talent for making pies and cakes. *She visits them on Feast Days, I bet!*

No. She's only asleep! I've been a bangy orc, and now I have to escape before she wakes up. As Lance slowly crawled out from under the bed, his grand-mother spoke. He stopped immediately and held his breath.

In that moment, his grandmother poured out her heart to the One Above All. To his surprise, her prayers focused not on her bad back, nor her sore knees, nor even his grandfather, but on him. He listened more intently than ever before, as his grandmother talked to the creator of the Cosmoverse about him.

She started by thanking him for his love and mercy, and then asked him to protect Lance and help him with his schoolwork. She asked the One

Above All to surround him with true friends and to help him be good and remember to pray. Lance felt awful, and wondered what the One Above All thought as he looked down and saw him hiding under the bed.

"And as he grows, Lord," she continued, "help him to make the right choices. Help him to seek you in times of need and to praise you in times of plenty. I know you made him special, just like his father. As his new-found abilities awaken, help him to use them wisely. And to turn to you and never let go."

Lance didn't understand everything she said. But he started to cry and couldn't stop. He covered his mouth, knowing she'd hear him and then there would be a spanking and disappointment. But she finished her prayer, got up and walked out of the room, leaving the door open. *That's strange,* he thought. *She never leaves her bedroom door open. Now I know she heard me!*

He crawled out and nervously stepped out into the living room, but didn't see her anywhere. A few minutes later, he heard her in the kitchen. He waited nervously for her to return and give him a spanking, but she never did. When she did finally come into the living room, she gave him a hug and told him lunch was ready. He was sorry for what he'd done, and never went into her bedroom again.

That's the first time I've thought of Mamaw since she passed away over a decade ago, Lance realized. As then, sadness swept over him, not just over her death, but also for every bad thing he'd ever done. *So many of the things my Mamaw prayed for me, I let slip away without a thought. After she died I never looked back.* With the memory and contrite heart came tears. A weight lifted from him and he no longer felt the dirt pressing down on his rug coffin. As clarity came, he realized it was even more than that. He no longer felt anything but the blinking of his eyes and the tears running down his face. And then he went into a deep slumber.

That evening, stationing himself within view of the cows, Trendle propped himself up against a tree. He counted the herd several times, and routinely got up to stretch his legs and walk about, always mindful of the skies—and of cow pies. He thought about the dead cow Volensidar had shown him and recalled the strangely clothed corpse the old elf described to him. *All covered in sores . . . I bet that was a sight!* It reminded Trendle of the stories his father had told him about the Black Death. They were just stories—his father hadn't lived through them, but there was something to be learned from them, and so he had passed them on to Trendle.

At Trendle's initiation into the knighthood, his father pulled him aside and said, "Don't fear what you can see, Trendle, fear what you *can't* see. That's where true power lies. Love and hate can crush kingdoms. Defeat and victory are close cousins, often decided by wisdom, not merely talent, Trendle, so if you don't have wisdom, find it." There was little that he could recall agreeing with when it came to his father, but he saw the wisdom in those words and kept them close.

He wondered what he would do if the wyrm did appear. After all, it had been snatching cows more frequently than usual lately, and he suspected it was merely taunting the townspeople. If this was the case, then Volensidar's attack might have been taken as a challenge, in which case Kali and her father could well be in danger. On the other hand, it might simply avoid the farm in search of easier game.

If he hoped to slay the wyrm, he knew he'd have to strike first, which meant ambushing it, something he really didn't feel up to, and besides, it didn't seem very honorable. *There are precious few places to hide anyway. Perhaps if I confront it—try to reason with it—I can convince it to leave the barony,* he thought.

About an hour and a half later, after growing increasingly uncomfortable and itchy, Trendle began noticing a rash of sores on his hands and arms. And he could feel others on his neck and cheek, and on the back of his head. Within no time, he grew thoroughly miserable, able to think of nothing but the pain in his limbs. Then he remembered the cow and the description of the outlander's body, and his face blanched. *The Black Death has returned, and I'm its next victim!*

Realizing he would be of no use to anyone even if he did survive the night, he decided to see the town doctor. So, he asked Kali to fetch her father when she snuck out to see him around eleven o'clock that night.

"Could be contagious. You didn't touch him, did you, Kali?" Volensidar asked, wiping sleep from his eyes.

"Papa, he needs us. If the Black Death has returned, wouldn't Mather have it, too, and you as well?" Kali said, obviously worried.

Volensidar shuddered. He had only been a boy when his grandfather fell ill, but he could never forget watching him slowly succumb to the Black Death one sore at a time. Many were healed during those horrific times, but many more died. Heavily populated regions of Cathor had been subjected to the curse no less than three times, and more times still did the curse resurface in pockets, wiping out villages and entire towns over the centuries. He had lived through one such event, and it had left an indelible memory that seeped into his nightmares on occasion. Many high and grey elves had died during that last one, though far more humans and dwarves perished. It had been worse still among the orcs, and by the end, even giants and other great races fell victim to the Black Death.

There were many theories surrounding the plague. Most suggested a divine cause, while others insisted arcane magic was to blame. For as long as Volensidar could remember, there had been arcane accidents both great and small, the worst resulting in the deaths of nearly a million souls. But the Black Death felt different. He shuddered again at the thought that the curse might have returned and mouthed a short prayer to the sun goddess, Mithra, to protect those he loved.

"Papa, you and Mather were both around the bodies. Mather hasn't complained about any sores. You haven't manifested any, have you?" Kalisen asked, her face marred with fear.

Volensidar didn't answer immediately. He was getting up in years and these days was never feeling quite right—there was always some ache or pain to remind him that he'd lived through over three hundred winters. He considered how he was feeling and sighed in relief. *No sores, at least,* he thought. Realizing his silence was making Kalisen uncomfortable, he blurted out, "Of course not. There's no reason to assume the worst. Even so, you ought to be more careful . . ."

Trendle was slumped over in the rocking chair beside the window and began moaning loudly. Volensidar sighed again, knowing what had to be done.

Slipping into his boots and overcoat, Volensidar yoked the old bog and hitched it to the cart. That great lizard was clearly in no mood to be woken up so late, much less to be tasked with pulling the cart. Once the bog was properly hitched, Kalisen and her father helped Trendle into the back of his cart.

Kalisen started to climb on board, but Volensidar held out a hand to block her. "Not this time, Kalisen. Straight to bed and no arguing," he said and picked up the reins.

"But Papa—" Kalisen said, falling silent when she caught sight of Trendle lying in the back of the cart writhing in pain.

"He'll live, Kalisen, and I imagine I'll be back by morning," the aging elf said. He snapped the reins hard on the bog's leathery back and the huge lizard lurched forward into the night. After several moments, Volensidar heard the front door slap shut and began to notice the deepening chill.

Trendle moaned the whole way to town, worse each time they hit a bump, which on these old roads was often.

Volensidar liked Trendle well enough, but had never been convinced he was knight material. He knew he wouldn't be able to talk the knight out of his quest, but tried anyway. It beat just sitting there listening to him moaning, or listening to his own thoughts, for he felt a little responsible for the knight's condition. While he had never liked Doc Catchet, the man could do wonders at times. He also knew Catchet purchased healing potions from the temple of Mithra, in Narchen to cover for his failings in medicine, though he'd never admit it.

"Doc Catchet will fix you up, Trendle, and then you can hunt down this dragon of yours if you still want to. But perhaps it would be better to allow the town guards to do it? They're a lazy bunch and have gone soft. You would be doing them a favor."

"I've been trained for this—they haven't. No, I need to do it, Volensidar."

"Need?" Volensidar said, concerned for Trendle and aware that many in the town made a habit of teasing him. "I hope you aren't doing this to prove—"

"I'm doing this because it's the right thing to do," Trendle interrupted. "I'm sorry, my friend, but someone has to stand up to the dragon! These frightful sores won't keep me from fulfilling my quest . . . but I should lie down for a while yet still. I do hope Doc Catchet can—ah—oh!"

Trendle's breath ripped from him as the cart jerked, despite Volensidar's attempts to find the best path over the old road. After that, Trendle's breathing became more ragged and he didn't speak again for the rest of the trip. Volensidar felt awful for the knight, knowing there would be more bumps ahead.

The Black Death? Is that what they're calling us now? I wonder if any of my brothers are still hunting on this world or if they've moved on to another? the reaper wondered. He waited in the shadow of the farm's choicest cow, hoping the dragon would return before Volensidar and the knight. *And if the dragon doesn't, will it ever?*

Worried that Trendle would complicate its new quest to shadow the dragon, the reaper had gone straight to work on the knight, approaching its latest victim like an aspiring artist, taking its time and relishing each new sore. After a time of delightful torment, he stopped suddenly, realizing he had made yet another mistake.

From the way the knight was talking with the girl earlier, he was getting close to sorting out the location of the dragon's lair, but now he's in no condition to lead me to it. I don't know if the dragon will even return to this farm, and I've no idea where to even start looking for it. In my excitement, I wasn't monitoring the knight as closely as I should have been. Could I have inflicted more damage than I'd thought? It has been thousands of years since I've hunted the locals, but I'm fairly certain the knights of old had more mettle than this Trendle fellow.

Spotting one of the moons in the sky as he searched for a sign of the dragon, the reaper was reminded of its former prison and wondered if it was the same moon. *Why do I keep doing this to myself? I must be going bangy. From here on, I'm fasting until I find this dragon . . . or a giant perhaps. No, they're stupid and boring. It has to be a dragon!*

As the hours passed, the shadow reaper accepted the likelihood that the dragon would not be making an appearance and grew concerned for the knight's welfare. *There's no way that knight could defeat a dragon by himself, which suits me fine as I reserve that pleasure for myself. Get well soon, Trendle. We've work to do . . .*

Trendle submitted to prodding and leaches and more questionable treatments, that in some cases hurt worse than his sores, but his condition seemed to be stabilizing. Even so, he continued to wince and moan.

Finally, the following afternoon, the good doctor gave Trendle a special drink. Trendle asked if the cinnamony drink was a magical potion. Catchet acted offended and insisted the concoction was a special blend of goat's milk and medicinal herbs. Feeling considerably better after drinking the glowing brew, Trendle was bombarded by Doc Catchet's boasts regarding his medical prowess, attributing the knight's quick recovery to his own genius.

Catchet was apparently counting on a healthy reimbursement for his seemingly magical treatments, as he drummed into the knight's head again and again how grateful he ought to be. Catchet pointed out that it was only right that he receive an equal share in the dragon's treasure hoard for saving Trendle's life. Trendle just shrugged noncommittally. He hadn't thought twice about treasure. He just knew it was his duty as a knight to protect Muldon from harm.

Doc Catchet had not been alive during the last Black Death and made it clear he didn't believe it had returned to Muldon of all places. "This is the least significant town in the Narchen barony—in all of Vraedia for that matter. Even if the gods were responsible for the Black Death—which I doubt—they wouldn't pick Muldon. They'd be lucky to find us on a map!"

Trendle wasn't entirely sure he believed the doc hadn't used magic to at least assist in the healing process, but he didn't care. He was just happy to be feeling good again. Whenever Catchet spoke, it was either to praise his own genius, accost Trendle for not taking better care of himself, or remind the knight of his debt. The doctor even rented Trendle his bog and cart for hauling off the dragon's treasure, for a modest, daily fee appropriate to someone coming into a large sum of money.

"I have to recoup at least some of my exorbitant expenses for housing one such as you, and nursing you back to health," Catchet reminded. "You owe me, Trendle, and I know you will want to make good on your promise!"

Trendle vaguely recalled agreeing to something earlier when the good doctor started applying leeches. The knight had felt light-headed and would have said anything to end the pain. Now, he was honor bound, it seemed, however questionable the situation that facilitated the pact.

After a final once-over at Trendle's request, Doc Catchet sent him out to chop wood, prescribing it as an essential part of his recovery. An hour later, the knight ran into the doctor's study and reported a new blister and asked if it was a sign of the Black Death.

"One sore isn't a sign that you're dying. Now go, before people start to talk of cowardice. I can't pretend you're still ill, if that's what you're hoping?"

Trendle's face twisted in disgust. "Of course not. I just want to be in top shape before going after the dragon. I will need all my strength and concentration."

"Yes, well, you're fine now."

"Are you sure, Doc? After seeing that cow's body all covered in sores . . . I don't want to die from these things," Trendle said, realizing he was afraid.

"What's this about a cow?"

"A cow died from the same illness I had, and Mather found a stranger dead and covered in sores as well. Didn't I tell you? I sure hope it's not the Black—"

"Enough!" Catchet said in a huff. "I don't want to hear another word about it. Focus, Trendle! Let that sore remind you of all the pain I spared you. Now go, and don't come back until you've filled my cart with the dragon's hoard. Then we'll settle up on your debt to me. I have full confidence in your ability to rid the town of this beast once and for all. And," he paused, placing a firm hand on Trendle's shoulder and displaying a concern Trendle thought he didn't possess, "While I have every confidence in your ability with that sword of yours, may I suggest . . . attack it while it's sleeping. That way, you're bound to hit it once anyway, and with any luck that'll be all you need!"

"But . . . that's not the honorable way," Trendle said. Still, something told him it was wise advice. "As you say, then," he continued, "but do you really think I can do it?" Trendle regretted putting the doctor in the position of actually having to speak his mind.

"You're a dragon Slayer aren't you?" the doctor said, noncommittally.

"Well, I want to be. That is, I've trained and researched everything I can on dragons, I've done all I can to be one."

"Then I suppose by definition you are one," Catchet said, adding somewhat more energetically, "if not by your knowledge of dragons and your sharp blade, then by your sheer determination. My treatments have made you stronger and more durable than ever . . . and you're not staying for lunch, besides, so don't get any ideas. Now go!"

Trendle sighed, waved goodbye, and climbed aboard the good doctor's cart for the trip. On the seat beside him bundled in a leather satchel were his journal and an annotated map of the region. On the map, symbols represented dragon sightings and probable locations to search for a lair, though he felt certain one bore more promise than the others, and that's where he was heading.

As he was leaving the town proper, a nosy merchant stopped him and demanded the status of his quest.

"Why yes, I'm still pursuing the dragon," Trendle replied. "I had become deathly ill, I'm afraid, but now—"

"You mean deathly afraid!" retorted the merchant. "Afraid to get out of bed. What will be your next excuse, Trendle?"

"I was sick. Ask Doc Catchet! But he healed me, and now I'm on my way to slay the fire dragon." Not bothering to wait for the skeptic to reply, Trendle rushed past him without looking back. Reminding himself of all he had done to prepare for this day, his courage slowly returned.

Searching the hills tirelessly, Trendle returned to an old road that ran above the mill near the river, where he stopped to camp for the night.

Cracking open his journal, Trendle reviewed his notes on the dragon but his eyes grew heavy. He hadn't meant to fall asleep, and awoke in a start the following morning, upon hearing a strange sound, which he imagined was the dragon feeding on his bog. Instinctively, he reached for his long-sword, then realized what he'd heard wasn't the dragon, but Catchet's bog, tugging on its tether, in its quest for a tuft of grass just out of reach.

More alarming than the sound was the smell and presence of freshly baked muffins and a slab of cheese he found in a basket beside the tree.

"Seen anything yet, Trendle?" came a familiar voice. "I haven't," Kali said as she climbed down from the tree the knight had been sleeping under.

"Kali, you startled me half to death," Trendle remarked, embarrassed.

The girl wore a flowery skirt and a smile.

Trendle quickly checked himself to ensure he was properly attired and sighed with relief. "What are you doing here?" he asked, feeling grumpy and annoyed at not having heard her approach.

"Trendle, you're practically in my backyard," Kalisen said, exaggerating. "You were a mess, but I'm glad to see you're feeling better, and so soon! I had my worries about Catchet, but I guess he—"

"Does your father know you're here?"

"Of course not. He stayed up so late last night worrying about his cows that he won't be up for at least another hour or two. Besides, I finished my morning chores—mostly. I thought you could use a hand!"

"No. Absolutely not. Well, yes, perhaps, but not from you. It's too dangerous!"

"You're looking good. Sores all gone, I hope?"

Trendle glanced down at his blistered thumb for a moment, then said, "All gone."

"Great, then let's eat." Spreading out the goodies on the scrap of cloth she'd brought with her, Kalisen sat down on the soft scrub near the edge of the old road.

Trendle was too hungry to argue. Several muffins later, he managed a weak retort, "You should be getting home now, Kali. When Volensidar wakes up, he'll be looking for you. Obeying your father and doing your chores are just as honorable as fighting dragons—and far less deadly."

"But I grew up around here, Trendle. I know these hills. I seem to recall there being some caves around here. I found them when I was just a kid, and maybe—"

"Just a kid?"

"Don't go there, Trendle." Kalisen warned, not wanting to be thought of as a child. "I'm older than you, remember?"

"True, but elves age differently than humans. Anyway, I'm certain the dragon makes his lair not far from here, so you're probably right about the caves." Finishing off another muffin, he donned his helmet and stood. "I suppose you can come along, Kali, but only as far as—" he stopped short, hearing something behind them. Drawing his longsword, Trendle scanned first the hills on one side of the road and then at the forest on the other. *Nothing. I could have sworn . . . the sky!*

Knowing how swiftly dragons can fly once they've had time to pick up speed, he wasted no time on looking, and instead lunged toward Kali. He scared her half to death, but couldn't bear the thought of anything happening to her and wanted to shield her with his body. *I might have only seconds left to act!*

Startled, the girl fell backwards, landing hard on the ground, knocking the wind out of her. *Did she see it?* Trendle wondered. *She looks scared!* He shielded her as best he could with his armored body, pinched his eyes closed, ready for death to come, and pointed his sword skyward. If the dragon were descending, he hoped it might impale itself on his blade, however unlikely.

"What . . . was that . . . for? Kalisen said, gasping for air, a hint of annoyance in her tone.

"Shh," Trendle said as he crouched low over her, sword still raised. When pain and then death didn't come, he glanced over his shoulder and was relieved to see the sky empty, but that was quickly replaced with a strong sense of embarrassment. *Would it have killed the dragon to have flown over just then? I can't believe I—no, she's safe and that's more important than my pride.*

"Did you see it?" Kalisen asked with wide eyes.

"Did you?" Trendle questioned, uncertain whether she meant the dragon really had flown over them, and wondered if he had simply missed it—again, or if she hadn't seen it and was wondering if he had. *If she did see it, then that means I didn't screw up after all, or maybe she's just wondering why I'm practically laying on top of her? I should get up. I don't think she saw it. I can't believe I—* "Are you all right?" he asked, staring down into her eyes noticing how beautiful she was for the first time.

"I don't know whether to be mad at you, or flattered that you were ready to sacrifice your life for me," Kalisen said, her chest heaving up and down with each breath.

When did she grow breasts? He wondered for but a moment. "I just want to be clear about one thing, Kali."

"Oh—kay," she said, and had an odd look of expectation on her face.

"Did you see the dragon or not?"

Kalisen sighed and said, "I think I would have heard if a dragon was swooping down on top of us, Trendle," she said, near breathless. I'm a high elf, remember?" After a moment, her face softened and she wrapped her arms around him.

Trendle blushed, but he did not get up. Not yet, and he didn't know why.

Kalisen laughed. "Your face is turning as red as a fire dragon's belly," she said, then leaned forward and planted a kiss on his nose guard.

Trendle's heart stopped and he was overcome with emotions he thought long abandoned. He quickly pulled away, deeply embarrassed, both in thinking the dragon was attacking and in finding himself attracted to her. Never before had he thought of Kalisen as a woman, but now . . . now she scared him.

"I—I'm sorry, Kali," Trendle blurted, and quickly got back to his feet and helped her up.

Once back on her feet, Kalisen didn't immediately let go of his hand. "I'm fine," she said, finally, and turned away, looking embarrassed. Trendle had never understood human women, much less young elven ladies, but he suspected he'd done something wrong, though he couldn't be sure what it was.

Kalisen brushed the leaves and dirt from her skirt and walked past him toward the cart. "We'd better get moving, Trendle," she said and climbed aboard the cart, adopting the reins as her own. "I'm driving."

Still embarrassed, Trendle didn't object, and quietly climbed aboard and sat down beside her.

"You're a knight, Trendle. Driving is such a menial task, especially driving a cart. I can be your squire," she said.

"Squire?" He remembered with some regret when he was his father's squire, but as he was preoccupied with the prospect of finally finding the dragon, he didn't argue the matter. "Careful Kali," he said, concerned for her driving skills.

She gave him a sour look, after which he kept his comments to himself. A short time later, she stopped the cart, turned to him and wrinkled her nose. "What's that stench?"

"I need you to go home now, Kali," Trendle said firmly. He was mad at himself for letting things go this far, and was worried she'd try to talk her way into hanging around longer than was safe. "Right now," he added, more forcefully than he'd meant to. *She looks surprised. I must exude confidence. And why shouldn't I? I've trained and I . . . well, if not confident, I'm surely well rested.*

"According to the map I made, we're near an optimal location for a dragon's lair. Now, I'll be fine, Kali, but if you stick around, it will only cause me to lose my concentration worrying over your safety."

"I understand," Kalisen said, surprising him, but quickly added, "Of course you'll need help loading up the treasure, so I'll hide behind a tree and join you once your work is done."

"I'm sorry, Kali—no. Your father would kill me if he knew you were in harm's way. I really need you to listen to me on this one." Sweating in his armor, despite the cold, Trendle removed his helm and wiped his brow, then glanced around. The helm had always limited his vision and he figured that if the dragon bit him on the head, the helm wouldn't do much good anyway. Even so, he had worn it for that's what knights do.

"Trendle . . ." Kalisen said, her voice barely a whisper. She rested her small hands on his vambraces and had a serious look on her face. "You might want to take your sword out now. I recognize this place. There's a large cave midway up that hill, and a smaller one on the far side. The dragon's there. I know it."

Trendle glanced up at the hills and then fixed his eyes on Kalisen, "You promise me whatever happens, Kali, you'll not go looking for trouble, nor worry about me?"

"You say that like I won't see you again. You're scaring me."

"I'm sorry. I just meant that, you have your whole life ahead of you, and worrying never changes anything. Whatever happens was supposed to happen. Now you'd better go. You mean too much to me to see you in harm's way."

"I do?" she smiled.

Again, he felt something stir within him. "Yes, you're a dear friend."

"A friend . . ." she repeated, her smile fading. It was replaced by an odd look he couldn't quite discern.

"Yes. My best friend," the knight said. He took a deep breath, and without another word, walked over to the cart and pulled out his shield.

When he turned back again, he noticed Kalisen had been wiping at the corner of her eyes. He leaned the shield against one leg and was about to don his helm when Kalisen said, "You have a good heart, Trendle. You're a swell knight, really, and I like you a lot—but . . . you don't have to do this and I won't think any less of you—"

"Kali . . ."

"Okay, okay. I'm going, but keep your shield up," she said, seeming to barely hold her tears at bay.

Trendle nodded and took his helm in his hands and lifted it up to slide it down over his head when he felt Kalisen's arms wrap around him once again.

With her high elven stature, Kalisen didn't have to stand on her tiptoes when she suddenly kissed him on the lips. She released him and took a step back.

Trendle had only been kissed once before—when he was visiting a neighbor's farm with his father. He'd only been seven or eight at the time. The girl was much older and bigger than he was, and caught him alone and off-guard. He remembered how she shoved him down into the mud and then straddled him near the feeding pens and kissed him hard, again and again till he could no longer breathe. Then she laughed and ran off behind the barn.

Trendle just stood there staring at Kalisen until she finally smiled and said, "Don't get killed on me, Trendle."

Realizing he had been staring, Trendle nodded. "I won't," he said, and then slid his helm over his head and drew his sword.

Kalisen turned around and ran back in the direction of town. Trendle stood as bravely as he could, holding back the tears until she was well out of view, then steeled himself and started up the hill.

The smell of dung became disarming as he drew nearer to the cave. It didn't take long to spot the source of the abomination, a dark pool midway up the hillside near the smaller mouth of the cave. It was partially concealed by a cluster of bushes. Anxious to get out of view in case the dragon wasn't inside, but circling high above, Trendle slipped inside the opening of the smaller cave. Hoping the beast was home and sound asleep, he edged slowly forward. With the sunlight peeking through the opening behind him, his shadow led him down the tunnel.

Then he heard it, snoring loudly. Stopping several times to listen and gather his nerve, Trendle finally drew his shield in close to his chest, tightened his grip on his longsword, and moved on until he was within thirty feet of the magical creature. He stood silently for a moment and watched its great bulk heaving up and down with each breath. It was a magnificent, yet frightful sight. It reminded him of seeing Kalisen's chest rising and falling with each breath. She was breathtaking and frightening in her own way. He had more to tell her, and regretted not doing so before she left. Trendle was certain he would never see her again, but was glad for the friendship they had shared nonetheless.

The shadow reaper, now within close proximity of his target, no longer needed Trendle, and stood, solidifying just inches away from the knight's face. The creature grinned at the poor knight, and then exposed his cavernous, toothy mouth, so startling Trendle that the knight froze, unable to move. The reaper just stared at him, allowing the horror of its presence to sink in. He had no doubt fear was spreading through the knight like a forest fire.

Flustered, Trendle clumsily sliced at the air with his longsword, but the reaper had already become incorporeal again and the blade passed harmlessly through his midsection and left arm.

The reaper stood there grinning and made no move to dodge the knight's blade.

Trendle swung again, this time striking the side of the tunnel with a loud clang that awoke the dragon. The knight ran back out of the cave faster than the reaper thought possible for one in armor. Accidentally bumping into the side of the entrance with his shield, the knight tumbled down the steep hillside.

The reaper slipped back into the shadows as the dragon stirred. Its large, piercing eyes snapped open and searched the room as its long snout sniffed the air. The fire dragon unfurled its massive wings. Its tail swept over the gold-strewn cave like a great log, ready to trip any would-be assassins.

The muscles on its limbs rippled under its weight, as it rose to full height and stretched, pushing sleep from its limbs and stealing a peek down the narrow tunnel.

"Yes . . . perfect," the reaper whispered from its hiding spot in plain view as a mere cave shadow. For a moment, the dragon seemed to stare right at him, then ducked its head down, tucked in its wings, and lumbered down the larger of the two tunnels.

Unable to control his descent, Trendle landed face first in the pool of dragon dung. He told himself it was only mud to ease his mind, but his nose knew better. Somewhere in the muck was his shield. Abandoning his search for it, he waded to edge of the pool and began climbing out, then stopped as the dragon burst forth from the main tunnel in a cloud of dust and pebbles.

Trendle watched in horror as the great, crimson wyrm spread its wings to their full glory. He lowered himself back into the cesspool and tried to ignore the slush oozing into his ears and down around his eyes, raising his eyebrows to stave off the flow long enough to determine the dragon's intent. Not only did the pool break his fall, leaving him with a larger bruise on his ego than on his body, it also had the effect of concealing his scent, for which he was grateful.

With angry emerald eyes, the dragon scanned the hillside and then the Vraeden Forest beyond, scrutinizing every bush and tree for something out of place. One great beat of its wings carried it to the bottom of the hill. In the waning sun, the dragon's scales seemed less brilliant than Trendle had expected, though no less formidable. He'd heard that being slammed by a great wyrm's wing alone could snap a man's back, and the weight of its tail could crush a man. Their great claws were said to be like swords, long and deadly. He aimed not to find out.

Sniffing the air for signs of the intruder, the fire dragon clawed at the ground in frustration and then angrily spewed fire into the air, before returning to its lair.

Trendle had ducked back down, submerging into the filth. He held his breath until his whole body tightened like a vise, desperate for release. *Better to face the dragon and die like a man than cower in muck*, he thought. But he made no move to retrieve his sword, which was lying only a few feet away. He came up for air several times, but it was nearly an hour before he crawled free of the dung pool and fled into the wilderness.

Never had anything gripped him, controlled him, held him so utterly powerless than when his shadow took form and faced him. It had been even more startling than the dragon itself. The whole affair chilled him to the bone as he tried to make sense of what had happened. He tried flushing the memories from his mind, but the smell of sulfur and dung clung to him—and the realization of something worse, something much worse.

"Make every encounter an opportunity to learn and grow," he reminded himself what his father had said so many years before. "Learn from your fear." The words held no more comfort now than they had then, but they were starting to make sense to him.

He no longer felt compelled to face the dragon—not when it was awake, and not with that shadow demon lurking about. Still, the dragon was a creature of flesh and bone, at least. He could imagine it as a huge animal, and get a sense for how it thought and fought. *But how can I hope to defeat a creature with no more tangibility than my own shadow? I would need an enchanted sword at the very least*, he realized.

An even weightier matter troubled him. While he had always tried to please his father, deep down, he knew he was never meant to be a knight. Now that he'd actually seen the dragon, he figured at best he would only manage to anger the beast, which would put Muldon's residents in further danger. Further, confronting the dragon meant honoring his father, not himself. While he desired to honor his father, he was no longer certain that facing a dragon was necessary, and did not believe he was called to die this day.

Ironically, it was his father's own advice that finally prompted Trendle to leave the knighthood. For a moment he'd felt as if he were running away, but then he realized what he was actually doing was taking a stand, confronting his own destiny. His encounter in the dragon's lair had indeed taught him something about himself. From now on I'm Trendle—not

Trendle the Knight, and certainly not Trendle the Sewing Knight, or the Farm Knight— just Trendle. For the first time in his life, that was enough.

Discarding his smelly armor, Trendle bathed in the river before heading off into the Vraeden forest to start a new life. He would miss Volensidar and especially Kali, but hoped at least she would understand his decision. With any luck, the dragon would tire of Muldon and move on, and the shadow demon would return to whatever hell it crawled out of. Whatever the case, Trendle knew his destiny lay elsewhere.

Never revealing himself to his host, the shadow reaper was careful to keep the dragon just weak enough that it stayed home and harmless. The dying wyrm no longer had the strength to leave its lair, much less offer any serious challenge.

Now that he had tamed the great beast, the reaper found he was growing restless, even bored with his daily torture routine. Soon, he would have to begin the hunt anew, and wondered whom he would shadow next. Dragons were near the top of the food chain, but he realized with a sinking heart that he actually preferred clever hosts to powerful ones. Many dragons were clever, though this one seemed less so, and the reaper's thoughts kept returning to Lance, who had seemed mediocre at first, but revealed a potential the reaper had not expected. He hoped he would meet another who could offer a serious challenge and keep him from dying of boredom.

One afternoon, the reaper found a piece of architechnology hidden amid the gold and gems in the dragon's lair. The creature switched to its solid form to study the device more closely, finding it fascinating. Having spent the previous three days tormenting its now dozing host, within a short time, the reaper too fell asleep.

An hour or so later, the enchanted beast must have rolled onto its side, for the reaper was nearly crushed to death. The reaper had to switch back to its incorporeal state in order to escape, for great was the dragon's weight bearing down on him. After that, the reaper was much more careful to stay incorporeal and was in such a state that it was days before he continued his work. By then, the reaper was in a foul mood, and simply killed the dragon outright.

Curious, the reaper glanced about for the exotic technology it had found earlier, and realized the dragon's corpse was likely lying on top of it. Briefly, the reaper considered the other treasures heaped in piles around the drag-on's lifeless body and grinned. He made himself comfortable and waited, knowing it was just a matter of time.

The last thing Trendle wanted was to run into someone he knew, as that meant answering difficult questions. But traveling without provisions was hardly a proper way to start a new life. Trendle had returned from the attic he was renting on the edge of town where he had grabbed his coat and the last of his munchies: a leather bag of nuts, raisins and cheese. The former knight was pleased that the attic was accessible by an external staircase, as he was able to go in quietly without being noticed. Still, he felt guilty sneaking around. As it was, he'd run through his food stores almost immediately and spent most of his time hunting and gathering edibles in the forest, and wood for the fire.

So far, near as he could tell, no one had seen him, but he had no horse nor bog, tent nor other special provisions, only the clothes on his back and his sword. Even his armor had been left behind in the forest, for it reminded him of his past—a life that was dead and gone.

The night was especially frigid and the bone cold breeze only enhanced it, so Trendle dragged his log up closer to the fire pit. He hugged himself to stay warm until the fire grew, and wished he'd bought a thicker coat when he'd had the money. For hours, he just sat and stared at the fire till he began to doze and nearly fell off the log. Realizing he was too close to the fire and might roll into it should he doze again, he stood up and dragged the log back far enough that he could lie down and use it as a pillow. As he did so, he heard a noise and drew his blade, his knightly training kicking in instinctively.

Paranoid, he scrutinized every tree and bush for what seemed like hours. Smoke filled his nostrils and made him squint. Surrounded by shadows, he knew he was vulnerable. Haunted by dark memories, he wanted to run, but held his ground. Finally, he told himself it must have been a rodent or other smallish critter and sheathed his dagger, returning to the fire.

Late in the night, he heard a voice and sat up with a start, realizing he was now on the ground beside the fire—and a bit too close at that. Scrambling to his feet, Trendle drew his sword and spun around to face the darkness.

"Easy now, I'm just a traveler myself and that fire would do my old bones good, if you don't mind a little company?" a stranger said, holding a bow with an arrow nocked. "I mean you no harm—if you feel likewise."

Trendle saw him lower his weapon, but the bowstring was still taut. *His voice is too deep and confident to be a child, and he's too lanky for a dwarf,* he thought. *He's dressed like a warrior. A short warrior.* "I'd prefer to be alone actually," Trendle replied, able to make out little more than a shadow shaped like a short human wearing a longcoat. Again, he considered running, but remained rooted beside the fire. *He relaxed the tension on the bow and now the arrow's gone. I didn't see his hand move. He's quick, and could have killed me as I slept.* "I suppose that'd be all right," he said finally, having changed his mind.

"I'm sorry if I startled you," the stranger said and stepped within the firelight. Though close enough that Trendle felt certain he should have been able to make out the stranger's features, oddly, the visitor was still draped in shadows.

"Why are you concealing your appearance?" Trendle asked, drawing his sword once more. The grip was ice cold. He almost dropped the blade, but remained perfectly still, staring at the shadows clinging to the man's face.

"Sorry, but I'm a skree. My kind was fashioned from the Shadow Realm. I sometimes forget to withdraw the shadow magic flowing around me. I know it makes people feel uncomfortable, but it was dark, so I thought nothing of it. I'm afraid I'm not used to being around others." As he spoke, the shadows withdrew . . . and Trendle noticed the man's skin was purplish, and his ears were similar to an elf's.

"A skree? I've never seen one before, though I've heard . . . well, if you've come to rob me, I have to warn you I have nothing of value. You should also know I'm a knight and—"

"As I said, I've just come for the fire."

After a moment, Trendle said, "Why are you out skulking in the middle of the night?"

"I was sleeping in the woods but heard a noise. I'd stay in Muldon, but they don't seem fond of my kind."

"Uh-huh."

"My name's Gaerdrik. I'm a bounty hunter, though I confess I haven't had a contract in too long. May I?" He pointed at the fire.

Trendle nodded yes. He felt more at ease and even a sense of commonality with the stranger now. "I've never felt welcome in Muldon, either, nor anywhere else for that matter. My name's Trendle."

"So you're a knight? I would think you'd be welcomed in Muldon. They have need of protection, after all. Being a knight must be glamorous."

"Not really, but the truth is, I just quit."

"Ah, well, I'm not trying to pry. Don't feel like you have to explain to me. I'm sure you had reasons for—"

"I don't deserve the title of knight," Trendle said, struggling to hold back the floodwaters of his mind. "I was never meant to be a knight and now I'm not." Trendle thought he was done talking. He wished he could just go back to sleep and never wake again. *Maybe it would have been better had he slain me in my sleep. I'm no use to anyone.* Somewhere within Trendle's troubled mind, a dam broke and all he'd been holding back since childhood flooded out of his mouth. He felt helpless to close it. Before he knew it, he'd told of how his father pressured him into becoming a knight. How he had accidentally killed a pig, and other blunders. And he told of how the townsfolk made fun of him.

He mentioned how he stood before a sleeping dragon and was about to go into the gory details, when the tears began falling, and instead, he summed it up with, "I entered the cave . . ."

"Really, there's no need to—"

"I fled. I was . . . terrified. The whole town was counting on me and I failed them. I'm a coward and don't deserve the title of knight." After that, he dragged the log back toward the fire and sat down. Exhausted, Trendle fixated on the flames once more.

It was a long time before either of them spoke again. Finally, Gaerdrik sat down beside him and pulled a small leather pouch out of his longcoat and started fiddling with its contents. The bounty hunter had several parts in his hands and was trying to fit them together. He tried for a half hour and had only managed to become frustrated.

"It doesn't look broken, just in pieces," Trendle said, glancing over. "It's better if you don't force the components. If they're meant to fit together, they will."

"If you know so much, you try it," Gaerdrik said and handed him the pouch and pieces in his hand.

"You sure that's all of them?" Trendle asked.

Gaerdrik nodded. "Someone bumped into me in town and I dropped it. The thing just fell apart. Be careful. I'm not sure if it's a weapon or . . . it's not from around here. It's not even from Cathor, I reckon."

"It was a good find, then," Trendle said with a smile. "I can't promise anything. I haven't had much luck lately, but I'm pretty good at fixing things." He began analyzing the components.

"I don't have any money to pay you if you fix it, but maybe I can trade you something?"

"Why? You need my help and I have nothing better to do," Trendle said with a shrug and snapped two pieces together. "I've found exotic technology before in my travels." Trendle's tongue lingered in the corner of his open mouth as he worked. "I've always been good with puzzles. You just have to know which order the pieces go in and have a little patience."

"It's amazingly lightweight. I've no idea what it's made of," Gaerdrik said, watching Trendle work. He stood up for a few moments and rubbed his hands together over the fire and then shoved them back into the pockets of his longcoat and sat down again, his eyes never leaving the device in

Trendle's hands.

"It has a few scratches on it, but I don't think it's broken," Trendle said, adding, "That doesn't mean I can get it to do anything. I still have no idea what its function is, but it isn't like the other technology I've found. It's . . . a simpler design, actually, though still far beyond anything the artificers of Vraedia have produced, I'd wager if I were a gambler." He rotated a strangely shaped piece several times before realizing another fit inside it like a glove. Finding a socket that looked like a good match, Trendle slid the combined pieces inside the socket and heard a satisfying snap.

"You've gotten a lot farther than I ever have!"

Trendle smiled, finding the puzzle challenging, but also deeply satisfying. He was pleased too that Gaerdrik approved. It felt good to know someone appreciated him. Someone beside Kalisen. The sudden thought of her weighed heavily on him and he did his best to push her out of his thoughts. She was tied to his past life, and though he knew he would miss her terribly, he felt he was doing what was best for both of them.

A few minutes passed in silence and then Trendle heard himself say what was on his mind again. "My father thought puzzles were a waste of time, but I think they help teach you to be observant. Of course, puzzles don't save towns from dragons . . . or other creatures."

"You never know," Gaerdrik said. "I've seen some strange things in my time."

After a moment, Trendle nodded. "Me, too. Very scary, strange things and you never know what experiences—or puzzles—might help you defeat your next problem."

"Trendle, you know why I don't hunt dragons?"

The ex-knight shrugged.

"Because I don't have what it takes. Not yet. Maybe never will."

"I tried to tell my father I wouldn't make a good knight, but he wouldn't listen," Trendle said.

Gaerdrik sighed deeply. "You know it isn't cowardice to stop doing something you weren't meant to. You stood up when no one else would."

"I don't want to talk any more about it, Gaerdrik. I ran. Period."

"But first you took a stand. That's something to be proud of."

"I said I don't want to—"

"You tried," Gaerdrik said more firmly. "Trendle, that's more than many would do. How many in town came with you to face the dragon?"

Only Kalisen, Trendle thought. *And I sent her away.* He didn't regret that decision, but was surprised merely thinking of her had dredged up memories and feelings he didn't care to entertain.

Gaerdrik continued. "You had the wisdom to recognize your own limitations. And you had the courage to stand again and to take a different path. It might not have been what others wanted, but it was what was right for you."

"I . . . I ran." *I didn't take another path. I'm still running,* Trendle thought, ashamed.

"You started over. There's no shame in that," the bounty hunter said.

Can I start over? Once they find out what a failure I am . . . What would I even do?

Trendle bit his lower lip till it nearly bled, steeled himself and focused on the task at hand. Almost immediately when Gaerdrik had handed him the parts, Trendle had noticed a depressed area—a button, if he wasn't mistaken, on the shell that housed the puzzle's various components. It was then that he found two small pebbles wedged in between the button and the housing. Taking out a knife, he pried out the pebbles, then slid two pieces of the housing together until they snapped into place over the internal components. Together they formed a disk that was flattish on one end and bulged out on the other to accommodate an oval of glass-like material. He'd never seen anything like it. On a whim, he reached his hand into the parts bag and felt around to make sure it was empty and frowned when he found a small component inside. He took out the tiny part and held it between his lips as he began taking the whole thing apart again.

"What are you doing? You had it!" Gaerdrik said, sounding frustrated.

Trendle showed him a small coil he found. "This is supposed to go inside somewhere." He squinted to see what he was doing.

"You sure that little piece is needed? It's so small."

Trendle nodded. "Sometimes it's the smallest of things that make the most difference in life. I'm afraid I need more light."

"I have that going for me, at least," Gaerdrik said, adding, "I can see perfectly fine in the moonlight, but when it comes to puzzles, I have no idea what I'm doing."

"If you would be so kind," Trendle said, standing, "do me a favor and help me move this log closer to the fire."

Almost immediately, Trendle dropped the tiny coil and they spent the next ten minutes searching for it.

"Found it!" Gaerdrik said, finally, and handed Trendle the tiny piece. "Sorry—guess it would have been better for us to wait till morning."

"Yes, that would have been easier, but it has been a fun distraction, none-theless," Trendle said. Once he had sorted out the only place the coil fit inside the device that would allow it to interact with other components, he was able to reassemble it much faster, remembering how it all fit together. "Sometimes you have to . . . no," Trendle said, after pressing down on the button and nothing happened. He took it apart again and reassembled it, this time flipping over one of the nearly symmetrical components and reinserting it on a whim.

Once back together, he pressed the button again and a beam of light lanced out, flooding the immediate area as if a sunbeam had dropped out of the sky. Startled, he almost dropped it.

"You did it, Trendle. You fixed it!"

"You just press it here," Trendle said, smiling, and pressed the button again with his finger. The light died away, after which, he handed it back to Gaerdrik.

"Excellent work, Trendle," Gaerdrik said, smiling as he slid the disk back into his pocket. "You sure you don't want something in trade?"

"No, I've never taken payment for fixing things."

"You should. It's a talent."

"It's a hobby," Trendle said with a shrug. "I'm glad I was able to help. That's reward enough." A moment later his stomach grumbled and he added, "Unless you've got a little food. My stomach isn't very happy with me, I'm afraid."

"I think I've got some jerky left," Gaerdrik said and rifled through his pack. He brought out some jerky and a chunk of bread and gave Trendle half of what he had.

"Thanks!" Trendle said and smiled again. Aside from Kali and her father—now part of his past life—he didn't have any friends. He just wanted to put his past behind him, and start fresh, though he still hadn't sorted out what he was going to do next.

They sat around the fire well into the night—mostly just dozing, but talking too at times, and Trendle was surprised how much they had in common.

Gaerdrik pulled the device out of his pocket again and pushed the button, marveling at the light it produced.

"It's amazing how bright the light is, considering it's not even magical," Trendle said as he put some dry branches onto the fire. "At least I didn't see any parts that appeared arcane in origin. I must admit, I don't know much about magic, but I've seen technology like that before. No one on Cathor knows how to make it—that much I'm sure of."

Gaerdrik nodded, flicked the button again and stowed the strange object in his pocket without another word.

"I'm sorry if you were hoping it was a weapon. I guess you being a skree, you won't have much use for a light source. I've heard the Masked Man who lives in the Vraedon Forest collects gadgets like that. I'm sure there are plenty of people who would pay well for it."

"Wild magic," Gaerdrik muttered.

"That's what most everyone in the kingdom calls it, but I don't believe there's any magic to it. I don't know how it works, maybe it's part mechanical and part magical. I dunno. The artificers in Brandal called such devices architechnology."

"If you say so, but it looks like magic to me."

Trendle glanced at the shadowy trees surrounding them and shivered. He was pleased to have company on a night like this—on any night these days. "Most of the exotic technology I've found over the years was broken, or maybe it just needed fuel—magic or something to make it work. I hear there are enchantments for that sort of thing—as long as an artificer has a bit of fuel left or knows what it needs, they can use magic to make more."

Nodding, Gaerdrik said, "I've heard as much. Sword work is not an easy thing, but I've never been able to wrap my head around magic, so I stick with what I know. Technology might as well be magic—it all makes my mind hurt when I think of it, but I find it stimulating just the same."

Trendle picked up a branch and stoked the fire as he scanned the forest around them. As with staring up at the daytime clouds, he now saw shapes, some of which, if they really were what he imagined, would doom them both. But they were just shadows. *Just shadows?* he thought, knowing he'd never look at another shadow the same again, and shivered.

The fire snapped and drew his attention back to the present. The former knight scolded himself for being paranoid and turned back to Gaerdrik. "I've found a few intact gadgets, but haven't had much luck fixing the broken ones. I spend a lot of time by myself and enjoy trying to put things back together again. Most of the time I can't get the things to work, or I get them to work for a time and then . . ."

"Maybe it is just a matter of fuel, and they simply run out, like you said," Gaerdrik offered.

"Maybe," Trendle said, adding, "just like how a f'lantii runs on magic. I once found an automaton—a little armored man, like a boy's doll, that could move and talk some. Well, after spending two weeks working on it, I finally got it to move around on its own. It said a few words in a language I didn't understand." He laughed recalling how the little soldier ran around in circles, bumping into things. "It worked for about twenty minutes and then just stopped. Never did get it working again."

"Well, you're very good at it. You're a mechanic, if you ask me. I think I'll hold onto this latest find. I've already thought of a possible use for it."

"I could have used one of those while I was trying to see well enough to repair it," Trendle said and then yawned deeply. He sat back down onto the log and sighed pleasantly.

A few minutes later, Gaerdrik said, "I don't suppose you know how to read Traders Tongue? I copied something down in my journal the other day and have been dying to ask someone to read it for me."

"My father taught me to read Traders Tongue when I was a boy, but it has been a few years since I've needed it."

"Why Traders Tongue?" Gaerdrik asked. "Sure, plenty of folks speak it in Vraedia, but most signs and documents I've seen are written in Tathra, or one of the major languages like elven, dwarven or gnomish."

"My father had a book written in Traders Tongue on swordplay and made me read it and practice the techniques. It's an old language, but it's more common in the western kingdoms where my father was born. It's still in use in many regions, though not so much the written word. But there's no saying, 'No,' to my father. Show me."

"It can wait till morning," Gaerdrik said and smiled, stifling a yawn of his own. "Then I'll be on my way and won't bother you again."

"No, it's okay," Trendle said, rather enjoying Gaerdrik's company. He motioned at the outer pocket on Gaerdrik's longcoat as he continued, "so long as you let me read it with your—"

"Lightbringer?" Gaerdrik said with a smile.

"You named it after Kane, the god of light," Trendle remarked and returned the gesture. "That's what his priests call him, I believe. It's a good name, Gaerdrik. I think it does him justice."

"I thought so, too. Some don't like Kane because he opposed the goddess Mithra for choosing peace over vanquishing evil. But there's a time for peace and a time for war, too. We must each know what we're called to, otherwise we're just taking up space, going through the motions."

Trendle felt his stomach turn and looked away. "I feel like that now. No clear path before me. No purpose. I'm not lazy, mind you. I'm just not sure what I'm meant to do."

"Oh, I didn't mean you, Trendle. Every new journey requires a time of introspection and planning. You'll find your way. I know you will. Anyway, I like writing my thoughts down in a journal. You might try it sometime. It can be calming."

"I dunno. Sometimes my thoughts scare me . . ."

Gaerdrik stared at him for a moment and then shrugged. "Well, not everything we think is worth quoting, but even our doubts can be helpful to note. I find that even in my darkest moments—if I try, I can usually think of something uplifting. A new dawn for every dusk, as they say."

Trendle nodded, but he wasn't sure what he thought. And he wasn't sure he was ready yet to face a new day.

Gaerdrik continued, "We shouldn't ignore our worries, Trendle, but we should make a point to focus the bulk of our attention on making the best of things."

Trendle just stared at the skree, astounded by his words. *I've never met anyone like him,* he thought. He watched as the bounty hunter opened his longcoat and took out a leather-bound journal.

Flipping to a particular page, Gaerdrik seemed about to hand it to Trendle, when he stopped and said, "I waterproofed one of my pockets to keep it safe. Are your hands clean?"

Trendle recalled how he, too, liked to keep his things properly maintained. *I'm so glad I managed to retrieve my tools from the attic before leaving town,* he thought. *I understand completely.* He stared down at his left hand in the firelight.

"Here," Gaerdrik said, and shined Lightbringer on Trendle's hands.

Trendle frowned and wiped his hands on his sides, then held them out for inspection. "They're pretty clean, I think," he said.

"All right," Gaerdrik said and handed over Lightbringer and the journal. He pointed at the crude letters on the right side of the page.

There was a drawing of a pretty, young woman on the left-hand page and Trendle's eyes were drawn to it. "Did you draw this? It shows much talent. She a friend of yours?"

Gaerdrik nodded sheepishly, "From a long time ago. I keep drawing her. I don't know why. I'll never see her again . . . but I didn't want to forget what she looks like, and I enjoy practicing my sketching."

"You're a good artist," Trendle noted and was reminded of Kali. A sadness swept over him. "She's pretty."

"Never mind her, Trendle. Can you read that?" he said, pointing again at the letters on the right-facing page. "I copied it the best I could. It was written in blood."

"Blood?" Trendle said, and chewed on the word for a moment before reading the words. There were only four words. "No shadows, no threat." He said. Returning the journal and Lightbringer with a shrug, he added, "Don't know what that's supposed to mean, but that's what it says."

Gaerdrik slipped the journal inside his longcoat and took a deep breath, letting it out slowly.

Trendle wondered what Gaerdrik had seen and why someone would write anything in blood, but figured he'd ask in the morning. He had so many questions—so much to think about, but he was tired, too. It was far past his bedtime and he knew he would pay for it in the morning. Even so, he was glad they had met and decided a new dawn might not be such a bad thing after all.

Gaerdrik stared down at Lightbringer. "Thanks, Trendle. That actually confirms something I've been suspecting for quite some time now," he said, stowing the device. "I think I know what I need to do."

"Well, I've finally sorted out what I'm meant to do, too!"

"You have? That's great news!"

"Yes," Trendle said and smiled. "I'm meant to get some sleep. Good night, my new friend. It has been a pleasure," he said, still smiling, and sat down on the ground before the fire. He removed his boots and let the fire warm his toes. Leaning his head back against the log, he shut his eyes and sighed.

"Sleep well, my friend, and thanks again," Gaerdrik said.

Trendle heard the skree get down onto the ground and then the log shifted slightly as the bounty hunter joined him.

"As I said, I'll be leaving first thing in the morning, but I do hope our paths cross again."

"Indeed," Trendle replied. It felt good to have a new friend, and Gaerdrik had said much that Trendle still wanted to think on. *I hope our paths do cross again . . .*

It was late in the morning when Trendle awoke, feeling refreshed and looking forward to talking with his new friend. Gaerdrik had said some things that encouraged him and made him think that perhaps things weren't as gloomy as he had thought. But when he glanced over, he saw that Gaerdrik had already gone. Once more, sadness came over him, but he chased it away. *This is a new day . . . and that's a good thing.*

Glancing up at the sky, he saw that he had slept in. Then he noticed a leather pouch resting on top of the log. Inside was a pound of dried fruits and nuts. Trendle was sad to see his new friend go, but was eager to start his new life. As he cleaned up in a brook nearby, he thought about all that the skree had said and decided to travel to Delathen and look for work as a mechanic. He doubted anyone knew him there, and that, too, was a good thing.

Realizing he hadn't taken a break since the day his father pushed him into the knighthood, Trendle decided to spend some time relaxing and improving his hunting skills first.

The old mill outside of town had fallen into disrepair when the owner died. His family lived in Harwik and were unable to find a buyer at the price they were asking. A few years later, as the property was slowly being reclaimed by nature, a more modern mill house was built further up stream, making it even less likely the old mill house would ever sell.

Rather than risk sleeping in the forest or hills where bandits and wild animals roamed, Trendle spent most nights in the old mill for a time. He stayed out of sight during the day and avoided the mill house's rickety staircase and the rotting planks in the floor.

When the time is right, I'll make my way to Delathen and start over there. Trendle smiled at the thought. While he had no idea what the future held, he knew one thing for sure: He wasn't running anymore.

A few days after Trendle's disappearance, Kalisen returned to the hillside where she had last seen him, and found Doc Catchet's cart. The bog harness was broken and the great lizard was nowhere to be found. As Trendle had told her dragons weren't known to eat bogs, she surmised it must have gotten spooked or hungry enough to break free of its harness and fled. She also found that she couldn't bring herself to enter the cave she'd played in as a child, afraid of what she might find there. She also decided not to tell Catchet she'd found his cart.

Weeks passed and rumors spread. Kalisen spent much of her spare time anguishing over Trendle's disappearance, and to assuage her own fears, came up with theories regarding his fate. There had been no dragon sightings since Trendle entered the cave, yet Doc Catchet had been telling everyone the knight was a coward and never even went into the dragon's lair.

Kalisen publicly praised Trendle's courage and prowess in combat, insisting he had vanquished the dragon. To strengthen her claim despite knowing her father wouldn't be pleased, she admitted she had hidden nearby and witnessed Trendle enter the cave before turning back for home. When asked why Trendle hadn't returned, she suggested that he simply went off in search of other towns and villages in need, rather than the idea that he lie dead inside the dragon's lair from wounds he'd suffered during battle. She had another theory, too, but kept it to herself.

As Catchet never could adequately explain the disappearance of the dragon, and because he'd always been an overbearing braggart, many in the town believed Kalisen's theory. Even so, she knew Catchet had been redoubling his efforts to deflate her version of Trendle as a hero.

Seeing the doctor on the road coming home from the marketplace, she decided to confront him in the hopes of ending their quarrel. She was nervous and her palms were sweating, but she knew it would be better to face him on the road than in the inn where he might rally support from Morse or others.

Kalisen ran to catch up. Without his cart, Catchet had to go everywhere on foot. Presently, he was carrying a basket of fruit and vegetables. "Doctor?"

"Ah, Kalisen, what a pleasure it is to see you," he said, frowning. "I was just thinking of you."

"You were?" Kalisen said, suspicious.

"Yes," Catchet continued. "I was having a good chuckle recalling the fanciful stories you've been telling about Trendle. You are as creative as you are clever, but we both know that's all they were—stories."

"I was there, Doctor. I saw Trendle enter the cave. You can't deny the dragon's gone!"

"I can't deny that out of the goodness of my heart, I loaned Trendle my cart, and he never brought it back! Now I have to go everywhere on foot. As Trendle's closest friend, I'm sure you wouldn't mind helping me get this basket home while we have a nice little chat?" He held the basket in his outstretched arms and wore a tired smile.

"I suppose . . ." Kalisen said with a sigh and took the basket. It was heavier than she thought it would be. *I should heed Papa's advice and just drop the whole thing, but for Trendle's sake—*

"Now then, what was it that you wanted to discuss?" Catchet said, continuing down the road at a faster pace.

Kalisen tried to keep up, but it wasn't easy with the heavy-laden basket. "I'll make you a deal."

"Oh? What sort of deal?" he said, walking faster still.

If it weren't for her long stride, Kalisen would have fallen behind. "In exchange for promising to retract your earlier comments and refrain from speaking ill of Trendle ever again, I'll take you to your cart and to where the dragon's treasure can be found. There's no way Trendle could have hauled off all the treasure on foot."

"There's no way Trendle could have defeated a dragon, either!" Catchet said. "I don't know what he did, but that, I do know."

"If you didn't think he could do it, why'd you loan him your cart?"

"I assumed he had enough sense to attack it while it was sleeping. How hard can it be to slay a sleeping dragon? Now that I think of it, Trendle could screw that up . . ."

"Please, just . . . you want your cart back, don't you?"

Catchet stared at her for a moment, but didn't say anything.

Kalisen's arms were aching and her legs begged to stop, but she kept going.

"My cart is the very least that I am due," he said. After a moment, he added, "Frankly, young lady, I don't believe there is a treasure to be had, but I am tiring of this whole affair as well."

Kalisen's spirits lifted. "You'll need to bring along your other bog as the one you loaned Trendle fled. I presume the dragon scared it off."

"Oh, I'm sure that must have been it. I'm sure Trendle didn't steal the bog to use it to get as far away from the dragon as he could. Yes, you must be right."

"I told you, I saw him go inside! Besides, Trendle doesn't like riding. It makes him woozy—just a little. But with the dragon's treasure, you could buy as many bogs as you like."

Catchet sighed. "I'm sure," he said in a way that made Kalisen think he was anything but sure. "If you know where my cart is, then take me to it, girl, and I won't say another word about Trendle."

"You promise?"

"Yes, I promise."

"And you'll take back what you said—publicly?"

"If I get the dragon's treasure I'll take back everything I said. Now, hurry up!"

Kalisen nodded and smiled to herself. After a moment, she looked up at him and said, "It's a deal, then!"

"Yes, it would seem to be. Come around first thing in the morning and we'll head out. I hope it isn't far."

"It isn't," she said with a smile, and found the strength to continue on.

Kalisen got up extra early the next morning, finished her chores, and met up with Doc Catchet. His hireling was there with a fresh bog, and pulled the lizard along behind them. Kalisen led them out past the old mill and to the cart and cave, but didn't enter, fearing what she might find there.

Catchet waited outside the cave with Kalisen, while his hired hand investigated the cave's depths. As they were waiting, Kalisen recalled her Papa's warnings about not associating with the doctor. She realized that once Catchet had the treasure in hand, there would be nothing to keep him from breaking his promise to her. She feared she had betrayed Trendle somehow, and ran all the way home in tears.

A few days later, when Volensidar sent her into town to buy supplies, she was surprised to hear everyone talking about Doc Catchet. Apparently his maid found him lying dead in bed, covered with running sores from head to foot. Locked up in his barn was a cartload of gold.

Slowly, almost imperceptibly, Lance became aware that he was awake, and with that awareness came the certainty that he had been changed forever. A strange calmness had come over him and he no longer fought to free himself, to breathe, to stop hurting, to live. He hadn't given up—quite the opposite, but such matters didn't weigh heavily on him. The urgency to escape had passed. The pain was gone. *I should be freaking out. I should be in pain,* he thought. *What's happened to me? Am I dreaming? I've gone bangy. Brain dead. No, that's not it, but something's definitely wrong—or right.*

He felt the need to both eat and drink, but they were duller sensations, no longer screaming for his attention. As before, he felt the roughness of his odorous rug coffin, but with his pain now absent, he thought of it more as a cocoon. Something had changed that he didn't understand. The stench of his own diseased flesh, blood and poison remained. There was a smell of dried mud and filth, too, but he was in no pain. And that was as intensely satisfying as it was baffling. Even so, his calm demeanor remained. Staying sane amid his circumstances wasn't so much a conscious act as it was a condition he was simply aware of. *The calm before the storm? I can't just stay here forever . . .*

Lance moved his head, straining to see more. As he did so, he let in a little light. He could not, however, see outside his prison. He felt something move near his mouth, and he twitched. *Something's in here with me! It's attached itself to my face and neck,* he thought, once more catching a panic. He glanced down to see what it was, but that cut off his light source. He thrashed, but knew it was hopeless. *I've tried this before. I—*he stopped struggling and managed to calm himself once more, though he knew not how. *Whatever it is, it doesn't hurt. It doesn't seem to be eating me. It's just—itchy.*

I've grown a beard, he realized. Leaning his head as far down as he could and turning it side to side while working his jaw, he felt the ends of his beard tickling the hairs on his neck, and the hairs above his lip tickled his nose. He sighed in relief.

It feels like hundreds of little worms crawling on my face and neck, just as with the beards I've tried to grow in the past. That's why I gave up on the idea of wearing a beard in the first place. That's what I feel every time. I wonder if it ever goes away? This one feels long and thick, too. It takes me weeks to grow a modest beard. Months to grow one as thick as this one feels. How long have I been sleeping? Days? Weeks? I should be dead. I should be, but I'm not—or if I am, this is all moot, though still very curious.

Why am I alive? There must be a reason. Am I alive so that I can kill the shadow reaper? It's my fault it's running loose down here, after all. As he considered this, he reminded himself that such a thing could only happen if there were an intelligence behind it—if this wasn't an accident. He also realized that he didn't desire to get revenge, so much as protect others from the creature. *I wish I could kill it, but at the very least, people need to know what they are up against,* he thought. *Who knows how many it might have already killed?* The thought crushed his spirit and made him feel miserable all over again.

Recalling his earlier vision, the words his grandmother had spoken in secret when he was just a little boy, returned to him now.

"I know you made him special, just like his father. As his newfound abilities awaken, help him to use them wisely. And to turn to you and never let go." She had said other things and he recalled them as well, and they brought him comfort.

A clarity came over him as baffling as the calmness he felt. It was then he remembered the orc superhero, Toro, and what Nevins and Harding had said about augments. *That's it. That's what I've become.* No other explanation made sense to him. *Unless the One Above All is keeping me alive like he did Jonah inside the fish. Or perhaps he died, and I died, too, and was brought back? Or Jonah was an augment, too? No, he brought Jonah back to complete his mission, whether he was an augment or not. That, I'm sure of, just as he has brought me back. The only thing I can think of that would come close to a mission would be my desire to stop that creature from killing anyone else.*

Whether by the One Above all, the GodStorm or by trauma, or all three, I've been given a second chance. I don't know how long I have to live, he thought, and threw his shoulders to one side and then the other again and again. *But I know one thing— I'm not going to spend the time I have left cooped up in a hole.* He tried kicking backwards with his legs, but still couldn't budge them. *No. I can move them, just not much,* he realized. He stopped squirming and focused on his feet, realizing he'd given up too soon before. *Now that I'm calmer and can think clearly . . .*

Lance took several deep breaths and relaxed his mind and body, then pushed his legs as straight as he could, contracted them, and then repeated the movements. It seemed fruitless, but after ten minutes or so, he noticed he could straighten them a little, and the weight on his back had lessened. *If I can do that, I can do more,* he decided, and he was right.

Over the next forty minutes, he exercised, rolling from side to side, followed by leg thrusts while lifting his chest as far as he could. He took breaks between each set, careful not to overexert himself. Every inch of the rug was wet, which also meant it was hard to gain traction.

If I were a worm, this prison would have been easy to escape. It would be even easier, if I were the shadow creature. All I would have to do is—

His thoughts were shattered by an intense vision that commandeered his senses and made it impossible to see or think of anything else. Before his eyes, light appeared, and as it grew, he saw a cobblestone road, each bump in the road blocking his view as if he were a worm navigating among the cobblestones. Before him was a pair of legs. *Small feet wearing sandals. A child,* he realized.

The child was walking down the road past buildings. The feet came upon a rock and kicked it, then moved toward the rock and kicked it again. The view remained low, right at street level. A moment later, there was a sound off to the child's left—people were talking and the view swung toward the voices—two women walking along. They appeared to be human, young, carrying baskets of fruit and vegetables. The view swung away again, back to the feet. A minute later, the feet stopped and the view ascended until the child's entire body could be seen. It was a human boy. The child squatted down and watched a spider crawling over a discarded apple, or something that looked like an apple, save for its odd, bluish color. The boy lifted his foot to smash the spider, then paused, and lowered his foot down, kicked it aside, and continued walking.

What is this? Is this real? What's happening to me? Lance wondered, and as he considered if what he was seeing was real or not, the vision faded. He thought about the creature once more and again, the vision returned. At once, his mind focused on something else and the vision faded. *I think I was seeing through the reaper's eyes, and I could pick up emotions, little details— or maybe I only imagined them. It hasn't harmed the kid yet. It's following him home, though. Probably so it can take out his whole family. Whatever power has enabled me to survive also gave me the power to see through the creature, to understand what it's thinking—at least a little. I wonder what I could accomplish with more practice? What are my limitations? Does my power work only on the creature, or does it work on others, too?* He tried to focus on the boy he saw, wondering if he could see through the boy's eyes. *This is absurd. I don't even know if the boy exists. I could be hallucinating. Just try it. Utterly ridiculous,* he thought, but focused on the boy anyway. *Nothing.* He thought about the creature again, and once more he saw through its eyes. *It's in a town. I have to warn everyone, but how. I can't even . . .*

He continued his exercise with fresh determination. A few minutes later, when he was rolling side to side, he was rewarded with a small increase in his cocoon's diameter. *I must have loosened up the outer end of the rug. I've been laying on it the whole time,* he realized.

He pressed outward with his elbows and knees again and again as he rolled side to side.

Exhausted, he rested until he could no longer wait, fearing the child would be killed. The reaper is taking its time, shadowing the boy, but that won't last long. I have to get free! He continued moving despite his exhaustion. Soon, he felt the rug's diameter increase a little more, and then he was able to get his arms free enough to cross his chest, slide them up over his face and slowly force them over his head. Excited, he clawed at the slimy insides of the rug, trying to pull himself out, but it was too slippery and his jumper was impeding his progress. It had become bonded with the rug in places.

By now it must be completely ruined, he realized, and lowered a hand to unzip the front far enough for him to squirm out of it, thanks to the additional room. Once he had gotten free of it, he was able to roll onto his back, and within a minute or so, crawled free of the hole on his belly. Covered in sludge and breathing hard, he rested on the edge of the hole.

The sun was bright and hurt his eyes. He closed them and continued resting. A few minutes later, reminding himself that the reaper wasn't resting, he squinted and looked over his body. He was a mess, covered from head to toe in sludge, but was grateful to be free of the pain, and free of his prison. Wiping off as much of the sludge as he could from his body, he was surprised to find the skin smooth and hairless, free of any blemishes, and as soft as a baby's skin. Even the scar on his ring finger was gone. He'd had it since he was a boy playing with his father's knife.

He stared at the skin on his arms. No sunspots. No freckles, and best of all, no sores. Madness. He still had his beard, but as he ran his hand over his head, he realized he was bald. Lance gasped, startled by his new body, his augmented self. *Aside from being a little winded, I feel great,* he realized. *Better than I have in a long time.* He lay there trying to catch his breath, and thirstily drank in the fresh air. *I need clothes, and eventually some food and water. Aside from that, once I've rested a bit, I'm good to go. But go where?* He thought of the shadow reaper, and at once saw through its eyes. *It's still following the boy through town. The kid's standing in front of a bakery staring in the window . . .*

Lance ended the vision and pulled the now only partially buried rug out of the hole and spread it out flat before him. *I can't believe I was down in that filth,* he thought. Here and there were bits of flesh. Inside the jumper itself were long, gooey sheets of flesh. He found his bottle of pain meds, but there was nothing else worth taking. Even his boots were ruined.

My guns, the beamer, even that architechnological thingy I'd put in my cargo pocket is gone.

Somewhere in the wreckage is Lorego's pistol and more medical supplies. And… he gasped again, as a snapshot of Janys flashed across his mind and for several moments, he was gripped with sadness. *I'll never see her again. I'm not even sure where to look . . .*

Glancing around, he saw that he was likely in the same region as before, but he didn't recognize the tree line, and the rows of corn were further down. *This is a different field, but maybe the same farm. My ship can't be far from here. The farmer must have found my body and buried me. I need to get back to my ship, but the town needs me more. I have to warn them.*

He stood in his blood-stained CDF-approved underwear at the edge of the field and glanced around, spotting several tombstones. The graves were very small and he realized it must have been a pet cemetery. He tried to get his bearings, reviewing what he had seen shortly before crashing and then right after. *I didn't see much,* he realized. *It was dark when I brought the shuttle down. There. That's where Lorego had said the settlement was. I think. It shouldn't be far, but it's far enough that I can't afford to stand around. I'll stay close to the tree line. I should eventually come to a house or road.*

Lance tossed the jumper onto the rug, rolled it up again and pushed it down into the hole. A few steps from the hole was a shovel. He picked it up and then threw some shovelfuls of dirt on top of the decrepit rug. Behind him was a forest. *I'd better stay out of sight until I find some clothes and until I'm sure I won't be in any danger.* With a sigh, he walked a short distance into the woods and then followed the tree line.

He came upon another field where there were several cows standing around. On the far side of the fence were rows of corn. *That's probably the same corn,* he thought. *I doubt they loaded me up and carted me miles away just to bury me. Maybe whoever moved me dropped some of my things. It's close enough to check.* He risked going out into the open and then sprinted across the field with shovel in hand, running faster than he remembered being able to, and reached the far fence.

Walking along the fence line, he came upon a freshly painted plank. *This is it,* he realized. There were dried dots of paint on the grass below the newly painted plank. The area also smelled a little like him and there were flies about. *They must have painted over the message I wrote.* He quickly searched the grass on both sides of the fence and several yards in both directions along the fence line, but didn't find anything. He sighed in frustration, knowing he'd wasted precious time. *No, at least I know where I am now and I think I can find my way back to the ship from here.* He turned and glanced in the direction he believed the ship to be in and was tempted to go to it.

Lance recalled how thrashed the ship had looked in the moonlight, like the skeleton of some great giant. As he was imagining it, the ship appeared before his eyes as if he were standing at the back of it. There in the shadows, he saw the damaged hoverbed and he gasped at seeing the body lying there. Overcome with emotions, the vision quickly faded. "I'm so sorry, sweetheart. I'm so sorry . . ." he whispered. Beside the body of his wife, still sitting in the seat beside the hoverbed, was Lorego, covered in blood.

Lance's breath was ragged and his heart was racing like mad. He walked over and leaned against a fence post and tried to pull himself together. Reminding himself that the village boy was in danger, he ran along the fence line instead of crossing the field again. *I'll just dip into the cornfield if I need to hide,* he decided. As he ran, he wondered what else he was capable of.

Even if I find the shadow reaper, all I have is a shovel. I wasn't able to kill it with a gauss rifle, so unless I have the power to fire laser beams out of my eyes, this may not go well. Warning the community is the best I can hope for. He passed another field and saw a farmhouse in the distance. There was even a clothesline with clothes hanging from it, but they were all much too small. *Clothes for a girl,* he thought, and kept running.

Passing by a tree bearing the blue, apple-like fruit he'd seen in the vision, he snatched one and kept running, eating it as he went. *It tastes like a cross between an apple and a pear. Very sweet,* he realized, grateful for having found it. *I should have grabbed two! I wonder how long it's been since I've eaten? I don't have time to go back. Hopefully I'll see another apple tree along the way.*

Coming upon a road, he struggled to determine which way to go. Neither ran straight toward the location in his mind. He glanced as far as he could in both directions, picked the one that seemed the least discouraging, and took it, running as fast and far as he could until he grew tired. Then he rested for a few minutes and continued running. After a short time, he came upon a bridge. Stopping to catch his breath, he glanced over and found a shallow stream. He ran down a slope of grass and right out into the middle of the water and sat down. Splashing icy cold water all over himself, he began shivering, but didn't care.

Finding a deeper spot, he submerged his whole head into the water and scrubbed his bald scalp and face vigorously. He then began wiping down his body. A thought came to him and he quickly removed his head and wiped his eyes. *I sure hope this world doesn't have piranhas or anything like piranhas. Or eye biters for that matter. Anything that bites. I should have been more careful. This world may have sentient, humanoid life, but it's still an alien world. And looks can be deceiving. Those people in my vision may have looked like humans, but they might be a different species entirely. Shapechangers, even.* He shook his head. *Madness.* Glancing down at the water, a thought came to him and he frowned. *I hope no one drinks from this creek for a while.*

Although he hadn't finished washing, Lance got out and walked further upstream. Kneeling down at the water's edge, he looked in the water for anything suspicious. Once satisfied, he scooped up a handful and drank, realizing what he needed more than anything was a drink.

I should have died in that hole. No, I should have died well before that.

The air was frigid, so he wiped off the excess water from his skin and then took off running again. As he ran, he came to a realization. *I should be utterly xhausted, but instead, I feel my strength returning. Actually, I feel better than I have in a long time. Somehow it's all linked to the GodStorm. That's when my sleep pattern became disrupted. That's when everything started to change . . .*

Normally, most of the tables in the inn were well illuminated by windows along three of the walls during the day. On this particular day, a heavy shadow fell across the table in the far corner, at which a lone figure sat, listening to the locals talk. No one saw him enter, nor were aware of his presence.

"Yes, of course I looked up. It was the first thing I thought of!" said an old orc sitting in the middle of the room, gnawing on a hunk of bread. He frowned at the scoffers sitting at the bar: an aging dwarf and a nobleman wearing delicate garments. "What else could have cast the shadow?"

"That's what I've been saying," the nobleman said, nodding. "Okun, you saw some great bird, or maybe the dragon really isn't dead, or—"

"Or maybe he's been drinkin' too much," the dwarf said, shaking his head.

"Morse, I said I looked. I think I would have noticed a dragon, and it weren't no bird, neither. The sky was as empty as your head."

"How would you know, bein' so full of ale your boots were leakin'?"

"Good one, Morse," the nobleman said, grinning.

The orc raised his voice to nearly shouting and said, "I'm tellin' you it was the shadow of a humanoid. It moved right across my path on its own accord, with no creature casting it—and no, I'm not bangy!"

The dwarf chuckled and said, "No, just drunk as an orc out of work."

"You should talk, Morse."

"Least I can hold my liquor," the dwarf said, finishing off his mug of ale. "Orcs are such—"

"Bartley saw the shadow too, Morse," the server said as she entered the room with a bowl of stew in one hand and a pint of ale in the other. "At least he claims to have—when he was comin' out of Jeb's Mercantile yesterday." The old woman smiled at Okun as she slid the bowl down in front of the orc.

The orc grunted pleasantly and laid some coins down on the table.

"What are those?" She asked, winking at Okun. Turning to the dwarf, she said, "Morse, have you ever seen these odd round disks?" She held out the coins, staring at them as if beholding rare gems.

The nobleman started laughing, but the dwarf elbowed him and he fell silent.

The woman then set down another mug of ale before Morse and lingered.

Morse jabbed the nobleman in the ribs again and the delicate man slid some coins onto the table with a frown. At that, Morse smiled again and took another swig. "Thank you, Flaxton. Now I don't have to mention your little problem . . ."

The woman glanced over, apparently curious.

Flaxton wiggled his empty mug in front of her. "What about me? Be a dear, Sura . . . my mug seems to have a leak."

"Uh-huh," she said and frowned. "Flaxton . . . Morse—others seen it, too, or at least mentioned seeing shadows acting in strange ways lately." Seeming to notice the shadowy corner of the room for the first time, she paused briefly and considered it, then shrugged and began wiping down the tables with a rag. "You two could try treating people decently," she said, glancing over at Okun sympathetically. "Give folks the benefit of doubt once in a while. See how that goes . . ." Once more she glanced toward the shadow-draped corner table where the stranger sat, and muttered, "Don't recall that corner being so—"

"The orc saw what he saw and I believe him. You should too, dwarf," a short, purplish-blue-skinned humanoid in mail said as he stepped forward from a table in the shadows where he'd been observing them.

Everyone was surprised at the stranger's presence and immediately gave him their attention.

Morse scowled and stood up, taking a step forward and folding his massive arms. "When did you slink in here, skree? Spying on us, are you?"

Flaxton sneered at the stranger and stood as well, but kept behind Morse. "You might have noticed there are no temples to Ranos in this barony. Your kind isn't welcome here." Glancing over at the old woman, Flaxton said, "Sura, tell 'm he has to leave."

"Me?" Sura said, looking at each of the patrons in turn, the skree last of all.

Still draped in unnatural shadows, despite the light coming in the windows, the skree said, "My name is Gaerdrik. I'm a bounty hunter, quick with my bow and my blade, but I turned away from the Shadow Lord when I was just a young boy. Not all of the skree follow Ranos." The skree removed his wide brim hat, exposing his pointy ears and eyes, but the shadow remained over them. He rested a hand on a strange, shiny pistol in a new holster on his side. His own shadow moved over him to stand before him, then back again and vanished completely. "As you can see, I have power over shadows. And I know enough about them to tell you that the orc isn't bangy, or at least his story isn't proof that he is. I don't know him personally, so I can't say." *Don't get too cocky.* He had been trying to present himself as one with power, confidence and authority, hoping to control the small crowd and gain the information he sought, but now wondered if revealing his power over shadows would count against him.

"So you're the one causing all the trouble," Morse said, confirming his fears. The dwarf took a step back, nearly stepping on Flaxton, cowering behind him. "Shoulda known. I heard there was a skree slinking around in town. You were born of shadow stuff, weren't ye? That's how you're able to control 'em? Why don't you go back to the Shadow Realm where you belong?"

"I can understand your being afraid of me, and you're correct. My kind was fashioned from the fabric of the Shadow Realm itself, but every creature spawned there has different powers."

"I'm not afraid of you," Morse muttered, backing up further still, accidentally putting his considerable weight on Flaxton's left foot. The nobleman blanched, gasping slightly and wriggled free. Morse didn't seem to notice.

"Ah, my mistake," Gaerdrik said, noticing Flaxton's expression and enjoying a brief smile before continuing. "To clarify, my grandparents were born in the Shadow Realm, but they fled to Cathor. I was born in Attus, across the Storm Curst Sea. My parents served The One Above All, as I do."

"Told you all I saw what I saw," Okun said, jabbing a thumb in the skree's direction. "Like he said I done." From what Gaerdrik had experienced being around orcs over the years, they were rough around the edges, but less prone to racism than some other species. He nodded at Okun.

Morse took a swig from his mug and wiped his mouth on his sleeve, his eyes never leaving Gaerdrik's.

"I'll just throw this out there. Anyone in town manifesting strange sores?" Gaerdrik asked.

"What do you know about all this?" Morse asked, his tone more like an order, his hand now resting on the small hammer dangling from his belt.

Sura eyed the stranger wearily and said, "We don't want any trouble, but to answer your question, sadly, yes. Three."

"I sure hope it isn't the Black Death," Flaxton said under his breath.

Morse turned and glared at him, then fixed his eyes on Gaerdrik and said, "What're you getting' at, skree?"

Gaerdrik could tell the dwarf was nursing a beer belly, and that his hammer was not made for combat. *You're no warrior, dwarf. Maybe a long time ago, but my guess? You're a blacksmith, or were one,* he thought, noticing the soot on the dwarf's high boots. *You're not a threat.* The bounty hunter glanced out the window. *It'll be dark soon. Finish this up.* Ignoring him, Gaerdrik turned his full attention to the old woman. "You have a shadow reaper in your midst. Sores are their trademark." *What's wrong, dwarf. What has you so upset?* he wondered, noticing the dwarf's countenance wither. "You were saying, Sura?" the skree continued.

Flaxton appeared skeptical, the orc and Sura, both concerned.

"Doc Catchet was found dead two days ago. His body was covered 'n sores head to foot. His laborer was also found dead behind the house, also covered in sores. The other one . . ." she said, pausing to glance over at Morse, who was now staring at her, his face beet red, "I'm sorry, Morse. The other is—"

"My daughter," the dwarf said as a tear trickled down his face and vanished into his speckled beard.

He understands now, Gaerdrik realized. His heart sank. The dwarf may have been a jerk, but nobody deserved this.

In a softer voice, void of arrogance, Morse said, "She did Catchet's laundry once a week. She fell ill early this morning. She's at home. Her mother's lookin' after her. I didn't realize . . . I didn't know Catchet had . . . that he . . ."

"I can't swear to it, but it seems likely that . . ." Gaerdrik trailed off, deciding he shouldn't speculate on such a serious matter. The girl could still be alive if what his mentor had taught him about the shadow reapers was true—that they prefer to take their time with their victims and kill them slowly. There was a chance she was still alive. He quickly buttoned up his longcoat.

"Do you think she's—"

"We need to move quickly, Morse," Gaerdrik said and rushed over to the corner of the room to retrieve his bow and quiver.

Behind him, he could hear Morse sobbing quietly. "I'm sorry, Morse. I sensed the creature earlier, but it got away from me. Take me to her."

The dwarf regained his composure and nodded. They ran toward the door.

"Morse, I . . ." Flaxton started, but seemed unable to finish and just stared at them as did Sura.

Okun got up quickly and followed.

Morse guided Gaerdrik down one street and then another. They were halfway to his house when Gaerdrik stopped, as a strange sensation washed over him.

"Why are you stopping? Please, my house is this way!" Morse said, barely holding it together.

Gaerdrik ignored him. He closed his eyes and focused, confirmed what he'd sensed, and tried to ascertain the direction. Surveying the area, he saw a small boy walking along the side of the road kicking a rock, two men unloading a barrel of wine from a cart, a young mother crossing the street carrying her baby in a basket, her dog padding along beside her, an elderly grey elf sitting on a bench beside a rickety table watching folks walk by as his companion mulled over his next move in the game they were playing.

Where are you, reaper? Come on . . . come on—the boy!

"Please . . . my daughter!" Morse pleaded.

The skree quietly pulled out his bow and readied an enchanted arrow.

"What are you doing?" Morse asked, then turned to Okun, "What's he doing?"

Okun shrugged nervously.

Gaerdrik drew the bow and held his breath, waiting, aiming it in the boy's direction.

A woman walked out of a bakery across the street, saw Gaerdrik and screamed. The boy, like everyone else in the area, stopped and turned to stare at the skree. Gaerdrik remained focused.

There. He fired and the arrow stabbed into the ground at the boy's feet. For a moment, the ground shimmered strangely, but Gaerdrik doubted anyone noticed. The arrow was ruined.

Startled, the two men who were unloading the cart dropped the barrel, which slapped the ground hard and gushed out wine. The boy was trembling, but didn't move. Everyone saw Gaerdrik nocking another arrow, and seemed oblivious to the presence of the shadow reaper, who had cried out and slithered away from the boy. It was injured, but still alive.

Several people were shouting now and the boy took off running. Gaerdrik reloaded, then spotted the laborers barreling toward him. Everyone else scattered except the grey elf waiting for his turn at the game.

"Gaerdrik?" Okun said wearily.

The grey elf spotted the shadow reaper's flat shadow slither under a horse tethered outside of a supply store and was shouting, pointing at it. Only Gaerdrik seemed to pay him any attention.

Without a word, Gaerdrik bolted toward the horse, leaving Morse and Okun standing in the middle of the street gawking and calling his name. Finally, Morse turned and ran home.

I'm so sorry, Morse, but if the shadow reaper left her, she's probably already dead, Gaerdrik thought, but said nothing. There wasn't time. He was close enough now that he still sensed the creature's general location and knew that the closer he got, the more accurately he would be able to detect it. But the shadow reaper was fast and slipped into an alleyway, hiding in its shade, then continued on, slipping from shadow to shadow. Gaerdrik's only advantage was that the reaper could only cross a well-lit area for a few seconds before its body would become like a statue.

Entering the alleyway, the skree continued chasing it, and was himself being chased by a growing number of locals as he ran another block, then another, trying to catch up to the creature. He only had a small number of enchanted arrows and didn't want to waste them. He still had his enchanted dagger, but the reaper was fast.

Following it behind a small warehouse where dilapidated farm equipment sat scattered amidst tall weeds, Gaerdrik frowned. Before him sprawled the enormous Vraedian Forest. Somewhere ahead in the shadows was the creature. Gaerdrik's ability to sense it was fading. *Too late, perhaps, but maybe not, he decided. If it stops, I'll know. It can't bear the notion of going for long without shadowing something. I have that, at least.*

He didn't like leaving things unfinished in Muldon, but knew he couldn't return to town. There would be too many questions, and as before, he figured he would be blamed for something he didn't do. The boy seemed unhurt and would survive even if he had some sores—he was just casually walking along after all, not limping, but that wouldn't stop the accusations of attempted murder. Perhaps Morse would come forward on his behalf, or the orc, Okun, but he couldn't count on it. They didn't seem to notice the shadow reaper.

And so he followed the reaper deeper into the Vraeden Forest, unwilling to give up pursuit. All around him, the trees were draped in shadows. "One Above All, guide my path," he prayed and pushed onward, deeper and deeper into the woods.

Recalling the message Trendle had read back to him, "No shadows, no threat," Gaerdrik repeated it aloud, understanding what the offworlder had meant, that he could capture and then kill the reaper if he managed to either remove all light from its location, or immerse it with light. If the creature tried to shadow him, it would become trapped and helpless within his own shadow, unless he withdrew the shadow magic into his own body. *And if it comes too close, I have Lightbringer.*

Reminded of Trendle again, Gaerdrik realized that unlike the former knight, he was born to hunt, and found satisfaction knowing he was doing what he was meant to. He said a prayer for his new friend and then smiled, realizing the reaper kept going almost beyond the range of his ability to detect, then would slow down and then take off again, almost as if it were waiting for him. *Good,* he thought. *I can't keep up this pace forever. And if I get too tired, I'm likely to get sloppy.*

The creature's still heading deeper into the woods, straight toward Delathen, if I'm not mistaken. I'm making a lousy bounty hunter, accepting work without concern for payment, but I don't care. This one's on me.

Up the road coming toward him, Lance noticed an elderly human woman riding a cart. She hadn't seemed to notice him yet, or at least if she had, she didn't react. Several concerns popped into his mind all at once and he began to panic. Instead of being pulled by a horse or donkey or oxen, it was pulled by a huge lizard. This concerned him, as he wasn't sure how aggressive the creature might be, but bigger worries warred for his attention. He stood off to the side of the road with his shovel and stared at her. *She seems human and she's dressed simply, not so different than what I'd imagine a primitive farming culture might dress like, but how will I communicate with her? The Traders Tongue has spread to hundreds of worlds, but this one? If she doesn't know that, all I've got is the Humanus language.*

Deciding he would be taken as less of a threat if he continued walking on the far side of the road, away from the lizard's mouth, and just walked along casually with his shovel as if he belonged there, despite being nearly nude, he kept going.

If we can communicate, I know what the boy looks like and can describe him. Maybe she knows him and I can warn her. Soon enough, she began staring at him and as she came nearer still, she muttered something in a language he didn't understand and then started laughing. She covered her mouth, but laugh she did.

This is probably a waste of time, but here goes. "Pardon me, but do you speak this language?" He said in Traders Tongue. She looked at him and then down at his briefs and continued laughing. He raised his voice and smiled. Then he switched to his native tongue. "Sorry for my appearance, but how about this language?" She continued laughing and shaking her head all the way down the road.

I've got to find something to wear. Lance turned around and continued running, but after only a few yards, he realized that it had been quite some time since he'd checked in on the boy and was hoping to recognize the area when he got there. *I should have been watching through the reaper's eyes the whole time,* he thought, and gritted his teeth with anger at his neglect. Then he realized it wouldn't have been safe to run blindly. He could have tripped or ran off the road and smacked into a tree or fallen into a ditch.

As he thought about the shadow reaper once more, the vision returned, but instead of seeing the boy walking along, he saw farming equipment and trees. *It's heading into the woods!* As the shadow reaper glanced back in the direction it had come, for a moment, Lance saw the backs of two buildings and realized the reaper was leaving town. A short, bluish-purple-skinned man seemed to be chasing after it with a bow. Others were running too, though whether they were truly chasing after the shadow reaper or after the purple man wasn't clear. *I hope the boy's safe!* When he took his mind off of the reaper, the vision immediately faded. *I'll have to be more careful,* he thought.

Ahead of him to the right was a grove, but it looked too small to be what he'd seen in the vision. *Most of this region is flat or hilly. There's only one forest, but it's big. Really big. Lorego showed it to me on his wristcomp. I copied it to mine,* he remembered, and glanced at his left hand, which still wore his wristcomp. He started running, and as he did so, he activated the holo and brought up the map projection of the area. The forest was far to his right. He ran alongside the grove, and could see numerous buildings beyond it. When he reached the end of the grove, he ran along the side of the town until he reached the end and saw a number of people had gathered and were staring off into the forest. *I can't be far. I recognize some of those people from the vision.* He bolted toward the forest, not stopping until he was sure he was well within and out of view.

Hiding behind a bush, he looked through the eyes of the reaper again. It wasn't moving. Instead, it was staring at the bowman from behind a tree. It waited until the purplish-blue-skinned fellow was almost on top of it, and then it took off again, dipping from shadow to shadow. It was considerably faster than the bowman, but kept stopping, as if it wanted him to catch up to it.

Lance ended the vision. *So, it's playing another game. I have to warn that bowman somehow. Neither should be far from my position, but they do have a head start. I'm fast. Faster than I was before, but . . . Just go. If nothing else, when you find him, you might be able to delay him long enough to save his life. He doesn't know what he's getting himself into.* He started running again, faster than he'd ever run before.

After twenty minutes without slowing down, Lance finally caught a glimpse of the bowman. With his eyes on the bowman—instead of where he was running—he didn't notice an exposed tree root, tripped over it, and tumbled headlong down a hill and smacked his head on rock. He lost track of his shovel on the way down. Immediately, Lance's vision blurred and he became dizzy. He lay on the ground for a time, disoriented. Finally, he forced himself to sit up, knowing the reaper and bowman were getting farther away. Blood ran down his cheek and into his beard. Lance wiped his brow.

Only moments later, the blood stopped flowing from the cut on his head, but his vision still hadn't cleared. Something felt odd with his right arm and he noticed a bleeding puncture wound. It was small, but deep. Near his foot was a splintered tree branch with a bloody tip.

Lance heard a whistle and looked up. A broad-shouldered masked warrior stared down at him from where he was perched atop a grassy mound. The stranger wore a hood over his head, and on his side was a large blade.

The warrior spoke and Lance recognized the language as the same one the woman on the cart had spoken. He just stared at the warrior, sighed and waved with his good arm. There was a haze all around the warrior and Lance couldn't make out any details, but after a few moments, his vision began to clear.

Lance was surprised just how big the warrior really was. He saw that the warrior's arms and legs were powerfully muscled. But his mask was a patchwork, and seemed to have been broken many times in the past. Even so, he was impressive to behold.

The warrior spoke again, this time in a different language, and then another. "You are clumsy and underdressed for hunting." He spoke in a deep voice.

Traders Tongue! Lance realized and smiled. "Yes. Yes, I am! I mean about my—doesn't matter," he said, shaking his head. "I'm so glad we can understand each other!" *Finally, a bit of luck.*

"That's because you are speaking the right language," the warrior explained and then glanced through the trees. He stood to his full height and hopped down to the ground more gracefully than Lance thought possible for a man his size. Once on level ground with Lance, the warrior stared down at him, wordless.

After a moment, Lance realized the masked man was focusing on the wristcomp on his left arm. He tapped the Home icon and the holo projection promptly vanished. His mind was exploding with possibilities. *I have so much to tell him, and to ask him, too! But there's no time. What should I say? Gosh, he looks like he could rip me in half. Better keep it simple . . .*

He started to get up, then thought better of it and sat back down. "My name is Lance Bendrik. I mean you no harm. There's a bowman in the woods and I'm trying to warn him about—"

"About what?" the masked warrior demanded.

"I was just about to say. There's a deadly creature out there," he blurted, pointing in the direction he saw the bowman running, and then continued. "It's called a shadow reaper. It hunts in the shadows and taints its victims with deadly sores."

The warrior stared off into the woods for a moment, then turned his attention back to Lance and said, "This is my forest. Nothing hunts here without my permission. I see no weapons—and where are your clothes? You are ill-prepared for walking around in the woods, much less for hunting."

"Oh, I'm not hunting," Lance assured him. "It's a long story and the creature is getting away."

"I know these woods better than anyone. There's no place it can go that I, the Masked Man, can't find it. I am also called the Lurker In The Forest, the bane of all of Aedenshire. Perhaps you've heard of me?"

"No, but I'm . . . *new* around here. It's good to meet you." Lance offered his hand.

The warrior just stared at his him until Lance retracted his hand. "Guess you don't shake hands on this—"

"Go home. Unless you want to trade me for that wild magic on your arm, you are of no use to me. It's time to start the hunt."

Wild magic? "Wait, are you off to hunt wild game, or do you mean you're going after the shadow reaper?"

"The shadow reaper, of course."

"Then I'm coming with you," Lance announced, and stood up, hoping the warrior wouldn't take his statement as a challenge.

"You're in no condition to assist me and I don't need the help."

Lance felt his head and the blood was dry. He glanced down at his arm and saw that the wound had already closed. *Amazing,* he thought. *Just a slight itch.* "What, this?" he said, motioning with his arms and laughed. "This is nothing. Scratches. I am far more resilient than I look." He glanced around for his shovel, but didn't see it. "I lost my weapon, but I can see through the creature's eyes. I can help you."

"You can see through its eyes?" the Masked Man asked, his tone dripping with skepticism.

"Yes. Anytime I want."

"I still don't need any help." the Masked Man said and turned to leave.

"It's getting away . . ." Lance muttered in Traders Tongue. "The creature can become incorporeal at will." Knowing that even in the Republic, not every culture speaking Traders Tongue used the same dialect, he wasn't sure if the warrior was understanding him clearly, and so he added, "it can only be hit by a weapon when it is solid."

"I know how incorporeal works. If I didn't, I would have said so."

"Right. Sorry."

"My sword is enchanted, so it can hurt even incorporeal creatures."

"Oh, well . . . you still need me. I can tell you where it is. I know how it thinks—to some degree. And I know how to kill it." *Well, that's not entirely true,* he realized. *It isn't a lie, but I know it won't be easy.*

The Masked Man considered him for a moment. His eyes seemed to be fixated on the wristcomp Lance wore. Finally, he turned around and walked off in the direction the bowman had headed. Without looking back, he said, "I work better alone," and continued walking.

Lance followed after. "I'm not going anywhere. I have no home. The creature killed my wife. It ruined everything that ever meant anything to me. I will kill it if I can, but I don't want the bowman or you, or anyone else getting hurt."

"Then I guess you'd better come with me," the warrior said, and kept walking. "I have a weapon stashed that you can borrow."

Lance glanced at him and saw at least half a dozen weapons visible.

"That bowman's in trouble and we're falling further and further behind,"

Lance pleaded. "Besides, couldn't I just use one of yours? You have so many. I promise to give it back, of course."

"I'm using all of them," the warrior said.

"I see … I don't suppose you have a flashligh— er, lantern or something, in your stash? Now *that* would be really useful. Shadow reapers are very sensitive to light."

"They are?"

"Very."

The Masked Man turned and smiled. "Follow me then, back in my lair. I have something that's far more luminous than a—" the warrior paused, and raised a hand holding a throwing dagger.

Lance hadn't seen the Masked Man draw a dagger. But when a short, blue-skinned humanoid stepped out from the shadow of a tree, Lance immediately noticed the gauss rifle slung over the stranger's shoulder— and a bow and nocked arrow aimed at his chest. The stranger said something to the Masked Man that Lance didn't understand. The Masked man answered. Whatever it was, neither made a move.

"How about we talk this out?" Lance said, afraid someone was going to do something that at least he would regret. *I hope he understands Traders Tongue,* he thought.

"Careful, bounty hunter," the Masked Man said finally.

He used the Traders Tongue. The old woman I met earlier didn't seem to know it, and the warrior didn't use it first with me, either. The Masked Man must want me to hear what he's saying. Which also means he either knows the bowman speaks the language, or thinks he might know it, too.

His dagger still poised to throw, the Masked Man continued. "You are hunting in my woods. I've never been fond of bounty hunters, much less, skree."

The pointy-eared skree kept his bow trained on Lance, but glanced over at the Masked Man briefly. "I know who you are, Masked Man, but I'm not hunting you."

"In that case, you have no reason to worry either," the Masked Man said.

Good. We can communicate, Lance thought. *Now if he'll just put down that bow …*

The skree motioned with his bow at Lance. "Something's amiss. I saw his corpse. At least I saw someone with his face propped up dead against a fence."

I dunno—it's complicated. I might have been dead, but I can't say that. Don't want to freak then out . . . "As you can see, I wasn't dead," Lance said, forcing a smile. "I'm sure I looked a mess—probably don't look a whole lot better now, but trust me. I'm fine now, except I just fell down the hill and—"

"He's very clumsy," the Masked Man explained.

"I was . . . distracted," Lance corrected.

The bowman frowned. "You are either the dead man's twin brother, a doppelgänger, or worse. Either way, you will explain yourself, and quickly."

"I'd be happy to. My name's Lance Bendrik. As you've probably guessed, I'm not from around here. I know I looked dead, but I wasn't," Lance said, careful not to come across as aggressive. He slowly raised his hands. "Someone found me—I'm guessing after you did, and buried me alive—thankfully in a shallow grave. They did a shoddy job, not that I'm complaining."

"You smelled dead too. Still do."

The Masked Man turned and reconsidered Lance for a moment and nodded in agreement. "You do smell worse than many of the beasts I've killed in these woods."

"The creature that attacked me is called a shadow reaper. It seems to be fond of killing its victims by manifesting sores on their bodies, but it also has long claws. It attacked me several times and left me for dead—covered in festering sores," Lance said, immediately realizing an obvious hole in his story. *Spit. I don't have a single sore on my body to offer as evidence that I'm telling the truth, and how do I explain—*

"I see no sores," the Masked Man stated the obvious.

Lance's heart sank.

"I was about to mention that," the bounty hunter said. "If you're telling the truth, you impersonated a corpse quite convincingly. And where have all the sores gone?" He lowered his bow, but did not return the arrow to the quiver on his back.

"I'm sure this wouldn't be the first time someone was mistaken for being dead," Lance said with a nervous laugh.

Neither the skree nor the Masked Man found him funny.

I can't believe this is happening. He stared at his gauss rifle for a moment and wondered if the local even understood how to use it. *Think. He has to notice you still haven't answered his question.*

"There's no way you could have survived," the skree announced. "Not without a miracle."

The Masked Man glanced over at the bounty hunter and said, "What game are you playing, skree? At best you are mistaken, at worst—"

"I'm not mistaken. That's him. Answer me, stranger. If you aren't a doppelgänger or a demon masquerading with a dead man's guise, then what happened to all the sores? How are you alive?" he asked, raising the bow once more.

"Enough! The word of a skree is not to be trusted," the Masked Man said. "Now lower your weapon before I feed it to you."

Lance remained very still, not wanting to give any reason for the bowman to shoot him over a misunderstanding.

"Have you ever even met a skree?" the bowman asked.

The Masked Man's frown deepened. He pointed off in the direction the bowman had been heading before confronting them. "The threat is out there, fool. This fellow seems harmless enough."

"So do the shadows," the bounty hunter said as he renewed the draw on his bow, adding, "until you realize that any shadow can be used as a gateway for a creature from the Shadow Realm. You didn't see how ruined the flesh was on the body I found."

The Masked Man glanced over at Lance, shook his head, and turned to leave. "The creature is getting away."

Closing his eyes, the bounty hunter relaxed his grip on his bow and seemed to be listening or meditating. He opened his eyes and turned toward the Lurker Of The Forest and said, "No, it's waiting for us. I don't know why, but it is."

"That's because it's playing a game," answered Lance. "It's fast, so it kept getting too far ahead of you and had to slow down and wait for you to catch up. It hunts for the challenge. If there's no challenge, it gets bored.

That's dangerous. I don't know if it's seen me yet, but if it does, I suspect it won't go far, unless there's something around here that interests it."

"Delathen is on the other side of these woods, but it's quite a journey," the Masked Man said.

The skree gave Lance an odd look. "I'm sure it was headed for Delathen. Plenty of people for it to hunt there, but it did seem to be waiting for me to catch up."

"If it grows bored, it kills its victims quickly and moves on," Lance said. "It must have found me amusing, because it took its time with me." He noticed the bowman had lowered his weapon slightly, but figured he was fast enough that lowering his weapon didn't mean much. Even so, Lance felt a little less queasy about the situation.

The Masked Man scanned the trees and shrugged, turning back to face them. "I don't see anything. In fact, I have never seen the sort of creature you speak of."

Lance stole a glance through the reaper's eyes again and said, "It's still out there, watching us from behind a bush."

"How can you know that?" The bounty hunter asked, his arrow still nocked, but the weapon remained lowered.

Although Lance hadn't seen him move, the Masked Man's dagger was gone and his right hand now rested on the pommel of his great sword. He grimaced at Lance and said, "Answer him. I humored you earlier when you were making outlandish claims, but you didn't deny the skree's accusation. What happened to the sores? I must warn you: Patience is not my forte. If you're just a human, how can your recent wounds have healed so quickly?"

Lance sighed and said, "The same way that I've managed to go weeks at a time without sleep, and to survive the shadow reaper's attack. The same way I can now run fast, heal faster . . . not to mention apparently excel at impersonating a corpse. Neither of you would understand, but don't feel bad, I'm not sure I do either. I just know it all started with a bizarre, magical anomaly called the GodStorm."

"The GodStorm?" the Masked Man repeated, glancing over at the skree. There was recognition on both their faces.

"I don't know what to tell you," Lance said. "I should be dead, but I'm not, and I figure I've been given a second chance for a reason. I don't want to see anyone else get hurt by that creature."

The purple-blue skree relaxed visibly and slid the arrow back into his quiver. "That's good enough for me. My name's Gaerdrik," he said, and offered his hand. I suppose you'll be wanting your rifle back?"

Lance smiled and shook the skree's hand, then glanced over to the Masked Man, but the warrior was gone.

Gaerdrik noticed too, and they looked around.

Assuming the shadow reaper was still nearby, Lance reached out with his mind and looked through its eyes. As he suspected, the reaper was staring at the Masked Man, who was walking stealthily through the woods, sword drawn. "The creature's hunting the Masked Man, or maybe it's the other way around," he said, once again looking through his own eyes.

Gaerdrik handed Lance the gauss rifle and said, "Take good care of it. That thing's worth more than I'll likely ever make as a bounty hunter, especially if I keep hunting for free. As for the Masked Man, if half the legends I've heard are true, he can take care of himself. But just to be safe, we'd best see if we can lend a hand." The skree broke into a run.

"I thought I heard talking," came a friendly voice, stopping Gaerdrik in his tracks.

The skree looked off to his right and then smiled.

Lance looked in the direction he'd heard the voice and saw a dirty-faced human with an unkempt beard smiling back from behind a bush.

"Trendle!" Gaerdrik said, seemingly pleased. "It's good to see you, my friend, but now's a bad time. You shouldn't be out here. There's a deadly creature about."

"The Masked Man?" Trendle said and shrugged. "I have a feeling he's not so bad once you get to know him. Puts on a good show, but I suspect —" the former knight paused, noticing Lance standing there all but naked and smeared in dry blood.

Nodding at Trendle, Lance half-smiled, but his thoughts were elsewhere. He was worried for the Masked Man. After losing his whole crew to the shadow reaper, he feared even the great warrior was not up to the challenge. "The Masked Man needs our eyes and senses," he said to Gaerdrik and bolted past him out of the clearing.

"Trendle, I was talking about a shadow reaper, not the Masked Man. Come on," Gaerdrik said, and followed after Lance.

Lance spotted the Masked man and glanced back, forgetting that his enhanced body had sped him well ahead of Gaerdrik, who might also have been distracted with the newcomer. "Over here," he shouted.

The Masked Man turned around and sighed deeply. "Must you be so loud?"

Lance glanced back toward the clearing. The moment Gaerdrik came to mind, Lance found himself looking through the skree's eyes at the dirty-faced newcomer Gaerdrik had called Trendle. They were rushing out of the clearing more or less in his direction.

So I can see through the eyes of—oh, I think I get it. If I'm right, I won't be able to see through Trendle's eyes. Nope, he thought, confirming his suspicions. I've been in contact with both Gaerdrik and the shadow reaper, but not Trendle or the Masked Man. Interesting, now if only I can figure out how to avoid doing it until I'm ready . . .

Gaerdrik and Trendle came up alongside Lance, and motioned for the Masked Man to join them.

"We need to travel together if we're going to keep everyone safe," Gaerdrik said.

"Another one? Ah, Trendle, is it?" the Masked Man said and lumbered back toward them looking miserable. "I don't suppose it would do any good to say that I work better alone?"

Lance stepped off to the side and looked through the eyes of the reaper, trying to recognize landmarks that would give him the creature's approximate location.

Gaerdrik turned to Trendle and said, "What are you doing out here?"

"I'm on my way to Delathen to find work as a mechanic. What's a shadow reaper and why's that man going around naked?"

At hearing "naked," Lance's concentration was broken and he glanced back at the others. "The creature's about twenty meters awa— I mean a stone's throw from here, but seems to be backing up. I think it's—there, he pointed, spotting a strangely bent tree that had been only a few feet to the shadow reaper's right side.

Gaerdrik nodded. "It's on the run again. Guess it wants us to follow."

Lance confirmed it using his second sight, and nodded too. "We need to stop it before it gets to this Delathen you spoke of. I assume that's a town or something?"

The Masked Man sneered. "A den of lazy, evil men."

"Oh, It's not *that* bad," Gaerdrik muttered.

"What's a shadow reaper?" Trendle asked again, but this time his voice was different.

He sounded scared, Lance thought. *But with Gaerdrik's senses and my second sight, we should be able to keep tabs on it. Kill it, even.*

Gaerdrik turned to Trendle and said, "I believe the creature's heading straight for Delathen. If you're heading there too, we should travel together."

"I've faced a creature made of shadows awhile back. If this is the same one, I'm not sure—"

"Don't worry my friend. I was born for this sort of thing, and the Masked Man has survived what would have killed a hundred normal men. I can sense the creature. This fellow here . . . Lance—he can see through its eyes, and is apparently extremely resilient. He was touched by the GodStorm and has amazing abilities I can't understand, but that's the GodStorm for you. Who can know its ways?"

"It blesses some and curses others," the Masked Man said, shaking his head.

Trendle glanced at Lance again. "I'm Trendle. Um . . . where are your clothes?"

"That's a very long story," Lance said and offered his hand. Without looking back, he said, "Don't worry, Masked Man, we're about to head out."

Gaerdrik glanced over and smiled. The Masked Man had seemed about to slip behind a tree. Instead, he sighed and waited. The skree announced, "There's no place the shadow reaper can hide that we can't find it. And my arrows can kill it."

"So can my sword," the Masked Man said, turning to face him. His blade was jet black and there were hints of glowing jade throughout the massive blade.

"The past is behind us, my friend," Gaerdrik said, and rested a hand on Trendle's shoulder. "Remember what I said earlier. Your path is your own and I'll not ask you to walk mine or anyone else's. But if you're heading for Delathen, we might as well travel together. There is safety in numbers, and together, we can accomplish far more than we ever could alone."

Trendle nodded and smiled. "I thought I might never see you again."

Lance couldn't help but smile at Gaerdrik's words. Already, he was finding he liked the purplish-blue-skinned fellow and wondered if his species had gotten a bad rap like the orcs had in the Humanus Republic. A thought came to him. "I have a feeling the creature will go after me again. It's probably dying to find out how I survived."

The Masked Man frowned. "How can a creature die by lack of information?"

"Sorry. Figure of speech. I meant it is no doubt very curious about me. After it satisfies its curiousity, it might well try to kill us all, but we'll be ready for it. If it comes close enough, we'll kill it. We just have to keep things interesting so it doesn't get bored and attacks the people of Delathen," Lance said.

"We can't let that happen," Gaerdrik said.

"As I was telling the Masked Man, the shadow reaper hates bright light. We're on our way to retrieve a special lantern of sorts. I used to have a . . . light source of my own, but I must have dropped it somewhere. Even a torch would help. Gaerdrik?"

Gaerdrik sighed as he reached inside his longcoat and pulled out Lightbringer. "Is this what you were talking about?" he said, holding out the flashlight Trendle had repaired for him. "Since you're not dead, I suppose I should give back the pistol, too," he said and took it out of his belt. "Just for the record, it isn't easy for me to acquire such wonderful treasures only to lose them again. Don't get me wrong, I'm glad you're alive, but . . ."

Lance smiled. "I'll make it up to you, I promise," he said and took back the flashlight. "You can keep the pistol, for now at least. But let me show you how to use it before you—"

"That's okay. I figured it out," he said, stowing the pistol in his belt again. "Lightbringer was broken, but Trendle fixed it," Gaerdrik said, pointing at the flashlight.

"Oh?" Lance muttered and pressed the button to activate the flashlight. A shaft of light appeared and the Masked Man looked at it hungrily.

Turning to Trendle, Lance said, "Gaerdrik's right. It only makes sense to stay together. We are headed in the same direction, after all."

"See now?" Gaerdrik said and smiled.

Lance was surprised the Masked Man hadn't objected again and turned to look. The others glanced over as well, but once again, the Masked Man was gone.

"How does he do that?" Lance said, baffled that anyone so big could be so quiet. *It's almost as if he's an augment, too. Either that or he's right and I talk too loud.*

"Don't worry, he couldn't have gotten far, and by now he must realize he won't be rid of us so easily," Gaerdrik said. "We're a team, at least for this hunt anyway. I'm not sure if we can trust him, but as you said, Lance, we don't want that creature hurting anyone else.

Gaerdrik patted Trendle on the back and said, "With your ability to repair architechnology, you are destined to be a great mechanic in Delathen, my friend."

"You know how to fix the wild magic?" the Masked Man asked as he stepped out from behind a tree.

"I have had some success, yes," Trendle said and smiled. "I'm better with mundane farming equipment, and—"

"He's being modest," Gaerdrik said. "He is an excellent mechanic and can fix just about anything."

At hearing this, the Masked Man smiled, too, and rejoined them. He looked over at Lance and Gaerdrik and said, "Lead on, since you two are so intimate with the creature's ways."

Lance and Gaerdrik set out toward Delathen, following along behind the creature at a distance. Behind them, the Masked Man and Trendle lagged behind. Lance could here the warrior talking excitedly.

"Trendle, we've ran into each other twice in these woods and you never mentioned you knew how to repair wild magic," the Masked Man said as they walked along.

"You barely spoke to me. 'No hunting,' and, 'Go home' were about the extent of our conversations," Trendle said.

"There are many who wish me dead."

"Why?"

"That, too, is a long story. I don't think you will like it in Delathen. Lord Laygur is a nasty man and I'm no friend of the Sword of the Lord, either. Gaerdrik alone can't protect you. The Vraeden Forest is a dangerous realm. But I, the Masked Man, will keep you safe, and in return, you will repair a few things for me. Fair enough?" the Masked Man said as he slapped Trendle on the back, almost knocking him to the ground.

"I . . . I would be more than happy to try," Trendle said. "I love fixing things. I do reserve the right to decide about Lord Laygur for myself, however. And, I would like to at least attempt to find work in Delathen. Sometimes people are not what they seem. They have a rough exterior, but inside, they aren't so bad, or at least have potential for good."

"That's not the case as far as Lord Laygur is concerned, Trendle, but suit yourself. Just remember what I said. I'll do you a favor and then you will do me one. Come. It's time to kill a shadow reaper and then return to my lair. I have acquired some artifacts I think you would find most interesting."

Gaerdrik stopped and turned around. "With all due respect, O Lurker Of The Forest, do you have to be so loud?"

Lance stifled a laugh. From the look on Gaerdrik's face, Lance could tell he was trying to keep a straight face.

The Masked Man grimaced. Turning to Trendle, he whispered. "We'll talk later." Moving to the front of the line, he announced, "I believe we were going to stop at my lair first to pick up that wild magic item I was telling Lance about—unless the reaper attacks us before then, of course."

"That's right. If it's as special as you say, it might prove quite useful," Lance said.

Glancing over his shoulder at Trendle, the Masked Man smiled and said, "It's just one of several fascinating items I have collected over the years."

'Is that so?" Trendle said, returning the smile.

"Only I know the way to my secret lair," the Masked Man said, and turned off to the right, pushing through a thick wall of brush, making his own path. "If you tell anyone where my secret lair is, I'm afraid I would have to crush you all like bugs," he warned. "The lair is neither far, nor close. My senses are as sharp as my blades, but do warn me if you sense the creature approaching. And do try to keep up."

I wonder if he has a bat cave? Lance mused, smiling, but as they continued on their way, a sadness soon came over him. He recalled the events leading up to this point. Inevitably, Janys came to mind, and Lance wished things had gone differently. That Raeden had never sent them down to Moon Thirty-Seven. That Janys was still alive. *I miss her so much,* he thought. A tear came to his eye as a snapshot of his wife lying dead in the shuttle flashed across his mind.

If only my powers would have manifested sooner. Maybe I could have saved Janys and the rest of the crew. Maybe I should have tried to—no. That's a path more dangerous than hunting a shadow reaper, he realized. *I can't change the past. I can only move forward and make the best of things.*

He glanced over at Gaerdrik. The skree was smiling to himself. *I don't know him—not really, but I sense good in him,* Lance realized.

Gaerdrik turned to him and the skree's smile deepened. He must have sensed Lance was struggling with something because he nodded and smiled anew. He briefly patted Lance on the back, startling him, and said, "I don't know what you've been through, my friend, but we aren't bound by what's gone before. I'm not saying we should forget our past, but we shouldn't allow it to cripple us, either." He glancing over at Trendle. "Today's a new day. A new opportunity, and that's something we can get excited about."

Lance nodded and his spirits were uplifted.

"If nothing else," Gaerdrik said with a wink, "between the four of us, we ought to be able to cobble together enough coppers to get you some clothes." At that he laughed. Glancing over at the Masked Man, he quickly piped down. "I'm afraid the nights are chilly this time of year."

Lance smiled. "So far, so good." *I can't believe I'm actually looking forward to the days ahead, but Gaerdrik's right: Today's a new day. This time, the shadow reaper is in over its head. This time it's the one being hunted. We will stop it. It's just a matter of time.*

Painting by Mike Antrim

Thank you for reading The Shadow Reaper!

ABOUT THE AUTHOR

Bob Whitely is an author, editor, game designer and commercial artist.

Passionate about blending genres, he created both the *Cosmoverse* and *Toonaria Campaign Settings*, two homologous, blended-genre universes. He also created the *Cosmothea Roleplaying Game* for his gritty *Cosmoverse*, and is developing *Epic Destinies*, a rules-lite roleplaying game for his seemingly light-hearted *Toonaria*.

After winning first place in a *Dungeons & Dragons* Monster Design contest, designing over two dozen board and card games and writing piles of stories, Bob decided it was past time to start sharing his creations and founded QT Games LLC. He has also written and directed numerous plays and skits over the past eighteen years, and has acted in some of them locally and abroad.

Currently, Bob is working on completing a bucket list of creative projects, after which he hopes to get out another bucket (he bought a truck load before realizing he'd never have time to fill them all.) He lives in Las Vegas, Nevada, where he pursues his greatest passion, his adventures with his wife, sons and an adorable chieweenie.

Arcane Synthesis:
A Blended-Genre Anthology

Eight epic stories from the 31st Century: a blend of fantasy and science fiction, horror and hope, by new and established authors—different voices revealing a single, blended-genre vision. The Cosmoverse is a place where one seemingly insignificant person can change everything—not merely in one city or on one world, but perhaps even across the dimensions. 400+ pages: 7 novellas + 1 novelette.

Sea of Worms

Sea of Worms marks an important turn in the life of Mojori, a student of the arcane arts. Young "Mojo" serves a ruthless spell-dueling champion who travels the worlds going from tournament to tournament. During his apprenticeship and schooling at the Academy of Arcane Arts, Mojo learns the secrets of magic, encounters exotic creatures and advanced technology, visits fantastic places and gets into delicate situations. He records his own epic adventure in journal format, including lore, maps and illustrations.

VOICES

(One of the novellas presented in *Arcane Synthesis*)

An excerpt . . .

Peeking out from under his covers, Anton stared at the glowing strip of light below his bedroom door. The shouting escalated, and with it came other sounds: frantic footsteps, heavy breathing, threats, objects careening off walls and bodies and doors, shattering or crumpling to the floor.

"Pleasepleaseplease don't hit her again," Anton whispered, not daring to draw attention to himself. Tears had always come easily for him, but he tried not to cry around Ford. That only made things worse. Alone in the dark, he made no attempt to stop them.

Mother told me to hide or pretend to be sleeping whenever Ford gets like this, Anton reminded himself.

But he felt too vulnerable and slipped out from under the covers. He quietly scooted underneath his bed frame, as he sometimes did when he was afraid, and laid tummy down, on the cold, dusty tile, vanishing into his own little world.

Anton cupped his tiny hands to his ears, pinched his eyes closed, and tried to visualize snugglebunnies playing in a field; their over-sized paws and ears flopped as they hopped about. His therapist told him to visualize those big-nosed, bright-eyed, pink fur balls from Toonaria whenever he was scared or frustrated.

But the voices made it difficult to focus on such things. His therapist didn't seem to understand. Neither did his mother.

At first, Anton didn't realize he was hearing things others were not. He didn't question it.

As time went on, his problem became more apparent. His mother assumed he was just trying to get attention whenever he claimed he was unable to sleep due to noises she couldn't hear—music playing on a neighbor's headphones, water running through the sprinkler pipes, people talking in the surrounding houses—let alone nearby sounds.

Apparently it wasn't normal to hear folks whispering in their bedrooms across the street. One voice in particular—a girl's, he only heard in his head.

He could often be found sitting in his room covering his ears, crying. When his mother questioned him, he said things she thought strange, and knew things she said he shouldn't. So she took him to a therapist and he'd been going ever since.

Anton tried to think about Snugs, his favorite snugglebunny ever.

Of course they aren't really bunnies at all. "They're better than bunnies!" he told his mother when they were out shopping a week before Christmas the previous year.

It was the night before she met Ford at a Christmas party and the first time she'd ever left Anton with a sitter. More sitters followed, but he was pleased at least, that Christmas came with a soft, cuddly snugglebunny and a picture book about faraway Toonaria, where all the gubbies lived.

Anton tried to visualize one of the stories from the book, which started out: "Toonaria is a happy place of never-ending adventure, a realm filled with magic and all your friends!"

He loved to sit on his mother's lap and listen to her read. It was her voice that calmed him, even more so than the stories themselves. Sometimes he wished they could escape together to Toonaria.

Ever since Ford moved in, his mother seemed too busy for talk of snugglebunnies, chocolate rivers, and candy cane rafts. With Ford came shouting, tears, and pain.

Reciting the names of each member of his beloved Gubby Gang in the hope of blocking out the voices, Anton recalled their greatest adventure: *Down the White Chocolate Rapids.*

Together, the voices blended into an overwhelming cacophony: neighbors watching the big game, two boys walking down the street debating the merits of a computer game, the little maltipoo across the street yipping endlessly in the window, a baby crying in a passing car . . .

"One day, I'll make you go away!" Anton said in a small voice, hating the man who had moved in and ruined everything.

The shouting stopped. Anton listened carefully, hoping desperately Ford had left, never to return. Of course, Ford always came back, and always got mad.

Something heavy fell over that jingled. *The Christmas tree!*

His mother screamed.

Ford threatened.

His mother ran, her legs slender and quick. Another crash—Anton's bathroom door slammed shut and locked.

Silence.

Anton had no idea whether this marked the end, or the beginning of something worse.

A tidal wave of emotions swept over him. He was no longer under his bed, but wedged beside the toilet and tub in his bathroom. He felt the shower curtain and tub pressing up against his back, and beyond the toilet, the sink to his left, and the bathroom door straight ahead. The knob rattled.

He blinked and he was under his own bed again, the vision gone, and with it his strength. His mother's anxious thoughts spun inside his mind: pain, fear, sadness, anger, hatred, and confusion. The conduit broke as something bounced off his bedroom door in a loud thump that caused him such a start that he hit his head on the bottom of the bed frame.

"I hate you!" he said through the tears, his strength slowly returning as his anger mounted.

Heavy footsteps stomped toward him. His bedroom door was at the end of the hall, right next to his bathroom. He heard her inside, whimpering.

Standing just outside Anton's door, Ford's heavy shadow blotted out most of the light.

Ford's voice was surprisingly calm and tender when he spoke again, his knock on the bathroom door, gentle. "Lori?"

Silence.

"Please open the door. let's . . . talk this out, babe."

Silence.

"It was an accident, Lori. I'm sorry about the tree and . . . I didn't mean to—babe, you know I hate talking to doors! It's Christmas. Let's start over, okay? Open the door."

"No," Lori said in a tormented voice.

Something along Anton's peripheral vision moved, startling him. His snugglebunny had fallen to the floor when he slipped out of his bed and as he watched in horror, it began convulsing. Its pink, wavy fur bristled. The doll ascended out of sight along with a handful of marbles and a pile of plastic colonial marines he'd forgotten to put away before bed.

"Open the door, Lori." Ford's voice intensified as he continued until he was shouting. "Lori? You hear me? Open the frickin' door! Right. Frickin'. *Now, Lori!*" Ford slammed his fist against the door twice in quick succession.

Anton knew she would never open the door as long as Ford was standing there, but he also knew Ford. Both the door and door jamb were new; they'd been replaced twice in the past six months at his mother's expense.

Inside the bathroom, his mother was wedged between the toilet and the tub, hands over her face, whimpering and praying to the One Above All for a miracle.

Anton's breathing pushed the dust bunnies out toward the edge of his bed. For a moment, he imagined he was betraying them, exposing them to the dangers of the larger world. Surprising himself, Anton followed after them, crawling out from under the foot of the bed. He stood trembling— just like the time Ford shook him to get him to stop crying.

"Stop it!" Anton shouted at the top of his lungs, now too angry to care whether Ford heard or not. Anger welled up within him, worse than ever before.

He was unaware that he too was now hovering above the tile floor.

"Leave her alone!"

The house grew coffin quiet.

Even the voices in the distance seemed to hold their breath, save for the maltipoo barking its head off.

Anton's door swung open, flooding the bedroom with light. Ford's massive shadow loomed like a Toonarian minotaur over him. He stood in the doorway, his breathing heavy, pumping alcohol-laced stench into the room.

"What's the matter, Anton? Not enough presents under the frickin' tree this year? Spoiled brat!"

Knowing Ford would hurt him regardless, Anton struggled to think of something terrible to say to hurt him first. "Leave my mother alone you … ugly old minotaur!"

Faceless in the doorway, Ford just stood there and laughed. "You're a freak, Anton. You know that, right? Flush, you think I'm afraid of you? Do you?" Ford said, undoing his belt. Not waiting for an answer, he glanced at the bathroom door and shouted, "Lori? I'm gonna teach this little freak of yours some manners."

Anton remained still, refusing to give Ford the pleasure of seeing him cower.

Ford's belt, at first invisible under a swath of belly and shadow, appeared out of nowhere, slapping the peeling paint on the wall, leaving a mark as the minotaur gave it a final, prophetic yank, freeing it from its loops. Shirtless, Ford was covered in a carpet of hair, sticky with sweat and booze.

Everything not tied down in the room shot up to join the rest, as if invisible dobbers, pranksters of Toonaria, were playing their little game.

Ford swayed as he glanced about with wild, angry eyes. "What are you doing in here, you bangy freak?"

"I hate you so much!" Anton screamed, not moving an inch from the foot of the bed, though he remained pressed up against it, little fists tightly balled, his gubby shirt wet with tears and covered with dust bunnies. With chest out and eyes welded shut, Anton stood his ground and waited for the pain to come. His head was on fire and time slowed. He couldn't breathe, couldn't think.

The shouting intensified, but Anton was a million miles away. There were muffled sounds … of a door opening, and of a struggle. A strong, icy breeze blew over him, like someone had let the window open and all the world's air was rushing in. The room grew freezer-cold. Though his eyes were still shut, Anton's eyelids were bright and he was certain the room was full of light as bright as the sun. When he opened his eyes again, everything was gone.

Arcane Synthesis: A Blended-Genre Anthology
Story Summaries

Voices
By Bob Whitely
A homeless boy struggles to silence the voices in his head and master his burgeoning mental powers.

Wisdom of the Shell
By Robert Duran Jr.
After bonding with a plant companion in the swamp, a naive mage finds wisdom and acceptance.

Spectre of War
By Allen Farr
Trapped on a magic-scarred world, the descendants of a crashed mech carrier learn to live without technology.

Emeraldeaths
By Steven E. Schend
A secret order of knights face overwhelming odds to stop a powerful being from the future.

Down and Out in Magetown
By Lee Hammock
On a world obsessed with magic, a stranded mech pilot turned private eye is hired to crack a murder case implicating technology.

The Voskree Net
By Darrin Drader
A ragtag band of opportunists race to find a world-shattering weapon before their enemies do.

The Sword of the Lord
By Ed Greenwood
The truth about a missing child lies in a treacherous forest harboring lethal ancient technology.

The Train Less Traveled
By Bob Whitely
A sentient train and its crew uncover a secret that threatens everything they hold dear.

A note from the Publisher

QT Games launched two imprints to share the universes Bob Whitely has been exploring through stories and games over the past four decades. As evidenced with *Arcane Synthesis: A Blended-Genre Anthology*, we also publish other authors, but our focus is on blended-genre stories set within either the *Cosmoverse* or *Toonaria*.

As a small publishing house in a sea of much, much larger publishing houses, our biggest hurdle is not coming up with new ideas—we have far more than we will ever have the time or resources to publish. No, our biggest hurdle is finding people who already love blended stories and games. We know they are out there, but finding them hasn't been easy. We're hoping you are one of them! If you are, and if you'd like to see more from QT Games or know someone who would, please consider spreading the word. Thanks in advance!

Running on a limited budget means we spend the vast bulk of our meager resources on pro editors and pro artists, instead of on marketing and promotion. We can't do both effectively, and we insist on publishing only high-quality products.

Reviews are an invaluable tool for both readers and publishers alike. They help folks decide whether a book is right for them. And that's also why if you mention one of our books online to a friend, or even post a review on Amazon, Goodreads, Facebook, Twitter or other social media, well, that makes a world of difference to us! After all, if we have to toot our own horn, not only is that far less effective than a reader sharing their heart, but we wouldn't have time to write nearly as many stories.

We also want to know what you think so we can improve what we do. Therefore, we're not just open to feedback, we'd truly *love* to hear from you! Have a question or comment? We're all ears!

Curious about QT Games? Check out our website! We are also developing board games and roleplaying games set in both the Cosmoverse, and our other sprawling universe: *Toonaria*. We're all about blended-genre stories. Embrace the blend!

Join our newsletter to get a FREE novella and to stay up-to-date on upcoming Cosmoverse fiction and tabletop games.
Website: qtgames.com | Email: info@qtgames.com

What is the Cosmoverse?

The Cosmoverse is a blended-genre, multi-dimensional reality. It has some things in common with our own "real" universe, in that there is an Earth (though you'll find it on few galactic maps). The Cosmoverse also overlaps with our pre-twenty-first century historical records, and due to a fondness for certain books, comics and movies, there has been a tip of the hat to favored works as well.

As for the Earth, it has been quarantined and most of humanity has moved on. It's a whole new ball game and while humans are still on the playing field, they are but one of many species roaming the galaxies. Let's stop by the thirty-first century Cosmoverse and take a peek . . .

The Cosmoverse is dying as a result of the exploitations of imperfect gods, god-like AI, rogue superhero "augments," and horrors from the far reaches of space. No single event caused this downward spiral, though magical and technological blunders were major factors.

The GodStorm took nearly everyone by surprise, sweeping away both gods and entire dimensions in its wake, and absorbing their energy. The storm has raged for over four hundred years, sometimes slipping between dimensions and then resurfacing without notice. Rather than diminishing over time, the storm continues to spread, changing and tainting everything it touches.

In many cases, the GodStorm's passing resulted in merely bizarre, yet relatively harmless effects, but in others the damage has been great. At times the GodStorm leaves behind an abscess that warps a region into a nightmarish version of itself, fracturing galactic kingdoms and cutting off worlds, leaving them to fend for themselves against the coming darkness.

Many prayers go unanswered as worshippers cry out to gods already absorbed by the storm. As the dimensions hemorrhage and blend together, ruptured by the storm, new religions have fixated on the GodStorm, and mysterious beings of power have arisen. Such forces contend for control over unwatched worlds or clamor against the followers of ancient gods who yet live, but are scrambling to find their own place in the collapsing universe.

In the chaos, galactic communications networks have fallen into disarray, resulting in sluggish response times to raiders and border violations. Some galactic kingdoms, struggling to both guard their borders and protect member worlds, have turned to megacorp fleets to lend a hand. Without proper oversight, such corporations have themselves become a threat.

Land, air and space-based stargates dot the Cosmoverse, some built by mages and gods, others by advanced races and AI. Together with

JumpGate ships, such conveniences have at times caused those living on distant worlds and galaxies to feel claustrophobic, despite the vast gulfs of space between their kingdoms. With such means of speedy confrontation, controlling such gates is a universal goal as wars and rumors of wars, paranoia, and conspiracy theories abound. Bizarre sightings and discoveries in ancient ruins, together with dark prophecies and political scandals have reinforced the growing fear among mortals and gods alike.

In hidden corners of the Cosmoverse, dark forces gather to prepare for conquest, seemingly unfettered by the GodStorm, while others are consumed in civil wars. Some isolated worlds have slipped backwards technologically, never recovering from wars or other calamities. Other worlds are obsessed with magic. Some live in isolation, rejecting technology and the kingdoms beyond their sun. Others appear unscathed and forgotten amid the chaos, consumed with their own trials.

It seems there is nothing anyone can do to prevent the Cosmoverse's demise. Those responsible for many of the trials the universe now faces had, eons ago, left behind artifacts, clues, experiments, and caches of highly advanced technology, which lay dormant and may be activated intentionally or unintentionally by the flip of a switch, the placement of an artifact, or the casting of a spell. As a consequence, one seemingly insignificant person can change everything in the Cosmoverse – and not merely in one city or on one world, but perhaps even across the dimensions.

Any thoughtless act—as simple as randomly pushing a button on an ancient machine or opening a long-forgotten vault—may trigger a cascade of unforeseeable events. So may a small act of compassion. So may a big gamble. So, what will you choose to do?

What is Toonaria?

Toonaria is a realm of epic magic, advanced technology, superheroes, skyships, fallen gods, secret agendas, secret societies, adorable, but dangerous monsters, towering kaiju, sky pirates, and much, much more. On the surface, Toonaria might seem like a silly universe being that the heroes are adorable monsters and giant kaiju (and so are many of the bad guys), but it's really so, so much more than that.

Our newsletter, blog, and website have been slowly unveiling the grittier, just below the surface events going on in that seemingly happy-go-lucky universe. Keep an eye out for updates. We're working hard on a few special projects that will reveal more about Toonaria's dirty little secret.

Good things are in the works . . .

CPSIA information can be obtained
at www.ICGtesting.com
Printed in the USA
BVHW041417290719

554583BV00006B/163/P